Praise for the incomparable bestsellers of
JUDITH McNAUGHT,
"One of the finest writers of popular fiction."*

NIGHT WHISPERS

"Never miss a McNaught! *NIGHT WHISPERS* heads like the *Titanic* toward its iceberg of a climax—with shocking revelations. . . . Judith McNaught has written her most stunning work of fiction to date. Sexy, smart, and page-turning, this is a must-read."

—barnesandnoble.com*

"Fans of romantic suspense will shout that the great Judith McNaught has written something wonderful with her perfect novel, *NIGHT WHISPERS*. . . . A tender triumph that will leave readers awed. . . . The characters are warm and charming, and will long be remembered."

—BookBrowser.com

"McNaught has truly outdone herself with *NIGHT WHISPERS*. It is a testimony to her impressive talent. . . . Equal parts romance and suspense, this is a must read for mystery and romance fans alike. . . . You'll find yourself delighted with this excellent book."

—*Rendezvous*

REMEMBER WHEN

"[A] clever take on the ultra-affluent, ultra-cynical social scene of McNaught's hometown of Houston. . . . McNaught has a lot of fun with a marriage of convenience that turns out to be anything but."

—*Chicago Tribune*

"McNaught delivers another well-written, cleverly plotted tale of a successful businessman and woman who find love amid the cold practices of commerce."

—*The Advocate* (Baton Rouge, LA)

"A powerfully written novel that captures the reader and leaves her wanting more. Ms. McNaught has combined an appealing heroine with a sexy hero. . . . One of the best stories I've read this year. Excellent!"

—*Rendezvous*

"Romantic, witty, and entertaining. . . ."

—*San Antonio Express-News*

"Excellent. . . . Judith McNaught once again works her unique magic in this newest charming and sparkling tale of romance."

—*Romantic Times*

UNTIL YOU

"Delicious. . . . A perfectly wonderful story, with lively, funny, well-rounded characters. *Until You* is a laughing, loving book, a page-turner and a delight."

—*The Advocate* (Baton Rouge, LA)

"Judith McNaught comes close to an Edith Wharton edge with *Until You*. . . . I was captivated. . . . McNaught has a lot of fun with a mistaken identity plot."

—*Chicago Tribune*

WHITNEY, MY LOVE

"The ultimate love story, one you can dream about forever."

—*Romantic Times*

"A wonderful love story . . . fast-paced and exciting . . . great dialogue!"

—Jude Deveraux,
New York Times bestselling author of *The Blessing*

Books by Judith McNaught

JUDITH McNAUGHT

NIGHT WHISPERS

POCKET BOOKS
New York   London   Toronto   Sydney

This book is a work of fiction. Names, characters, places and incidents are products of the author's imagination or are used fictitiously. Any resemblance to actual events or locales or persons, living or dead, is entirely coincidental.

POCKET BOOKS, a division of Simon & Schuster, Inc.
1230 Avenue of the Americas, New York, NY 10020

Copyright © 1998 by Eagle Syndication, Inc.

Originally published in hardcover in 1998 by Pocket Books

ISBN: 0-671-52574-3

First Pocket Books paperback printing July 1999

20 19 18 17 16 15 14 13 12

POCKET and colophon are registered trademarks of Simon & Schuster, Inc.

Cover design by Lisa Litwack
Front cover photo by Comstock

Printed in the U.S.A.

For information regarding special discounts for bulk purchases, please contact Simon & Schuster Special Sales at 1-800-456-6798 or business@simonandschuster.com

TO NICHOLAS MICHAEL SHELLEY—

Dearest Nicky,

As your first birthday approaches, it is time to offer you some guidance to help steer you through life. The dedication page of this novel seems a rather good place to do that, and so I give it to you here:

> Aim high—like your mom.
> Shoot straight—like your dad.
> Fight hard for what you believe in—like your uncles.

Each time you succeed, no matter how tiny the success, stop for a moment and listen for a cheer. You'll hear it in your heart. Do you hear it now?

That's me, my darling.

No matter where I am, or where you are, I'll be cheering for you.

Always. Forever.

ACKNOWLEDGMENTS

My gratitude and affection to the two people whose kindness and support especially enriched my life during the creation of this novel . . .

Tamara Anderson, negotiator and strategist par excellence
Joe Grant, knight in legal armor

And to the following people whose expertise and invaluable assistance enriched the novel, itself . . .

Don K. Clark, Special Agent in Charge, Federal Bureau of Investigation, Houston
H.A. (Art) Contreras, U.S. Marshal, Southern District
Alan and Jack Helfman, my personal "magicians" with contacts in all the right places
Michael Kellar, Criminal Intelligence Division, Houston Police Department
John Lewis, a guardian angel

Last, but far from least, to . . .

Cathy Richardson, my right arm
Judy Webb-Smith, my other right arm

1

He'd been following her for three days, watching. Waiting.

By now, he knew her habits and her schedule. He knew what time she got up in the morning, whom she saw during the day, and what time she went to sleep. He knew she read in bed at night, propped up on pillows. He knew the title of the book she was reading, and that she laid it facedown on the nightstand to keep her place before she finally turned off the lamp.

He knew her thick blond hair was natural and that the startling blue-violet color of her eyes was not the result of the contact lenses she wore. He knew she bought her make-up at the drugstore and that she spent exactly twenty-five minutes getting ready to go to work in the morning. Obviously, she was more interested in being clean and neat than in enhancing her physical assets. He, however, was very interested in her considerable physical assets. But not urgently and not for the "usual" reasons.

At first, he'd taken great care to keep her in sight while ensuring that she didn't notice him, but his precautions were more from habit than necessity. With a population of 150,000 people, 15,000 of them college students, the little city of Bell Harbor on Florida's eastern seaboard was large enough that a stranger could move unnoticed among the population, but not so large that he would lose sight of his prey in a jumble of metropolitan expressways and interchanges.

Today he'd tracked her to the city park, where he'd spent a balmy but irksome February afternoon surrounded by cheerful, beer-drinking adults and shrieking children who'd come there to enjoy the Presidents' Day picnic and festivities. He didn't like children around him, particularly children with sticky hands and smudged faces who tripped over his feet while they chased each other. They called him, "Hey, mister!" and asked him to throw their errant baseballs back to them. Their antics called attention to him so often that he'd abandoned several comfortable park benches and was now forced to seek shelter and anonymity beneath a tree with a rough trunk that was uncomfortable to lean against and thick gnarled roots that made sitting on the ground beneath it impossible. Everything was beginning to annoy him, and he realized his patience was coming to an end. So was the watching and waiting.

To curb his temper, he went over his plans for her while he turned his full attention on his prey. At the moment, Sloan was descending from the branches of a big tree from which she was attempting to retrieve a kite that looked like a black falcon with outstretched wings tipped in bright yellow. At the base of the tree, a group of five- and six-year-olds cheered her on. Behind them stood a group of older adolescents, all of them boys. The young children were interested in getting their kite back; the adolescent boys were interested in Sloan Reynolds's shapely suntanned legs as they slowly emerged from the thick upper branches of the tree. The boys elbowed each other and ogled her, and he understood the cause of the minor male commotion: if she were a twenty-year-old coed, those legs of hers would have been remarkable, but on a thirty-year-old cop, they were a phenomenon.

Normally, he was attracted to tall, voluptuous women, but this one was only five feet four with compact breasts and a slender body that was appealingly graceful and trim although far from voluptuous. She was no centerfold candidate, but in her crisp khaki shorts and pristine white knit shirt, with her blond hair pulled up in a ponytail, she had a fresh wholesomeness and prim neatness that appealed to him—for the time being.

A shout from the baseball diamond made two of the older boys turn and look his way, and he lifted the paper cup of orange soda toward his mouth to hide his face, but the gesture was more automatic than necessary. She hadn't noticed him in the past three days as he watched her from doorways and alleys, so she wasn't going to find anything sinister about a lone man in a park crowded with law-abiding citizens who were enjoying the free food and exhibits, even if she did notice him. In fact, he thought with an inner smirk, she was incredibly and stupidly heedless whenever she was off duty. She didn't look over her shoulder when she heard his footsteps one night; she didn't even lock her car when she parked it. Like most small-town cops, she felt a false sense of safety in her own town, an invulnerability that went with the badge she wore and the gun she carried, and the citizens' sleazy secrets that she knew.

She had no secrets from him, however. In less than seventy-two hours, he had all her vital statistics—her age, height, driver's license number, bank account balances, annual income, home address—the sort of information that was readily available on the Internet to anyone who knew where to look. In his pocket was a photograph of her, but all of that combined information was minuscule in comparison to what he now knew.

He took another swallow of lukewarm orange soda, fighting down another surge of impatience. At times, she was so straight, so prim and predictable, that it amused him; at other times, she was unexpectedly impulsive, which made her unpredictable, and unpredictable made things risky, dangerous, for him. And so he continued to wait and watch. In the past three days he'd collected all the mysterious bits and pieces that normally make up the whole of a woman, but in Sloan Reynolds's case, the picture was still blurry, complex, confusing.

Clutching the kite in her left fist, Sloan worked her way cautiously to the lowest branch; then she dropped to the ground and presented the kite to its owner amid shouts of "Yea!" and the sound of small hands clapping excitedly. "Gee, thanks, Sloan!" Kenny Landry said, blushing with pleasure and admiration as he took his kite. Kenny's two front teeth were missing, which gave him a lisp, both of which made him seem utterly endearing to Sloan, who had gone to high school with his mother. "My mom was scared you'd get hurt, but I'll bet you never get scared."

Actually, Sloan had been extremely afraid during her downward trek through the sprawling branches that her shorts were snagging on the limbs, hiking up, and showing way too much of her legs.

"Everyone is afraid of something," Sloan told him, suppressing the urge to hug him and risk embarrassing him with such a show of public affection. She settled for rumpling his sandy brown hair instead.

"I fell out of a tree once!" a little girl in pink shorts and a pink-and-white T-shirt confessed, eyeing Sloan with awed wonder. "I got hurted, too, on my elbow," Emma added shyly. She had short, curly red hair, freckles on her small nose, and a rag doll in her arms.

Butch Ingersoll was the only child who didn't want to be impressed. "Girls are *supposed* to play with dolls," he informed Emma. "*Boys* climb trees."

"My teacher said Sloan is an honest-to-goodness hero," she declared, hugging the rag doll even tighter, as if it gave her courage to speak up. She raised her eyes to Sloan and blurted, "My teacher said you risked your life so you could save that little boy who fell down the well."

"Your teacher was being very kind," Sloan said as she picked up the kite string lying on the grass and began winding it into a spool on her fingers. Emma's mother had been another classmate of Sloan's, and as she glanced from Kenny to Emma, Sloan couldn't decide which child was more adorable. She'd gone to school with most of these children's parents, and as she smiled at the circle of small faces, she saw poignant reminders of former classmates in the fascinated faces looking back at her.

Surrounded by the offspring of her classmates and friends, Sloan felt a sharp pang of longing for a child of her own. In the last year, this desire for a little boy or little girl of her own to hold and love and take to school had grown from a wish to a need, and it was gaining strength with alarming speed and force. She wanted a little Emma or a little Kenny of her own to cuddle and love and teach. Unfortunately her desire to surrender her life to a husband had not increased at all. Just the opposite, in fact.

The other children were eyeing Sloan with open awe, but Butch Ingersoll was determined not to be impressed. His father and his grandfather had been high school football stars. At six years old, Butch not only had their stocky build, but had also inherited their square chin and macho swagger. His grandfather was the chief of police and Sloan's boss. He stuck out his chin in a way that forcibly reminded Sloan of Chief Ingersoll. "My grandpa said any cop could have rescued that little kid, just like you did, but the TV guys made a big deal out of it 'cause you're a girl cop."

A week before, Sloan had gone out on a call about a missing toddler and had ended up going down a well to rescue it. The local television stations had picked up the story of the missing child, and then the Florida media had picked up the story of the rescue. Three hours after she climbed down into the well and spent the most terror-filled time of her life, Sloan had emerged a "heroine."

Filthy and exhausted, Sloan had been greeted with deafening cheers from Bell Harbor's citizens who'd gathered to pray for the child's safety and with shouts from the reporters who'd gathered to pray for something newsworthy enough to raise their ratings.

After a week, the furor and notoriety was finally beginning to cool down, but not fast enough to suit Sloan. She found the role of media star and local hero not only comically unsuitable but thoroughly disconcerting. On one side of the spectrum, she had to contend with the citizens of Bell Harbor who now regarded her as a heroine, an icon, a role model for women. On the other side, she had to deal with Captain Ingersoll, Butch's fifty-five-year-old male-chauvinist grandfather, who regarded Sloan's unwitting heroics as "deliberate grandstanding" and her presence on his police force as an affront to his dignity, a challenge to his authority, and a burden he was forced to bear until he could find a way to get rid of her.

Sloan's best friend, Sara Gibbon, arrived on the scene just as Sloan finished winding the last bit of kite string into a makeshift spool, which she presented to Kenny with a smile.

"I heard cheering and clapping," Sara said, looking at Sloan and then at the little group of children and then at the kite-falcon with the broken yellow-tipped wing. "What happened to your kite, Kenny?" Sara asked. She smiled at him and he lit up. Sara had that effect on males of all ages. With her shiny, short-cropped auburn hair, sparkling green eyes, and exquisite features, Sara could stop men in their tracks with a single, beckoning glance.

"It got stuck in the tree."

"Yes, but Sloan got it down," Emma interrupted excitedly, pointing a chubby little forefinger toward the top of the tree.

"She climbed right up to the top," Kenny inserted, "and she wasn't scared, 'cause she's *brave*."

Sloan felt—as a mother-to-be someday—that she needed to correct that impression for the children. "Being brave doesn't mean you're never afraid. Being brave means that, even though you're scared, you still do what you should do. For example," she said, directing a smile to the little group, "*you're* being brave when you tell the truth even though you're afraid you might get into trouble. That's being really, really brave."

The arrival on the scene of Clarence the Clown with a fistful of giant balloons caused all of the children to turn in unison, and several of them scampered off at once, leaving only Kenny, Emma, and Butch behind. "Thanks for getting my kite down," Kenny said with another of his endearing, gap-toothed smiles.

"You're welcome," Sloan said, fighting down an impossible impulse to snatch him into her arms and hug him close—stained shirt, sticky face, and all. The youthful trio turned and headed away, arguing loudly over the actual degree of Sloan's courage.

"Miss McMullin was right. Sloan is a real-life, honest-to-goodness hero," Emma declared.

"She's really, truly brave," Kenny announced.

Butch Ingersoll felt compelled to qualify and limit the compliment. "She's brave for a *girl*," he declared dismissively, reminding an amused Sloan even more forcibly of Chief Ingersoll.

Oddly, it was shy little Emma who sensed the insult. "Girls are just as *brave* as boys."

"They are not! She shouldn't even be a policeman. That's a man's job. That's why they call it police*man*."

Emma took fierce umbrage at this final insult to her heroine. "My mommy," she announced shrilly, "says Sloan Reynolds should be chief of police!"

"Oh, yeah?" countered Butch Ingersoll. "Well, my grandpa *is* chief of police, and he says she's a pain in the ass! My grandpa says she should get married and make babies. *That's* what girls are for!"

Emma opened her mouth to protest but couldn't think how. "I hate you, Butch Ingersoll," she cried instead, and raced off, clutching her doll—a fledgling feminist with tears in her eyes.

"You shouldn't have said that," Kenny warned. "You made her cry."

"Who cares?" Butch said—a fledgling bigot with an attitude, like his grandfather.

"If you're real nice to her tomorrow, she'll prob'ly forget what you said," Kenny decided—a fledgling politician, like his father.

2

When the children were out of hearing, Sloan turned to Sara with a wry smile. "Until just now, I've never been able to decide whether I want to have a little girl or a little boy. Now I'm certain. I definitely want a little girl."

"As if you'll have a choice," Sara joked, familiar with this topic of conversation, which had become increasingly frequent. "And while you're trying to decide the sex of your as-yet-unconceived infant, may I suggest you spend a little more time finding a prospective father and husband?"

Sara dated constantly, and whenever she went out with a new man—which was regularly—she systematically looked over his friends with the specific intention of finding someone suitable for Sloan. As soon as she selected a likely prospect, she began a campaign to introduce him to Sloan. And no matter how many times her matchmaking efforts failed, she never stopped trying because she simply could not understand how Sloan could prefer an evening alone at home to the company of some reasonably attractive man, no matter how little they might have in common.

"Who do you have in mind this time?" Sloan said warily as they started across the park toward the tents and booths set up by local businesses.

"There's a new face, right there," Sara said, nodding toward a tall male in tan slacks and a pale yellow jacket who was leaning against a tree, watching the children gathered around Clarence the Clown, who was swiftly turning two red balloons into a red moose with antlers. The man's shadowed face was in profile and he was drinking from a large paper cup. Sloan had noticed him a little earlier, watching her when she was talking to the children after the kite rescue, and since he was now watching the same group of children, she assumed he was a father who'd been assigned to keep his eye on his offspring. "He's already someone's father," she said.

"Why do you say that?"

"Because he's been watching that same group of children for the last half hour."

Sara wasn't willing to give up. "Just because he's watching the children doesn't mean one of them belongs to him."

"Then why do you suppose he's watching them?"

"Well, he could be—"

"A child molester?" Sloan suggested dryly.

As if he sensed he was being discussed, the man tossed his paper cup into the trash container beneath the tree and strolled off in the direction of the fire department's newest fire engine, which had been drawing a sizable crowd.

Sara glanced at her watch. "You're in luck. I don't have time for matchmaking today anyway. I'm on duty in our tent for three more hours." Sara was staffing her interior design firm's booth, where brochures were being dispensed along with free advice. "Not one reasonably attractive, eligible male has stopped to pick up a brochure or ask a question all day."

"Bummer," Sloan teased.

"You're right," Sara solemnly agreed as they strolled along the sidewalk. "Anyway, I decided to close the tent down for twenty minutes in case you wanted to get some lunch."

Sloan glanced at her watch. "In five minutes, I'm scheduled to take over our tent for another hour. I'll have to wait until I'm off duty to get something to eat."

"Okay, but stay away from the chili, no matter what! Last night, there was some sort of contest to see who could make the hottest chili and Pete Salinas won the contest. There are signs all over his chili stand stating that it's the hottest chili in Florida, but grown men are standing around trying to eat the stuff, even though it's half jalapeño peppers and half beans. It's a guy thing," Sara explained with the breezy confidence of a woman who has thoroughly and enjoyably researched her subject, and therefore qualifies as an expert on men. "Proving they can eat hot chili is definitely a guy thing."

Despite Sara's qualifications, Sloan was dubious about the conclusion she'd drawn. "The chili probably isn't nearly as hot as you think it is."

"Oh, yes, it is. In fact, it's not just hot, it's lethal. Shirley Morrison is staffing the first aid station and she told me that victims of Pete's chili have been coming to her for the last hour, complaining of everything from bellyaches to cramps and diarrhea."

• • •

The police department's tent was set up on the north side of the park, right next to the parking lot, while Sara's tent was also on the north side, about thirty yards away. Sloan was about to comment on their proximity when Captain Ingersoll's squad car came to a quick stop up ahead, beside the tent. While she watched, he heaved his heavy bulk from the front seat and slammed the door, then strolled over to their tent, carried on a brief conversation with Lieutenant Caruso, and began looking around the area with a dark frown. "If I'm any judge of facial expressions, I'd say he's looking for me," she said with a sigh.

"You said you still have five more minutes before you're supposed to take over."

"I do, but that won't matter to—" She broke off suddenly, grabbing Sara's wrist in her excitement. "Sara, look who's waiting over there by your tent! It's Mrs. Peale with a cat in each arm." Mrs. Clifford Harrison Peale III was the widow of one of Bell Harbor's founding citizens, and one of its richest. "There's a fantastic potential client, just waiting for your excellent advice. She's cranky, though. And very demanding."

"Fortunately, I am very patient and very flexible," Sara said, and Sloan smothered a laugh as Sara broke into a run, angling to the left toward her tent. Sloan smoothed her hair into its ponytail, checked to make certain her white knit shirt was tucked neatly into the waistband of her khaki shorts, and angled to the right, toward the police department's tent.

3

Captain Roy Ingersoll was standing at the table outside their tent, talking to Matt Caruso and Jess Jessup, whom she was due to relieve for lunch. Jess grinned when he saw her, Ingersoll glared at her, and Caruso, who was a spineless phony, automatically mimicked Jess's smile, then checked to see Ingersoll's expression and quickly switched to a glare.

Normally, Sloan found something to like in nearly everyone, but she had a difficult time doing that with Caruso, who was not only a phony but Ingersoll's full-time snitch. At thirty-three, Caruso was already sixty pounds overweight, with a round, pasty face, thinning hair, and a tendency to sweat profusely if Ingersoll so much as frowned at him.

Ingersoll launched into a diatribe as soon as she reached him. "I realize that doing your job here isn't as important to you as performing heroic feats in front of an adoring crowd," he sneered, "but Lieutenant Caruso and I have been waiting to go to lunch. Do you think you could sit here for half an hour so we could eat?"

Sometimes, his barbs really wounded, frequently they stung, but his latest criticism was so silly and unjust that he seemed more like a cranky child with gray hair and a beer belly than the heartless tyrant he frequently was. "Take your time," Sloan said magnanimously. "I'm on duty for the next hour."

Having failed to evoke a response from her, he spun on his heel, but as he stepped away, he fired one more insulting remark over his shoulder. "Try not to mess up anything while we're gone, Reynolds."

This time, his taunt embarrassed and irritated her because several people who were walking by heard what he said and because Caruso smirked at her. She waited until they were a few paces away; then she called out cheerfully, "Try the chili! Everyone says it's great." She remembered what Sara had said about the challenge of hot chili to men, and although Sara's notion had seemed completely inane at the time, Sara was an unquestioned authority on men and male behavior. "You'd better stay away from it if you can't handle jalapeño peppers, though!" she added, raising her voice a little to reach them.

The two men turned long enough to give her identical smirks of confident male superiority; then they headed directly for Pete Salinas's chili stand.

Sloan bent her head to hide her smile and began straightening up the stacks of brochures on neighborhood-watch groups, civil service employment opportunities, and on the new self-defense classes for women being taught at city hall.

Beside her, Jess Jessup watched Ingersoll and Caruso until they vanished into the crowd. "What a perfect pair. Ingersoll's an egotist and Caruso is a sycophant."

Privately Sloan agreed with him, but she automatically chose to soothe a difficult situation rather than make it more inflammatory. "Ingersoll's a good cop, though. You have to give him credit for that."

"You're a damned good cop and he doesn't give *you* any credit," Jess countered.

"He doesn't give *anyone* any credit," Sloan pointed out, refusing to let the discussion threaten the relaxed mood of the balmy afternoon.

"Unless he happens to like them," Jess argued irritably.

Sloan shot him an irrepressible grin. "Who does he like?"

Jess thought for a moment; then he chuckled. "No one," he admitted. "He doesn't like anyone."

They lapsed into comfortable silence, watching the crowd, returning friendly nods and smiles from people they knew or who knew them or who simply walked by. It began to amuse Sloan that several women had walked by more than once and that their smiles were becoming increasingly blatant and aimed directly at Jess.

It amused her, but it didn't surprise her. Jess Jessup had that effect on women no matter what he was wearing, but when he was in uniform, he looked as if he belonged in a Hollywood film, playing the part of the handsome, tough, charismatic cop. He had curly black hair, a flashing smile, a scar above his eyebrow that gave him a dangerous, rakish look, and a thoroughly incongruous dimple in one cheek that could soften his features to boyishness.

He'd come to Bell Harbor a year ago, after spending seven years in Miami with the Dade County Police

Department. Fed up with big city crime and big city traffic, he'd tossed a sleeping bag and change of clothes into his Jeep one weekend and driven north from Miami. With no particular destination in mind except a pretty stretch of beach, he found himself in Bell Harbor. After two days, he'd decided the little city was truly "home."

He applied for a position on Bell Harbor's police force and unhesitatingly left Miami behind, along with the seniority and pension he'd earned while he was there. Competent, witty, and energetic, he was nearly as popular with his colleagues on Bell Harbor's police force as he was with the city's female population.

Everyone at the department teased him about the increased number of emergency calls from "damsels in distress" that inevitably came in from his particular patrol area. The duty roster changed every three months, and wherever Jess's new assignment placed him, it was inevitable that the calls from ladies would begin to increase.

Everyone, from the secretaries to the desk sergeants, teased him about his attractiveness to women, and to his credit, he showed neither annoyance nor vanity. If it hadn't been for the fact that the women Jess dated were all tall, willowy, and beautiful, Sloan would have believed he was oblivious to looks, his own or anyone else's.

At the moment, a redhead and two of her friends had concluded a brief huddle and were now heading straight toward their table. Sloan saw them and so did Jess. "Your fan club approaches," she joked. "They've worked out a plan."

To her amusement, Jess actually tried to deter them by turning his head away from them and toward Sara's tent. "It looks like Sara has a customer," he said with unnecessary intensity, peering at that tent. "Isn't that Mrs. Peale with her? I should probably go over there and say hello."

"Nice try," Sloan teased. "But if you stand up and leave, they'll either follow you or wait for you. They have that glazed, determined look that women get when you're around."

"You don't," he said irritably, startling Sloan and then making her laugh.

All three women were in their late twenties, attractive, with sleek, tanned bodies that were so perfect and voluptuous that Sloan was struck with admiration. The redhead was the spokesperson for the group, and her first words made it obvious they already knew Jess. "Hi, Jess. We decided you looked lonely over here."

"Really?" he said with a noncommittal smile.

At closer range, it was apparent that they were all wearing a lot of makeup, and Sloan mentally adjusted their ages to early thirties.

"Really," the redhead said brightly, giving him a long, intense look that would have made Sloan blush if she'd tried it. When he didn't seem to react to the invitation in her gaze, she tried a more practical tack. "It's such a relief to know you're the one on patrol in our neighborhood now."

"Why is that?" he asked with a smiling perversity that Sloan had seen him use to discourage women before.

All three women looked startled but undiscouraged.

"There's a crazy man on the loose," one of them reminded him unnecessarily, referring to the wave of burglaries that had left several elderly women savagely beaten and near death in their homes.

"Women in this town are terrified, particularly single women!" the redhead put in. "And especially at night," she added, increasing the wattage of her gaze.

Jess smiled suddenly, acknowledging the message she was sending. "I can solve that for you," he said, his tone heavy with promise.

"You can?"

"I can." He turned abruptly to Sloan, forcing her from her comfortable position of amused observer to unwilling participant. "Would you hand me that clipboard and three of those brochures?" he said. Sloan did as he asked, and he gave a brochure to each of the three women; then he handed the redhead the clipboard. "Just put your names on that list."

They were all so willing to do anything he asked that they wrote their names and phone numbers on the list without question.

"What did I sign up for?" the redhead asked, handing the clipboard back to him.

"Self-defense classes," he said with a wicked grin. "We're giving four of them at city hall, and the first one is tomorrow afternoon," he added, carefully omitting the information that Sloan was teaching most of the class, and that he would only be present to help her demonstrate some physical moves women could use to fend off an attacker.

"We'll be there," the brunette promised, breaking her silence.

"Don't let me down," he said warmly.

"We won't," they promised before they walked away.

They looked like Las Vegas chorus girls, Sloan decided, noting the choreographed movements of tight derrieres, long legs, and high-heeled sandals. A slight smile hovered at the corner of her mouth as she tried to imagine herself in the role of uninhibited femme fatale. "Let's hear it," Jess said wryly.

"Hear what?" she said, startled to discover that instead of watching the three women, he'd turned in his chair and was staring intently at her.

"What were you thinking?"

"I was thinking they looked like Las Vegas chorus girls," Sloan said, bewildered and uneasy beneath his unwavering stare. Several times in the past, she'd caught him looking at her in that piercing, thoughtful way, and for some inexplicable reason, she had never wanted to ask for an explanation. At the department, Jess was renowned for his ability to extract confessions from suspects, simply by asking a question, then sitting across from them and staring at them until they began to answer. This gaze was less intimidating than that, but it was disconcerting nonetheless. "Honestly, that's what I was thinking," she insisted a little desperately.

"That's not all of it," he persisted smoothly. "Not with that smile . . ."

"Oh, the smile—" Sloan said, inexplicably relieved. "I was also trying to imagine myself in those heels and tight, skimpy shorts, strolling around in the park."

"I'd like to see you do that," he said, and before Sloan could even form a reaction to that remark, he stood up, shoved his hands in his pockets, and said something that left her gaping at him. "While you're at it, could you also slap on a half inch of makeup to hide that glowing skin. Dump some dye on that honey-blond hair, too, and get rid of those sun streaks."

"What?" she said on a choked laugh.

He gazed down at her, his expression bemused. "Just do something so you stop reminding me of ice cream cones and strawberry shortcake."

Her laughter bubbled to the surface, dancing in her eyes and trembling in her voice. "Food? I remind you of food?"

"You remind me of the way I felt when I was thirteen."

"What were you like at thirteen?" she asked, swallowing back a laugh.

"I was an altar boy."

"You weren't!"

"Yes, I was. However, during mass, my attention constantly wandered to a girl I liked who always sat in the third pew at ten o'clock mass. It made me feel like a letch."

"How did you handle that?"

"First, I tried to impress her by genuflecting deeper and appearing more skillful and adept than any of the other servers."

"Did it work?"

"Not the way I wanted it to work. I was so good I had to serve two masses instead of one all that year, but Mary Sue Bonner continued to ignore me."

"It's hard to imagine a girl ignoring you, even then."

"I found it a little unsettling, myself."

"Oh, well, win some, lose some, you know."

"No, I didn't know. All I knew was that I wanted Mary Sue Bonner."

He almost never talked about his past, and Sloan was intrigued by this unprecedented glimpse of him as an uncertain adolescent.

He lifted his brows. "Since piety and religious fervor didn't impress her, I caught up with her after ten o'clock mass and persuaded her to go to Sander's ice cream shop with me. She had a chocolate ice cream cone. I had strawberry shortcake . . ."

He was waiting for her to ask what happened after that, and Sloan was helpless to resist the temptation to hazard a guess. "And then I suppose you had Mary Sue?"

"No, actually, I didn't. I tried for the next two years, but she was immune to me. Just like you."

He was so damned handsome and so uncharacteristically disgruntled that Sloan felt a little flattered without knowing why.

"Speaking of you," he said abruptly, "I don't suppose you'd consider going to Pete's party with me tomorrow night?"

"I'm on duty, but I plan to go there later."

"And if you weren't on duty, would you go with me?"

"No," said Sloan with a jaunty smile to take the sting out of her answer, though she doubted he was stung at all. "In the first place, as I already explained, we work together."

He chuckled. "Don't you watch television? Cops are supposed to become romantically involved."

"In the second place," she finished lightly, ignoring that, "as I also told you before, I have a rule that I do not go out with any man who is a hundred times more attractive than I am. It's just too hard on my fragile ego." He accepted her refusal with the same unaffected good humor he had before, thus proving he didn't really care one way or the other.

"In that case," he said, "I might as well go and have lunch."

"This time, don't let the girls fight over who gets to buy it for you," Sloan teased as she began tidying up the table. "It's a terrible thing to watch."

"Speaking of admirers," he said, "Sara has evidently acquired a new one. He was hanging around, talking to her earlier; then she brought him by here and introduced him to me. His name's Jonathan. Poor bastard," Jess added. "If he doesn't have a few million dollars in the bank, he's wasting his time. Sara's a flirt." He stepped over the ropes that secured the tent to the stakes in the ground. "I think I'll give some of that chili you recommended a try."

"I wouldn't do that," Sloan warned, breaking into a mischievous grin.

"Why not?"

"Because I heard that it's so bad that the first aid trailer is dispensing prescriptions for a number of unpleasant stomach ailments."

"Are you serious?"

She slowly nodded, her smile widening. "Completely serious."

Jess gave a shout of laughter and headed off across the grass in the opposite direction from the chili stand, toward the booths where pizza and hot dogs were available. He paused to say hello to Sara, who was still engrossed in conversation with Mrs. Peale and was holding one of Mrs. Peale's cats while they chatted.

Afterward, he stopped to talk to a group of children. He crouched down so that he'd be closer to their height, and whatever he said to them made them laugh. Sloan watched him, wishing a little wistfully that she could simply go out with him and not worry about the outcome.

In view of Jess's preference for tall, gorgeous women, Sloan had been stunned when he asked her out to dinner a few weeks ago and even more shocked when he asked her out again. It was so tempting to say yes. She liked him immensely, and he possessed nearly all the qualities that she wanted in a man, but Jess Jessup was simply too good-looking for comfort. Unlike Sara, who wanted glamour and excitement in her marriage and who was determined to find a man who had it all—looks, charm, and money— Sloan wanted almost the opposite. She wanted "Normal."

She wanted a man who was kind, affectionate, intelligent, and dependable. In short, she wanted a life that was different from the one she'd known and yet similar enough to be comfortable—a simple life in Bell Harbor like the one she'd had, but with children and a husband who would be a loving, faithful, and reliable father. She wanted her children to be able to depend on their father's love and support. She wanted to be able to depend on that herself—for a lifetime.

Jess Jessup would have been perfect in so many ways, except that he attracted women like a human magnet, and in Sloan's opinion, that did not make him a good lifetime marriage prospect. The fact that he possessed all her other criteria in abundance made him too tempting and too risky, so she regretfully decided to avoid any sort of personal relationship with him, and that included dinner dates.

Besides, any sort of serious relationship with Jess or another police officer would surely become a distraction at work, and Sloan didn't want anything to compromise her performance. She loved her job and she liked working with the ninety law enforcement officers who made up Bell Harbor's police force. Like Jess, they were friendly and supportive, and she knew they genuinely liked her.

By four in the afternoon, Sloan was more than ready to go home. Caruso and Ingersoll had both gone home shortly after lunch, complaining of intestinal "flu," which meant Jess and Sloan were stuck there until dispatch could send over replacements.

She'd been on duty since eight o'clock that morning, and she was looking forward to a leisurely bath, a light dinner, and then finishing the book she was reading in bed. Sara had left an hour ago, after stopping by to tell Sloan that Mrs. Peale had invited her over Tuesday night to see her house and talk about redecorating the first floor. For some reason, the elderly woman wanted Sloan to be there, too, and after securing Sloan's agreement, Sara had dashed off to get ready for a date with the promising lawyer she'd recently met, whose name, she said, was Jonathan.

The approach of the dinner hour had temporarily emptied out most of the park, and Sloan was sitting beside Jess, her elbows propped on the table, her face cupped in her palms.

"You look like a forlorn little girl," Jess chided, leaning back in his metal chair and watching the people moving slowly toward the parking lot. "Are you tired or just bored?"

"I'm feeling guilty about Ingersoll and Caruso," she admitted.

"I'm not," Jess said, and chuckled to prove it. "You'll be a heroine again when the guys find out."

"Do not say anything," Sloan warned. "There are no secrets in Bell Harbor, not in our department."

"Relax, Detective Reynolds. I was only joking." His voice took on a warm, somber tone Sloan had never heard him use before. "For your information, I would probably go to amazing lengths to protect you from harm; I would not purposely cause you any."

Sloan's hands fell away, and she turned to him, her eyes searching his handsome, smiling face, her expression one of comic disbelief. "Jess, are you flirting with me?"

He looked past her. "Here come our replacements." He stood up and looked around for anything he might be leaving behind. "What are your plans for tonight?" he asked conversationally as Reagan and Burnby strolled toward them.

"I'm going to bed with a good book. What about you?"

"I have a hot date," he stated, banishing Sloan's

impression that he was flirting with her and making her laugh.

"Jerk," she called him affectionately; then she ducked into the tent to retrieve her purse. Officers Reagan and Burnby were standing at the table, ready to take over, when she emerged. They were both in their early forties, reliable and personable Bell Harbor cops who remembered when traffic violations and domestic disputes were about all they had to deal with, family men with wives who went to PTA and children in Little League. "Anything happening?" Ted Burnby asked her.

Sloan slipped the shoulder strap of her brown leather handbag over her shoulder and stepped over the tent ropes. "No."

"Yes," Jess contradicted. "Sloan just called me a jerk."

"Sounds like you're making progress," Burnby joked, with a wink at Sloan. "Sloan's right," Reagan contributed, grinning. "You are a jerk."

"Try the chili when you get a chance," Jess countered slyly, stepping over the tent ropes right behind Sloan.

She swung around so suddenly that she bumped into Jess, who had to grab the rope for balance. "Don't go near that chili," Sloan warned, looking around him at the others. "It made Ingersoll and Caruso sick."

"Killjoy," Jess complained, turning her around and giving her a light shove in the general direction of the parking lot. "Spoilsport."

Sloan's shoulders shook with laughter. "Idiot," she retorted.

"Hey, Sloan," Burnby called after her. "You're in the

news again. That domestic call you were on last night made the news on Channel Six. You did good, kiddo."

Sloan nodded, but she was far from thrilled. She'd seen the newsclip on the six A.M. news and forgotten about it, but it certainly explained why Captain Ingersoll was in a particularly surly mood today.

As she walked away with Jess Jessup, Burnby and Reagan studied them with fascinated interest. "What do you think?" Reagan asked, referring to the betting pool at the office. "Is Jess going to get her into bed, or not? I've bet five bucks that Sloan won't go for it."

"I've got ten bucks on Jess."

Burnby squinted into the sunlight, still studying the pair, who'd stopped to talk to some people near the edge of the park. "If Sloan finds out about the pool, all hell will break loose."

"I got news for you," Reagan said, his belly shaking with laughter. "I think Sloan *already* knows about it, and so there's no way she's going to let him win. I think she knows about the pool, only she's too smart and too classy to let on."

Sloan's vehicle, an unmarked white Chevrolet provided by the city of Bell Harbor, was parked next to Jess's. After waving good-bye to him, she paused with the car door open and her right foot on the floorboard. Partly from habit and partly from a vague sense of uneasiness, she looked around at the scene to assure herself that everything looked peaceful and normal.

Bell Harbor was growing so dramatically that dozens of unfamiliar faces were appearing every day. She didn't recognize the heavyset teenage girl who had a toddler by the hand, or the grandmother with twins chasing each other around her, or the bearded man reading the newspaper beneath a tree. The dramatic influx of new residents had brought prosperity and tax benefits to the city; it had also brought a dramatic increase in crime as Bell Harbor went from a sleepy seaside community to a thriving little metropolis.

No more than one hundred fifty people were enjoying the park. Clarence the Clown was taking an hour off for dinner, and so were the jugglers. Most of the booths and tents were deserted, save for the people who were manning them. The park bench near Sara's tent was empty, and there was no sign of a clean-cut stranger wearing a yellow cotton jacket that seemed out of place on such a balmy, sunny day.

Satisfied, Sloan got into her car, started the engine, and glanced in the rearview mirror. No one was behind her, and she slipped the gearshift into reverse and pulled out of the parking lot, driving slowly down the winding gaslit street that bisected the park.

Earlier, when Burnby had congratulated her, he'd been referring to the night before, when she had gently coaxed an enraged, drunken ex-husband, bent on killing his ex-wife's boyfriend, into putting down his gun. When he balked at going to prison for an "unfinished" crime, Sloan had persuaded him to look at his impending prison time as an "opportunity" to "relax" and to think about finding a more-deserving woman who would appreciate his "true qualities." No one would have known about that if the defendant hadn't granted an interview to the local television static and told the reporter what Sloan had said to persuade him to put down his weapon. Although the defendant hadn't seen the grim humor in Sloan's advice to him, the media caught on at once, and as of this morning, Sloan was once again an unwilling local heroine, only this time praised for her wit, not her courage, in adverse circumstances.

Last night, Captain Ingersoll had given her grudging praise for the way she'd handled the situation, but this morning's media coverage had obviously ticked him off again. To a certain extent, she could understand his attitude. She did get more attention because she was a female.

As she drove past the main intersection at the entrance to the park, Sloan deliberately switched her thoughts to something more pleasant, like the leisurely bubble bath she planned to take in a few minutes. She turned left onto Blythe Lane, a wide cobblestone street lined with fashionable boutiques and upscale specialty shops, each with a chic curved green canopy marking the entrance and a huge potted palm at the curb.

She rarely drove through the business district without being struck by the transformation it had undergone in the last few years. Although the population boom had originally evoked a bitter outcry, the complaints from longtime residents diminished abruptly as property values soared and struggling locally owned businesses became thriving enterprises, almost overnight.

Eager to continue attracting prosperous new taxpayers, the city council took advantage of the town's charitable ood by pushing through a series of mammoth bond ies designed to modernize and beautify the communi-
At the urging of Mayor Blumenthal's ambitious, influ-

ential wife, a team of Palm Beach architects was hired and the transformation began.

By the time it was complete, the widespread effect was one of carefully planned, prosperous charm that made Bell Harbor resemble Palm Beach—which was precisely what Mrs. Blumenthal had wanted. Using her influence and the taxpayers' money, she turned her attention from commercial buildings to the public buildings, beginning with city hall.

Holiday traffic was heavy, and it was nearly fifteen minutes before Sloan turned onto her street and pulled into the driveway of the gray-and-white stucco cottage on the corner that she loved. The beach was across the street, and she could hear the surf and the laughter of children and calls from parents.

A half block away, a dark blue sedan pulled into a parking space behind a minivan, but there was nothing unusual about that. It seemed like any other holiday weekend.

Sloan put the key in the front-door lock, already dreaming of soaking in a hot bath and spending the rest of her evening with the mystery novel she'd been reading in bed. Sara couldn't comprehend why Sloan would prefer to spend Saturday night with a good book rather than on a date, but Sara hated to be alone. For Sloan the choice between a date with someone she knew she could never be interested in and time spent alone reading a book was an easy one to make. She vastly preferred the book.

She smiled as she remembered that she didn't have to go on duty until tomorrow afternoon, when she taught her self-defense class.

4

The police department was located in the new city hall building, an attractive three-story white stucco building with a red tile roof and a wide, gracefully arched loggia that wrapped around it. Surrounded by a lush green lawn dotted with palm trees and antique gas lamps, Bell Harbor's city hall was not only inviting, it was functional.

Oak-paneled courtrooms and an auditorium that was used mostly for town meetings occupied the third floor; the mayor's office, the clerks offices, and the records department occupied the second; while most of the first floor was designated for the police department.

Sara's firm had been hired to plan the interior, and her flair was apparent in the mayor's lavishly appointed office and in the courtrooms, where the chairs were upholstered in an attractive dark blue and beige fabric that complemented the carpeting.

When it came to the area designated for the police department, Sara and her partners had been given a comparatively small budget and strict requirements that didn't allow them much room for flexibility or creativity.

The center of that vast area was taken up with thirty desks arranged in three rows, each desk with its own computer terminal, two-drawer file cabinet, swivel chair, and side chair. Glass-fronted offices designated for ranking police officers were at the front of the vast room, and conference rooms lined the left and right sides. At the rear of the area, concealed from view by a heavy door that was always kept closed, was a long, narrow lockup used for temporarily detaining offenders who were being charged and booked.

In a valiant effort to diminish the harsh institutional effect of a sea of beige linoleum, beige metal desks, and beige computer monitors, Sara's firm had had the center area covered with a dark blue and beige commercial carpet and ordered matching draperies hung at the windows. Unfortunately, the carpet was continually soiled by food, drinks, and dirt tracked in by the ninety police officers who used the room in three shifts, around the clock.

Sloan was one of the few officers who appreciated Sara's efforts, or even noticed them, but on that day, she was as oblivious to her surroundings as everyone else. Holidays were always a busy time for the police, but this one seemed even noisier and more hectic than usual. Telephones rang incessantly, and loud voices, punctuated with bursts of nervous laughter, echoed down the hallway from an anteroom where forty women were gathering for Sloan's first self-defense class. The conference rooms were all being used by officers interviewing witnesses and talking to suspects involved in a robbery by a group of teenagers that had ended up in a high-speed chase and then a huge pileup on the interstate. Parents of the teenagers and lawyers representing the families tied up the telephones and paced in the hall.

The pandemonium annoyed Roy Ingersoll, who wasn't feeling well, and he retaliated by prowling up and down the aisles of desks, gobbling antacid tablets and looking for something to criticize. Marian Liggett, his sixty-five-year-old secretary, who was hard-of-hearing and who regarded the newly installed telephone-intercom system as evil and untrustworthy, added her voice to the din by standing in his office doorway and shouting to him whenever he had a phone call.

Officers tried to concentrate on their paperwork and ignore the distractions, but everyone was finding that a little difficult to do—everyone except Pete Bensinger, who was so excited about his bachelor party that night and his forthcoming marriage that he was oblivious to Ingersoll's sour mood and everything else. Whistling under his breath, he sauntered down the aisles, stopping to chat with anyone who'd talk to him. "Hey, Jess," he said, stopping at the desk beside Sloan's. "How's it going?"

"Go away," Jess said as he typed out a report on a minor drug bust he'd made earlier in the week. "I don't want your good mood to rub off on me."

Pete's euphoric good cheer was undiminished by Jess's rebuff. Stopping at Sloan's desk, he leaned over and tried to sound like Humphrey Bogart. "Tell me, kid, what's a good-looking broad like you doing in a place like this?"

"Hoping to meet a smooth talker like yourself," Sloan

joked without looking up from the notes she was making on the class she was about to teach.

"You're too late," he crowed, throwing up his hands in delight. "I'm getting married next week. Haven't you heard?"

"I think I did hear a rumor like that," Sloan said, flashing him a quick smile as she continued to write. The truth was that she, and nearly everyone else on the force, had been directly involved in his entire rocky courtship. He'd met Mary Beth five months ago and fallen in love with her "at first sight" by his own calculation. Unfortunately, neither Mary Beth nor her well-to-do parents had been particularly enthusiastic about marriage to a police officer whose occupational and financial prospects were far less than dazzling, but Pete had persevered. Armed with a great deal of advice from his fellow officers, most of which was very bad advice, he'd pursued Mary Beth and triumphed against all the odds and obstacles. Now, with his wedding only a week away, his boundless enthusiasm was boyish and utterly endearing to Sloan.

"Don't forget to come to my bachelor party on the beach tonight," he reminded her. Jess, Leo Reagan, and Ted Burnby had originally planned to have a party with a female stripper and the usual sort of drunken revelry, but Pete wouldn't hear of it. His marriage to Mary Beth meant too much to him, he declared, to do anything right before it that he might regret . . . *or that she might make him regret*, Jess Jessup had added. To make certain he got his way, Pete had insisted that his bachelor party be a "couples" party, and he was bringing Mary Beth to it.

"I thought the party was tomorrow night," Sloan lied, sounding as if she might have a problem being there tonight.

"Sloan, you have to come! It's going to be a great party. We're going to light a fire on the beach and barbecue—"

"Sounds like a violation of the Clean Air Act to me," she teased.

"All the beer you can drink," Pete cajoled.

"Drunkenness and disorderly conduct—we'll all get busted, and the news media will turn it into a national scandal."

"No one will be on duty to make the bust," he countered happily.

"I will," Sloan said. "I'm splitting a shift with Derek Kipinski tonight, so he'll be at the beginning of your party and I'll be there later." Pete looked a little crestfallen, and she added more seriously, "Someone has to work the beach; we've got a serious drug problem there, particularly on the weekends."

"I know all that, but we aren't going to stop it by busting some small-time pusher under the pier. The stuff is coming in by boat. If we want to get rid of it, that's where we should be stopping it."

"That's a job for the DEA and they're supposedly working on it. Our job is to keep it off the beach and off the streets."

She glanced at the entrance and saw Sara walking in; then she jotted another note on her list of reminders for the self-defense class. "I've got to teach my class in ten minutes."

Pete gave her shoulder a brotherly squeeze and wandered off to his desk to make a phone call. As soon as he was out of hearing, Leo Reagan got up and crossed the aisle to Sloan's desk. "I'll give you ten-to-one odds he's calling Mary Beth," he said. "He's already called her three times today."

"He's completely besotted," Jess agreed.

Sara arrived, perched her hip on the edge of Sloan's desk, smiled a greeting at the two men; then she leaned around Leo and looked at Pete, who was leaning way back in his chair, grinning at the ceiling. "I think he's adorable," she said. "And based on the look on his face, he's definitely talking to Mary Beth."

Satisfied that Pete was preoccupied, Leo pulled an envelope out of his shirt pocket and held it out toward Jess. "We're taking up a collection to buy Pete and Mary Beth a wedding gift. Everyone is putting in twenty-five bucks."

"What are we buying them, a house?" Jess said. He dug into his pocket, and Sloan reached for her purse.

"Silverware," Leo provided.

"You're kidding!" Jess said as he put twenty-five dollars into the envelope and passed it to Sloan. "How many kids are they planning to feed, anyway?"

"I dunno. All I know is that Rose called some store where they keep a list of stuff the bride picked out. Would you believe your twenty-five dollars will only buy part of one fork?"

"It must be one hell of a *big* fork."

Sloan exchanged a laughing look with Sara as she slid

twenty-five dollars into the envelope. At that moment, Captain Ingersoll strolled out of his glass-enclosed office, studied the scene, and noticed the cheerful gathering around Sloan's desk, and his expression turned to a glower.

"Shit," Reagan said. "Here comes Ingersoll." He turned to leave, but Sara was untroubled by the captain's glower or his impending arrival.

"Wait, Leo, let me donate something toward the silverware." She put money into the envelope; then she turned the full force of her most flirtatious smile on the captain in a deliberate and unselfish attempt to alter his mood for everyone's sake. "Hi, Captain Ingersoll. I've been worried about you! I heard you got sick from that awful chili yesterday and had to go to the first aid trailer!"

His glower faltered, faded, then turned into what passed for his smile. "Your friend here recommended it," he said, jerking his head toward Sloan, but he couldn't pry his gaze from the hold of Sara's. He even tried to make a joke about the money she'd just given Reagan. "Don't you know that bribing a police officer is a felony in this state?"

He really had an atrocious sense of humor, Sloan thought as he added in a jocular voice, "And so is interfering with an officer in the performance of his duty."

Sara batted her eyes at him and he actually flushed. "How am I interfering?"

"You're a distraction, young lady."

"Oh, am I?" she cooed.

Behind Ingersoll's back, Jess opened his mouth and pretended to be sticking his finger down his throat. Unfortunately, Ingersoll, who was no fool, looked around at that moment and caught him in the act. "What the hell is the matter with you, Jessup?"

Sloan choked back a laugh at Jess's predicament and came to his rescue. "I think I'll get some coffee," she interrupted hastily, standing up. "Captain, would you like a cup?" she asked in a sweetly subservient voice designed to startle and disarm him.

It worked. "What? Well . . . yes, since you offered, I would."

The coffeepots were located on a table across the aisle, just beyond the copy machines. "Two sugars," he called when Sloan was halfway there. Sloan's telephone began to ring, and he picked it up solely to impress Sara with how busy he was at all times. "Ingersoll," he barked into the receiver.

The male voice on the other end of the line was courteous but authoritative. "I understood this was Sloan Reynolds's phone number. This is her father."

Ingersoll glanced at the clock. Sloan's class was scheduled to begin in three minutes. "She's just about to start a self-defense class. Can she call you back later?"

"I'd prefer to speak to her now."

"Hold on." Ingersoll pressed the hold button. "Reynolds—" he called out. "You have a personal call. Your father."

Sloan looked over her shoulder as she dropped two sugar cubes into his coffee. "It can't be for me. I don't have a father—"

That announcement was evidently more interesting than some of the other conversations in the room, because the noise level promptly dropped by several decibels. "Everyone has a father," Ingersoll pointed out.

"I meant that my father and I don't have any contact," she explained. "Whoever is calling must be looking for someone else."

With a shrug, Ingersoll picked up the phone. "Who did you say you were calling?"

"Sloan Reynolds," the other man said impatiently.

"And your name is?"

"Carter Reynolds."

Ingersoll's mouth fell open. "Did you say *Carter* Reynolds?"

"That's exactly what I said. I would like to speak with Sloan."

Ingersoll put the call on hold, folded his arms across his chest, and stood up, staring at Sloan with a mixture of awe, accusation, and disbelief. "By any chance, could your father's name be *Carter Reynolds?*"

The name of the renowned San Francisco financier-philanthropist exploded like a bomb in the noisy room, and in the aftermath, everything seemed to grow still and silent. Sloan stopped in her tracks with a coffee cup in each hand, then continued walking. Familiar faces in the room stared at her with unfamiliar expressions of suspicion, wonder, and fascination. Even Sara was gaping at her. Ingersoll took the cup of coffee she handed him, but he remained near her desk, obviously intending to eavesdrop.

Sloan didn't care that he was there; in fact, she scarcely noticed. She'd never received so much as a birthday card from her absentee father and whatever his reason for suddenly tracking her down now, it wasn't going to matter. She wanted to convey that to him very firmly and completely and impersonally. She put her coffee cup down on her desk, shoved her hair off her cheek, picked up the receiver, and put it to her ear. Her finger trembled only a little as she pressed down on the flashing white button. "This is Sloan Reynolds."

She'd never heard his voice before; it was cultured and tinged with amused approval. "You sound very professional, Sloan."

He had no right to approve of her; he had no right to any opinion whatsoever where she was concerned, and she had to fight down the impulse to tell him that. "This isn't a convenient time for me," she said instead. "You'll have to call back some other time."

"When?"

A recent newspaper picture of him flashed through her mind—a handsome, lithe man with steel gray hair who was playing doubles tennis with friends at a Palm Beach country club. "Give it another thirty years, why don't you."

"I don't blame you for feeling annoyed."

"Annoyed—*You* don't blame—!" Sloan sputtered sarcastically. "That is *extremely* nice of you, Mr. Reynolds."

He interrupted her tirade in a pleasant, but no-nonsense tone. "Let's not argue in our first conversation. You can berate me in person for all my paternal shortcomings, in two weeks."

Sloan took the phone from her ear momentarily and

glared at it in frustrated confusion, then returned it. "In two weeks? In person? I'm not interested in anything you have to say!"

"Yes, you are," he said, and Sloan felt a flash of furious admiration for his sheer gall and the force of his will, which seemed to prevent her from hanging up on him. "Maybe I should have said it in a letter, but I thought a phone call would accomplish things more quickly."

"Just what is it that you want to accomplish?"

"I—" he hesitated. "Your sister and I want you to join us at the Beach for a few weeks so we can all get to know each other. I had a heart attack six months ago—"

The "Beach," Sloan surmised, was clearly the insiders' term for Palm Beach. "I read about your illness in the newspaper," Sloan said, managing to convey studied indifference along with the reminder that all she knew of her own father was what she read. Geographically, Palm Beach was not very far away, but socially and economically, Palm Beach was in another galaxy. To add to its own prestige, the Bell Harbor newspaper always carried the Sunday social section from its illustrious neighbor to the south, and it was there that Sloan saw frequent pictures and mentions of her socially prominent father and her accomplished sister.

"I want the three of us to get to know each other before it's too late."

"I can't believe your nerve!" Sloan exploded, angry and bewildered by the unexpected sting of tears she felt at the emotionally charged phone call. "It is already much too late. I have no desire whatsoever to know you, not now, after all these years."

"What about your sister?" he countered smoothly. "Don't you have any interest in getting to know her?"

Sloan's mind promptly conjured up the same photograph at the country club. Her sister, Paris, had been her father's tennis partner. With her dark head thrown back and her right arm extended in perfect form for a perfect tennis serve, Paris hadn't looked as if her life was anything except . . . perfect. "I have no more interest in getting to know her than she's had in getting to know me," Sloan said, but she felt as though the words had a hollow ring.

"Paris feels as if she's missed out on a very important part of her life by not having known you."

According to the frequent mentions of Paris that Sloan had seen, Paris's life had been an endless succession of glamorous and fulfilling events—from her tennis and equestrian trophies to the lavish parties she hosted for her father in San Francisco and Palm Beach. At thirty-one, Paris Reynolds was beautiful, poised, and sophisticated, and she hadn't needed or wanted Sloan in her life before this. That knowledge hardened Sloan's weakening resolve to avoid any contact with the wealthy branch of her family. "I'm just not interested," she said very firmly. "Good-bye."

"I spoke to your mother today. I hope she can change your mind—" he was saying as she hung up the phone. Her knees began to shake in delayed reaction, but she couldn't give in to weakness in front of everyone. "That's that," she said brightly. "I'd better get going; I have a class to teach."

5

By the time Sloan reached her temporary classroom, she'd convinced herself that her emotions were firmly under control and that she could concentrate completely on what she had to do.

She walked into the room, closed the door behind her, and gave the group a bright, fixed smile. "We're going to be talking about correct ways for women to deal with several potentially dangerous situations. . . ." she announced; then she realized she'd forgotten to greet them or introduce herself. "By the way, my name is Sloan Reynolds . . ." she began again. *And my father has just contacted me for the first time in my life*, she thought.

Sloan shook her head to clear it. The classes she was about to give were vitally important to the women in the room, and the women were all important to her. They needed her advice; they were counting on her. Carter Reynolds was nothing to her.

Sloan thrust him out of her mind and began the first of her lectures. "We'll start with one of the most common scenarios where a lone woman suddenly finds herself in danger. Let's suppose you're alone on the road at night and you get a flat tire," she said. "There's very little traffic and the nearest lights—the nearest sign of people—are three or four miles away. What do you do?"

Several hands went up and Sloan nodded toward an attractive middle-aged woman who sold real estate. "I'd lock the car doors, roll up the windows, and stay in the car until a police car, or tow truck, or some sort of trustworthy help arrives."

That was exactly the answer Sloan expected to hear, and it was the wrong answer. "Okay," she said, preparing to illustrate her point. "Now, suppose that while you're locked in your car, a vehicle pulls over to the side of the road. A man gets out, comes over to you, and offers to help. What will you do?"

"Does he look trustworthy?" the realtor asked.

"I don't *know* what honest looks like," Sloan countered firmly, "and neither do *you*. I mean, who looked more wholesome than Jeffrey Dahmer or Ted Bundy? But let's suppose the guy who offers to help you *doesn't* look trustworthy. What would you do then?"

"I'd keep the window up, and—and I'd lie and tell him help is already on the way!" the realtor finished with the enthusiasm of one who has come up with an inspired solution. "Is that the right answer?"

"Well, let's see if it is or isn't," Sloan said as she walked over to a table where she'd set up a television and videocassette player. "If your man was a good guy who truly wanted to help, he'll leave. But what do you think he'll do if he's a bad guy who wants to rob or rape or murder you?"

"What can he do?" the woman replied. "I'm in the car with the doors locked and the windows up."

"I'll show you what he can—and will—do," Sloan said as she pressed the playback button on the VCR. The television screen lit up showing a nighttime scene exactly like the one Sloan had described, with an actress playing the part of the stranded motorist on the highway. On the screen, a second car pulled to a stop, and a clean-cut-looking actor got out and offered to fix her tire. When the woman politely declined his help, he suddenly grabbed the door handle and tried to open the car door. She began screaming in panic, and he ran to his car, but instead of leaving, he returned a moment later with a tire iron; then he bashed in her window, unlocked the door, and jerked the screaming, struggling woman out of the car, where he began bludgeoning her with the tire iron.

The brief film clip was so realistic that Sloan's students were silent and shaken after she turned off the VCR.

"Lesson number one—" Sloan said firmly, but with a smile to ease the tension in the room. "Do *not* stay in a disabled vehicle. If you do, you're turning yourself into a potential victim and advertising your plight to every criminal and creep who drives by."

"Then what should we do?" a pharmacist's wife asked.

"You have several choices, depending upon how far away you are from the nearest house or business. None of your alternatives are convenient, but they're not as 'inconvenient' as being robbed or worse. If you're within walking distance of a house or business, even if it's several miles away, start walking. If you can't go cross-country, then you'll have to walk along the highway, but be prepared to duck behind a bush or crouch in a ditch if you see car lights coming your way. If it's too far to walk, or if the climate would endanger your health, then you'll have to stay in the car, but be prepared to get out of it and hide somewhere as soon as you see headlights coming your way. If someone stops to check out the car, stay hidden."

Sloan paused to let all that sink in; then she said, "If there's some reason why you absolutely must remain in your vehicle until morning, then wait until you see headlights coming, get out of the car and go to your hiding place. From there, you can watch and see what he does and how he acts. If he tries to break into your vehicle, or vandalize it, or steal your hubcaps—or if he has a couple drunken buddies with him—then at least you'll know you're safer where you are."

Sloan reached behind her and picked up a small black object on the table. Smiling, she said, "If you really don't like hiking down highways and across fields in the dark— if you'd rather not spend a terrifying night jumping in and out of your car, hiding and fearing for your life—then I'm happy to recommend an alternative." Lifting her arm, she held up the cellular telephone she'd taken from the table, and her smile vanished. "Please get one of these," Sloan implored. "Please," she said again for emphasis. "You can buy one for under one hundred dollars, and if you only use it for emergencies, the monthly cost for airtime isn't much. I realize that for some of you the cost of a cheap cell phone and monthly service may put a strain on your budget, but you can't put a dollar value on your life, and it's your life you're risking without one. If you have one of these when you're stranded at night in a car, you don't have to spend the night hiking or hiding. You can phone a tow truck, or the police department, or your husband or boyfriend and tell them you'll be waiting near the car. After that, all you have to do is stay out of sight until the help you're expecting arrives.

"Oh, one more thing," she added as Jess walked into the room. "If you've phoned the police, stress that you'll be near the car, not in it. Don't just leap out from behind a bush when we get there."

"Why not?" Sara challenged, smiling directly at Jess.

"Because," Jess said dryly, "it scares the hell out of us when that happens."

Everyone laughed, but Sloan had a much different impression of that ostensibly innocent exchange between Sara and Jess. Sara, who was always nice to everyone, had actually meant to force Jess into admitting to fear in front of a roomful of women. Sloan knew that as surely as she knew that Jess, who never took any gibe—or any woman— seriously, had truly resented Sara's "joke." They were two of the most attractive, most personable people in all of Bell Harbor. And they couldn't stand each other. They were Sloan's closest friends, and the undercurrent of animosity between them had finally risen to the surface and was bursting out into the open.

Sloan finished her lecture with a reminder that the next session would include some physical self-defense moves and reminded them to wear suitable clothing; then she turned off the television set and removed the video cartridge from the VCR. She'd completely forgotten that Carter Reynolds had reared up out of the dark highway of her own past.

Unfortunately, her respite lasted only until Sara got her alone.

6

"I can't believe Carter Reynolds is your father!" Sara burst out excitedly the moment the heavy doors of city hall swung closed behind them. "I can *not* believe it," she repeated, thinking of the articles she'd seen about him in the "Palm Beach Social Section" of Bell Harbor's Sunday newspaper.

"I've never been able to believe it myself," Sloan said wryly. "Actually, I've never had any reason to believe it," she added as they walked across the parking lot toward her car.

Sara scarcely heard that; her thoughts were racing down another track. "When we were little kids, you told me your parents got divorced when you were a baby, but you forgot to mention your father is . . . is . . . Carter Reynolds!" she said, lifting her arms to the sky, palms up, as if addressing heaven. "My God, just his name makes me think of yachts and Rolls-Royces and banks and . . . money. Mountains and mountains of glorious money! How could you keep a secret like that from me all these years?"

Sloan hadn't had a private moment to think about his call, but Sara's awed exuberance only hardened her own determination to remain unaffected by Carter Reynolds's illness, his tardy attempt to get to know her, and especially his money. "He *isn't* my father, except in the biological sense. In all these years, I've never received so much as a birthday card or a Christmas card, or even a phone call from him."

"But he called you today, didn't he? What did he want?"

"He wanted me to come to Palm Beach for a visit so we could get to know each other. I told him no. Absolutely no," Sloan said, hoping to eliminate any debate from Sara. "It's too late for him to try to play father," she said as she slid her key into the lock on the door of her car.

Sara was intensely loyal to Sloan, and under ordinary circumstances she would readily have empathized with Sloan's decision to reject a parent who had rejected Sloan since babyhood. However, from Sara's point of view, there was nothing "ordinary" about being the daughter of a man who could make Sloan into an heiress. "I don't think you should be so hasty," she said, thinking madly for some sort of excuse she could offer for the inexcusable. She voiced the first lame possibility that came to mind.

"I don't think men need to be close to their children the way women do," Sara reasoned. "It's as if they lack some sort of parental chromosome, or something."

"Sorry," Sloan said lightly, "but you can't attribute his utter disinterest in me to defective genetics. From everything I've read, he positively dotes on my sister. They play tennis together; they ski together; they play golf together. They're a team, and a winning one. I've lost count of how many trophies I've seen the two of them holding on to."

"Your sister! That's right! My God, you have a sister, too!" Sara exclaimed, sounding amazed. "I can't believe it . . . you and I made mud pies together, we did homework together, we even got chicken pox together, and now I discover that you not only have a rich socialite for a father, but you also have a sister you've never told me about."

"I just told you nearly everything I know about her—which is only what I've seen in the newspapers. Beyond that, all I know is that her name is Paris and she's a year older than I am. I've never heard from her, either."

"But how did all this happen?"

Sloan glanced at her watch. "I've only got an hour to eat and change clothes, then I'm on duty until nine. If you really want to talk about this, could we do it at my place?"

Sara was almost as flexible as she was fascinated. "I really want to talk about this," she said, already starting toward her red Toyota two parking spaces away. "I'll meet you at your place."

The stucco house Sloan had bought years ago was on a corner directly across from the beach—a tiny two-bedroom place on a narrow lot in a ten-block neighborhood of tiny, forty-year-old houses. The aging neighborhood's proximity to the ocean combined with the diminutive size of the houses had made them extremely desirable to young people with the energy and determination to fix them up but without a lot of cash to do it. As a result of the imagination and dedication of these first-time home owners, the entire neighborhood had acquired a quaint, eclectic look with avant-garde clapboard houses existing in happy harmony next to storybook cottages of stucco and brick.

Sloan had invested all her savings and all her spare time in her own house and had turned it into a picturesque stucco cottage with white window boxes and sparkling white trim that flattered the slate gray color of the stucco. When she first bought her house, the stretch of beach across from it had belonged almost exclusively to the residents of Sloan's quiet neighborhood. Back then, the street had been quiet, the residents lulled by an undulating silence that deepened and withdrew as each new breaker flung itself onto the beach and receded into the sea.

Bell Harbor's population explosion had put an end to all that as families with young children looked for a beach without the noise and antics of the college crowd, and they discovered Sloan's beach. Now, when Sloan turned onto her narrow street at four P.M. on Sunday, it was lined with vehicles parked bumper-to-bumper, some of them directly in front of No Parking signs and others partially blocking residents' driveways. And although she knew the surf was still rising and falling, she couldn't hear it above the delighted squeals of the children and the music from their parents' portable radios.

Sara grabbed the only parking space in sight, and Sloan bit back a smile as she watched Sara force a dark blue Ford sedan to back up so that she could claim the space for herself. The driver let her bluff him out.

"You really *have* to do something about all those cars," Sara decreed as she hurried over to Sloan, brushing a smudge off her pants leg. "They're packed in so tight that I had to squeeze between my car and the one in front of it, and I got dirt on my leg."

"I count myself lucky when they're not blocking my driveway," Sloan joked, unlocking her front door. Inside, the house was cheerful and bright, furnished in casual rattan furniture with pillows covered in a print of palm leaves and yellow hibiscus on a white background.

"I'd count myself lucky if you'd tell me about Carter Reynolds. How did he know where to phone you today?"

"He said he called my mother."

"So the two of them have stayed in touch over the years?"

"Nope."

"Wow," Sara breathed. "I wonder what she thought of his sudden interest in you."

Sloan could have bet serious money on her mother's probable reaction, but instead of replying, she tipped her head toward the answering machine, where the red message light was flashing frantically and the call counter indicated that three new messages were waiting. Suppressing a weary smile, she walked over and pressed the message playback button. Her mother's voice burst out with exactly the tone of youthful delight Sloan had expected to hear. "Sloan, honey, it's Mom. You're going to get a wonderful surprise today, but I don't want to spoil it because I want you to be as surprised as I was. But here's a hint: Sometime today, you're going to get a phone call from a man who's very important to you. Call me at home this afternoon before you go on duty tonight."

The second message was recorded two minutes after the first one, and it was also from Kimberly Reynolds. "Honey, I was so excited when I left you the last message that I wasn't thinking straight. I won't be home until nine tonight, because we're having a sale on Escada and we're very busy at the shop, so I told Lydia I'd stay and help until we close. And you can't call me here at the shop, because it upsets Lydia so much when employees use the shop's phone, and you know how bad her ulcers are. I don't want to give her another attack. I can't stand the suspense, so please leave me a message on my answering machine. Don't forget. . . ."

Sara looked understandably stunned. "She's completely thrilled about his phone call."

"Of course," Sloan said, shaking her head in amused disbelief at her mother's typically naïve optimism. According to Sloan's birth certificate, Kimberly Janssen Reynolds was her mother, but the reality was that Sloan had raised Kimberly and not the reverse. "Why are you surprised?"

"I don't know. I guess I thought Kim would be carrying some sort of grudge."

Sloan rolled her eyes at that. "Are we talking about *my* mom—the same sweet woman who can't refuse anyone anything because she's worried she'll seem rude or hurt their feelings? The same woman who just let Lydia bully her into working an extra six hours, but who dares not use Lydia's telephone because she's worried that the overbearing witch will have an ulcer attack if she does? The same underpaid, overworked woman who has run Lydia's shop for her for fifteen years and who brings in more customers than all the rest of Lydia's clerks combined?"

Sara, who loved Kimberly almost as much as Sloan did, started to laugh as Sloan finished her comic diatribe. "I can't believe you actually thought the same woman who practically raised you could carry a grudge against Carter Reynolds, merely because he walked out of her life thirty years ago, broke her heart, and never looked back or contacted her again."

Grinning, Sara held up her hand. "You're absolutely right. I must have had a moment of temporary insanity to even suggest such a thing."

Satisfied with that, Sloan pressed the playback button again. Message number three was also from Kimberly and had been recorded only fifteen minutes before Sloan and Sara walked into the house. "Honey, it's Mom. I'm at a pay phone in the drugstore on my break. I called the police station, and Jess told me you'd already gotten a long distance phone call from your father, so I'm not ruining your surprise by leaving this message. I've been thinking about what you should take with you to Palm Beach. I know you've been spending every cent you can spare on your house, but we'll have to start shopping for a complete new wardrobe for you. Don't worry honey, by the time you leave for Palm Beach, you'll have loads of beautiful clothes."

Sara suppressed a chuckle while Sloan erased the messages and reset the answering machine.

Sloan picked up the phone, dialed her mother's number, and left a message on her answering machine as Kim had asked her to do. "Hi, Mom, it's Sloan. I spoke to

Carter Reynolds, but I am not going to Palm Beach. I have no desire to get to know that side of the family, and I told him that. Love you. Bye." With that, she hung up the phone and turned to Sara. "I'm starved," she announced as if the subject of Carter Reynolds were already buried and forgotten. "I think I'll fix a tuna sandwich. Would you like one?"

Silently, Sara turned and watched Sloan walk into the kitchen and begin opening cupboards. Now that the shock of the discovery was wearing off, Sara was as hurt as she was baffled by the realization that Sloan and Kim had kept this enormous secret from her. They were her family, closer to her than any family that she'd ever known.

Sara's own mother had been an abusive alcoholic who didn't care or even notice when her four-year-old daughter began spending most of her time next door with Kimberly and Sloan Reynolds. Seated beside Sloan at an old kitchen table with a white Formica laminate top and stainless steel legs, Sara had learned to draw with fat crayons in the coloring book Sloan was always willing to share with her, and it was Kim who lavished praise on Sara's efforts. The following year, when both girls went off to the first day of kindergarten, they were holding hands for courage and wearing identical Snoopy backpacks that Kim had gotten both of them.

When they came home, they were both proudly clutching drawings with big stars put there by their teacher. Kimberly promptly taped Sloan's drawing onto the refrigerator, but when the girls ran next door to present Sara's mother with her drawing, Mrs. Gibbon had tossed it onto a cluttered table, where it landed on one of the round wet spots left by her whiskey glass. When Sloan tried to explain about Sara's star, Mrs. Gibbon screamed at Sloan to shut up, which humiliated and frightened Sara to tears. But Sloan didn't burst into tears or even look afraid. Instead she picked up Sara's drawing and took Sara by the hand; then she led her back to her own house. "Sara's mommy doesn't have a good place to put her pictures," Sloan had explained to Kimberly in a small, fierce, shaking voice that sounded strange to Sara. Sloan got the tape out and hung Sara's picture next to hers. "So we'll just keep them right here, won't we, Mommy," she decreed as she pressed the heel of her hand hard against the tape to make sure it was secure.

Sara held her breath, fearful that Mrs. Reynolds might not want to waste such treasured display space on drawings Sara's own mother didn't want, but Kimberly hugged both little girls and said that was a *very* good idea. The memory was etched forever in Sara's mind, because she never again felt completely and utterly alone. It was not the last time Sara's mother caused misery, nor the last time that Sloan interceded for Sara or someone else while she fought back tears and terror. It was not the last time that Kimberly hugged them or consoled them or bought them expensive matching items for school that she couldn't afford. But it was the last time that Sara felt like a helpless outsider in a cruel, bewildering world where everyone except her had someone to turn to and trust.

In the years that followed, their childish drawings were replaced by their report cards and school pictures and newspaper clippings with their names underlined in red. Coloring books and crayons that had littered the kitchen table gave way to algebra books and term papers; conversational topics changed from teachers who were mean, to boys who were hunks, to money, of which there was never enough. By the time they were teenagers, Sloan and Sara realized that Kim simply could not manage money, and it was Sloan who took over budgeting; some of their other roles were reversed as well. But one thing remained constant, even as it deepened and grew: Sara knew she was a valued, essential part of a family.

Given all that, it was understandable that she was shaken by the discovery that there was one enormous family secret to which she had never been privy.

Sara sank down at the kitchen table and thought about how often she had sat at kitchen tables with Sloan and Kimberly. Thousands of times.

Sloan looked over at her friend. "Would you like a sandwich?" she repeated.

"I realize this is none of my business," Sara said, feeling a little like an outsider for the first time since she'd met Sloan and Kimberly, "but can you at least tell me why you kept all that about your father a total secret from me?"

Sloan swung around, startled by Sara's hurt tone. "But it wasn't a big secret, not really. When you and I were kids, we talked about our fathers, and I told you about mine. When my mother was eighteen, she won a local beauty contest and the first prize was a trip to Fort Lauderdale and a week in the best hotel. Carter Reynolds was staying at the same hotel. He was seven years older than she, impossibly handsome, and a hundred times more sophisticated. Mom believed it was love at first sight and that they were going to get married and live happily ever after. The truth was, he had no intention of marrying her or even of seeing her again until he found out she was pregnant, and then his disgusted family gave him no choice. For the next couple of years they lived near Coral Gables, scraping by on what he could earn, and Mom had another baby.

"Mom thought they were blissfully happy until the day his mother arrived at their house in a limousine, offered him a chance to come back into the family fold, and he grabbed it. While my mother was in tears and shock, they persuaded her that it would be selfish of her to try to hold on to a man who wanted his freedom, or to try to keep both his babies away from him. They convinced her to let them take Paris back to San Francisco with them for what Mom thought was a visit. Then they got her to sign a document agreeing to a divorce. She didn't know that in the small print she had relinquished all her rights to Paris. They left in the limousine, three hours after his mother arrived. End of story."

Sara was staring at her, her eyes filled with tears of sympathy and outrage for Kim. "You did tell me that story a long time ago," she said, "but I was too young to understand the . . . the ruthlessness of what they did and the torment they caused."

Sloan took instant advantage of Sara's own words to press home her point. "And now that you *do* understand, would *you* want to admit you're related to that man or his family? Wouldn't you want to forget it?"

"I'd want to kill the bastard," Sara said, but she laughed.

"A healthy reaction and honest description of the man," Sloan said approvingly as she put two tuna salad sandwiches on the table. "Since killing him was not an option to my mother and since I was too young to do it for her," Sloan finished lightly, "and since talking about him or my sister or anything associated with that day used to make her incredibly sad, I convinced her when I was seven or eight that we should pretend none of them ever existed. After all, we had each other and then we had you. I thought we had a pretty terrific family."

"We did. We do," Sara said with feeling, but she couldn't smile. "Wasn't there anything Kim could do to get Paris back?"

Sloan shook her head. "Mom talked to a local lawyer, and he said it would cost a fortune to hire the kind of high-powered attorneys she'd have needed to fight theirs in court, and even then he didn't think she'd win. Mom has always tried to convince herself that in living with the Reynolds family Paris has had a wonderful life with advantages and opportunities that Mom never could have given her."

Despite her objective tone, Sloan felt swamped by anger. In the past, her strongest emotion had been indignation on her mother's behalf and contempt for her father. Now, as she recounted the story, she was a grown woman, and what she felt was far more fierce than indignation; it was empathy and compassion so intense that it made her chest ache. For her father—that callous, selfish,

cruel destroyer of innocence and dreams—what she felt
for him was not merely contempt, it was loathing, and it
grew as she considered his presumptuous phone call earlier. After decades of neglect, he actually believed he
could make a phone call and his abandoned wife and
unseen daughter would leap at the chance for a reunion.
She shouldn't have just coldly dismissed him on the
phone; she should have told him she'd prefer spending a
week in a snake pit to a week with him anywhere. She
should have told him he was a bastard.

7

The fire had been noticed at approximately nine-thirty P.M., according to Mrs. Rivera's neighbor who saw smoke seeping under a front door and called 911. Within six minutes, the fire department was on the scene, but it was already too late to save the shabby frame house.

Sloan had been on her way home from work, intending to change clothes and walk across the street to the beach where Pete's bachelor party was underway, when she heard the radio call and decided to offer whatever help she could. By the time she arrived, the street was already jammed with fire engines, ambulances, and police cruisers, their emergency lights flashing like grim beacons in the night. Sirens were wailing in the distance, and fire hoses were stretched across the street, slithering over the yards like fat white snakes. Police officers were cordoning off the immediate area and trying to keep a growing crowd of curiosity seekers from getting too close.

Sloan had just finished taking statements from several neighbors when Mrs. Rivera suddenly arrived on the scene. The heavyset, elderly woman plowed past the officers and onlookers like a frantic linebacker heading for a touchdown, tripped over a fire hose, and landed in Sloan's arms, her momentum nearly knocking them both to the ground. "My house!" she cried, struggling to free her wrist from Sloan's grasp.

"You can't go in there," Sloan told her. "You'll get hurt, and you'll only get in the way of the men trying to save your house."

Instead of being calmed or deterred, Mrs. Rivera became hysterical. "My dog—!" she screamed, struggling to free herself. "My Daisy is in there!"

Sloan wrapped her arm around the woman's shoulders, trying to detain and console her at the same time. "Is Daisy a little brown-and-white dog?"

"Yes. Little. Brown and white."

"I think I saw her a few minutes ago," Sloan said. "I think she's safe. Call her name. We'll look for her together."

"Daisy!" Mrs. Rivera sobbed, turning in a helpless circle. "Daisy! Daisy—where are you?"

Sloan was scanning the street, looking for likely hiding places where a small, terrified animal might seek shelter, when a little brown-and-white face, covered in soot and grime, suddenly peered out from beneath an unmarked police car. "There she is," Sloan said.

"Daisy!" Mrs. Rivera cried, rushing forward and scooping the terrified animal into her arms.

After that, there was nothing Sloan could do except stand beside the bereft woman and offer the solace of companionship while they watched the ravenous flames devouring the roof, licking at the front porch. "One of your neighbors told me you have a daughter who lives nearby," Sloan said gently.

Mrs. Rivera nodded, her gaze riveted on her collapsing house.

"I'll radio for a car to pick her up and bring her here to you," Sloan offered.

By the time Sloan got home, she was already so late for Pete's party that she couldn't possibly take time to shower and wash her hair. She parked her car in her driveway, grabbed her purse, and hurried across the street, where she had to turn sideways to sidle between two of the cars parked along the street. As she edged between the cars' bumpers, she thought she saw someone sitting in the driver's seat of another car parked far down the row; then the shadowy figure disappeared, as if the person had slouched down in the seat or leaned over out of sight.

Sloan suppressed the impulse to investigate and walked swiftly across the sidewalk. She was in a hurry. Perhaps the person in the car—if it had been a person— had dropped something on the floor and reached down to pick it up. Perhaps he'd decided to take a nap. More likely, what she'd seen had been only a shadow on the windshield cast by palm fronds swaying across a street lamp.

Even so, she continued to watch the vehicle, a Ford, from the corner of her eye as she headed toward the long row of food stands on the boardwalk. As she started around the north corner of an ice cream stand, she saw the Ford's interior light go on, and a tall man got out of the car. He started walking slowly toward the beach, moving at an angle that kept him south of the row of food stands and along the edge of the sand dunes.

Sloan could no longer quell her uneasy suspicions, and she froze, using the side of the building to shield her from his view. North of the snack stands was a three-mile stretch of sandy beach dotted with circular kiosks used by beachgoers for barbecues and sheltered picnicking. That was the stretch of beach suitable for sunbathing, swimming, and parties, and it was there that Pete Bensinger's party was under way.

To the immediate south of the snack stands, where the stranger was heading, there was nothing except sand dunes covered in thick vegetation, dunes that offered little on a dark night except privacy for trysting couples and for people who were hoping to engage in other, less innocent endeavors.

Sloan knew she'd been jumpy and off-balance ever since her father's phone call that afternoon, but there was something about the male who got out of that car that made her feel distinctly, and professionally, uneasy. For one thing, he seemed vaguely familiar; for another, he wasn't dressed for a late-night stroll on the beach, and most important of all, there was something stealthy in his actions, both when he was in the car and now that he was out of it. There'd been muggings at the dunes, drug exchanges, and even a murder several years ago.

Sloan edged her way back to the corner of the ice cream stand, then began retracing her steps, staying close to the rear of the food stands so that she would emerge on the south end of the row of buildings. From there, she would be able to either watch him or follow him.

Silently cursing the sand that filled his shoes, the man waited beside the dunes, expecting his prey to appear on the beach, beyond the snack stands. She'd been so unsuspecting, so easy to follow, and so predictable, that when she didn't appear where he expected to see her, it didn't occur to him to be alarmed. She'd been in a hurry, and since she hadn't appeared on the beach, he assumed she'd forgotten something at home and returned to get it.

Rather than going after her and getting more sand in his shoes, he backed up a few steps and crouched down in the cleft of two dunes. Concealed by sand and vegetation, he reached for a roll of mints in his pocket and waited for her to reappear in his line of sight.

Removing the silver wrapper from the candy, he leaned forward, watching for a glimpse of her as she recrossed the street toward her house. The moon was behind a cloud, but the streetlamp was near enough to the snack bar to enable him to see her as she suddenly emerged from behind the south end of the buildings and disappeared almost immediately in the overgrown dunes.

Her unexpected maneuver tantalized him, it added a little flavor and excitement to what had been, until now, a thoroughly boring but necessary four days. She was up to something. Something private.

He stood up cautiously, craning his neck, his senses alert to any sound, any shadow, but she seemed to have vanished. Swearing under his breath, he turned and started to climb up the hill behind him. From higher ground he'd be able to spot her.

"Hold it right there—"

Her voice startled him so completely that he lost his grip on the tall stalks of sea grass and slid to the ground. Off-balance and unable to regain his footing in the soft sand, he twisted around, stumbled, and lunged forward at her. He tripped over something, felt a blow on the back of his neck, and landed facedown in the sand.

Blinking grit out of his eyes, he turned his face toward her. She was standing just beyond his reach with her feet planted slightly apart, her arms outstretched, a nine millimeter Glock clamped between her hands.

"Put your hands behind your back where I can see them," she ordered.

For the moment, he was willing to go along with her. She'd obviously realized he was armed when his jacket fell open, but now she was going to try to disarm him, and he had no intention of letting her do it. He smiled slowly, deliberately, as he put his hands behind him. "That's a big gun for a little girl like you."

"Clasp your hands together and roll over onto your back."

His smile widened knowingly. "Why? No handcuffs?"

Sloan did not have handcuffs; she did not even have a shoelace to bind his wrists. What she did have was an armed man on a populated beach who was cool enough—or weird enough—to goad and smile at her, a potential psychopath who was not exhibiting any normal reaction to his predicament. "Do as I said," Sloan warned, lifting her weapon a little higher for emphasis. "Roll over onto your back, on top of your hands."

Another bizarre smile drifted across his face as he considered her instructions. "Not a good plan. When you reach for my weapon, all I have to do is lift up a little, grab your wrist, and shoot you with your own weapon. Have you ever seen how much damage a nine millimeter does to a body?"

He sounded crazy enough to kill anyone on the beach who got in his way, and the last thing Sloan intended to do was give him that chance by trying to disarm him herself. Tense but steady, she leveled her weapon on a spot between his eyes. "Don't make me use this," she warned.

His eyes narrowed as he registered the subtle change in her aim; then he slowly rolled onto his back on top of his hands. "I'm carrying twenty-five thousand dollars in cash," he said, changing tactics. "You take it and I walk away. No one gets hurt; no one finds out."

Sloan ignored him. Stepping back, she aimed the Glock high and out over the water and fired off three rounds in rapid succession; then she pointed the gun at him again. The shots echoed in the darkness like small cannons fired in a canyon, and somewhere down the beach someone shouted in alarm.

"Why in hell did you do that?" he demanded.

"I've just sent for reinforcements," she replied. "They're right down the beach. They'll be here in a minute."

His entire demeanor altered before her eyes. "In that case, introductions are in order," he snapped, turning brisk and businesslike. "I'm Special Agent Paul

Richardson, FBI, and you're about to blow my cover wide open, Detective Reynolds."

Other than the fact that he knew her name and his personality had just undergone a radical change, Sloan had no reason to believe he was anything other than what he'd seemed to be moments before. And yet . . . "Let's see some identification."

"It's in my jacket pocket."

"Sit up slowly," she ordered, following his movements with her gun. "Take it out with your left hand and toss it over here."

A flat leather case landed in the sand beside her foot. Keeping her weapon trained on him, she bent down and picked it up, flipping it open. It bore his picture on one side and his credentials on the other.

"Satisfied?" he asked, already rolling to his feet.

Sloan wasn't satisfied; she was furious. She let her arm drop to her side, and her body began to tremble in delayed reaction to the extremely tense situation he'd inflicted on her. "Was that your idea of fun, or do you have some other excuse for scaring the living hell out of me?" she demanded.

He shrugged as he brushed sand off the legs of his pants. "I had an opportunity to find out how you react under stress, and I decided to take advantage of it."

As Sloan watched him, she suddenly realized why he'd seemed familiar, and she also realized he wasn't telling her the entire truth. "You were at the park yesterday, and in the parking lot at city hall earlier today. You've been watching me for days."

Instead of replying, he zipped his cotton jacket up

enough to conceal the brown leather holster at his arm; then he finally gave her his full attention. "You're right. I have been watching you for days."

"But why? Why is the FBI interested in what I do?"

"We're not interested in you. We're interested in Carter Reynolds."

"You're what?" she said blankly.

"We're interested in your father."

Sloan stared at him, speechless and disoriented. Her father had long ago ceased to exist for her. Carter Reynolds was simply a name that belonged to a famous stranger, a name that no one ever mentioned to her. And yet, in the last twelve hours, that man, that name, seemed to be rising up out of the ashes of her past and sticking to her like soot. "I don't know what you think he's done, but whatever it is, I'm not involved. I haven't had anything to do with him in my entire life."

"We know all that." He glanced toward the shoreline where three men were running in their direction, one of them with a flashlight, its beam bouncing and fanning the sand like a lighthouse beacon gone haywire. "It looks like your reinforcements are on the way," Richardson observed, taking her by the elbow and propelling her forward. "Let's go meet them."

Sloan moved automatically, but her legs felt like wood and her brain like sawdust. "Be casual," the agent instructed. "Introduce me. If anyone asks, we met in Fort Lauderdale two months ago when you were attending the police seminar, and you invited me to Bell Harbor for the holiday weekend. Now, smile and wave at them."

Sloan nodded and obeyed, but she couldn't think of

anything except that the FBI was investigating Carter Reynolds . . . and they'd been tailing her . . . and a few moments ago, this particular FBI agent had tried to see if she'd take a bribe!

Jess reached them first, well ahead of the others, his breathing unaffected by his run. "We thought we heard shots coming from here," he said, scanning the dunes. "Didn't you hear it?"

Sloan made a valiant effort to seem amused while she lied to a trusted friend who'd just raced to her rescue. "Those were firecrackers, Jess. Two teenagers set them off in the dunes and then split."

"It sounded like shots," Jess argued, planting his hands on his hips and staring beyond her shoulder.

Ted Burnby and Leo Reagan lumbered to a stop a few moments later. "We thought we heard shots," Ted panted, but Leo Reagan was incapable of speech. Forty pounds overweight and completely out of shape, he leaned over and braced his hands on his knees, trying to catch his breath.

"A couple of teenage boys were setting off firecrackers," Sloan lied again, feeling more awkward and resentful with each falsehood.

Leo and Ted accepted that far more readily than Jess, but then Jess was smarter and more streetwise, a big city cop who'd defected to a less violent community but whose instincts were still sharp. After a few moments more, he finally gave up his frowning visual search of the dunes and frowned at her instead. "Pete's party is almost over," he said bluntly. "We were wondering why you hadn't shown up."

In the current circumstances, there was only one possible, believable answer Sloan could give. "I was on my way there just now."

He dropped his hands from his hips, adopting a slightly less aggressive stance as he surveyed her companion. "Who is this?"

To Sloan's relief, the FBI agent decided to introduce himself. "Paul Richardson," he said, reaching forward to shake hands with Jess, then Ted and Leo. Positively exuding relaxed male cordiality, he added, "I'm a friend of Sloan's from Fort Lauderdale."

"If you plan to get anything to eat at Pete's party, you'd better get over there," Leo warned the agent, his thoughts ever reverting to food. "The nachos are already gone, but the chili dogs are good."

"I've had a long day," Agent Richardson regretfully replied; then he looked at Sloan and said smoothly, "Sloan, you go to the party without me."

Sloan panicked. He intended to vanish without answering any more questions! She'd unmasked him, and now he would simply disappear from Bell Harbor, leaving her in an agony of uncertainty, with no way of finding out why the FBI was watching her. She was so desperate to stop him that she actually clutched his arm. "Oh, but I want you to meet Pete," she insisted. "We'll only stay a few minutes."

"I'd really be a drag tonight."

"No you wouldn't," Sloan said breezily.

His eyes narrowed in warning. "I think I would be."

"You couldn't possibly be a drag. You're such an *interesting* person."

"You're biased."

"No, I'm not," she argued, and in desperation Sloan switched to veiled blackmail and said to her friends, "Let me explain how *really interesting* he is—"

"Don't bore them with any details, Sloan," he interrupted with a meaningful smile. "Let's go meet your friend Pete and get something to eat."

Leo brightened at the mention of eating. "Hey, Paul, you like anchovies?"

"Love them," Richardson said enthusiastically, but Sloan had the impression he was clenching his teeth.

"Then you're in luck because the pizza had anchovies on it, so there's a lot of it left. Never met anybody who likes anchovies, except Pete and now you."

Throughout the discussion, Jess had been intently studying the FBI agent; then he seemed to lose interest and patience. "If we don't get back to the party, the party's going to come looking for us."

"Let's go," Agent Richardson said agreeably; then he startled Sloan by curving his arm around her shoulders in what appeared to be a casually possessive, affectionate gesture. But there was nothing affectionate about the hard warning squeeze he gave her shoulders.

Jess, Leo, and Ted fell into step beside them, and the four men quickly struck up a conversation about sports. Soon the relative isolation of the dunes began to give way to a well-lit stretch of beach, where portable radios competed with the sound of the surf and beach blankets dotted the sand like colorful bandages, occupied mostly by young couples who were romantically inclined.

8

The kiosk where Pete's party was taking place was next to a barbecue grill, and the smell of charcoal lighter and overcooked hot dogs was enough to make Sloan's nervous stomach churn. Pete and his fianceé, along with the rest of the party guests, were standing a few yards away, listening to Jim Finkle, who'd brought his guitar and was playing a beautiful flamenco song. "He should have been a professional musician, not a cop," Jess remarked, and he continued on to join Jim's audience.

Leo hung back a moment, however. "Have something to eat," he instructed Richardson, gesturing expansively to a wooden table covered with open pizza boxes, large bowls encrusted with the remnants of cheese dip, chili, and potato salad, and a platter of cold hot dogs with buns. "Drinks are over there in the cooler," Leo added before he headed off to listen to Jim. "Help yourself."

"Thanks, I will," Agent Richardson said, and with his hand still on Sloan's shoulder, he forced her to remain at his side until they reached the table. Sloan knew he'd been angry at first, but on the way here, he'd seemed to truly relax, joking with Leo about men who like to cook, and even laughing at something she said. Since she hadn't actually given his identity away, she naturally assumed he was feeling more charitable toward her. He even smiled as he handed her a plate and said furiously, "If you so much as utter one word tonight that might somehow jeopardize me, I will bust your ass for obstruction of justice."

His continued anger caught her so off-guard that Sloan gaped at him while she automatically took the plate from him. Still smiling, he handed her a napkin, took one for himself, and snapped, "Got it?"

Having issued a warning that she knew was no idle threat, he spooned food onto his plate from each bowl and picked up a cold hot dog, but Sloan noticed he did not touch the pizza—not even when the guitar music stopped and Leo and the group were returning to the table. Evidently Agent Richardson's dedication to duty and country stopped short of eating an anchovy.

"I wasn't really going to tell them anything about you," she explained, adopting the tone of calm reason that she always used to neutralize violent emotional situations. "But I am entitled to an explanation, and I couldn't let you disappear without giving me one."

"You should have waited until tomorrow."

Sloan dipped a limp taco chip into some salsa and put it on her plate, determined to appear as nonchalant as he. "Really?" she retorted. "Exactly how was I supposed to find you tomorrow?"

"You couldn't. I would have found you."

"With what?" she said bitterly. "Binoculars?"

Her rejoinder almost seemed to amuse him, but the man was like a human chameleon, so she couldn't be certain. "I see your point."

"Hey, Sloan, where've you been?" Pete demanded. With his arm looped over his fiancée's shoulder and a beer in his hand, he strolled up to them, and Jess tagged along. Mary Beth was blond and slender, a shy, refined, pretty girl who managed to look as happy as Pete without saying a word.

"Honey, show them the locket I gave you as a memento of the week before we got married," Pete instructed as soon as Sloan finished introducing them to her "friend" Paul Richardson. "It's solid fourteen karat gold," Pete added proudly.

Mary Beth lifted the heavy, heart-shaped locket at her throat so they could properly admire it.

"It's lovely," Sloan murmured, trying to concentrate on everything happening around them, watching for anything that Richardson might consider as "jeopardizing" his case.

Agent Richardson leaned forward to study the locket as if he had absolutely nothing on his mind now except socializing with Sloan's friends. "It's beautiful," he said.

"Last month," Mary Beth confided to him, breaking her personal record for lengthy conversation with a stranger, "Pete gave me a gold watch as a memento of the month before we got married."

"He's obviously crazy about you," Agent Richardson remarked.

"He's *obsessed*," Jess corrected with a grin, but Sloan

scarcely heard him. Her attention had riveted on an unexpected and immediate threat to Agent Richardson's masquerade. Sara was strolling down the beach straight toward
them with her date, and Sara never forgot an attractive
male face. Earlier, Sara had said she didn't intend to stay
very long at Pete's party, yet here she was. Agent Richardson
seemed to notice Sloan's distraction and followed her gaze.
"There's my friend Sara," Sloan warned him as casually as
she could.

"Along with her current man-of-the-week," Jess said
sarcastically as he took another swallow of beer. "This one
drives an eighty-thousand-dollar BMW. Blue. His name's
Jonathan."

Sloan had bigger problems at the moment than the
senseless bickering of her two closest friends. She stepped
forward as soon as the couple neared their group. "Sara,
hi!" she said, talking fast, hoping to bluff her way out of a
potential disaster. "Hi, Jonathan," she added. "I'm Sloan,
and this is a friend of mine, Paul Richardson, from Fort
Lauderdale." While the two men shook hands, Sloan
tried without success to distract Sara from her scrutiny of
the FBI agent. "Did you hear those firecrackers earlier?
Everyone thought they were gunshots."

"No," Sara said, studying Paul Richardson's face; then
her expression went from puzzled to enlightened. "I know
who you are. You were at the park yesterday!"

"Yes, I was."

"I saw you there. In fact, I pointed you out to Sloan—"

At that conflicting piece of information, Jess Jessup
lowered his beer can, staring hard at Richardson, and

Sloan leapt into the breach. "Unfortunately, when you pointed Paul out, his back was to me," she said with a quick laugh. "He was looking for me at the park, but we missed each other and didn't connect until later."

Sara gaped at her. "You mean, you knew he was going to be in town?"

"Of course not," Sloan said, improvising madly. "When I invited Paul here, he didn't think he could get away, and I assumed he wasn't coming. At the last minute, he realized he *could* get away for part of the weekend, and he tried to surprise me."

Sara's interest switched from the peculiar logistics of Sloan's fledgling romance to the financial prospects of Sloan's potential boyfriend. "Get away from what?" she asked.

To Sloan's relief, the FBI agent finally decided to help her out of the impossible predicament she was in, and he contributed an explanation. "I'm in the insurance business," he said politely.

"Really!" Sara said with an enthusiasm Sloan knew she didn't really feel. Sara wanted a rich husband for herself and she was determined that Sloan should have one, too. "Insurance is such an interesting field. Do you handle commercial, residential, or personal?"

"We handle most types of policies. Are you interested in adding to your existing insurance?" he quickly inquired, sounding as if he were about to launch into a sales pitch. It was a masterful diversionary tactic, because absolutely no one wanted to be at a party while someone tried to sell them insurance, and he obviously knew it. In other circumstances, Sloan would have been amused and impressed.

"No, I'm really not," Sara said, looking panicked at the prospect that he would start trying to persuade her differently.

To Sloan's enormous relief, he decided to extricate Sloan and himself from the whole ordeal. "Sloan's been so busy this weekend that we've hardly had any time together, and I have to leave tomorrow," he told the little gathering around them; then he looked at her as if they were at least very close friends. "How about fixing me a cup of coffee before I go back to the hotel, Sloan?"

"Great idea," Sloan managed, and with a quick wave to her friends, she turned and walked away with him.

Sara watched them for a long moment; then she glanced at her date. "Jonathan, I left my sweater somewhere around here. I think it's on Jim's blanket. Would you mind getting it for me?" Jonathan nodded and walked away.

Jess eyed the other man with a cynical twist of his lips; then he took another swallow of beer. "Tell me something, Sara," he said sardonically, "why do all the men you go out with have three-syllable first names?"

"Why do all the women you go out with have two-digit IQs?" Sara countered, but her verbal thrust lacked force because she was preoccupied with Sloan and Paul Richardson. Standing beside Jess, she watched the couple walking across the sand toward the street. "He's very attractive," she remarked, thinking aloud.

Jess shrugged. "He doesn't do anything for me."

"That's because *he* doesn't look like a topless dancer."

"I don't trust him," Jess stated, ignoring her topless dancer remark.

"You don't even know him."

"Neither does Sloan."

"Yes she does or she wouldn't have invited him here," Sara argued loyally, but in reality she was staggered that Sloan had not mentioned him to her.

"I'm surprised you aren't already on your way to your office to run a Dun and Bradstreet report on him," Jess said sarcastically.

"I thought I'd wait until tomorrow morning," Sara retorted, refusing to give him the satisfaction of knowing he could rile her.

"You are one mercenary little bitch."

Never before in their long history of rivalry had Jess Jessup ever crossed the line from sarcasm to profane personal attack. Sara felt tears sting her eyes, which upset her even more. "You really have a hard time dealing with rejection, don't you?" she fired back.

"You can't reject something that was never offered. And while we're being so blunt," he continued ruthlessly, "can you explain to me why Sloan Reynolds would want a shallow, mercenary, flirtatious tease like you for her best friend?"

Sara felt as if he'd punched her in the stomach. Never in her life had she confronted such virulent contempt from any human being except her mother, and the childhood memories flooded over her, paralyzing her. He was waiting for her to fight back, and she couldn't. For some reason that wasn't even clear anymore, she and Jess had disliked each other from the beginning, but she hadn't realized, hadn't even imagined, that he genuinely despised her. She stared at him, her eyes bright with unshed tears; then she dropped her gaze and swallowed, trying to force the words out. "I'm sorry," she managed as she turned away.

"You're sorry?" he repeated. "What the hell for?"

"For all the things I must have done to make you despise me."

Jonathan arrived with her sweater and spread it over her shoulders, and they walked away. "I'd like to go home now," she told her date. "I'm a little tired."

Jess watched her walk away. "Shit," he said bitterly; then he crushed the beer can in his hand and flung it into a trash container.

9

Sloan nodded at one of her neighbors who was walking his dog on the beach, and she smiled at another couple who were talking with friends in their front yard, but the minute she stepped into her own living room, she dropped the charade. "Why am I under FBI surveillance?" she demanded.

"How about that cup of coffee while I explain?"

"Yes, of course," Sloan replied after a startled pause, and led him into the kitchen. If he was willing to stay long enough for coffee, then he must be planning to give her a genuine explanation, rather than the brusque brush-off she'd feared.

She went over to the sink and filled the coffeepot with water. As she spooned coffee into the basket, she looked over her shoulder at him, watching as he removed his navy cotton jacket and draped it over the back of the chair. He was about forty, tall and athletically built, with short dark hair, dark eyes, and a square jaw. Clad in a white polo shirt, navy slacks, and navy canvas deck shoes, he would easily pass for an attractive, clean-cut, casually dressed businessman—except that he was also wearing a brown leather shoulder holster with a nine millimeter Sig-Sauer semiautomatic protruding from it. Since he seemed to be unbending a little, Sloan kept her tone very polite and even gave him a little smile of encouragement as she prodded him to begin. "I'm listening."

"Two weeks ago, we discovered that your father was going to make contact with you," he said, pulling out a kitchen chair and sitting down at the table. "We know he planned to telephone you today. What did he tell you?"

Sloan plugged the coffeepot in, turned around, and leaned against the Formica countertop. "Don't you know that, too?"

"Let's not play games, Detective."

His clipped, autocratic reply irked Sloan, but she had a peculiar feeling that if she kept her cool and played her cards just right, he was going to tell her everything she wanted to know. "He said he'd had a heart attack and he wanted me to come to Palm Beach for a few weeks."

"What did you tell him?"

"I don't even know the man. I've never laid eyes on him. I told him no. Absolutely not."

Paul Richardson already knew all that. He was interested only in her attitude and her spontaneous, unguarded reactions to his questions. "Why did you refuse?"

"I just told you why."

"But he explained to you that he'd had a heart attack and that he wants to get to know you before it's too late."

"It is already thirty years too late."

"Aren't you being a little too impulsive here?" he

argued. "There could be a lot of money in this for you—an inheritance."

His notion that Carter Reynolds's money should, or could, influence her decision filled Sloan with scorn. "Impulsive?" she challenged. "I don't think you could say that. When I was only eight years old, my mother lost her job and we ended up living on hot dogs and peanut butter sandwiches for weeks. My mother wanted to call him and ask him for money, but I looked up peanut butter in a schoolbook and proved to her that it was one of the most nutritious foods on earth; then I convinced her I loved peanut butter more than chocolate. When I was twelve, I got pneumonia, and my mother was afraid I was going to die if I didn't go to the hospital, but we didn't have any insurance. My mother told me she was going to call him and ask him to guarantee the hospital bill, but I didn't have to go to the hospital. Do you know why I didn't have to go to the hospital, Agent Richardson?"

"Why?" Paul asked, unwillingly touched by the fierce pride, the ferocious dignity emanating from her.

"Because I got better that very night. And do you know why I made such a miraculous recovery?"

"No, why?"

"I made that miraculous recovery because I *refused* to do anything that would ever, *ever* force us to accept one cent from that creep."

"I see."

"Then you'll also see why I wouldn't touch his money now, when I'm neither sick nor hungry. In fact, the only thing I'd turn down faster than his money at this moment is his invitation to spend time with him in Palm Beach so that he can soothe his conscience." She turned back to the counter and reached into a cabinet for two coffee mugs.

"What would it take to make you change your mind about visiting him?"

"A miracle."

Paul remained silent, waiting for her curiosity to rise to the surface once her animosity ebbed. He thought it would take her several minutes to make the emotional transition, but in that he had also underestimated her. "Did Carter Reynolds send you here to try to change my mind?" she demanded. "Are you here officially for the FBI, or is it possible that you're doing a little moonlighting for him on your vacation?"

Her suggestion was completely off-base, but it told Paul she had a clever imagination and the ability to make quantum leaps in logic on her own. Unfortunately, he did not regard either of those qualities as an advantage to him in the particular role he had in mind for her.

"The bureau is interested in some of Reynolds's business activities and in some of his business partners," he replied, ignoring her accusation. "Recently we uncovered information that indicates he's involved in certain criminal activities, but we don't have enough evidence yet to prove that he's directly or even knowingly involved."

Despite her genuine indifference to her father, Paul noticed that she went very still at the realization that he was probably a criminal. Instead of feeling some understandable gratification at the news, as he'd hoped and expected she would, she evidently didn't want to believe that of him. She got past it within moments, however, and sent him a quick, apologetic smile; then she poured coffee into the mugs and carried the tray over to the table.

"What kind of activities do you think he's involved in?"

"I'm not at liberty to say."

"I don't understand what any of this has to do with me," she said as she slid into a chair across from him. "You can't think I'm involved in whatever he's doing," she added with such sincerity in her voice that Paul smiled against his will.

"We don't think that. You were of no interest to us until a few weeks ago. We have an informant close to him in San Francisco who tipped us off about you and about his intention to contact you. Unfortunately, as of yesterday, that informant is no longer accessible to us."

"Why not?"

"He died."

"Of natural causes?" Sloan persisted, unconsciously reverting to the detective she was trained to be.

Richardson's almost imperceptible hesitation told her the answer even before he spoke. "No."

While Sloan was still reeling from that, Richardson continued. "We've had him under surveillance, but we haven't been able to get enough evidence to persuade a judge to authorize a wiretap. Reynolds maintains an impressive suite of offices in San Francisco, but he transacts the business we're interested in elsewhere, possibly at home. He's cautious and he's clever. He's leaving for Palm Beach and we'd like to have someone in place close to him while he's there."

"Me," Sloan concluded with a sinking feeling.

"Not you. Me. Tomorrow, I'd like you to have a sudden

change of heart and call Reynolds. Tell him you've decided you would like an opportunity to get to know him, and that you'll join him in Palm Beach."

"What good will that do you?"

He gave her an innocent look that wasn't innocent at all. "Naturally, you'll want to bring a friend along so you won't feel all alone and self-conscious in your new surroundings, someone you can while away the time with when you aren't spending it with your newfound father."

Appalled by what he was suggesting, Sloan leaned limply against the back of her chair and stared at him. "That friend would be you?"

"Of course."

"Of course," she repeated dazedly.

"If Reynolds objects to your bringing this friend along, tell him that we were planning to spend your two-week vacation together and that you won't change your vacation plans unless I can come along. He'll give in. He has a thirty-room house in Palm Beach, so an extra guest won't matter. Besides, he's not in any position to impose limitations on you right now."

An overpowering weariness settled over Sloan. "I'll have to think this over for a while."

"You can give me your answer tomorrow," he stipulated; then he glanced at his watch, took a few swallows of his scalding coffee, and stood up, reaching for his jacket. "I have to get back to the hotel for a phone call. I'll come back here in the morning. You're off tomorrow, so that will give us time to work out a story that will satisfy everyone here and everyone in Palm Beach. You will not be able to disclose the truth to anyone, Sloan. That specifically includes Sara Gibbon, Roy Ingersoll, and Jessup."

Sloan found it a little odd and unsettling that he "specifically" included those people, but when he added, "That also includes your mother," she felt a little better.

"I can't overemphasize the need for absolute secrecy," he continued as they walked through the living room. "No one is to be considered trustworthy here, or when we get to Palm Beach. There is more at risk than you know."

"I haven't agreed to go to Palm Beach with you yet," Sloan reminded him very firmly at the front door. "Also, it isn't a good idea to meet here tomorrow. Sara will be bursting with questions about you, and my mom is going to try to talk me into going to Palm Beach, even though I left a message on her answering machine saying that I absolutely wouldn't go. Both of them will probably appear here first thing in the morning."

"In that case, where can we meet?"

"How about the same place that we met tonight—at the dunes?"

Instead of replying, Paul shrugged into his jacket and studied the young woman waiting for his answer. In the last hour, she'd dealt calmly and efficiently with a man she believed to be an armed attacker, and with only moments to make the adjustment, she'd adapted to the need to pass her attacker off as her friend. A few minutes ago, he'd watched her adjust to the fact that her socialite father could actually be a criminal. Despite her small frame and delicate appearance, she was physically fit and mentally agile. Even so, he could see that the day had taken its toll on her. She looked tense and exhausted, and he felt an unaccustomed pang of guilt for having doused her vitality and warmth. He made an effort to lighten her mood a little. "When you see me at the dunes, could you be a little gentler with me this time?" he asked dryly.

"Are you going to attack me again?" she countered, managing a smile.

"I didn't attack you; I tripped."

"I like my version better," she jauntily informed him, and Paul laughed despite his worries.

As he crossed her front yard, however, his amusement gave way to concern over the problems she was likely to cause him in Palm Beach. Originally, he'd rejected the idea of using her in such a complex undercover scheme. He'd seen enough inept, inexperienced, and corrupt small-town cops to have developed an instinctive mistrust of them all, and the fact that this particular small-town cop had turned out to be a remarkably savvy, squeaky-clean young idealist who looked like a wholesome college cheerleader wasn't totally reassuring to him either.

He wasn't the least bit worried that she'd refuse to go to Palm Beach with him. Based on everything he'd read about Sloan Reynolds in her FBI file as well as his own personal observations, he was certain she would go to Palm Beach. The same stubborn integrity that had made her choose peanut butter as an eight-year-old, rather than contacting her father for money, would now force her to swallow her pride, reverse the upright, moral stance of a lifetime, and go to him in Palm Beach.

10

The Ocean View Motel did not actually offer a view of the ocean except to the seagulls roosting on its roof, but it did have a swimming pool, a lounge that was open until two A.M., and cable television. All those facilities were in use at one A.M., when Paul pulled up in front of the main entrance.

The television set in the lobby was tuned to CNN, the sound drowned out by the jukebox in the lounge, where a half dozen people were drinking at the bar and ignoring the dance floor. He walked out a rear door and skirted around the swimming pool, where some teenage boys were playing water volleyball and keeping up a steady stream of friendly macho obscenities.

The telephone in his room was ringing when he let himself inside. Out of habit, not necessity, he let the phone continue to ring while he double-locked the door, checked it, and pulled the draperies over the windows; then he walked over to the bed and answered the phone. The voice on the cellular phone belonged to an agent whom Paul had known for years, one who'd been in Bell

Harbor for the last two days helping Paul check out Sloan Reynolds. "Well?" the other agent demanded eagerly. "I saw you with her on the beach at a party. Is she going to cooperate?"

"She'll cooperate," Paul said. Cradling the phone on his shoulder, he leaned over and flipped on the air-conditioner to high, and the smell of cold, moldy air hit him in the face.

"I thought you weren't going to make contact with her until tomorrow morning."

"I changed my mind."

"When?"

"It might have been when she came up behind me and knocked me on my ass. No, I think it was right after that, when she was holding a nine millimeter Glock on me."

His friend let out a guffaw. "She made you? You're kidding!"

"No, I'm not, and if you harbor any hope of my continued friendship, you won't bring it up again." Despite the gruffness of his tone, Paul couldn't help smiling at the remarkable indignities that had been inflicted on him tonight by a naïve, inexperienced female cop who weighed less than one hundred ten pounds.

"I heard three shots tonight. With all her marksmanship medals from the police academy, I'm surprised she didn't at least nick you."

"She wasn't firing at me. She'd cornered what she believed to be an armed assailant on a crowded beach, and she knew her pals were less than three hundred yards away. Rather than taking the risk of disarming me single-handedly, which could have ultimately jeopardized the safety of innocent bystanders, she fired into the air and signaled for help. It was a good call on her part. Prudent, expedient, and imaginative."

He paused to prop a pillow against the headboard and stretch out on the bed before he continued. "By the time her backup arrived a few minutes later, she'd discovered who I am, grasped what I needed her to do, and she assumed the role she needed to play and pulled it off. All things considered," he finished, "she showed remarkable skill and adaptability."

"She sounds like she's perfect for your job then."

Leaning his head back, Paul closed his eyes and battled with his private misgivings. "I wouldn't go that far."

"Are you still worried that once she's in Reynolds's Palm Beach palace, surrounded by all his wealth and rich friends, she'll be tempted to switch sides on you?"

"After talking to her tonight, I'd say that's extremely unlikely."

"Then what's the problem? By your own admission she's smart, she's adaptable, and she's also a better shot than you are." When his friend didn't rise to that bait, he added cheerfully, "I don't think we should hold it against her that she also happens to have great legs and a beautiful face." In the telling silence that followed, the humor vanished from his voice. "Paul, we've ascertained that she's not corrupt, you don't think she's corruptible, and now you've discovered she's clever. What the hell is bothering you, anyway?"

"What bothers me is that she's a Girl Scout. It's fairly

obvious she became a cop because she wants to help people. She rescues kites from trees and searches for mongrels in the street; then she stays on duty so she can comfort an old Hispanic woman whose house is burning to the ground. Given a choice between living on peanut butter when she was a kid, or asking her father for money, she chose the peanut butter. She's an idealist to the core, and *that* is what bothers me about her."

"Excuse me?"

"Do you know what an idealist is?"

"Yes, but I'd like to hear your definition, because until ten seconds ago I thought idealism was a rare virtue."

"Maybe so, but it's not an asset to me in a situation like this. Idealists have a peculiar habit of deciding for themselves what's right and wrong; they listen to their own voices; then they act on their own judgment. Unless idealism has been tempered, it bows to no authority but its own. Idealists are loose cannons in any situation, but in a sensitive operation like this one, a *naïve* idealist like Sloan Reynolds could become a nuclear warhead."

"I gather from that enlightening flight into philosophy that you're afraid she won't let you tell her what to think?"

"Exactly."

Sara said good night to Jonathan as soon as she reached her front door; then she took a hot shower, trying to steam away the chill of Jess's taunts. Somehow, the verbal combat had broken out between them soon after they'd first met, and she'd fallen into the habit of defending herself with periodic counterattacks. But tonight, he'd gone too far. He'd turned brutal. Worse, there'd been an element of truth in his words, which hurt her even more.

She was toweling her hair dry when her doorbell rang. Puzzled and cautious, she wrapped herself in a long robe, went into the living room, and peeked between the draperies before she went to the door. A Bell Harbor police cruiser was parked at the curb in front of her house. Pete must have decided to continue his party here, she thought with a weary smile, and the others would soon be arriving.

She opened the front door, and her smile abruptly faded. Jess Jessup was standing on her porch, his dark hair tousled as if he'd been running his hands through it—or, more likely, some eager woman on the beach had rumpled his hair after Sara left. Judging by the grim expression on his face, the lady's attentions must have been unsatisfactory. Injecting as much ice into her voice as she could, Sara said scornfully, "If you're not here on official police business, go away and don't ever come back here again. For Sloan's sake, I'll be polite to you if she's with you, but if she's not, you stay away from me!" She wanted to say more, and worse, but she suddenly felt like crying, which made her feel stupid and even angrier.

His brows snapped together as she finished her tirade. "I came here to apologize for the things I said tonight," he said, sounding angry, not apologetic.

"Fine," Sara said coldly. "You've done it. It doesn't change my mind." She started to shove the door closed, but he blocked it with his foot.

"Now what?" she demanded.

"I just realized I didn't come here to apologize." Before she could react, he caught her shoulders and pulled her toward him. "Get your hands off me—" she stormed; then his mouth swooped down and captured hers in a hard kiss that was easy to resist—until it softened. Shock and anger and an awful twinge of pleasure made her pulse race, but she stayed perfectly still, refusing to give him the satisfaction of struggling or cooperating.

As soon as he released her, Sara stepped back, her right hand groping for the doorknob. "Is assault a turn-on for those bimbos you date?" she demanded, and before he could reply, Sara gave the door a mighty shove that sent it slamming in his face.

Paralyzed, Sara stayed where she was until she heard his car start; then she slowly turned and leaned limply against the front door. Dry-eyed, she stared at the carefully chosen accessories she'd bought for her living room— a beautiful porcelain vase, an antique footstool, a small Louis XIV table. They were cherished items, of fine quality—beautiful symbols of the beautiful life she planned for herself and the children she would someday have.

11

It was dusk when Carter Reynolds hung up the telephone in his office at home and swiveled around in his chair, gazing out the large circular window behind him. The San Francisco skyline stretched out before him, shrouded in fog—mysterious, exciting. In two weeks, he had to exchange all this for the monotonous blue skies of Palm Beach in March, a pilgrimage that his family had taken for generations, a tradition that his grandmother would not allow him to forsake.

In recent years, he'd come to regard the biannual trips to Palm Beach as increasingly irksome, unavoidable intrusions on his life, but after this last phone call, the trip was suddenly ripe with life-altering possibilities. For nearly an hour, he remained where he was, contemplating a complex variety of scenarios; then he swiveled around and pressed a button on the telephone that activated the house intercom. "Where is Mrs. Reynolds?" he asked the servant who answered.

"I believe she's resting in her room before dinner, sir."

"And my daughter?"

"I believe she is with Mrs. Reynolds, reading to her, sir."

Pleased that the women were together, he stood up and headed for the third floor, where forty years ago, his grandfather's architect had decided the family's suites should be located. Ignoring the elevator, he walked up a broad staircase with an ornate black wrought-iron railing; then he turned to the right, down a paneled hall where portraits of his ancestors brooded back at him from their heavy, richly carved frames.

"I'm glad the two of you are together," he said when Paris answered his knock and let him in. The room made him feel claustrophobic with its maroon brocade draperies perpetually drawn over the windows to block out the light and the cloying scent of lavender hanging in the air. Trying not to let it depress him, he looped his arm over Paris's shoulder and smiled at his grandmother, who was seated in a baroque chair beside the fireplace. With her white hair in a chignon and her frail body garbed in a gray dress with a high collar held together by a large filigree and ruby broach, Edith Reynolds looked like a well-to-do Whistler's Mother, except her spine was more rigid.

"What is it, Carter?" she demanded in her imperious voice. "Do be quick, will you. Paris was reading to me, and we're in a very good part of the story."

"I have exciting news for you both," he said, waiting politely for Paris to be seated.

"Sloan just called me," he told them. "She's had a change of heart. She's decided to join us in Palm Beach and stay with us for two weeks."

His grandmother relaxed back in her chair, and Paris shot out of hers, their expressions as opposite as their physical reactions to the news.

"You've done well," his grandmother told him with a regal inclination of her head and a slight thinning of her lips that was the closest she ever came to a smile.

His chestnut-haired daughter stared at him like a tense thoroughbred about to bolt over the gate. "You—you can't just walk in here and spring this on me at the last minute! I thought she wasn't coming. This isn't fair. I shouldn't have to deal with this. I don't want to go to Palm Beach!"

"Paris, don't be ridiculous. Of course you're going to Palm Beach." He turned toward the door, his last words spoken politely but with the quiet force of an edict. "And while we're there," he added, turning to face her, "I will expect you to spend as much time as possible with Noah. You can't expect to marry a man when you avoid him at every possible opportunity."

"I haven't been avoiding him; he's been in Europe!"

"He'll be in Palm Beach. You can make up for lost time while you're there."

Courtney Maitland perched on the arm of a leather chair in front of her brother's desk, watching him load files into two briefcases. "You just got back from Europe and you're already leaving again," she complained. "You spend more time away than you spend here at home."

Noah spared a glance for his fifteen-year-old half-sister, who was wearing a tight, shiny, black spandex skirt that barely covered her upper thighs and a hot pink tank top that barely covered her breasts. She looked like a pretty, sulky, overindulged teenager with an appalling taste for lewd clothes, all of which was true of her in his opinion. "Where the hell do you shop, anyway?" he demanded.

"I happen to be dressed in the height of fashion—my fashion," she informed him.

"You look like a hooker."

Courtney ignored that. "So how long are you going to be gone this time?"

"Six weeks."

"Business or pleasure?"

"A little of both."

"That's the way you described that trip to Paraguay when you took me with you," she said with an eloquent shudder. "It rained all the time, and your 'business' friends carried machine guns."

"No they didn't. Their bodyguards had machine guns."

"Your business friends had guns, too. Handguns. I saw them."

"You were hallucinating."

"Okay, you're right, and I'm wrong. It was Peru where your 'business' associates had handguns poking out of their jackets, not Paraguay."

"Now I remember why I stopped taking you on business trips with me. You're a pain in the ass."

"I'm observant." A paper slid off his desk, onto the floor, and Courtney swept it up and handed it to him.

"The result's the same either way," he said as he took the paper, glanced at it, and added it to the items in his briefcase. "However, as it happens, I'm going to Palm Beach this trip, not Paraguay or Peru. Palm Beach—you remember—we have a house there? We go there every year when you're on winter break. Your father is there now. And you and I will be there tomorrow."

"I'm not going this year. Dad will spend all his time on the golf course. You'll spend all your time behind closed doors either in a bunch of meetings or telephone conferences, and when you aren't doing that, you'll be aboard the *Apparition*—having meetings and phone conferences."

"You make me sound duller than dirt."

"You are dull—" He glanced up at her, and the almost imperceptible change in his expression made Courtney hastily correct herself. "I mean you lead a dull life. All work, no play."

"A vivid contrast to your own life. No wonder you can't see the merit in mine."

"What lucky lady is going to be the fleeting object of your sexual attention while you're in Palm Beach?"

"You are begging for a spanking."

"I'm too old to spank. Besides, you aren't my father or my mother."

"That reaffirms my faith in God."

She decided to change the subject. "I saw Paris at Saks Fifth Avenue yesterday. They're leaving for Palm Beach, too. You know, Noah, if you aren't careful, you're going to wake up one morning married to Paris."

He tossed a gold fountain pen and pencil into one of the briefcases and snapped it shut; then he spun the combination lock. "That would be the shortest marriage on record."

"Don't you like Paris?"

"Yes."

"Then why not marry her?"

"For starters, she's way too young for me."

"You're right. You're forty and that's over the hill."

"Are you trying to be obnoxious?"

"I don't have to try; it comes naturally. If Paris were over the hill, like you, would you marry her then?"

"No."

"Why not?"

"Mind your own damned business."

"You are my business," she said sweetly. "You're the closest thing to a sibling I have."

It was a deliberate effort to soften and manipulate him, and Noah knew it. It was also somewhat effective, so he said nothing and decided to save his breath for the battle he was bound to have with her over going to Palm Beach. Her father was thinking of staying down there permanently and enrolling Courtney in school there, but Noah had no intention of getting involved in that war.

"Don't you want to get married to anyone?"

"No."

"Why not?"

"Because I've been there, done that, and didn't like it."

"Jordanna turned you against marriage completely, didn't she? Paris thinks Jordanna turned you off on all women."

He glanced up from the files he was sorting through, a

frown of impatience gathering on his forehead. "She thinks what?"

"Paris doesn't know about the women you take with you on the yacht, or the ones who sneak out of your hotel rooms that I see on those rare occasions when you take me somewhere with you. She thinks you're wounded and noble and celibate."

"Fine. Let her go on thinking that."

"Too late. Sorry. I told her all about them. The whole terrible, lurid truth."

Noah had been scribbling a note for his assistant, and he didn't stop writing or lose his concentration. "I'm taking you with me to Palm Beach."

"No way! You can't."

He stopped writing and focused the blast of a gaze on her that made his contemporaries shrivel. "Watch me," he said softly. "Now, start packing."

"I won't."

"Fine. I'll take you just the way you are, and you can live in that disgusting outfit you're wearing. You decide."

"You're bluffing."

"I don't bluff. You should know that better than most people, after all these years of confrontations."

"I hate you, Noah."

"I don't give a damn. Now, get packed and meet me downstairs in the morning."

She slid off the arm of the chair, her eyes glistening with unshed tears. The tears were futile. He was impervious.

12

Preoccupied with her impending departure for Palm Beach, Sloan didn't notice Jess's patrol car behind her until she was a mile from home and he flipped on his light bar. Startled by the flashing lights behind her, she glanced in her rearview mirror and saw him give her a thumbs-up. "Have a good vacation—" he called over his loudspeaker.

Sara's car was parked behind Kimberly's when Sloan pulled into her driveway, and Paul Richardson was there, too, rearranging luggage in the trunk of a bright blue coupe he'd probably rented for their trip. Sloan hadn't seen him in the two weeks since she'd agreed to go to Palm Beach, but he'd spent an extra few hours with her on Presidents' Day so he could have lunch with Sloan and her mother. He'd had a much easier time convincing Kimberly at lunch that he was romantically interested in Sloan than he was having now, trying to get the luggage into the car, Sloan noted. He finally gave up, pulled one of his suitcases out of the trunk, and opened the car door instead. "Do you need help?" she offered as he tried to shove his bulky suitcase behind the driver's seat and onto the car's backseat.

"No, I need a U-Haul," he said with a wry smile.

"I'll be ready to go in five minutes," Sloan promised. Since she'd packed only two medium-size suitcases that she'd borrowed from Sara, she assumed that either the car's trunk was very small or Agent Richardson's luggage was very large, but in any case, she didn't want to discuss suitcases or their contents. As soon as her mother and Sara had realized Sloan was going to Palm Beach, they'd started talking about clothing, and they'd kept right at it until Sloan couldn't bear another word on the subject.

She'd never liked to spend money on clothes, and unlike her mother and her best friend, Sloan *did* not regard this trip as a reason to change her spending habits or her "image." Of course, they didn't realize she was going to Palm Beach to spy on her father, so they both had big dreams for the trip, and to Sloan's frustrated amusement, their dreams seemed to hinge on what Sloan would be *wearing* when the right moment presented itself. "Carter will be dazzled," Kimberly happily predicted the day Sloan told her of her impending trip, "when he sees you in that black beaded cocktail dress in Faylene's window. I'm going to buy it for you."

Sara's hopes for Sloan were of a different kind: "I can see you now at the Palm Beach Polo Club," Sara said dreamily, "wearing my red linen sheath when 'Mr. Perfect' walks in . . . handsome, rich, exciting . . ."

"Stop it, both of you," Sloan had interrupted firmly.

"Mom, don't you dare spend one dollar on anything for me. If you do, I'll return whatever it is without wearing it. Sara, I appreciate your offer, but I refuse to play dress-up to impress Carter Reynolds."

"Okay, but what about impressing 'Mr. Perfect'?"

"He sounded perfect for you, not me," Sloan pointed out with an affectionate smile. "Besides, I'm taking Paul with me, remember?"

"Yes, but you're not engaged to him, so there's no harm in keeping your options open, and my red sheath is just perfect. It's 'flirty' but not 'forward'—"

"Please, don't start—" Sloan pleaded, covering her ears in her desperation to stop Sara from launching into one of her enthusiastic fashion narratives. "I'll make you a deal. I'll agree to keep my options open if you'll leave the subject of clothing closed." She stood up to illustrate her determination to permanently end discussion of the topic and announced she was going to bed.

But the discussion didn't end there; it raged on day after day, hour after hour, in her presence and in her absence. In fact, Kimberly and Sara had been so persistent that as Sloan finally hugged them both good-bye, she half expected Sara to produce yet another garment bag filled with more of her own clothes for Sloan to consider. Instead, they both instructed her to have a good time and waited in the doorway to see her off.

Kimberly watched Paul Richardson walk around the car and politely open the passenger door for Sloan. "She's going to look gorgeous in that black beaded cocktail dress," Kim predicted happily. "She has a beautiful new wardrobe to begin a beautiful new life, a life with her father in it, and Paul Richardson in it—"

"And my red linen dress in it—" Sara added with a nervous giggle.

The car began to move away from the curb, and both women waved a cheery good-bye, their expressions innocent. "Paul was very sweet about keeping the other two suitcases out of sight," Kimberly said.

"Yes, he was," Sara agreed, but her smile wavered with uncertainty. "I'd feel a lot better if this romance of theirs didn't seem so sudden. I mean, I wish Sloan knew him better."

"I don't," Kimberly announced cheerfully to an astonished Sara. "She's always been much too serious about life and much too cautious about men. To tell you the truth, I've wished for years that she'd be more . . . more . . . *impulsive!*"

Tipping her head toward the departing car, Sara grinned at the woman she loved more than her own mother. "I think you've gotten your wish, Mom."

13

They'd been on the road for nearly two hours, and Paul stole a worried glance at his silent passenger. She was sitting very still and straight, her features carefully composed, but with each passing mile, he could almost feel her dread increasing, her tension mounting, and he felt a pang of remorse for what she was being compelled to do.

In order to avoid giving her any information that might somehow cause her to back out of the trip, he'd spoken to her only once on the telephone since Presidents' Day. During that call, she'd tried to ask him several questions about her father and sister, but he'd insisted she save all that for the drive to Palm Beach. He was ready now to answer her questions, anxious to ease the way for her and reinforce her resolve, but she seemed unable to speak or even meet his eyes when he spoke.

He tried to come up with something encouraging that might come out of this for her. If she were an ordinary young woman who was about to meet her father and sister for the first time, she'd certainly have some hope of future closeness to fortify her for what lay ahead. But

Sloan wasn't going to them for sentimental reasons; she was swallowing her pride, acting out of duty, and she was going there to spy on them.

There was scant possibility of any remotely happy ending for her, so Paul invented one, partly to soothe his conscience and partly to lift her spirits. In his fairy-tale scenario, Carter Reynolds turned out to be innocent of any criminal activity, he developed a strong paternal attachment to Sloan, and the two of them ended up caring about each other.

Ignoring the astronomical odds against all that, Paul said, "Sloan, it may not seem like it to you now, but this trip could have a very positive outcome for your entire family." She stopped staring out the windshield and stared at him instead. Since it was the only encouragement she seemed able to give him, Paul forged ahead. "Right now, your father is merely a suspect who we're investigating. You're helping us to get closer to him and to the facts, and once we've done that, we may discover he's completely innocent of any criminal wrongdoing."

"What do you think the chances are of that?"

Paul hesitated. He didn't want to insult her intelligence or repay her trust by completely misleading her. "Slim," he said honestly. "But it is a possibility. Now, let's consider the situation on a more personal level: There's no doubt he's been a sorry excuse for a father, but he clearly has some regrets, or he wouldn't have contacted you. None of us really knows everything that happened to bring an end to your parents' marriage, but based on what you've told me, his mother was the instigator of the divorce proceedings and the custody arrangement. She's the one who came to Florida to bring him back to San Francisco after his father's stroke, correct?"

"Yes, but he went along with her plan."

"True, but he was only in his twenties at the time. He may have gone along with her out of weakness, or immaturity, or cowardice, or because she convinced him it was his sacred familial duty, who knows? Those are mostly character flaws, but they aren't necessarily unforgivable or permanent. All we really know for certain is that she died three months ago, and almost immediately afterward, your father is asking you for a reconciliation."

Sloan realized Paul was truly trying to be helpful, but he was also making her feel uneasy and uncertain when she was already strangling on other emotions she could scarcely contain. She wanted to ask him to stop, but some innate sense of justice or maybe simple curiosity prompted her to pursue his reasoning one step further. "What about my sister? What possible justification could she have for never trying to contact my mother?"

Paul glanced sideways at her. "Maybe she wonders why her own mother never tried to contact *her.*"

"Under the terms of the agreement they forced my mother to sign, she was not allowed to contact my sister."

"Maybe Paris doesn't know that."

Sloan stared hard at him, trying to suppress the first, silly flare of hope she'd felt in decades about a possible family reunion. "You said you had an informant in the household in San Francisco. Do you know any of this for a fact?"

"No. Paris was never of much interest to us. All I know

about her is that some people think she's aloof and cold, while others think she's quiet, refined, and elegant. Everyone agrees she's beautiful. She's a nationally ranked tennis player, a five-handicap golfer, and a master at bridge. When she plays in tournaments, she's usually teamed up with your father, who is also a nationally ranked tennis player, an excellent bridge player, and a scratch golfer."

Sloan expressed her sacrilegious disregard of such frivolous accomplishments by rolling her eyes and lifting her shoulders in a Gallic shrug—a gesture that was somehow so prim, and so unexpectedly cute, that Paul had to choke back a startled laugh. "Then there's Edith," he said, mentioning the last surviving member of the family. "She'll be in Palm Beach, too."

"Edith?" Sloan repeated.

"Your great-grandmother on your father's side," Paul explained, and bluntly added, "She's a ninety-five-year-old dragon with a quick temper who terrorizes and intimidates anyone who crosses her path. She's also a notorious cheapskate. She's worth about fifty million dollars, but she reportedly throws a fit if more than one lamp is lit in a room."

"She sounds delightful," Sloan said dryly; then she had to fight down the uneasy awareness of her own frugality—Sara had called her a miser just last week, and her own mother lamented that Sloan hated to part with money. But then, Sara and Kimberly were both hopeless spendthrifts, Sloan reminded herself bracingly. She, on the other hand, lived on a tight budget because she'd learned the necessity of it in childhood and because her salary as a police detective left her very little money to spare. If she had plenty of money, she'd certainly spend it. Well, some of it.

Satisfied that he'd relieved a little of her anxiety with his best-case scenario, Paul left her pretty much to her own thoughts after that, but as they neared the Palm Beach exit off the highway, he knew he had to bring her back to reality. After his efforts to make her relatives seem human and possibly likable, he now had to remind her that her father was a criminal suspect and her role was to spy on him. "Your father's house is about ten minutes from here," he said. "Earlier, I gave you my best-case scenario. I'm afraid we have to prepare now for a worst-case scenario. Let's go over our stories again, so we can do our jobs."

She turned in her seat, giving her full attention to him. "Okay, go ahead."

"We're going to tell them we met in Fort Lauderdale five months ago, when I was attending an insurance seminar there," he explained, reminding her of the personal details about himself that they might expect her to know. "My father's name is Clifford; my mother's name was Joan. She died several years ago. I was an only child; I grew up in Chicago and graduated from Loyola University. I still live in Chicago and work for Worldwide Underwriters Inc. You and I haven't been able to spend much time together because we live so far apart, and that's why it was so important to us to spend these two weeks together." He flipped on the turn indicator and changed lanes, preparing to take the next Palm Beach exit. "Clear so far?"

Sloan nodded. They'd discussed all this on Presidents' Day, but now her curiosity was piqued. "Is any of that true?"

"No," he said in a flat tone that discouraged any further

effort to inquire into his real personal life. "My cover is in place, and it will hold up if Reynolds decides to check me out, but I doubt we'll need it. Once your family realizes we haven't known each other long or spent a lot of time together, they won't get suspicious when you don't know everything about me. They won't be particularly interested in me anyway, so they won't ask many questions. I'll be there to come up with answers when they're needed. If I'm not around, say whatever you want but remember to fill me in later. Now, let's go over your background. Have you decided on a suitable career for yourself?"

"Yes."

They'd both agreed that it would be foolish to tell Carter Reynolds that Sloan was a police detective. According to Paul's San Francisco informant, Reynolds hadn't known anything whatsoever about Sloan when he called Kimberly to get her phone number, and there was no reason to think he'd learned anything at all when he called her at work. Paul was still elated about that. "I can't get over how lucky we were that your mother didn't have a chance to tell him anything about you the day he called her."

"Luck didn't have anything to do with it. My mother was dying to tell him all about me, but he didn't give her the chance because he's heartless and rude. He hasn't called her in thirty years because he doesn't care how she feels or what she thinks. When he finally did call her, he told her he didn't have time to talk, he only had time to get my phone number. As soon as she gave him my direct number at work, he told her he'd call her again sometime when he was less rushed, and he hung up!"

"I see your point."

Sloan didn't mean to dampen his spirits. "You got your lucky break later, when he called me," she said with a smile. "I've quizzed Sara without her realizing it, and she says she remembers exactly how Captain Ingersoll answered my phone and exactly what he said to Carter. Nothing Ingersoll said would have alerted my father that he'd called the police station or that I'm a cop. *That* was lucky."

"I was due for a lucky break in this case," Paul said wryly. "Now tell me what career you picked out for yourself."

"In college, I majored in marine biology and then mathematics before I switched to law enforcement, but you said you wanted me to pick a career that Reynolds will regard as frivolous or innocuous. A career in science or mathematics doesn't qualify, and I don't have enough knowledge in either of those fields to pull it off. I was still trying to think of a solution last week while I was waiting for Sara to finish talking to a client—and that's when it hit me—the perfect career."

"Don't keep me in suspense; what is it?"

"For the next two weeks, I'm an interior designer."

"You're right." He laughed. "It's just what I had in mind. Do you know enough about it to pull it off?"

"I know enough about it to bluff." For years, she'd listened to Sara rhapsodizing over furnishings and accessories, and Sloan was reasonably certain she'd absorbed enough jargon and information to fake her way through a few superficial conversations with Carter Reynolds, who would surely find the subject boring, anyway.

"There's one more thing we need to discuss," he said, his voice taking on an implacable quality. "I want to be absolutely certain you're clear on your role in Palm Beach and on the legalities involved if you deviate one inch from it."

Sloan realized exactly where he was going, but she was curious to hear his logic anyway.

"Legally, your father is entitled to a reasonable expectation of privacy in his own home. Because you're going there at my request, you are technically working for the FBI. Since the FBI does not have a search warrant, any evidence you *or* I discover will be thrown out of court unless it was in plain view and in a place he allows us to be. You may pass along information to me, but you cannot search for it. Am I making this clear? I don't want you to so much as open a drawer unless someone asked you to get something out of it."

Sloan suppressed a smile at the fact that Paul felt the need to explain what was elementary legal information. "Actually, I learned a little about this on an episode of *Law and Order*."

He relaxed a little, but his tone remained emphatic. "As to conversations you might overhear, the same rules apply. Make sure you're somewhere you're allowed to be, and that you had a legitimate reason to be there. It would also help if you happened to be in plain sight of someone at the time. As to telephones, there's to be no eavesdropping on extensions. We're going to play this completely by the book. Got it?"

Sloan nodded. "Got it. The thing is, no matter how

scrupulous we are, his lawyers will shower motions to suppress on the court like pamphlets."

"Your job is to make certain you haven't done anything to make a judge feel inclined to grant them. The point to remember is that our primary reason for being here is not to look for evidence. I'm here to keep an eye on him. He spends a lot of time in Palm Beach during the year. I want to know what he does while he's here, where he goes, and who he meets. You're here because it's the only way I could get in and because you may be able to pass along helpful information that you come across. You aren't here to look for that information."

"I understand."

Satisfied, Paul tried to think of something more lighthearted to discuss, and after a moment, he brought up the topic they'd been on before this. "I think passing yourself off as an interior decorator is an inspired choice. Reynolds won't feel threatened in any way. It's perfect."

Sloan nodded, but as the time for her masquerade approached, the idea of faking a career, particularly Sara's, didn't feel perfect at all to Sloan. She was going into unknown territory where she was going to have to interact with lofty strangers, and in hiding her true career, they were not only eliminating a major topic of safe conversation, they were erasing her life.

"Sloan?" Paul prodded as he turned onto a wide boulevard lined with imposing oceanfront mansions. "Are you having second thoughts about being able to pass yourself off as an interior decorator?"

"Interior designer," she corrected him with a sigh.

"No, I'll be all right. It's all a matter of taste anyway; so if I make some sort of blunder, they'll just assume I don't have any taste."

"That works for me," he announced cheerfully, annoyingly pleased by the possibility that she might actually disgrace herself in such a way. "After all," he explained, "the more Reynolds underestimates you, the more likely he'll be to let his guard down. Feel free to seem inept, gullible, and even foolish whenever possible. He'll go for it."

"What makes you think he'd believe I'm any of those things?"

"Because, according to our information, that's approximately how he remembers your mother," Paul said, choosing his words carefully. He didn't want to tell her that Reynolds had actually referred to Kimberly as "a nitwit," "a hopeless Pollyanna," and "the quintessential dumb blonde."

"I just know I'm going to hate that man." Drawing a long, calming breath, Sloan said, "What does his opinion of my mother have to do with what he'll believe about me?"

Paul gave her a wry smile. "You look like her."

"I don't think so."

"Well, you do," he said flatly. "Reynolds will think so, too, and he'll naturally assume you are as"—he paused to choose the least offensive of the words Reynolds had used to describe Sloan's mother—"as gullible as she was."

Sloan had the alarming impression that he'd already arrived at some decision about all this, but that he was easing her toward it because she wasn't going to like it.

"I gather you'd like me to reinforce his misconception about my mother's and my intellect, is that right?"

"If you can."

"And since you knew I was probably going to hate this idea, you decided to save it until we were practically in his driveway."

"Exactly," he said unashamedly.

Sloan leaned her head against the headrest, closed her eyes, and indulged in a rare moment of self-pity. "Oh, great. This is just great."

"Look, Sloan, you've come here to do a job, not make Reynolds admire you, right?"

Sloan swallowed. "Right," she sighed, but mentally she cringed as the next two weeks unfolded in her imagination.

He flipped on his turn signal as they approached a palatial Mediterranean-style villa with a flagstone driveway and huge iron gates blocking the entry at the street.

"One last thing before we go in there. I know it's going to be hard, but you *must* hide your hostility from Reynolds. He's no fool, and he has to believe you want a reconciliation. Can you hide your feelings about him?"

Sloan nodded. "I've been practicing."

"How do you practice a thing like that?" he asked dryly as he turned into the driveway.

"I stand in front of the mirror and think about something awful he's done; then I practice smiling until I actually look happy about it."

Paul laughed aloud and covered her hand in a brief, encouraging squeeze; then he pulled up to the gates. He lowered his side window and reached out to press a button on a brass box mounted on a pedestal beside the car door; then he paused and looked at Sloan. "Smile for the camera," he instructed with a meaningful nod toward the tiny, glass-covered hole in the metal box on the pedestal.

He pressed the button on the box.

"Yes?" a male voice spoke.

"Sloan Reynolds and Paul Richardson," he said.

The gates parted in the center and swung open.

14

Whenever Sloan had imagined this moment, she'd pictured her father opening the door and greeting her personally, so now she braced herself to look pleasant but noncommittal. Her effort was successful but entirely wasted on the tall, fair-haired butler who actually opened the door and who managed to seem almost as pleasant and even more noncommittal than she. "Good afternoon, Miss Reynolds. Good afternoon, Mr. Richardson," he intoned in a deep voice that bore faint traces of a Nordic accent. "The family is expecting you. Please follow me."

He led them down a wide, tiled hallway with archways on both sides that opened into numerous spacious rooms, all of them furnished in European antiques. At the end of the hall, a door opened suddenly, and Sloan had her first look at her father as he strode forward to greet her himself. Since he'd had a heart attack, and since he'd been so anxious for an opportunity to make amends, she naturally expected him to appear remorseful and haggard, but the man striding toward her was lithe, tanned, and very handsome. "Sloan!" he said, stopping in front of her and holding out his hand.

Sloan automatically held out her hand for what she

presumed would be a handshake, but he covered her hand with both of his and kept it. "My God, you look so much like your mother that it's almost eerie," he said with a warm smile; then he added with simple sincerity, "Thank you for coming."

Sloan's entire body was shaking with nervous tension, but somehow her voice sounded steady and normal. "This is my friend, Paul Richardson."

The two men shook hands; then Carter's gaze returned to her. "For some reason," he admitted ruefully, "I assumed the friend you were bringing with you was female. Nordstrom had two guest rooms made ready, but—"

"That will be fine," Sloan said swiftly.

His smile warmed even more, and Sloan had the impression that her father was pleased that she wasn't so brazen that she wished to share a bedroom in his home with her "boyfriend." She wasn't quite certain how he managed to communicate that to her, and she had to remind herself that she didn't care what he thought. "Nordstrom will take care of your luggage," he said. "Now, come along with me. Your sister and your great-grandmother are in the solarium."

As they started forward, a slender man of about thirty-five with thinning hair and wire-rimmed glasses walked out of a room near the main staircase carrying a sheaf of papers that he was reading. Carter stopped him and introduced him to Sloan and Paul as Gary Dishler. "Gary is my assistant," Carter explained. "Whatever you need while you're here, just ask Gary if I'm not here."

With a pleasant smile and a manner as informal as the

open-collared shirt he was wearing, Gary shook hands with both of them. "Please don't hesitate to call on me for any reason," he said. "I'm sort of a jack-of-all-trades."

The solarium was a huge, octagonal glass room at the back of the house, filled with full-size trees, tropical plants, and a little Asian bridge that crossed a miniature stream. Wicker settees with plump pillows were arranged in groupings beside pots filled with exotic blooms and beneath trellises covered in flowering vines. Near the footbridge, surrounded by towering trees and white orchids, two women watched the trio approach, and Sloan braced herself for a meeting that felt as odd as the setting in which it was taking place.

Paris's newspaper pictures had not done her justice, Sloan realized as she approached her glamorous sister. With her ivory skin, large brown eyes, and dark and glossy shoulder-length hair, Paris was the epitome of stylish elegance in a jade linen dress with a narrow skirt, wide sleeves, and tight cuffs decorated with bright gold buttons at the wrist. Still and silent, her hands folded loosely in her lap atop what appeared to be a sketchbook, she gazed at Sloan without betraying any emotion whatsoever.

Annoyed with her own attack of nervousness, Sloan concentrated on putting one foot in front of the other. Since she couldn't look as blasé as her sister, she focused instead on the ancient, thin woman seated beside her. Paul had described Edith Reynolds as a dragon, but Sloan thought she looked more like a frail hawk. Dressed in a stark black dress with a thick pearl choker at her throat, the old woman had a narrow patrician face, white skin as pale as her pearls, white eyebrows, and white hair pulled back into a severe chignon. Her light blue eyes were the only spot of color on her entire being, but they were as sharp and intense as twin laser beams as they focused on each and every feature of Sloan's face.

There was nothing frail about her voice either when she cut Carter off at the beginning of his attempted introduction. "Our identities must be obvious to her, Carter," she snapped. She transferred her glare to Sloan as if daring her to contradict that; then she said brusquely, "I am your great-grandmother, this is your sister, and you are Sloan."

Since her attitude verged on rudeness, Sloan decided to reply with nothing more than a silent nod of agreement, which caused the old woman to look a little taken aback. She switched her attention to Paul and attacked him instead. "Who are you?" she demanded.

This time, common courtesy required Sloan to speak. "This is my friend Paul Richardson," she said evenly; then she glanced at her father, who seemed to be completely unconcerned by the old woman's bizarre attitude. "I did make it clear that I was bringing a friend," she told the white-haired woman.

"Yes, but we naturally assumed you meant you were bringing a female with you," Edith Reynolds informed her. "I hope you do not intend to share a bedroom with him here."

Sloan had a swift, sudden urge to either laugh or leave, but since neither reaction fitted the personality Paul wanted her to assume, she tried to look completely oblivious to the old woman's provoking attitude. "No, ma'am, I didn't."

"Do not call me ma'am," she snapped. "You may address me as Great-grandmother," she decreed after a moment. She sounded like a monarch reluctantly granting an undeserved favor to a lowly peasant, and Sloan instantly decided never, ever, to address her in that way.

Oblivious of Sloan's mental mutiny, she turned her dagger gaze on Paul. "How old are you?"

"Thirty-nine."

"In that case, you are old enough to understand that in my house, certain rules of decorum are followed, regardless of whether anyone is around to watch you. Do you take my meaning?"

"I believe I do. Yes," he added when she scowled.

"You may address me as Mrs. Reynolds."

"Thank you, Mrs. Reynolds," he replied courteously, managing to sound exactly like a chastened prep-school student instead of an FBI agent capable of bringing disaster down on her entire family.

Sloan's father finally stepped in. "Paris," he prompted his daughter, "I know you've been looking forward to this moment—"

Paris Reynolds took her cue and stood up in one graceful, fluid motion, her gaze fixed politely on Sloan. "Yes, I have." She said this in an exquisitely modulated but cautious voice and held out a perfectly manicured hand. "How do you do?" she asked.

How do I do what? Sloan wondered irreverently (or a little desperately). The phrase *Stepford Sister* flitted through her mind. "I've been looking forward to meeting you, too," Sloan replied, shaking hands with the cultured stranger who was her sister.

Edith Reynolds had already wearied of the social niceties. "I'm sure that Sloan and Mr. Richardson would like to freshen up and rest before dinner," she said. "Paris will show you both to your rooms," she informed Sloan. "We gather for dinner at seven. Do not be late. And do *not* wear pants."

Sloan had dreaded and expected a long and awkward interview with her father and sister as soon as she arrived, so she was surprised and a little relieved that she was being given a two-hour reprieve by the old dragon. Although, her instincts told her that if Edith Reynolds had known Sloan wanted a reprieve, she probably would have insisted on the interview.

"Paris will make certain you're comfortably settled in," Carter Reynolds interjected with a warm, conciliatory smile at Sloan and then Paul. "We'll see you both at dinner."

Sloan followed in Paris's wake with Paul walking beside her, his hand touching her elbow in a polite, familiar way that fitted his assumed role as her boyfriend. She was so bemused by these peculiar people that she scarcely noticed the rooms they passed as they walked toward the foyer and climbed a long curving staircase with a wrought-iron railing and thick brass handrail. Thus far, the most "human" of the three was Carter Reynolds, whom she'd expected to be the most unlikable.

At the top of the staircase, Paris turned left and continued walking until they were almost at the end of the hall. "This is your room, Mr. Richardson," she intoned as she

swung the door open on a spacious room decorated in
jade green with massive Italian furniture. His suitcases
were lying open on the bed. "If you need anything at all,
just press the intercom button on the telephone," she
said, and finished off her impeccably courteous speech
with an equally courteous smile before she started down
the hall again.

Paul had said people thought she was cold and aloof.
She was worse than that—she was completely lifeless,
Sloan decided with a twinge of disappointment that surprised her with its sharpness. Paris even moved as if the
simple act of walking was actually a precisely orchestrated
dance—her feet balanced on the high heels of her sandals, not too much hip movement, no swinging of the
arms, shoulders back, head up.

"I'll see you at dinner, Sloan," Paul called softly.

Startled that she'd momentarily forgotten to play her
part in the pretense, Sloan turned and said the first thing
that came to mind. "Have a nice nap."

"You, too."

At the end of the hallway, Paris stopped at another door,
opened it, and made the identical speech she'd made to
Paul, complete with identical vocal inflections and matching perfunctory smile, but this time she hovered in the
doorway as if waiting for something. She was probably
expecting some sort of reaction to the accommodations,
Sloan assumed as she glanced around at a spectacular
suite decorated in shades of pale rose and cream-colored
silks with delicate French furnishings glowing with gold
leaf. Beneath her feet, the Oriental carpet was so thick it

was like walking in sand. "This is—lovely," she said lamely, turning to face her sister in the doorway.

Paris made a graceful gesture toward a pair of French doors. "The balcony has a view of the ocean that's particularly nice at sunrise."

"Thank you," Sloan said, feeling increasingly awkward.

"Nordstrom brought up your suitcases," Paris observed with a regal nod in the direction of the canopied bed at the far end of the suite. "Shall I send someone up to help you unpack?"

"No, thank you." Sloan waited for her to leave, *wanted* her to leave, but she hovered there in the doorway, her hand on the doorknob. Sloan belatedly realized that the dictates of social etiquette that seemed to govern her sister's thoughts, words, and actions must now require that Sloan take a turn at some sort of conversation. She said the only thing that came to mind. "Are you an artist?"

Paris looked at her as if she'd spoken in a foreign dialect. "No. Why do you ask?"

Sloan nodded at the large tablet in her hand. "I thought that was a sketch pad."

"Oh, I forgot I was carrying this. Yes, it is. But I'm not an artist."

Frustrated by her unhelpful reply, Sloan looked at the sleek brunette posed in the doorway like a *Vogue* model and suddenly wondered if Paris could possibly be shy, rather than aloof. Either way, carrying on a conversation with her was like trying to give yourself a backrub, but Sloan tried again. "If you're not an artist, what do you use the sketchbook for?"

Paris hesitated; then she walked forward and offered her sketchbook to Sloan like a queen holding out a scepter. "I'm designing my own line of women's apparel."

Clothes! Sloan thought with an inner groan. Sara loved to talk about clothes; Kim loved to talk about clothes; Sloan didn't have a fashion-conscious corpuscle in her entire body. Sloan accepted the sketchbook and followed Paris to the bed, where she sat down and opened the cover of the book.

Even to Sloan's inexpert eye, it was immediately obvious that Paris wasn't designing clothes for the average woman. She was designing high-fashion, high-style cocktail dresses and formal gowns that Sloan knew instinctively would cost as much as a good, late-model used car. Trying desperately to think of something articulate and appropriate to say, Sloan turned the pages in silence until she came to a sheath dress and suddenly remembered how Sara had described her own red one. "Oh, I like this very much!" she burst out a little too enthusiastically, she thought. "It's 'flirty' but not . . . um . . . 'forward'!"

Paris peered over at the sketchbook to see what had taken her fancy and then looked rather disappointed. "I think it's a little common."

Sloan had no idea if that was intended as a deliberate insult to her taste in clothes, but she closed the book and opted for unvarnished honesty. "I'm really not a good judge," she explained. "My mother and my friend Sara love clothes, but I'm always too busy to shop. When I do go shopping, I can never decide whether something new is really 'right' for me, so I end up buying the same styles I already have; then I wear them until they're practically ready to fall apart so I don't have to go shopping again. Sara says the only way she can tell that I've bought something new is when it's a different color."

Sloan was aware that something she said had actually captured Paris's interest, but she didn't realize what it was until she was finished and Paris asked, "Does she love clothes? Your mother, I mean?"

Your mother. *Our* mother.

The weird irony of the situation hit Sloan with sudden force, but any empathy she might have felt for Paris was offset by the fact that Paris could afford the clothes she loved, while "their" mother had to work in a dress shop and sell what she loved to others. "Yes," Sloan said flatly. "She does." She got up and walked around the bed to her suitcases, as if suddenly intent on unpacking.

Sensing her dismissal, Paris stood up. "I'll see you downstairs at seven," she told Sloan in an equally flat voice.

Feeling absurdly guilty for cutting the conversation off so abruptly, Sloan bent over and unzipped Sara's large fold-over suitcase while she watched Paris leave the room and close the door behind her. Preoccupied with her thoughts, she opened the suitcase, removed a black cocktail dress on a hanger from it, and had turned to look for a closet before it finally hit her that something was wrong. . . .

She hadn't borrowed Sara's big fold-over case because she hadn't needed it.

And she had never laid eyes on the black beaded cocktail dress with the short chiffon skirt that she was holding in her hand.

She swung back to the bed and stared at the open suitcase. A long, periwinkle blue silk skirt was on the next hanger. Sloan didn't recognize that either, or the matching top beneath it, or the red sundress . . .

"Oh, Mom, no!" Sloan whispered fiercely as she sank down on the bed beside the suitcase. Without looking, she already knew that everything else in that suitcase was new, and she knew exactly how her mother had managed to pay for it. A white envelope was tucked beneath the straps of a new pair of yellow sandals, and she reached for the note while resolving to return every single item as soon as she got home. So long as she didn't wear any of these things, the stores would be willing to return her mother's money. Sloan was sure of that—until she read her mother's note.

"*Darling—*" her mother had written in her rounded, pretty script, "*I know you're going to be upset when you see these clothes, but I didn't use my charge card, so you don't have to worry about my making those awful interest payments that seem to get bigger and bigger no matter how many payments a person makes. I used the money I've been saving for my cruise, instead.*"

Sloan groaned, and reminded herself again that the clothes could be returned.

You wanted me to have a dream vacation, but at this very minute you're making the biggest dream I've ever had come true. After all these years, your father is finally going to get to know you, and I want you to look as beautiful on the outside as you are on the inside.

This is the only dream I have left, darling. You've made all my other dreams come true, just by being you.

Now, have a wonderful time in Palm Beach! Think only happy thoughts, be carefree, and wear the beautiful clothes I bought for you.

I love you.

Mom

P.S. Just in case you're tempted to wear only a few of your new things, I think you should notice that I cut the labels out, so nothing can be returned. Have fun!

With a teary laugh, Sloan stared at the blurry words of the letter; then she looked at the top layer of clothes in the suitcase. She could not be "carefree" in Palm Beach, nor "think only happy thoughts," but while she was spying on her father, she was definitely going to "wear the beautiful clothes." With typical selfless generosity and an uncharacteristic streak of guile, her mother had left her no choice in that.

She brushed the tears out of her eyes and carefully unpacked all the beautiful new things in that suitcase before she realized there was another large suitcase of Sara's on the floor that she hadn't packed herself.

She wrestled it onto the bed, opened the locks, and lifted the top.

The first thing she saw was Sara's red sheath. The second thing was another white envelope. Inside the envelope was a short note from Sara.

You're always taking care of everyone else, but Mom and I wanted to take care of you this time. So don't be upset

*when you realize my clothes are in this case. And don't be
upset when you realize your clothes aren't in any of the others, either.*

Love, Sara

*P.S. We took pictures of all the outfits and put them in
your makeup case. That way, you won't have to think about
which accessories go with which outfit.*

Irate, Sloan glared at the note. She could not *believe*
they'd done this to her, and without betraying even a hint
of their scheme!

Her glare gave way to a helpless smile, and then to
laughter.

As soon as she finished unpacking, she opened the
French doors and walked out onto her balcony. Her room
was situated at the northeast end of the house, overlooking a deep lawn that ended in a sandy beach about three
hundred yards from the house. Tall clipped privacy
hedges marked the side boundaries of the estate and
extended almost to the beach, concealing a high iron
fence. Sloan couldn't see it.

Clumps of palm trees, crepe myrtles, and giant hibis-
cuses were scattered about the grounds, with tennis courts
situated on the far left, near an olympic-size swimming
pool and cabana. In the center of the lawn, a little flag
fluttered from a short pole, marking the center of a
putting green with short, dense grass that looked as if each
blade had been clipped with manicure scissors.

Amused by the incredible extravagances indulged in

by the ultrarich, Sloan leaned over the balcony railing and looked to the right, along the house, wondering if Paul's room also had a balcony and if he might be outside. She could see several iron railings like the one she was leaning over, but the balconies were all recessed into the structure of the house itself, so it was impossible to see if anyone else was outside.

Disappointed that she couldn't exchange even a wave with her coconspirator, she turned away. In addition to a pair of chaise lounges with thick cushions, her balcony also provided a round iron table and a pair of chairs, but it was so muggy she didn't feel like staying outside.

Wishing there were some way to find out if the FBI agent's first impression of her family was anything like her own, Sloan went back inside and walked over to the bed. The house was the size of a hotel, and the telephone on the nightstand had six telephone lines and twelve other buttons that weren't labeled. Even if she could figure out how to call his room on this phone, she realized they wouldn't be able to talk freely for fear that someone somewhere in the house might pick up an extension and overhear them.

Sloan considered going to his room, but she didn't want to risk getting caught by some browbeaten servant who might be required to report any infractions of the rules to that domineering old woman who actually thought she deserved to be addressed as Great-grandmother by Sloan.

Reluctantly, she postponed the idea of conferring with her coconspirator until later tonight when there was a suitable opportunity and location.

Too keyed up to sleep, Sloan decided to read the mystery novel she'd started before Paul Richardson arrived in Bell Harbor and disrupted her entire life. She folded back the bedspread, propped some pillows against the headboard, and stretched out. Cognizant of Edith Reynolds's sharp warning not to be late for dinner, she reached over and set the clock radio for six P.M., just in case she fell asleep. On the telephone, a light was illuminated now, indicating one of the six lines was in use, and Sloan wondered if the telephone was simply that, or if it was part of a system used to operate the house.

In Bell Harbor, when prosperous new residents built a new mansion or restored an old one, they invariably installed modern multiline telephone systems. The telephones that went with some of these systems not only provided intercom service to all the rooms, they enabled the homeowner to control everything—from lighting and security systems to heating and cooling systems—with a telephone.

As long as the homeowner remembered what codes to use, the telephones did their job, but when the homeowner made a mistake, the results could be chaotic, and the resultant tales of such incidents that circulated among Bell Harbor's firefighters and police officers were frequently hilarious.

With a stab of amused nostalgia, Sloan thought back to last month when Karen Althorp picked up her phone and inadvertently keyed in the number five for a fire emergency, when she meant to key in a six and turn on her Jacuzzi. When the fire department broke through a window and charged through the house into the backyard, they discovered the curvaceous divorcée cavorting naked in the hot tub with her gardener.

Nude but indignant, she threatened to sue the hapless firefighters for damaging her property, and ordered them to leave.

A week later, instead of keying in a six, she keyed in a nine, which sent out a silent police alarm. Jess Jessup had arrived first at the darkened house and he'd found Karen Althorp reclining by the pool, gazing up at the stars, stark naked.

She was so startled when Jess announced his presence that she screamed, then invited the handsome police officer to take off his clothes and join her.

Dr. and Mrs. Pembroke had installed a similar system in their new house, and it was responsible for their divorce. Dr. Pembroke later tried to sue the manufacturer for seven million dollars—the amount of the cash settlement he had to give Mrs. Pembroke in the divorce.

With a mental shrug, she opened her novel. *Death Stops Here* was a spine-tingling best-seller, and within minutes she was thoroughly engrossed.

The sudden buzzing of the alarm made Sloan jump. Intent on finishing the chapter, she groped blindly for the clock radio and turned it off. A few minutes later, she reluctantly laid the book facedown on the nightstand and got up.

15

Paul knocked on her door a few minutes before seven o'clock, and Sloan called to him to come in. "I'm almost ready," she told him, leaning around the corner of her dressing room. He was wearing a gray pinstripe suit, white shirt, and a red-and-gray patterned tie. Sloan thought he looked extremely nice, but she wasn't certain it was appropriate to comment on his appearance in their circumstances. "Better leave the door open, so no one gets the wrong idea and squeals on us to Her Highness," she warned.

Standing in front of the full-length mirror in the dressing room, she checked her appearance with the Polaroid snapshot. The light blue–purple silk skirt was long and straight with a slit to the knee, and the matching top had a wide cowl collar that was meant to be worn off the shoulders, according to the snapshot. Sloan felt a little odd with bare shoulders, but when she tried to tug the collar up, the soft silk slid back down to the tops of her arms, so she left it that way.

She checked the picture again and fastened the matching belt around her waist; then she stepped into the silver sandals that were in the picture. She clipped on the silver earrings and the bracelet she was supposed to wear; then she picked up the silver choker that was in the photograph and put it on, too. She felt as if she was wearing an awful lot of jewelry, but she was a fashion neophyte, while Sara and her mother were experts on the subject, so she decided to adhere to their pictorial advice.

Paul's reaction to her appearance was so flattering that Sloan was instantly glad she'd adhered to the layout in the picture. "You look stunning," he said with a smile of pure masculine appreciation. "What do you call that color?"

"I don't know. Why?"

"Because it's the same color as your eyes."

"In that case, I would call this color 'blue,' " Sloan told him with an unaffected smile.

At the bottom of the staircase, a uniformed maid was waiting to show them to the living room, where cocktails and hors d'oeuvres were being served to a gathering that included the three members of the family and a man who was talking to Paris, his back to the doorway.

Her father looked up as soon as they walked in and put his glass on the coffee table. "Right on time," he said with a welcoming smile as he stood up.

He introduced the stranger as Noah Maitland. Sloan's first reaction had been surprise that a guest was included in such an awkward family situation, but when Noah Maitland turned and looked at her, she felt like a dazzled teenager.

Tall, tanned, and black-haired, he had a smile that could heat a room, eyes the color of cold steel, and a cultured baritone voice that had the same effect as a beautiful piece of music. He was such a study in contrasts, he had so much sex appeal, and he looked so fantastic in his impeccably tailored dark suit and striped tie that Sloan lost her concentration when he reached out to shake her hand. "Beautiful women certainly run in this family," he said, his gray eyes warm with admiration as they looked straight into hers.

"How do you do?" Sloan managed. "Thank you," she added awkwardly, hastily withdrawing her hand and her gaze from his. He was Sara's "Mr. Perfect" in the flesh.

On the way into dinner her father quietly confided, "Paris and Noah are practically engaged."

"They make a beautiful couple," Sloan said honestly, watching her sister walking beside Noah into the dining room. She felt a little sorry for Sara's missed opportunity, but as soon as the meal began, she had larger problems because Paul and she immediately became the focal point of the conversation.

"This is a momentous occasion for our entire family," her father intoned with a glance around the table that specifically encompassed Noah Maitland, who was seated directly across the table from Sloan. "Sloan, tell us all about yourself."

"There isn't much to tell," Sloan replied, trying not to notice that Noah Maitland's entire attention was now focused on her. "Where do you want me to start?"

"Start with your career," Carter prompted. "What do you do?"

"I'm an interior designer."

"Artistic women also seem to run in the family," he observed with a smile at Paris.

"*I* am not artistic," Edith pointed out bluntly from her position at the foot of the table. "Did you go to college?" she demanded of Sloan.

"Yes."

"What did you study?"

The time had come to portray herself as the frivolous, not-too-bright woman Paul Richardson needed her to be. "Oh, I studied a lot of things," Sloan said, staying as close to the truth as possible so she'd be less likely to accidentally contradict herself later. "I couldn't decide what I wanted to do with my life. I kept changing my major." She paused for a spoonful of the soup that had been put in front of her.

Her great-grandmother didn't see a need to eat. "How were your grades?"

"Fair."

"Are you a good interior decorator?"

Sloan took petty gratification in correcting her. "Interior *designer*," she said.

Paul Richardson spoke up then. Smiling fondly at Sloan, he said, "I think she's very good."

Edith Reynolds refused to be convinced. "All the interior decorators I hear of are homosexuals," she announced. "In this day and age, I would have hoped young women like Paris and you would do something more useful with your lives."

Sloan stole a look at Paris to see how her silent sister was reacting to this not-so-subtle criticism that encompassed both of them, but if Paris felt anything, she didn't show it. Wearing a red sarong-style dress with a mandarin collar and her dark hair swept up on the top of her head, she looked beautiful, exotic, and composed. "What sort of career would you choose?" Sloan asked the white-haired woman.

"I believe I would be a tax accountant," Edith declared. "I know I could have done a better job and found more deductions than my accountants find."

"Unfortunately, Sloan doesn't have a head for figures," Paul said proudly and patted Sloan's hand.

"What about sports?" Carter asked her. "Do you play golf?"

"No."

"Tennis?"

Sloan played tennis, but she knew she wasn't in their league. "A little. Not much."

He switched his gaze to Paul. "Do you play, Paul?"

"A little."

"Let's get together tomorrow morning at nine, Paris and I will help you polish up your game. You should have some golf lessons while you're here, too. Paris is an excellent golfer." He looked at Paris. "Will you take Sloan out to the club tomorrow afternoon, make sure she has whatever she needs, and give her some pointers?"

"Yes, of course," Paris instantly replied, flashing Sloan a quick, polite smile.

"I really don't like golf," Sloan began.

"That's because you don't play," he argued. "What about hobbies? What do you do with your spare time?"

Sloan was beginning to feel a little badgered. "I, um . . . I read."

"What do you read?" he asked, sounding a little disappointed in her.

"Magazines," Sloan told him, intending to add to his disappointment. "I just love *House and Garden*. Don't you, Paris?"

Her sister looked startled to be included and Sloan was certain she was lying when she replied, "Yes, very much."

"What about your other interests?"

The interrogation had gone on too long, Sloan decided. She was hungry and broke off a piece of her dinner roll. "What do you mean?"

"What about current affairs?" he pressed.

Lowering her eyes to hide her laughter, Sloan buttered her roll. "I *love* current affairs. I watch the Entertainment channel on cable all the time, just to find out who is having an affair with who. Or is it 'whom'?" Affecting an expression of innocent confusion, she raised her gaze and caught Noah Maitland's look of amused disgust before he hid it. He had just written her off as an idiot, she realized with a surprising twinge of regret.

Evidently, her father had decided not to let her disgrace herself further or add to his guest's boredom. "What do you think is going to happen to the market?" he asked, looking at Noah.

When Sara referred to "the market" she meant the semiannual introduction of new products at the design centers in Dallas and New York. "At the Dallas market, rose and gold tones were really 'in,' this year," Sloan said with sham delight, knowing perfectly well Carter meant to discuss the stock market. "And at the New York market, I saw some really *divine* new jungle prints."

"You and Paris will have a great deal to talk about later," Carter Reynolds said.

With a mixture of relief, amusement, and mortification, Sloan heeded his unspoken request to be quiet. She was a little worried that she'd carried her act too far, but when she stole a look at Paul, he gave her a wide grin that told her she'd done even better than he'd expected.

Satisfied that she needn't worry on that score, Sloan pretended to concentrate on her eight-course meal while she listened to her father and Noah Maitland's animated discussion about the world economy. The two men differed radically on several points, but they were both so well-informed that Sloan was fascinated and a little awed.

In addition to her contributions to her pension fund at the police department, Sloan deposited a percentage of every paycheck into a retirement account of her own, and she'd insisted her mother follow suit. By the time dessert was cleared away, she was so impressed with Noah Maitland's logic that she decided to change her entire investment strategy.

Edith Reynolds reached for her cane and struggled to her feet while the last dessert plate was being lifted off the linen tablecloth. "It is time for me to retire," she announced.

Paul and Noah both stood up to assist her, but she waved them off. "I do not need to be treated like an invalid," she informed them brusquely. "I am as healthy as the two of you!"

Despite her claim, Sloan saw the awkward stiffness of her movements as she leaned heavily on her cane, and Sloan realized it was sheer force of will, rather than physical strength, that propelled the elderly woman to the far side of the enormous room.

In the doorway, she paused and looked back at the group seated at her gigantic baroque dining room table beneath a spectacular chandelier. Sloan expected the white-haired matriarch to say some sort of formal goodnight. "Do *not* forget to turn off the lights!" she barked instead, and Sloan hastily looked at her lap to hide her mirth.

Edith's departure seemed to signal the immediate end of the dinner. "If you young people will excuse me," Carter announced, standing up, "I have some work to do."

"I think I'd like to take a walk," Paul said, already pulling out Sloan's heavy chair. "Sloan?"

"I'd love a walk," she replied, absolutely dying to get out of there.

There was no way for Paul to avoid inviting the other couple to join them, but Sloan breathed a sigh of relief when they declined.

Outside, Sloan waited to speak until they were almost to the putting green and out of hearing of anyone at the house; then she turned and looked at Paul with unconcealed mirth. "I cannot *believe* I'm actually related to these people," she confided.

"Neither can I," he admitted with a chuckle.

"My great-grandmother must be a direct descendant of Genghis Khan," Sloan continued.

"For appearances' sake, I should either hold your hand or put my arm around you, in case anyone is watching. Do you have a preference?"

"No, either one is fine," Sloan said, so preoccupied with her subject that she scarcely noticed when he took her hand. "And then there's my sister! She's so lifeless. No wonder people think she's cold and haughty."

"Do you think she is?"

"I don't know yet."

"What do you think of your father?"

"I have an impression, but it isn't completely formed yet. At least I think I understand what my mother saw in him. She was only eighteen at the time, and he has a lot of charm, a lot of polish, and he's very handsome. I can see how dazzled she must have been by all that."

"What did you think of Maitland?"

The question surprised Sloan, since he wasn't a family member or of professional interest to either of them. "Handsome," she reluctantly admitted.

"He certainly thought you were attractive. He couldn't take his eyes off of you at first."

"You mean until dinner, when he discovered I'm actually a complete idiot?" she said ruefully.

In a spontaneous gesture, Paul let go of her hand, put his arm around her shoulders, and gave her a light hug. "You were absolutely perfect."

Startled by the gruff sincerity in his voice, Sloan gazed at his moonlit profile. "Thank you," she said, and for the very first time, she actually felt as if she had merit to him as a partner.

"You haven't left your badge or weapon where anyone might find them, have you?"

"No, they're well-hidden in my room."

"We may as well call it a night. I know you're dying to get back to your book."

Sloan turned back toward the house, and while he seemed in a more relaxed mood, she decided to press him for a little more information. "I wish I knew what you were specifically looking for here," she began.

"If I had a specific answer for that," he said, "I'd be able to get a judge to sign a search warrant, in which case, I wouldn't have needed you to get me in here."

In a lighter tone, he said, "No matter what happens, my time here won't be completely wasted. I heard some very interesting things at the dinner table tonight when Maitland and your father were talking about the world economy."

"Like what?"

He laughed at her intent expression. "Like the fact that I need to change my stock market investment strategy. Interesting, isn't it, that their opinions differ so much? Your father controls a bank with branches all over the world, and Maitland has investments all over the world. They both have common interests and a global outlook. I expected them to have a reasonably similar philosophy."

"I thought the same thing," Sloan said. "Fundamentally, it seemed to me that they both think the same things are going to happen, but they disagreed on the effect and the timing. I noticed they seem to do a lot of off-shore investing."

He slanted her an odd smile. "I noticed that, too."

• • •

He walked her to her bedroom door, but instead of saying good night in the hall, he followed her into the bedroom and closed the door; then he waited.

"What are you doing?" Sloan asked, already halfway across the room and removing her earrings.

"Kissing you good-night," he joked.

When he left, Sloan decided to write a letter to Sara while all the events of the evening were still fresh in her mind. A television set was concealed inside the antique armoire across from her bed, and she turned on CNN; then she went to work on the letter.

16

The first hour after dawn was Sloan's favorite time of day to run along the beach, but it was nearly seven o'clock when she woke up. Anxious to get started, she hurried out of bed, pulled her hair into a ponytail, and put on a pair of shorts and a tank top that Sara hadn't removed when she repacked Sloan's suitcases.

The house seemed deserted as she walked silently along the hallway and down the stairs, but outside, two men were pruning a hedge along the side of the property. Sloan waved to them as she jogged across the lawn, her spirits already beginning to lift as she breathed in the salty air and felt the familiar presence of the sea. Lazy waves lapped the sand beside her feet as she ran along the water's edge, and gulls wheeled by, their boisterous cries as uplifting and soothing to her as music.

Overhead, the sky was crystal blue with fat white clouds floating by on a gentle cooling breeze. On her left, the ocean filled the entire horizon, majestic, beautiful, untamed. On her right, the horizon was obscured by a procession of mansions, a few of which were even bigger than her father's, and there was some sort of activity at all of them. Gardeners were looking after flower beds, servants were tidying patios and taking care of swimming pools, and sprinkler systems were spraying water on lawns that sparkled like wet emeralds in the morning sun.

Concentrating her gaze on the ocean, Sloan ran three miles along the water's edge and then turned back. She kept up the pace until the little flag on her father's putting green was visible; then she slowed to a jog. Palm Beach residents evidently slept later than their Bell Harbor counterparts, she decided, because she'd had the beach almost to herself on the first half of her run, but now there were several other people running along the sand. Runners here were also less friendly, avoiding eye contact instead of greeting each other as they passed with a nod or smile.

Sloan was pondering that when she was distracted by an elderly gardener in a long-sleeved shirt who'd been working in a flower bed near the edge of the lawn. He stood up; then he clutched his left arm and doubled over. Sloan ran toward him, already scanning the grounds for someone to help her if help was needed, but he seemed to be the only one working at that house.

"Take it easy," she said gently. "I'll help you. Lean on me." She wrapped her arm around his waist, wondering if he could make it to the iron bench that encircled the trunk of a nearby tree. "Tell me what's wrong."

"My arm," he gasped, white-faced with pain.

"Are you having any chest pains?"

"No. Had surgery . . . on my . . . shoulder."

Enormously relieved that it wasn't a heart attack, Sloan

guided him over to the tree and eased him onto the white iron bench. "Take a deep breath and let it out slowly," she coached. "Do you have any medicine to take for the pain?"

He took a deep breath and then another, following her instructions. "I'll be all right . . . in a minute."

"Take your time. I'm not in any hurry."

After a few more deep breaths, the gardener lifted his head and looked at her, and Sloan noticed his color was already improving. He was a little younger than she'd thought—probably in his late sixties—and he looked thoroughly chagrined. "When I stood up, I forgot and leaned on my left arm," he explained. "I felt like my shoulder was going to tear loose from the rest of me."

"How long ago was your surgery?"

"Last week."

"Last week! Shouldn't you be wearing some sort of brace?"

He nodded. "Yes, but I can't use my arm with that contraption on."

"Surely someone else here could take over your work while your shoulder heals, and you could do their work."

He stared at her as if that had never occurred to him and yet the possibility fascinated him. "What sort of work do you think I could do here?"

"This must be one of the biggest estates in Palm Beach. There must be something to do here that isn't heavy labor. You should talk to whoever owns this place and explain your condition."

"He already knows about my shoulder. He thinks I should stop doing everything until it heals."

"He won't give you another job to do?" Sloan said, angry at the callous indifference of the very rich to the financial plight of the less fortunate.

He patted her hand, touched by her indignation on his behalf. "I'll be fine if you just sit here and talk to me for a while. Conversing with a sweet, pretty little thing like you is better than any painkiller I could take."

"Will you get into trouble by sitting out here with me?"

He smiled, thinking that over. "I can't see how, but it's a delightful prospect to contemplate."

Several things struck Sloan at once: his hand was smooth, his speech was educated, and his attitude was almost flirtatious. Embarrassed, she started to stand up. "You're not the gardener. I made a foolish mistake. I'm sorry."

He tightened his grip on her hand to prevent her from standing, but he let it go when she sat back down. "Don't run off and don't be embarrassed. I was very touched by your concern and glad of your help. Few young people here would have stopped to help an old gardener in pain."

"You *aren't* an old gardener," Sloan persisted, amused by his audacity.

"I'm a *new* gardener. I needed a temporary hobby while my shoulder heals. I had the surgery on an old injury that was beginning to ruin my golf game." His voice took on a truly dire note as he confided, "I developed a hook in my drives that I couldn't get rid of, and my short game was atrocious."

"That's . . . tragic," Sloan sympathized, trying not to laugh.

"Exactly. And this house belongs to my son, who is so heartless that he not only played golf without me yesterday, he also had the insensitivity to shoot a seventy-two!"

"He's a monster!" Sloan teased. "He doesn't deserve to live!"

He chuckled. "I love a woman with a sense of humor, and yours is showing. I'm intrigued. Who are you?"

Sloan's father's house was only a few houses down the beach from this one, and there was every chance the two men were acquainted. She didn't want to reveal that she was Carter Reynolds's daughter, and yet she'd be in plain view of this man when she left here and returned to the house. "My name is Sloan," she evaded.

"Is that your first name?"

"Yes. What's your name?" she added quickly, before he could ask for her last name.

"Douglas, and I haven't seen you around here before."

"I live in Bell Harbor. I'm visiting some people down the beach, but only for a few days."

"Really, what people? I know most of the families along this stretch of the beach."

Sloan was trapped. "Carter Reynolds's family."

"Good heavens! I've known the Reynoldses forever. You must be a friend of Paris's?"

Sloan nodded and looked at her watch. "I really should go."

He looked so crestfallen that she felt guilty. "Couldn't you spare a few more minutes to brighten the day of a lonely old man? The doctor won't let me drive, and my son is either working or out somewhere. I assure you, I'm completely harmless."

Sloan was a sucker for the plight of the elderly, including the wealthy elderly, who she now realized must also suffer from loneliness. "I guess I have a little while before I have to play tennis. What would you like to talk about?"

"Mutual acquaintances?" he suggested at once and with unabashed delight. "We could have a good gossip— tear their reputations to shreds! That's always amusing."

Sloan burst out laughing at his tone and his suggestion. "That won't work. The only people I know in Palm Beach are the Reynolds family."

"It wouldn't be much fun to gossip about them," he joked. "They're dreadfully dull and as upright as trees. Let's talk about you instead."

"I'm dull, too," she assured him, but he was not to be derailed from his chosen topic. "You're not wearing a wedding ring, which means you're not married, which means you must occupy your time in some other way. Do you have a career?"

"I'm an interior designer," Sloan replied, and quickly added, "but that's not a very interesting topic. Let's talk about something that interests you, too."

"I'm quite interested in beautiful young women who, for some reason, do not want to talk about themselves," he said with a sudden perspicuity that surprised and alarmed Sloan after his seemingly lighhearted, innocuous banter. "However," he reassured her, "I won't pry into your secrets. Let's see—we need a mutually interesting topic. I don't suppose you're fascinated with corporate mergers, high finance, world politics—that sort of thing?"

Sloan nodded eagerly. "I heard some interesting theories on the future of the world market at dinner last night."

He looked staggered, gratified, and impressed. "A beautiful woman with a soft heart, a sense of humor, and a fine mind. No wonder you aren't married—I'll bet you frighten young men your own age to death." He flashed her an engaging smile that made Sloan wonder if he was quite as harmless as he'd said; then he slapped his knee and announced, "Let's talk about the Russian economy. I *love* to hear myself talk on *that* subject. I never fail to amuse myself with my own wisdom and insight . . ."

Sloan laughed, helplessly charmed by his humor. And then she listened. And was impressed.

When she left, Douglas Maitland stood at the edge of the lawn, watching her; then he strolled back to the house and sauntered into the kitchen. "Good morning," he told his son and daughter as he helped himself to a cup of coffee. "You should have watched the sun come up today. It was beautiful."

His son was sitting at the kitchen table, reading *The Wall Street Journal*. His daughter was removing a bagel from the toaster. They both looked up in surprise at his buoyant tone. "You're in remarkably good spirits this morning," Noah observed.

"I've had a remarkable morning."

"Doing what?" his daughter, Courtney, challenged skeptically. "In the first place, you haven't gone anywhere.

In the second place, there's nowhere to go. Palm Beach is the *pits*. I can't believe you actually expect me to live here permanently when I could stay in California and board at school."

"I must be a masochist," Douglas told her cheerfully. "However, to answer your original question, my morning was made remarkable by the presence of a fascinating young woman who noticed that my shoulder was causing me pain, and who offered assistance and then conversation."

Courtney's eyes narrowed. "How young a woman?"

"Under thirty, I'd guess."

"Oh, great! The last two times you met 'a fascinating young woman' who was 'under thirty,' you married her."

"Don't be sarcastic, Courtney. One of those women was your mother."

"The second one was too young to have children," she lied.

Douglas ignored her and described Sloan to his son. "She mistook me for a gardener—an understandable mistake, considering that I was digging in the dirt. We had a delightful discussion. You'll never guess who she is—"

"Let me try," Courtney interrupted. "While you talked to her, was she sitting on a tuffet, eating curds and whey?"

Both men ignored her. "Who is she?" Noah asked.

"If you had dinner with Carter last night, you probably met her. I would have asked her about that, but I rather hated to admit I had a son your age. My vanity had already taken a blow by being mistaken for the gardener. Her name is Sloan."

Noah gave a bark of laughter. "You have to be joking! What on earth did you find to talk to her about?"

"Many things. We discussed world affairs, the economy—"

"You must have done all the talking," his son said sarcastically. "She couldn't carry an intelligent conversation in a basket."

"She did it very well this morning. She mentioned she'd heard a similar discussion last night. When she told me what she'd heard, it sounded like it came from you."

"I'm amazed she was able to repeat it, but believe me, she didn't understand it."

"You're making her sound like a parrot! Really, Noah, I think I qualify as a reasonably good judge, and I can guarantee that she's not only beautiful, she is also very smart. And she's witty, too."

"Are we both talking about Carter Reynolds's daughter?"

It was Douglas's turn to look shocked. "His what?"

"Carter has two daughters. Paris is older by a year."

"I've known Carter for decades and he's never mentioned having another daughter."

"He told me last night that the girls were divided in the divorce when they were babies and Sloan remained with her mother. After his heart attack, Carter decided to try to heal the family breach, so he invited her to come for a visit. Until yesterday, the two branches of the family have had no contact."

"Why not?"

Noah pushed his newspaper aside and stood up. "I

have no idea. Carter didn't volunteer any more information, and I didn't feel it was appropriate to ask."

"I sensed she had a secret!" Douglas said, smiling at his perception. "I fooled her by letting her think I was a gardener, so she tricked me by keeping her own identity a secret. She must have known I'd find out who she is. Tit for tat. She's amazing! I told you you'd underestimated her."

"Maybe," Noah replied, unconvinced but definitely curious.

Courtney finished spreading cream cheese on her bagel and brushed past Noah on her way to the table. "I can see how all this is going to turn out," she predicted. "My brother is going to marry Paris, my father is going to marry her sister, and I'm going to go on the *Sally Jessy Raphael* show and talk about incestuous stepfamilies. It will be very intense."

"I've told you before that I am not going to marry Paris," Noah snapped.

"Well, you can't marry Sloan, because our father plans to do that. And you can't marry her after he does, because that's old stuff and it won't get me on Sally's show. They've already done 'my sister-in-law used to be my stepmother' programs."

"Knock it off!"

Courtney waited until Noah was out of earshot; then she looked at her father, who was opening Noah's newspaper. "Why do you let him talk to me like that?"

Douglas ignored her attempt to provoke a quarrel and turned to the editorial page.

"He's not my father; he's only my brother. Why do you let him talk to me like that?"

"Because I'm too old to spank you and he refuses to do it."

"He'd probably enjoy it. He likes violence."

"What makes you say that?" Douglas inquired mildly.

"You *know* why," she shot back, "only you pretend you don't because you lost most of our money but he's making so much of it now that we can go on living like this. Are you going to pretend you didn't know when he gets caught? Are you going to go see him on visiting days?"

17

On the tennis court, Sloan's father and sister not only looked good in their winter tans and tennis whites, they had the grace and power of two perfectly matched thoroughbreds, and Sloan couldn't help being impressed at the beginning of the first game of the set.

By the end of that game, Sloan realized something else: Her father played tennis as if the court were a battlefield, and he showed no mercy to the enemy even though it was obvious that Paul and Sloan were hopelessly outmatched. Furthermore, he showed no mercy to his partner either. Whenever Paris made what he perceived to be a mistake, no matter how minor, he lectured or criticized her.

That made Sloan so uncomfortable that she felt like cheering when there was only one game left. Instead, she stood next to Paul on their side of the net, trying to pretend she couldn't hear her father chastising Paris for the way she'd scored the last point: "You've been staying too close to the net all morning! The only reason Paul missed your last lob was because you got lucky. Losers rely on luck. Winners rely on skill. You know that, don't you?"

"Yes," she said, as composed and polite as ever, but Sloan knew she had to be thoroughly embarrassed, and Sloan wondered if he behaved like this toward her when they played elsewhere.

"This is unbelievable!" Sloan whispered to Paul. "Why doesn't she stand up to him and tell him she's doing her best."

"She isn't doing her best," Paul replied. "She's been trying to play well enough to suit him, but not so well that we'll feel completely outclassed over here."

Sloan's heart sank. She'd had the same impression, but when Paul put it into words, he made it a fact and that made it impossible for her to ignore the angry sympathy she'd been feeling for Paris.

Carter's personality underwent a complete change for the better as soon as the match was over. With all the cordial charm he'd displayed yesterday, he trotted over to the net and gave Sloan an approving smile. "You have a lot of natural talent, Sloan," he told her. "With good coaching, you could become a real contender. I'll work with you while you're here. In fact, I'll give you a lesson right now."

That announcement startled a horrified laugh from Sloan. "That's very nice of you, but I think I'll pass."

"Why?"

"Because I don't particularly enjoy playing tennis."

"That's because you don't play to the best of your ability."

"You may be right, but I'd rather not try."

"Okay. You're in good physical condition. You run. What else do you do?"

"Nothing much."

"What about that self-defense course you took? They must have taught you a little tae kwon do or jujitsu?"

"A little," Sloan said evasively.

"Great. I studied martial arts for a few years. Let's go over there and you can show me what you can do."

The man was not merely athletic, he was a compulsive competitor, Sloan realized with a shock, and he was not going to give up until he took her on in one form or another. She also knew Carter Reynolds didn't like to lose, and since she was here to ingratiate herself with him, it didn't seem like a good idea to humiliate him.

"I really don't think that's a good idea."

"I'll go easy on you," he insisted. Ignoring her protest, he laid his tennis racquet on the grass and walked a few steps away. "Come on."

Sloan threw a helpless glance at Paul, and noticed Noah Maitland walking across the lawn toward them with a large brown envelope in his hand.

Carter saw him, too, and waved. "I didn't know you were coming over this morning, Noah."

"I brought some papers over for you and Edith to sign," the other man explained.

"I'll be with you in a few minutes. Sloan took a self-defense course recently, and she's about to show me what she learned."

"Take your time," Noah said.

With great reluctance, Sloan laid her tennis racquet in the grass beside her father's. Paris looked uneasy but said nothing. Paul looked uneasy, too, but Sloan wasn't certain whether he was worried she'd get hurt or whether he was worried she'd hurt their host. Noah Maitland folded his arms on his chest and looked skeptical, which unnerved Sloan more than what she was about to do. "I really don't want to hold up your meeting," she told Noah, hoping to evoke a last-minute reprieve. "I'm sure those papers are much more important than this."

"Not to me," he said and tipped his head toward Carter. "Have at it."

Sloan thought his attitude seemed a little odd, but she had no choice except to do as he suggested. She walked over to her father, reminding herself that no matter how he behaved, it was not a good idea to toss him on his back.

"Ready?" he asked her with a brief, formal bow.

Sloan nodded and returned his bow.

He moved so suddenly that Sloan didn't react in time and he scored his point with embarrassing ease.

"You weren't alert," he said in the same infuriating tone of censure and condescension he'd used on Paris during the tennis match. Instead of giving her time to return to her position, he nailed her again, catching her off-balance. "Sloan, you're not concentrating."

Sloan decided it was a very *good* idea to toss him on his back. He moved in, thought he saw an opening, and lunged. Sloan pivoted and with a high, hard kick sent him sprawling onto the grass. "I think I was concentrating better that time," she sweetly replied.

A little warier now, he stood up and circled, looking for a new target. Mentally Sloan acknowledged that he was really very good, but he was also overconfident. He lunged; she countered with a block and struck back at his solar plexus, taking his breath away. "I was more alert that time," she confessed.

Sloan was no stranger to angry predators, and when she scored the next hit, she realized he had become one. He doubled over, his face red with embarrassed anger, and his movements lost all grace and style. He waited for an opening; then he pivoted and kicked but missed her. The instant he recovered, Sloan scored another hit; then she decided it was time to end this "exhibition" before she was forced to either hurt him or risk being hurt if she didn't.

Plunking her hands on her hips, she backed out of his reach. "That's enough for me," she laughed, trying to diffuse the tension. "You play too rough."

"We're not finished," he said, dusting grass off his shorts.

"Yes, we are. I'm worn out."

To Sloan's surprise, it was Noah Maitland who came to her rescue. "Carter, it's impolite to assault your guests on the second day of their visit."

"That's right," Sloan joked. "You're supposed to wait until the *third* day." She turned to reach for the tennis racquet lying at Noah Maitland's feet, but he picked it up instead and held it out to her.

"My father sends you his regards," he said, and the glamour of his lazy white smile was so unnerving that Sloan had difficulty concentrating on his words as she reached for the racquet.

"Pardon me?"

"My father told me he had a fascinating discussion with you this morning. He was very impressed."

"I had no idea that was your father," Sloan uttered, horrified.

"So I gathered." He looked over at Carter, and Sloan seized that as an opportunity to flee. "Carter," he said, "if you want to sit in on your Tuesday night poker game at the club, I'd like to take Sloan and Paul and Paris to dinner."

Sloan was already starting to the house with Paul, but she heard her father say, "That's a great idea! Sloan—" he called, "is that all right with you and Paul?"

It was not a "great idea" and it was not "all right." Sloan turned but kept walking backward in a silly compulsion to keep a maximum distance from Noah Maitland. "Sounds nice," she called. To Paul she said softly, "I wish we could find a way to get out of that."

He slanted her a sideways look. "I wish I knew about those documents Maitland needs to have signed."

"Is Noah Maitland a suspect in some way?"

"Everyone is a suspect, except you and I. And," he joked, "I'm not completely sure about you." Sobering, he said, "I wonder what sort of documents would require Edith Reynolds's signature. If we knew, it might point us in a direction we haven't thought to look."

Sloan had a feeling he wasn't telling her the whole truth, but she knew it was pointless to question him further.

"How did you happen to meet Maitland's father this morning?"

"On my way back from running this morning, I saw a man digging in a garden and when he stood up, he was obviously in pain. I stopped to help and stayed there to talk to him for a few minutes. I thought he was the gardener at first."

"You didn't tell him anything, did you?"

"Nothing that would harm us and no more than was necessary. In fact, I only told him my first name, but I couldn't avoid telling him where I was staying. Have I created some sort of problem?"

He considered that for a moment. "Absolutely not," he said with an inexplicable smile. "Maitland's father isn't the only one you've impressed today. I think you've impressed the son as well. I think he's a little intrigued."

"By me? No way!"

"I saw the way he was looking at you. You noticed it, too. It made you jumpy."

Sloan chuckled at the absurdity of his conclusion. "Men like Noah Maitland generate enough sexual electricity to light up New York City, and they know it. It's a power they have and they use it on whoever happens to be nearby. I happened to be nearby. I felt a little shock, and it made me 'jumpy.' "

"Is that how it works? How many 'men like Noah Maitland' have you known?"

"I have an inherited understanding of his 'type,' " Sloan said firmly, "and therefore a genetic immunity to it."

"What are you talking about?"

"My mother. Based on what she's told me and on what I can see with my own eyes, my father must have been just like Noah Maitland. Did you know Paris is in love with him? They're practically engaged."

They were near the patio steps, and he lowered his

voice. "Paris isn't in love with him. Your father is pushing her to marry Maitland. She doesn't want to do it. Unfortunately," he added philosophically, "that doesn't necessarily mean she won't cave in and do it anyway. Both men completely dominate and intimidate her."

"How do you know all this?"

"She confided the first part to me at breakfast this morning. I figured the second part out myself."

"She told you that?" Sloan repeated in shock. "It's hard to imagine her opening up that much with anyone. And why you?"

"Because I don't dominate her. On the other hand, I'm male, and she's intimidated by males, so when I gently asked her a blunt question, she felt compelled to answer."

"That is so sad," Sloan said softly as they stopped near the back door to the house. "I didn't expect to like her. I don't *want* to like her."

He chuckled at that. "But you do, and you will. And you will also try to shield her from both men while you're here."

There were times when Paul Richardson's all-knowing attitude got under her skin. "What makes you so sure of yourself? What makes you think I'll do anything of the kind?"

Her ire didn't faze him in the least. "You won't be able to help it," he stated implacably, but not unkindly, "because *you* have a compulsion to help people who need you."

"*You* are not a psychiatrist."

"True," he said with a grin as he reached out to open the back door for her, "but I recognize a soft heart, and yours is as soft as a freshly toasted marshmallow."

"That sounds disgusting."

"Actually, it was a compliment," he replied blandly. "I'm crazy about toasted marshmallows. Just don't let your soft heart interfere with your judgment or your job here."

Gary Dishler intercepted them in the kitchen, so Sloan was deprived of the opportunity to reply to that last gibe. "It's been a fun morning," she lied. "I'm going upstairs to take a shower—"

"Excuse me, Miss Reynolds," Dishler said. "Mrs. Reynolds wants to see you in the solarium."

"Oh." Sloan looked down at her grass-stained shorts and smudged arms. "I have to take a shower and change clothes first. Would you tell her I'll be there as soon as I can?"

"Mrs. Reynolds said she wants to see you *immediately*," he informed her.

The summons sounded dire, and Paul noticed it, too. "I'll go with you," he said.

Gary shook his head and very firmly informed Sloan, "Mrs. Reynolds said she wants to see you *alone*."

The solarium overlooked the back lawn, and when Sloan saw the sour expression on Edith Reynolds's face, she assumed the elderly woman had seen the brief self-defense contest and had not approved. "That was quite an exhibition you put on out there!" She paused to pass a condemning look over Sloan's mussed hair and stained shorts. "Well-bred young women do not roll around in the grass, and they do not parade around in soiled clothes."

Sloan bridled at the injustice of the attack. "I did not want to give that exhibition. In fact, I did everything I could to avoid it, but your grandson insisted on it. Furthermore, I would have changed clothes before I came here, but Mister Dishler insisted you wanted to see me immediately."

Her face froze at Sloan's rebellion. "Are you finished?"

Sloan nodded.

"That is quite a temper you have."

"I've had quite a morning."

"So I have observed. In the last few hours, you've run on the beach and attempted to rescue Douglas Maitland, I understand from Noah. You returned in time to play tennis—but not well—and then you completed your busy morning by throwing your own father on his back, not once but twice. If you have any more excess energy after lunch, kindly devote it to your backhand."

"What?"

"There is room for much improvement in your tennis game."

"Mrs. Reynolds, I am not a member of the idle rich. I work for a living, my time is valuable, I like to spend it doing what I like to do, and I do not like tennis!"

"I held trophies in my day. The Reynolds family has always excelled at tennis. Branches of our family hold tennis championships at the finest country clubs all over the country. Your game is a disgrace to the family name at present; however, with serious practice, I believe you could live up to our standards."

"I have neither the intention nor the desire to do anything of the sort," Sloan scornfully informed her. "I am not a member of the Reynolds family."

"Foolish girl! You don't look like us, but you are more Reynolds under the skin than Paris is. Where do you think you got that proud defiance you're demonstrating to me at this very moment? Why do you think you refused to let Carter humiliate you out there? Look at you right now—unbending, sure of yourself even though you're dirty and appallingly dressed, confident as a king that you have every right to stare me right down in my own home because you think you're right and I am wrong. If that isn't Reynolds superiority, I don't know what you'd call it."

"If you think I should be flattered, I have to tell you I'm not."

"Hah!" she said, and slapped the arm of her chair in gleeful triumph. "Spoken like a true Reynolds! You think you're better than we are even though we could buy and sell the city you live in. How I wish Carter's mother were still alive to see this. When she went to Florida to bring him home, she intended to bring back the child who would be most like us. Despite all her scheming, that evil, foolish woman took the wrong girl!"

"Which was certainly lucky for me."

"Enough pleasantries. I think we understand each other very well and can now arrive at a deeper understanding very quickly. Sit down, please."

Caught between ire and amusement at her use of the word "pleasantries" to describe what they'd been doing thus far, Sloan sank into the wicker chair next to hers.

"I'm going to stop pussyfooting around," she

announced, causing Sloan a fresh surge of amused dread. "I insisted you be invited to join us here, and I did so for several very good reasons—Why do you look so surprised?"

"I was under the impression this was my father's idea. He said he'd had a heart attack and wanted to get to know me while there was still time."

She hesitated, fiddling with the ever-present strands of pearls at her throat, then she said reluctantly, "You have it wrong. In the beginning, he objected even more strenuously than Paris."

"Paris objected?"

"Of course. She was extremely distressed when she discovered you'd decided to accept the invitation."

Sloan averted her gaze to the pink azaleas blooming beside her chair while she tried to assimilate all this without feeling any emotion. "I see."

"I don't think you do. When Paris was still a small child, Carter's mother completely convinced her that your mother was unfit to be around little children, and that a judge made a special law to keep your mother away from her. Later, she was led to believe you would naturally turn out to be just like your mother."

She paused a moment to let that sink in; then she said, "As for Carter, he had several reasons for not wanting to bring you into the family at this late date. For one thing, he didn't think it would be kind to introduce you to a life you've never had. Moreover, I suspect he felt guilty for leaving you behind. In which case, it's understandable that he would not relish coming face-to-face now with the person he wronged. I would have forced this little reunion long ago, but I could not do it until Carter's mother, my daughter-in-law, did me the surprising favor of preceding me in death."

"Why not?"

"Because she would have driven you off in ten minutes. You would never have tolerated the treatment she would have subjected you to, and I did not want to subject you to it. I could have come to see you, I suppose, but that wouldn't have mended the breach between Paris and Carter and you. And that is my goal."

Sloan was staggered to discover that her goal was evidently to mend, when all she'd done so far was humiliate, criticize, and anger Sloan.

"Once Carter's mother died, I realized I could bring you to us, and I forced Carter to go along with the plan. He had no choice."

"He didn't?"

"Of course not," she announced with a gruff laugh. "Because I hold the purse strings."

Sloan blinked and cleared her throat. "You do what?"

"I control the Hanover Trust, which owns a major portion of the Reynolds fortune," she declared, as if that single piece of information should clarify everything to Sloan.

"I don't understand," Sloan said.

"It's quite simple. My father, James Hunsley, was a handsome, penniless rogue from a fine family, but he'd gambled away his own inheritance by the time he was twenty-five. To support his lifestyle, he had to marry an heiress, and he selected my mother, who was heiress to the Hanover fortune. My grandfather saw right through him and refused to consent to the marriage, but my mother loved him, and she was a spoiled, headstrong girl. She threatened to elope, and my grandfather gave in, but not until he'd arranged things so my father could never get full control of my mother's fortune. Grandfather Hanover set up a trust and gave *her* control after his death, but only with the advice and consent of the other trustees he'd appointed. Under the terms of that trust, control remains in the hands of the oldest surviving Hanover descendant, not the spouse of a Hanover. At present, I am that descendant."

Sloan decided not to reply to that revelation. "Your father must have been disappointed when he found out about the trust."

"He was furious, but once he realized that his life was not going to improve unless he made money of his own, he did just that. His was a modest fortune, nothing like the Hanover fortune, and of course half of it belonged to my mother and ended up in the trust. Carter inherited my family's business acumen, and he's increased the Reynolds fortune many times over," she stated with pride. "However, I didn't send for you to discuss Carter. It's Paris I want to talk about. You see, despite everything she was led to believe about your mother and you, she told me last night, she thought you seemed quite nice."

Until then, everything she'd said had been so negative that Sloan was completely unprepared for the praise that followed.

"It is clear to me that you have spunk and spirit, and I'd like Paris to have a little more of that. Perhaps you could keep that in mind when you're with her?"

She broke off at the sound of Paris's footsteps and waited in silence until Paris had pressed a kiss to her cheek. "Your game was off this morning," she said sternly. "You were playing too close to the net. What got into you?"

"I was having an off day, I guess."

"Nonsense. You were trying not to hurt Sloan's feelings because her game is deplorable. Enough about that," she interrupted when Paris started to reply. "I believe you and Sloan are playing golf this afternoon?"

"Yes, we have a tee time later today."

"Good, I want the two of you to spend plenty of time together. What are you planning tonight?"

"Noah wants to take Paul and Sloan and me out to dinner."

"Excellent," she said with an emphatic nod. "Your father has his heart set on a Christmas wedding for the two of you. You need to spend more time with Noah, too."

Sloan didn't want to play golf, and she knew Paris didn't want to marry Noah. Carter and Edith Reynolds apparently had no interest in what those under their control wanted. Sloan wasn't certain what she wanted; she was still reeling with shock from the things Edith had said, and she was anxious to repeat the pertinent parts to Paul. Beyond that, the only thing she was certain of was that she did want to get to know Paris better.

"I need to take a shower," Sloan said to both of them; and then she deliberately smiled at Paris as she stood up. "I, for one, would like to thank you for taking it easy on Paul and me on the tennis court. It was very kind."

"Nonsense!" Edith interrupted. "She should have used the time to hone her skills not let them rust!"

Sloan realized that this old woman was not going to respect anyone she or her son could walk on, even though she took it as her right and privilege to do the walking. "Paris is aware that Paul and I are your guests, and so her first priority would naturally be to make us feel comfortable. I think I read in an etiquette column in the newspaper that this is the first and most important duty of a hostess. Isn't it?" Sloan finished, trying to look innocent.

Edith Reynolds wasn't fooled. "Young woman, are you presuming to lecture me on manners?"

There was something indefinable about her tone; although it was indignant, it was not quite angry.

Sloan bit her lip to hide a smile. "Yes, ma'am, I think I was. Just a little."

"Outrageous girl," she pronounced in a gruff voice that lacked genuine anger. "I can't stand to see you wearing all that dirt another moment. Run along and take your shower."

Dismissed, Sloan started away.

"And don't waste water," Edith called out irritably.

When Sloan was gone, Edith focused her pale blue eyes on Paris. "She is an impertinent young woman. No respect for authority. Little enough for money. What do you think of her?"

Long ago when she was a child, Paris Reynolds had accepted that it was useless and unwise for anyone, including her, to oppose a member of her family. They were indomitable and unforgiving, while she was a coward and a weakling. And yet, in the last hour, she had seen her younger sister stand up for herself and then for Paris. In view of that, it seemed imperative for Paris to now do the same. Nervousness made her palms damp, and she rubbed them on her shorts. "I—I'm sorry, Great-grandmother," Paris said, her voice shaking from unfamiliarity with taking an opposing stand, "but s-s-she—"

"Stop stammering, child! You overcame that speech impediment years ago."

Shaken but still determined, Paris lifted her chin, looked her great-grandmother in the eye as Sloan had done, and announced, "I think she is great!"

"Well, then, why didn't you come out and say so in the first place?"

Unable to answer or endure a lecture, Paris glanced at her watch. "If I don't hurry and take a shower, we'll miss our tee-off time at the club."

"Take a look at the clothing she brought with her," Edith called out. "Make certain she won't disgrace herself or us while she's here. She'll be meeting our friends at the club and in town. If she needs clothes, see that she has them."

Paris turned in dismay. "I can't go through her closet and belittle her clothes and tell her they aren't right."

"Of course you can. You have an excellent sense of style. You design clothes."

"Yes, but—"

"Paris! Take care of the matter. And Paris—" she called as Paris started off. "There's no reason to throw money away at the expensive shops here unless you don't have something to lend her."

18

Sloan had no idea how much the FBI knew about her father or his finances, or even what they suspected him of doing, but it seemed important to tell Paul what she'd learned. Frustrated that the information exchange was strictly a one-way street, she knocked on the door to his room. When there was no answer, she went down the hall to her room and discovered its door was locked. She rattled it. "Hello, is someone in there?" she called.

The door opened so suddenly that she stepped back and stared in confusion at Paul, who was wearing shorts and holding her paperback novel with his forefinger inserted between the pages as if to keep his place.

"My room doesn't have a balcony, so I thought I'd borrow yours and read for a while, until you came back," he explained.

Sloan knew he was lying for the benefit of anyone who might overhear them in the hall. She followed him inside and closed the door. "What are you really doing?"

"Checking for bugs. I didn't find any."

The idea of a private home being bugged by its owner seemed preposterous, and Sloan said so.

"It was just a precaution. Your father is known to be an extremely cautious man."

"Not that cautious or we wouldn't be here," Sloan joked.

"And speaking of why we're here," she added with a pleased smile, "I just had an enlightening conversation with my great-grandmother. Did you know she controls the major portion of the family money?"

"You're referring to the Hanover Trust?"

A little deflated, Sloan nodded.

"What did she tell you?"

Sloan repeated the pertinent parts of her conversation with her great-grandmother almost verbatim.

"Nothing new there," he said. "At least nothing significant. You were down there quite a while, what else did she talk about?"

Sloan told him the rest, and he seemed far more pleased by it than by the information she'd thought was important. "If she wants you to spend quality time with Paris, do it. I'll hang around here and see what I can find out."

"About *what*?" Sloan demanded, throwing up her hand in frustration. "What do you suspect him of doing? I think I'm entitled to some sort of a minimal explanation."

"You're on a need-to-know basis. When I think you need to know, I'll tell you."

Striving to match his blasé tone, Sloan said, "And, when I have something *I* think *you* need to know, I guess we'll have to negotiate."

She expected him to react to her threat with either amusement or annoyance, but he did neither.

"There are two men in Palm Beach you never want to try to negotiate with, Sloan. I'm one of them."

"Who is the other one?" Sloan asked, taken aback by the veiled threat she heard in his voice.

"Noah Maitland. Thanks for letting me use your balcony," he said for effect as he stepped into the hall.

The door closed behind him, and Sloan slowly headed into the bathroom to take her shower.

He was completely unreadable, unpredictable, and single-minded, but there were times when he'd also seemed charming and rather kind.

Now she had an uneasy feeling that this last might be a facade.

19

Paris was waiting in the foyer when Sloan came downstairs. "I brought the car around in front," she said, and Sloan followed her outside.

A pale gold Jaguar convertible with the top down was parked in the driveway, and as they drove past the main gates, Sloan watched the sunlight gleaming on Paris's chestnut hair. She was thinking how perfectly her sleek sister suited her sleek car when Paris glanced sideways and caught Sloan looking at her. "Did you forget something?" Paris asked.

"No, why?"

"You had an odd look on your face."

After what she'd seen and heard of Paris today, Sloan wanted desperately to breach Paris's barrier of formality and get to know her sister. She seized on Paris's question as an opportunity. "I was thinking that this car is very beautiful and that it suits you."

Paris almost lost control of the steering wheel as she turned and looked at Sloan. "I don't know what to say."

"You could say whatever you're thinking."

"Well, then, I guess I was thinking that that was the last thing I expected you to say."

Sloan had given up on any further voluntary conversation when Paris blurted, "And I was thinking that it was such a *nice* thing for you to say." She infused the word with so much warmth that Sloan knew Paris meant it as a very great compliment.

They turned left onto a large boulevard, and Paris hesitatingly said, "Does it feel odd to you to be here in the car and know that we're . . . we're sisters?"

Sloan nodded. "I was just thinking that very thing."

"You're not at all what I expected."

"I know."

"You do?"

"Yes. Your great-grandmother told me what you'd been told."

Paris slanted her a shy look. "She's your great-grandmother, too."

Some demon of mischief made Sloan say, "Somehow I find it much easier to believe you're my sister than she is my great-grandmother."

"She's a little hard to get to know. She intimidates people."

Including you, Sloan thought.

"Does she intimidate you?"

"Not really. Well, maybe just a little," Sloan admitted. "Most people are terrified of her."

"She's not exactly a typical great-grandmother, at least not my impression of one."

"What is your grandmother like?"

"You mean our mother's mother?" Sloan said gently.

"Yes."

"She died when I was seven, but I remember she was very—cuddly. She smelled like cookies."

"Cookies?"

Sloan nodded. "She loved to bake. She was plump, which is why I guess I said 'cuddly.' She always had cookies for Sara and me."

"Sara?"

"A childhood friend, who is still my best friend."

An awkward silence ensued, the silence of two people who want to move forward but who are so relieved by where they are that they're afraid to take the next steps. Sloan drew a long breath and prayed that she was saying the right thing. "Would you like to know what your mother is like?"

"If you want to tell me. It's up to you."

Lifting her face to the wind, Sloan tipped her head back and contemplated Paris's evasive answer. "If we aren't honest and frank," she said with quiet sincerity, "we don't have a chance of really getting to know each other, and I don't want to miss out on that. Do you think we could make a pact to tell each other the truth and say what we really feel? That's going to take blind trust, but I'm willing to try it. Will you?"

Paris's hands tightened on the steering wheel as she considered Sloan's pact. "Yes," she whispered finally. "Yes," she declared again with a shy smile and a firm nod.

Sloan put the new pact to its first test. "In that case, would you like to know what your mother is really like?"

"Yes, I would."

"That's easy," Sloan said happily. "She's very much like my impression of *you* so far. She's kind. She doesn't like to hurt anyone's feelings. She adores beautiful clothes, and she works in the most fashionable dress shop in Bell Harbor. Everyone who knows her, loves her, except Lydia, the owner of the shop. Lydia bullies and browbeats her terribly and takes constant advantage of her, but Mother makes excuses for her bad disposition." Sloan broke off as the country club entrance came into view. "Paris, let's not play golf. Let's do something else, instead."

"But Father wanted you to have a lesson."

"I know, but suppose I tell you I absolutely refuse to do it. In that event what will he do?" Sloan wondered if he ranted and raged or worse. He had the temperament of a bully. "Will he shout at you?"

Paris looked shocked by the suggestion. "No, but he'll be extremely disappointed."

"I see. You mean 'disappointed' in the way he was disappointed in your tennis game this morning?"

"Yes, only he'll be extremely disappointed in both of us this time. This morning he was disappointed in me alone. He doesn't get over disappointments as quickly or easily as some people do," she explained as if that were her problem, instead of his—a justifiable fact that Sloan should accept and understand in the same way Paris did.

Sloan understood it perfectly: Her father was not physically abusive. He engaged in emotional tyranny instead, a more subtle but equally effective form of brutal domination. "If I absolutely refused, then he can't be disappointed in you, can he?"

"No, I guess not."

"Do you *want* to play golf?"

She hesitated for so long that Sloan wasn't certain whether Paris didn't want to answer or didn't know what she wanted, period. "No, I really don't. I'm not as fond of golf as Father would like me to be."

"If we could do anything you wanted right now, what would it be?"

"We would have lunch somewhere and just talk."

"I'd love that! Since I absolutely refuse to play golf, he can't be disappointed in you, so let's have lunch and talk instead."

Biting her lip, Paris hesitated; then she made a sudden right turn. "I know just the place. It's a little café and we can eat outside. No one will bother us or rush us."

In Bell Harbor a "café" was a very casual eating place, a first cousin of a diner. Paris's café was a swanky French restaurant with canopies over the entrance, an enclosed patio with a fountain, and valet parking. The valet knew her by name and so did the maître d'.

"We'd like to eat outside, Jean," Paris told him with that genteel smile that Sloan admired now that she realized it was genuine.

"May I bring you something to drink?" he asked when they were seated at a table near the fountain with a view of the shops across the street.

Paris looked at Sloan for a decision, then abruptly made it herself. "I think we should have champagne— some very good champagne—for a special occasion."

"A birthday?" he guessed. Paris shook her head and looked shyly at Sloan. "More of a rebirth."

When he left, an awkward pause followed while they both tried to think of a place to begin getting acquainted. On the sidewalk in front of them, a mother wheeled a baby in a handsome buggy and a teenager swooped around her on a twelve-speed. "I got my first two-wheel bike when I was five," Sloan said to break the silence. "It was too big for me, and I ran into everyone I passed until I finally learned to balance it. The crossing guard said I was a menace."

"Did you always know you wanted to be an interior designer?"

Although Sloan had to conceal a few things about her present life, she was determined to be honest with Paris about everything else. "Actually," she confessed, "my original career goals were to be Superwoman or Batwoman. What about you?"

"As soon as I got my first doll, I started worrying about an appropriate layette for her," Paris admitted. "So I guess I was always interested in fashion."

A waiter arrived with a bottle of champagne in a silver stand, and Sloan waited for him to finishing serving their drinks while a young teenage couple strolled by, holding hands. "They look awfully young to be dating and holding hands, don't they?" she remarked, and when Paris nodded, Sloan seized on that as the next topic of conversation. "How old were you on your first date?"

"Sixteen," Paris said. "His name was David, and he took me to my sophomore dance. I had wanted to go with a boy named Richard, but Father knew David's family and felt he would be a more acceptable escort."

Sloan was instantly intrigued. "How was it?"

"It was awful," Paris confessed with a smile and a shudder. "On the way home from the dance, he started drinking from a flask; then he parked the car and started kissing me. He wouldn't stop until I finally burst into tears. How was your first date?"

"A lot like yours," Sloan said, laughing. "I went with Butch Bellamy, who was a foot taller than I and couldn't dance. He spent most of the night in the locker room, drinking beer with his buddies on the freshman football team. On the way home, he parked the car and started kissing me and grabbing me."

Laughing, Paris guessed the ending of the story: "And you burst into tears, too, so he would take you home?"

"No. I told him if he didn't let me out of the car, I'd tell all his friends on the team that he was gay. Then I took off my first pair of heels and hiked two miles in my first pair of panty hose. They were not a pretty sight when I got home."

Paris laughed, and Sloan lifted her glass in a toast. "To us—for surviving our first dates," she said with smiling solemnity.

Paris clinked her glass against Sloan's. "To us, and to all girls with first dates like ours."

The waiter appeared just then and handed each of them an open menu. Anxious to maintain the spirit of cheerful closeness that had sprung up between them, Sloan peered over the top of her menu. "What's your least favorite food?"

"Brussels sprouts. What's yours?"

"Liver."

"They say that if liver is fixed with—"

Sloan shook her head. "There is *no* way to fix liver and make it edible. Maybe we aren't genetic sisters, after all. Maybe I was adopted and—Why are you laughing?"

"Because I was only repeating what people say. I *hate* liver. It makes me gag."

"The gag reflex is the ultimate proof. We're definitely related," Sloan happily decreed, but Paris turned very solemn.

"Not necessarily. This is the ultimate test question, so take your time before you answer: How do you feel about tomato soup?"

Sloan shuddered, and they both burst out laughing.

The waiter had put a basket of fresh bread sticks on the table, and Paris reached for one. "Have you ever been married?" she asked.

"No," Sloan replied. "Have you?"

"Almost. I got engaged when I was twenty-five. Henry was thirty-two, and we met in Santa Barbara at a theater party. Two months later, we got engaged."

Sloan paused in the act of selecting a bread stick for herself. "What happened?"

"The day after we got engaged, Father discovered Henry had an ex-wife and two children living in Paris. I wouldn't have cared if he hadn't lied and told me he'd never been married before."

"That must have been awful for you."

"It was at first. Father hadn't trusted him from the very beginning."

Sloan could imagine how little sympathy Paris must have gotten from Carter Reynolds, and she felt a pang of angry sadness that Paris hadn't had Sloan or her mother to help her through it. "How did your father discover that?"

"He's your father, too," Paris reminded her with a beguiling smile; then she answered Sloan's question. "When Henry and I began seeing a lot of each other, Father had him investigated, but the report from Europe didn't get back until after we announced our engagement."

Sloan tried not to sound as mistrustful of Carter Reynolds's motives and integrity as she was beginning to feel. "Does he usually have your friends investigated?"

To Sloan's shock, Paris nodded as if that were the most normal thing in the world for a parent to do. "Not just my friends, but other people he doesn't know who start spending a lot of time around us. Father believes it's best to be careful about people you associate with. He doesn't give his trust easily." She glanced at the bread stick in her hand; then she lifted her gaze to Sloan's. "Let's talk about something else. My broken engagement doesn't deserve another minute of our valuable time."

After that, the hours flew past, filled with hesitant questions, honest answers, and warm smiles, as two strangers, who had started out to form a bond, discovered that the bond was already there. Ignoring the waiters, their meals, and the admiring looks of men, a beautiful brunette and an exquisite blonde sat at a sidewalk table beneath a striped umbrella and carefully constructed a bridge to span thirty years.

20

Sitting beside Paris in the late-afternoon traffic on the way home from the café, Sloan felt as if the magic of the last few hours had spread its beauty over all of Palm Beach. Overhead, the sky was a brilliant blue, the clouds whiter, fluffier. The ocean was more majestic, the beach prettier. Colors were more vivid, sounds were soothing, and the sea air blowing against her face was a benediction, not just a breeze.

Yesterday, Paris and she had been strangers who thought of each other as adversaries; now they were sisters who thought of each other as allies. She glanced at Paris, and Paris's answering smile was filled with the same wonder and delight that Sloan felt.

"We didn't have time to talk about Paul and you," Paris said as they neared the house. "Are you serious about him?"

Sloan hesitated, struck by the sudden, unhappy realization that this wonderful, fragile new relationship with her sister was going to be jeopardized in the future by the lies she and Paul had perpetrated on Paris. If Paul found no evidence that incriminated Carter, then Paris could at least be spared the truth about their reason for coming to Palm Beach. In that event, Sloan would have to come up with some reason for having kept her job a secret. But if the evidence did turn up, then Paris would soon know the full extent of their deception, and Sloan was afraid of how she'd react.

Either way, Sloan was trapped. She couldn't say anything that might impede Paul's investigation, so she resolved to stick as closely to the truth as possible so that Paris would have fewer reasons to feel duped no matter what happened to Carter. "The truth is we're just friends. I was . . . uneasy . . . about coming here. Paul convinced me I should, and he . . . volunteered . . . to come with me."

"For moral support," Paris concluded. "He's so nice. He's someone you just know you can trust."

Sloan made a mental note never to rely on Paris's judgment of men. "What about Noah and you?" she said, eager to shift the focus away from herself. "Carter told me the two of you are practically engaged."

"Father is determined to make it happen. I've told him I don't want to marry Noah, but he just can't understand."

"Why not?"

Paris flashed her a winsome smile. "Probably because Noah is gorgeous, brilliant, and incredibly rich, and women make fools of themselves over him. However, Noah doesn't want to marry me either, and so we made a secret deal that solves the whole problem."

"What sort of deal?"

"Noah *isn't* going to propose," she said with a laugh as she turned into the driveway. The gates opened automatically, without Paris stopping to press the call button or using any kind of electronic opener. Sloan's attention switched to the house's security system out of concern for Paris's safety, and then because she realized the information might also be vital to Paul and her. "Aren't you ever afraid here?"

"Of what?"

"Thieves. Prowlers at night. This place is the size of a museum. If I were a thief, I'd figure there were lots of things inside it worth stealing."

"We're very safe," Paris assured her. "Besides the fence, we have infrared beams all around the perimeter of the property. They're turned on automatically with the alarm system at night. Also, there are ten cameras positioned around the property. Are you afraid here?"

"I—I guess I always think about security and safety," Sloan said, trying to stick as closely to the truth as possible for the sake of her future relationship with Paris.

"That's why you took a self-defense course," Paris concluded, and immediately tried to reassure her with more information. "If you get worried, you can turn on any television set in the house and see whatever the cameras are seeing. Tune to channel ninety, then go right on through to channel one hundred. That will show you all the camera views of the property. At least, I think those are the right channels, but Gary will know for sure. I'll ask him. Father had Gary arrange for the new security system."

"Thank you—" Sloan said lamely.

"Also, if you hear or see something that really scares you, you can pick up any desk-style phone in the house, press the pound key, and hold it down. But don't try that unless you really think there's a problem. I did it accidentally once when the system was first installed. I was trying to open the gates from the house, but I forgot to press the intercom button before I held down the pound key."

"What happens when you do that?"

"Everything," Paris said with a giggle. "An alarm goes directly to the police station, the sirens on the house start screaming, and all the lights on the property, inside and outside, turn on and start flashing."

Sloan thought that sounded rather like the integrated telephone-security setups that had caused Karen Althorp and Dr. Pembroke so much embarrassment in Bell Harbor.

Paris drove around the side of the house to a six-car garage, and one of the garage doors opened automatically. "I haven't seen you use a gate opener or a garage door opener," Sloan said.

"There's an electronic gadget hidden somewhere on our cars. When you drive up to the garage, the gadget on the car talks to the gadget on the correct garage door and opens it. The same gadget opened the gates for us when we turned into the drive just now."

"It sounds like no one who shouldn't be here can get in or out," Sloan observed as Paris parked the car in her garage stall.

"Anyone can get out once Nordstrom has let them in. There are sensors under the pavestones that open the gates when the weight of a car rolls over them. Otherwise,

Nordstrom would have to be on hand to open the gates every time a delivery truck or servant needed to leave."

"You are truly part of the electronic age," Sloan told her with a smile.

"Father is extremely security conscious."

Sloan was afraid he probably had more than one reason for that.

21

Gary Dishler materialized in the hallway from a room by the stairs as soon as Paris and Sloan walked past it. "Mrs. Reynolds has been asking for you," he told Paris. "She's upstairs in her room."

"Is she feeling all right?" Paris asked worriedly.

"If she's suffering from anything, it's boredom," he reassured her.

While Paris confirmed that television channels ninety through one hundred showed the images from the security cameras, Sloan studied the butler, who was nearby. Nordstrom was well over six feet tall, with blond hair, blue eyes, a ruddy complexion and a muscular physique. On the way upstairs, she confided her thoughts. "He looks more like a security guard than a butler."

"I know," Paris returned with a smile. "He's really huge."

They were still smiling as they walked into Edith Reynolds's bedroom. The old lady was seated on a fringed, maroon velvet sofa at the end of a room that was nearly the size of Sloan's entire house and filled with so much dark, very ornate furniture that Sloan felt a little claustrophobic.

Mrs. Reynolds scowled as she took off her glasses and laid her book aside. "You've been gone all day," she accused. "Well," she said to Paris. "How was Sloan's golf lesson?"

"We didn't go to the club," Paris said.

Edith's white brows snapped together, but before she could say anything Sloan spoke up. Trying to simultaneously shield Paris from the old woman's displeasure as well as improve her mood, Sloan deliberately made a joke of her refusal to play golf. "Paris tried to make me play golf, but I begged her for mercy; then I refused to get out of the car. She tried to drag me out of it, but I'm stronger than she is. She tried to clobber me with a putter; then I reminded her that you do not approve of public spectacles, and she had to give in."

"You are being impertinent," Edith declared, but she was having trouble maintaining her dark scowl.

Sloan let her amusement show. "Yes, ma'am, I know, but I just can't seem to help it."

"I told you to address me as Great-grandmother!"

"Yes, Great-grandmother," Sloan quickly amended, sensing that yielding on that point would accomplish her goal. She was right. Edith Reynolds's lips were twitching with reluctant laughter.

"You are also outrageously stubborn."

Sloan nodded meekly. "My own mother has said so."

On the brink of losing their battle of wits, Edith saved face by dismissing Sloan with a flip of her hand. "Go away. I've had enough. I want to talk to Paris privately."

Satisfied that Paris wouldn't be reprimanded for the aborted golf lesson, Sloan did as she was told, but not before she noted Paris's dazed expression.

When Sloan was gone, Edith nodded to the chair in front of her. "Sit down. I want to know what you did and what you talked about."

"We had lunch at Le Gamin and we talked about everything," Paris said as she sat down. For over an hour, Paris tried to repeat what Sloan had said, but she was interrupted constantly by her great-grandmother's probing questions. "It was wonderful," Paris said when the inquisition was finally over. "I could have stayed there all day and all night. Sloan felt the same way. I know she did."

"And now," Edith said coolly, "I suppose you want to go up to Bell Harbor and meet your mother?"

Paris braced for a storm of opposition, but she did not back down as she would normally have done. "Yes, as a matter of fact, I do. Sloan told me all about her, and she's nothing like Father and Grandmother described."

"You have known Sloan for less than two days, and you are willing to take her word over theirs, is that it?"

Paris concentrated on her words so she wouldn't stutter. "I'm not taking anyone's word. I simply want to make my own decision."

Instead of verbally flaying her as Paris expected, her great-grandmother leaned back in her chair and stared at her. After a prolonged, tense silence, she said, "It appears that Sloan's defiance and stubbornness are remarkably contagious."

"I hope so," Paris said, lifting her chin.

"If you are still interested in anyone else's advice on anything, I suggest you refrain from sharing your new opinion of your mother with your father."

Paris nodded and stood up. "May I go now?"

"By all means," Edith replied.

Edith Reynolds watched her leave, and for several minutes she was perfectly still, lost in thought; then she reached for the telephone beside her chair and dialed a private unlisted phone number. "I have some work for you to do, Wilson," she told the man who answered. "It must be done very discreetly and very quickly." Then she told him what she wanted.

22

"How was your day?" Noah asked as he walked into the family room, where his father was watching an ancient John Wayne movie and Courtney was slouched in a chair, thumbing through a magazine, with headphones over her ears. Courtney tugged off the headphones, and Douglas looked up.

"My day has been boring," he complained in the aggrieved tone of an invalid who thinks everyone should suffer his confinement with him. "I read and I took a nap. Where were you all afternoon?"

"I took some papers over to Carter's house this morning; then I ran a few errands and met with Gordon Sanders."

"I don't trust Sanders," Douglas said; then he asked eagerly, "Did you see Sloan when you were at Carter's?"

"As a matter of fact I did," Noah replied with amused irony. "I got there just as he was challenging her to a match to prove what she'd learned in some self-defense class she'd supposedly taken."

"It's a sorry state of affairs when women have to take

self-defense courses before they feel safe on the streets! Poor little Sloan. She's as sweet and gentle as a dove."

"Your sweet little dove tossed Carter on his ass. Twice."

Douglas was momentarily dumbstruck. "Really? Well, I still feel sorry for today's women. Imagine living in fear of being mugged."

Noah chuckled. "Save your pity for her mugger. If Sloan doesn't have a black belt in karate or whatever it was she used on Carter, then she's damned close to it." He glanced at his watch. "I have a phone call to make."

"Are you going out tonight?" Douglas said, belatedly noticing that Noah was wearing a suit and tie.

When Noah said he was, father and daughter both looked at him as if he were abandoning them to an unspeakable fate by leaving them alone with each other. Courtney even sounded bitter. "So, who is the lucky lady tonight?"

"I'm having dinner with Paris and Sloan—"

"The man has no shame!" Courtney announced to the ceiling. "He's hitting on sisters. It's incestuous!"

"—and Paul Richardson," Noah added, ignoring her and speaking to his father.

"Who is he?"

"Sloan's friend."

"Poor guy," Courtney mocked as she pulled her headphones back over her ears. "He's about to lose his girlfriend to Palm Beach's most eligible, most devastatingly handsome bachelor."

Courtney's prediction was far from accurate. In fact, as far as Noah could tell, Sloan Reynolds barely knew he was part of the foursome at the Ocean Club, which wouldn't have bothered him except that she was beginning to intrigue him. For one thing, it was difficult to assimilate that the delicate, golden-haired beauty seated across from him in a sexy black cocktail dress was the same disheveled athlete who'd thrown Carter on his ass that morning.

When he listened to her chatting with Paris or Paul Richardson, Noah couldn't imagine how he'd mistaken her for being boring or witless last night, but if he asked her a direct question himself, she seemed unable or unwilling to piece together a long sentence. If he didn't address a comment directly to her, she avoided looking at him altogether.

Richardson was another enigma. Although he'd come with Sloan, he was paying as much attention to Paris, and Sloan didn't seem to mind. Paris was full of surprises, too. Noah had known her for years, but tonight she was more animated with two strangers than she'd ever been with him or anyone else he'd ever seen her with. Moreover, Noah had the impossible impression that Paris was developing a genuine fondness for her sister's boyfriend.

If he hadn't been being made to feel like an outsider, Noah would have found the evening completely fascinating.

The dance floor at the Ocean Club was separated from the dining room by a trellis covered with tropical plants, and while they were waiting for dessert to be served, Noah decided to get Sloan on the dance floor, where she couldn't ignore him as easily. He actually anticipated that she'd decline if he gave her the opportunity, so he got up and walked around to her chair before he asked her to dance.

Her head jerked up and she stared at him in surprised dismay. "Oh, no. Thank you. I don't think so."

Caught somewhere between amusement and annoyance, Noah looked at Richardson. "Do you have trouble getting her on the dance floor, or is it just me?"

"Sometimes," he admitted with a relaxed grin; then he looked at Sloan and jokingly said, "Noah is going to look like a wallflower if you leave him standing there. Men have feelings, too, you know. Have a heart and dance with him."

Noah noticed how slowly and reluctantly she stood up, and he noticed that she seemed unaware that every man she passed on the way to the dance floor stared at her. In his experience, beautiful women were always conscious of their appeal, and the fact that she either didn't care or didn't know, further added to her allure. When he took her in his arms on the dance floor, she held herself as far from him as possible and focused her gaze on the third button on his shirt.

Sloan was so tense that her body felt like a piece of plywood. Noah Maitland had been watching her like a hawk all evening, and now she was forced to dance with him. He made her so nervous that she couldn't come up with a coherent sentence when he asked her a direct question. He was so incredibly good-looking that women had given her envious looks on the way to the dance floor, and the men stared at her, too, wondering what possible attraction she could hold for someone like him. He was Sara's dream, but he was Sloan's nightmare.

She realized that the more she ignored him, the more interested in her he seemed to become; therefore, she thought it was logical that the best way to turn him off would probably be to act interested in him. Except Sloan couldn't do that, because that would require flirting with him or at the very least looking straight into those mesmerizing silver eyes of his, and she couldn't make herself attempt either thing.

Noah moved automatically to the music, trying to remember the last time he'd danced with anyone who acted as distant as Sloan, and he gave up when he got as far back as prep school. He decided to loosen her up with a little flirtatious conversation. "What do the men in Bell Harbor do to impress you?"

Startled by the new, slightly intimate note in his baritone voice, Sloan said the first thing that came to mind. "They don't."

"That's a relief."

"What is?"

"It's a relief that they don't impress you either. That way, I can soothe my wounded pride with the knowledge that I'm not the only one who can't get anywhere with you."

For a second, he thought she wasn't going to bother answering; then she finally focused those remarkable purple-blue eyes on him. "I meant they don't try," she said, looking at him as if he were being absurd.

Noah abruptly abandoned the rules of sophisticated repartee by which he normally lived and took a direct approach. "Tell me something?"

"I'll try."

"Why is it you're perfectly able and willing to carry on a conversation with everyone but me?"

Sloan felt as stupid as she knew she sounded. "I can't explain it."

"But you do notice it?"

She nodded.

Noah looked down into those long-lashed eyes that she finally raised to him, and he forgot how frustrated he'd been a moment before. He smiled. "What can I do to help you relax?"

Sloan heard something distinctly sexual in that, and it completely unnerved her. "Are you flirting with me?" she asked bluntly.

"Not very successfully," he replied just as bluntly.

"I wish you wouldn't try," she said honestly. Softening her tone, Sloan added, "But if you ever come to Bell Harbor, I have a friend I'd like to introduce to you. Sara would be perfect for you."

She was trying to fix him up with a girlfriend, Noah realized with disbelief, and that was as unprecedented as it was insulting. "Let's revert to silence. My ego can't handle any more of this."

"I'm sorry."

"So am I," he said curtly. He took her back to the table the instant the dance was over, and Sloan knew he never intended to bother with her again. She should have felt very relieved. She felt . . . let down. He asked Paris to dance, and the moment they were away from the table, Paul turned on her with a frown. "What is your problem with Maitland?"

"I don't have a problem, exactly. I just don't know what to do with him. He was trying to flirt with me."

"Then flirt with him."

Sloan twisted the stem of her wineglass in her fingers. "I'm not very good at flirting, and he's *very* good at it."

"Well, practice on Maitland. Pretend he's someone you're investigating, only smile at him when you ask him questions about himself, and then remember to smile at him while he's answering. Look straight into his eyes. No, not like that!" he said with a sharp crack of laughter. "You looked catatonic."

"Just what do you suggest I ask him *about?*" Sloan retorted, stung by his laughter.

"What's the first thing you wondered about after he picked us up tonight?"

"I wondered how much he pays for a tune-up for his Rolls-Royce!"

"Well, don't ask him that," Paul warned with another laugh.

"We don't exactly have a lot in common," Sloan said, irritated anew by his mirth. "He's a rich, spoiled aristocrat from another universe. Just look at the suit he's wearing. How much do you think it cost?"

"Don't ask him that, either," Paul said.

"I'm not completely stupid. However, I'm glad you think this is so funny."

She sounded genuinely hurt, and Paul sobered. "Sloan, you have a job to do. I'd like to know about those documents he brought over to the house this morning. Make peace with him. Better yet, make friends with him.

Friends tell each other things. Your father regards Maitland as a friend, and he's undoubtedly mentioned things to Maitland in passing that we might find interesting even if they don't seem significant to Maitland. Understand?"

Sloan decided to take advantage of their remaining moments of privacy to discuss something else. "If you're interested, I know the security layout at the house."

"I'm interested."

The music was winding down, and Sloan hurriedly added the rest of the information she needed to share with him: "One more thing—Paris asked me today about my relationship with you, and I told her that we aren't romantically involved."

She told him what she'd said and why she'd done it, and Paul nodded. "Okay. That's good. Actually, the way things are working out, I think it's going to be very much to our advantage if she and Maitland both know that."

"Paris likes you," Sloan warned. "She thinks you're trustworthy."

"I like her, too."

"You know what I'm trying to say."

"I do, and stop frowning at me. It looks odd." Sloan smoothed her frown into a smile. "That's better. You concentrate on Maitland. I'll worry about Paris."

Sloan had neither the desire nor the opportunity to follow Paul's instructions on that matter, because Noah Maitland treated her with chilling courtesy for the rest of the evening.

23

Courtney poked her head into the kitchen, where a stout woman in her early sixties was stirring chopped pecans into pancake batter. "Morning, Claudine. Where is everyone?"

"Your brother decided to have his breakfast on the terrace," she said without looking up. "Your father is outside, too."

"I'll have a waffle. I'm glad you don't get sick very often. Yesterday we had to fend for ourselves at breakfast. I burned my bagel."

"It's a miracle you survived," Claudine unsympathetically replied.

"When I have my own cook, *I'm* going to have a French chef!"

"Good, then you'll get fat from all that rich food, and it will serve you right."

Satisfied with their ritual morning sparring session, Courtney grinned and retreated back through the doorway. "I think I'll have French toast instead of pancakes."

Outside, she stopped at a serving cart where Claudine

had set out a pitcher of fresh orange juice. She poured orange juice into a glass; then she sauntered down the terrace steps to the second level, where Noah was seated at a table beneath a bright yellow umbrella, reading one of several newspapers stacked near his elbow.

"How did you make out with Sloan Reynolds last night?"

"I didn't."

"You're kidding," Courtney said with unconcealed delight as she slid into the chair next to him. "You struck out?"

He turned to the financial section before he answered. "I crashed and burned," he murmured without looking up.

"The woman must be blind!"

Noah mistook her remark for loyalty and flashed her a brief smile. "Thank you."

Courtney was quick to correct his mistake. "I meant she must be blind, or else she can't read, because she obviously hasn't had a look at your financial statement. If she had, she'd be sitting in your lap, right now." When that failed to evoke a reaction from him, she looked over her right shoulder across the lawn, toward the beach. "Where is our father?"

"The last time I saw him, he was digging in a flower bed near the edge of the lawn."

Courtney leaned back and peered around a clump of trees, looking for him. "That's not what he's doing now. He's standing around like he's watching for someone. I'll bet he's watching for Sloan! It was about this same time yesterday when he saw her."

That got Noah's attention, Courtney noticed. He twisted around in his chair and squinted into the sun.

"Just because you struck out doesn't mean he will. Maybe she prefers older men. I would love to have a look at this woman. I think I'll go down there and hang around with him."

"No you won't. Don't embarrass us."

"I like to embarrass us."

Noah had a feeling she was right about their father's reason for lingering by the shrubbery at the edge of the lawn, and he sighed in disgust. "Roger Kilman called for him a little while ago. Run down there and tell him he had a phone call. It's absurd for him to be standing around like that."

"Jealous?"

"That's enough!" Noah warned sharply; then he instantly regretted his tone. "Will you just do what I asked you to do without an argument for a change?"

"Possibly," Courtney replied with a sudden smile, watching her father wave at someone and start forward. A moment later a blonde in running shorts and a tank top jogged into view on the beach and stopped to talk to him. Courtney watched for a few moments. "I'll bring him back here no matter what it takes," she promised enthusiastically, already sliding her chair back.

Sloan had given Douglas Maitland several reasons why she couldn't accept his invitation to join him for breakfast on the terrace, but he overrode her protests with charming insistence, pointing out that her family were all late sleepers; then he put his hand beneath her arm and marched her forward.

A sloping, beautifully landscaped lawn stretched the two-hundred-yard distance from the beach to the house, where it ended in a broad limestone terrace with three levels. Umbrella tables, chaise lounges, and white wrought-iron chairs with bright yellow cushions were invitingly arranged on each level, and as they neared the terrace, Sloan belatedly realized that one of the tables was already occupied by a man and a girl.

Sloan didn't need to see his features to be certain the man was Noah Maitland. She had seen him only three times, but his chiseled profile, his glossy black hair, and his wide-shouldered physique were emblazoned on her brain, and her nervous system reacted to the stimulation of his presence with an annoying jolt of adrenaline.

Sloan was trying to think of some last-minute excuse for a hasty retreat when the girl at the table jumped up and trotted down the terrace steps, heading straight toward them.

"You are about to meet my daughter, Courtney," Douglas warned her cheerfully, and tightened his grip on Sloan's elbow as if he sensed her desire to flee and somehow automatically attributed it to the girl's impending arrival. "It is an experience most people find difficult to forget. Her mother was my fourth wife. A lovely woman, but she realized she didn't want children after Courtney was born. Courtney has only seen her a few times, so she hasn't had the benefit of a mother's influence. We make allowances for that."

Tall and thin, the teenager had permed dark hair that she wore in a thick ponytail over her left ear, and she walked with a coltish exuberance that didn't fit with Sloan's image of the spoiled, conceited, whiny teenager whom she assumed Douglas was warning her about. Courtney's first words didn't fit with that image either. "You're Sloan, aren't you?" Sloan started to nod, and Courtney put out her hand. "I've been dying to meet you. I'm Courtney."

Sloan was not only taken aback; she was more than a little charmed by the child's enthusiasm, her mischievous smile, and her familiar gray eyes. "I'm very happy to meet you," Sloan said, shaking her hand.

"People sometimes start out feeling that way, but they usually change their minds."

Sloan dealt with teenagers all the time in Bell Harbor, and she had a feeling that if she didn't follow through with Courtney's opening salvo, she'd be showing Courtney a lack of interest rather than good manners. "Why is that?"

"Because I say whatever I think."

"No, my dear," Douglas contradicted mildly, "it is because you refuse to think at all."

Courtney ignored him and rushed toward the terraced steps, forcing them to hurry to keep pace with her. "Noah is going to be so glad to see you," she predicted as they approached him from the side. "Noah, look who I found—"

He was *not* glad to see her, Sloan noted. He glanced over his shoulder, and Sloan saw annoyance flash across his face before he laid down his newspaper and politely stood up. "Good morning, Sloan," he said with flawless formality and no warmth.

"I ambushed her on the beach," Douglas confessed, pulling out a chair for Sloan across from Noah's and settling into one on her right. Courtney took the chair on Sloan's left, and a woman appeared on the terrace carrying a tray with a coffeepot and cups.

"We're going to be four for breakfast, Claudine," he told her. "Sloan, what would you like to have?"

"Whatever you're having will be fine," Sloan said, trying not to think about how unfriendly Noah seemed and how stilted and awkward that was going to make the meal for her. She needn't have worried. While Claudine was still filling the coffee cups, Courtney lit a conversational bonfire. Perching her chin on her fists, she looked from Douglas to Noah and then to Sloan. "How does it feel to be the only woman in Palm Beach to have both Maitland men chasing you? And who is the leading contender?"

Sloan thought she must have misunderstood her. She blinked. "I'm sorry?"

"Courtney, please—" Douglas started to intervene, but he changed his mind when Courtney explained, "Noah said Sloan shot him down last night."

Douglas turned an intrigued smile on Sloan. "Did you really?"

"No, I—" Sloan glanced at Noah, who was scowling at Courtney, who wasn't daunted in the least.

"Yes, she did," Courtney told her father. "Noah said so this morning." Turning to Sloan, she said, "I asked him how things went with you last night, and he said he 'crashed and burned'—"

"No," Sloan blurted desperately. "You misunderstood. He—he didn't even get off the ground—"

She didn't realize what she'd said until Douglas gave a bark of laughter and slapped his knee. Sloan felt as if the Cheshire Cat from *Alice in Wonderland* were going to materialize next if she didn't get the situation under control. Since Noah seemed to be the only other relatively normal person at the table, she looked directly at him. "What I meant to say," she explained very clearly and concisely, "is that you couldn't have 'crashed and burned' because you weren't even trying to—to—"

A flicker of amusement lit his gray eyes, "to get off the ground?"

"Exactly," Sloan said emphatically. She'd been at the table for less than two minutes and she felt as if she'd already fought her way through a treacherous minefield. "Thank you," she added feelingly.

Noah had intended to make an excuse to absent himself from the meal, but the beguiling gratitude on Sloan's face changed his mind. "Don't thank me yet. This could get worse."

"I guess you weren't in very good form last night, Noah," Courtney concluded.

"I guess I wasn't," he said.

Courtney decided to switch to a more vulnerable target and aimed at Sloan. "Noah said you have a black belt in karate and that he saw you throw Carter on his ass—"

"That wasn't karate," Sloan interrupted, trying not to look shocked.

"What was it?"

"They were some martial arts moves taught in self-defense classes. They probably came from tae kwon do or jujitsu."

"Do you know any karate?"

"Yes."

"Do you have a black belt?"

"I teach self-defense to women," Sloan evaded. "As a volunteer."

"Would you show me some moves so I can defend myself?"

"We're the ones who need to defend ourselves from *you*," Douglas said dryly.

Sloan was inclined to agree with him, but she couldn't resist the irrepressible teenager. "Yes, if you'd like."

"Promise?"

"I promise."

Stalling for time, Sloan took a sip of water while she tried to think of some way to divert Courtney from the inquisition in which she clearly took unrestrained delight. She almost choked when Courtney helpfully suggested, "At this point, most people ask me what courses I'm taking at my school and what my college plans are."

Sloan bit back a guilty laugh, looked away, and encountered Noah's knowing gaze and sympathetic grin. She'd assumed he lived a life of elegant leisure, far above the stresses inflicted on ordinary humanity, and the realization that he had "to endure" the whims of a precocious teenager made him seem very human and very likable. Unaware that her expression had softened as much as her attitude, she smiled at him and then turned to Courtney.

She wanted to say something that was true and not superficial, and after a moment, she said with quiet sincerity, "I'll bet your IQ is off the scales."

"You're right. So is Noah's. Now, where did you go last night? Where were you when you shot Noah down and he crashed and burned?"

"We went to the Ocean Club, and I *didn't do—*" Sloan said desperately.

"We were on the dance floor," Noah clarified piously. "I was trying my best to carry on a flirtation, and she volunteered to fix me up with a friend of hers."

Douglas laughed out loud, and Courtney studied her with wide-eyed respect. "Are you really immune to his great looks and legendary wealth? Or—were you just playing hard to get?"

Mortified, Sloan looked at Noah, who waited to hear her answer.

"Don't keep us in suspense, my dear," Douglas prodded with an expectant grin.

The entire conversation was so outrageous that Sloan covered her face with her hands, leaned back in her chair, and started to laugh. She laughed so hard she made the others laugh, and when she tried to explain, the expressions on their faces made her laugh again. "I don't . . . don't know the first thing about flirting," she told Courtney. "If I'd had a . . . a telephone, I'd have called my friend Sara from the dance floor . . . and asked her . . ."

"Asked her what?" Courtney said eagerly.

"I'd have asked her what I should say to a man who asks what he can do to . . . to impress me."

"You mention jewelry," Douglas promptly advised. "You bring up a diamond bracelet."

That incredible suggestion sent Sloan into fresh peals of laughter. "Is that what wealthy Palm Beach women do?" she managed between giggles. No longer self-conscious, she lifted her gaze to Noah's. "What would you have done if I'd . . . I'd mentioned a diamond bracelet?"

Noah looked at her soft, provocative mouth and lifted his gaze to her face. Beneath a heavy fringe of russet lashes, her shining eyes were an amazing lavender blue, mesmerizing in their lack of guile, and her smooth cheekbones were flushed a becoming pink. Strands of hair had escaped from her french braid, and they glistened like spun gold at her temples. Plucky, unpretentious, and unaffected, she sparkled from within and glowed on the surface. She was, he decided, the most wholesomely beautiful female he'd ever seen. She was also becoming embarrassed by his scrutiny, her laughter fading from her trembling lips, her long lashes flickering down to hide her eyes.

"On second thought," Douglas joked as he correctly interpreted Noah's thoughts, "don't bother with a bracelet, Sloan. You can go straight for a diamond necklace."

Time passed very quickly after that. By the time the breakfast plates were being cleared away, Sloan felt almost as if she were a family friend, and much of that was due to Courtney. With democratic impartiality, the outspoken teenager had switched her attention from Sloan and aimed a series of equally impertinent, and frequently hilarious, comments at her father and then her brother. No one was spared, and by the end of the meal, her three

victims had bonded with each other in shared helpless-
ness, sympathy, and laughter.

In that short time, Sloan learned an amazing amount
about both men from Courtney, including the fact that
Noah had been married for three years to someone
named Jordanna, who had supposedly soured him on
marriage, and that two of Douglas's wives had been
Sloan's age.

Courtney gave her father absolutely no quarter, and he
let her get away with it, but Noah had limits, Sloan
noticed, and those limits evidently involved his work. He
ignored Courtney's numerous gibes about his personal
life and even some of the women he'd been involved
with, but when she started to make a remark about his
"business associates," Noah's jaw tightened and his voice
turned ominous. "I wouldn't go there, if I were you," he
warned her.

To Sloan's surprise, the irrepressible fifteen-year-old
stopped in midsentence and did not "go there."

Claudine arrived with a coffeepot and started to refill
Sloan's cup, but Sloan looked at her watch and shook her
head. "Those were the most delicious pancakes I've ever
had," she told the cook, and Claudine beamed at her. "I
have to go," she said to the others. "Everyone will be looking for me."

"Wait," Courtney said, trying to forestall her departure.
"Why did you learn martial arts?"

"To make up for my lack of height," Sloan said lightly
as she shoved her chair back and stood up; then she
smiled down at her youthful hostess and said, "Thank you

for the most memorable meal I've ever had. And thank you for making me feel like a member of your family."

It registered on Sloan that Courtney actually seemed at a loss for words for the first time since she'd set eyes on Sloan, but she was distracted by Noah who stood up and said, "I'll walk you home."

In silence, Courtney and Douglas studied the pair as they strolled side by side across the lawn.

Propping her bare feet on Noah's chair, Courtney crossed them at the ankles and wriggled her toes, studying the brownish red lacquer she'd applied to her toenails. "Well?" she said finally. "What do you think of Sloan now?"

"I think she's lovely and utterly delightful," Douglas replied. "I also think," he added mildly as he stirred a spoonful of sugar into his coffee, "that you went beyond reasonable bounds with some of your comments. In the past, you've always exercised a modicum of restraint in front of strangers, but this morning, you didn't."

"I know," Courtney cheerfully agreed. "I was *great!* Noah should double my allowance for what I accomplished today."

"What do you think you accomplished?"

"It's—like—so obvious! I made Sloan relax. She was uptight at first, and who could blame her? I mean, she doesn't know anyone in Palm Beach; she doesn't even know her own family. She's lived in a small town her entire life, she doesn't know how to flirt, and you can bet she's never had any money."

"I'm certain Carter provided very well for her mother and her."

"Well, if you'd have been listening to the way she answered my questions, instead of staring at her big, beautiful—"

"Courtney!"

"—eyes. I was going to say 'eyes,' " she said truthfully. "Anyway, if you'd have been listening instead of staring, you'd have found out that her mother works as a clerk in a boutique and Sloan went to a local college and worked part-time. Are you following me so far? Can you see where I'm going with all this?"

"Not yet, but I'm trotting along in your wake, trying to keep up."

Courtney rolled her eyes at his obtuseness. "Considering all the stuff she revealed about herself, can you imagine how overwhelmed she must be by Noah? I mean, besides the fact that he's tall, dark, gorgeous, and sexy, he is also rich and sophisticated. I went to a lot of trouble to make him seem more normal and approachable to her."

"Ah, I see," Douglas said dryly. "I suppose that explains why you found it necessary to refer to his ex-wife as 'The Wicked Witch from the West' and to imply that his mistress has buckteeth?"

"I never referred to Nicole as his mistress!" Courtney protested indignantly. "The word 'mistress' has an elitist sound to it that might have scared Sloan off. I referred to her as 'Nicole.' "

She leaned forward to inspect a possible chip in her pedicure and sighed dramatically. "Poor Sloan. Noah is going to turn on the charm. He'll take her out on one of the yachts, lavish her with attention, dazzle her with a trinket, and he'll lure her into bed. She'll fall for him, just like women always do; *then* she'll find out he's as hard as nails and the only thing he really cares about is making money. He'll get too involved in 'business' to bother with her; she'll sulk; he'll get bored; then he'll dump her and break her heart. You know," she concluded cheerfully, "if I weren't his loyal, devoted sister, I'd warn Sloan that he's really a complete bastard!"

The shy self-consciousness that Sloan thought she'd overcome at breakfast began to return as he walked beside her, but Noah eased it by asking her if she liked to go sailing and then telling her about the time Douglas and Courtney nearly capsized in a storm off the coast of Nassau.

Two houses away from her father's house, a group of youngsters were building a sand castle. The youngest, a chubby little toddler of about a year and a half was still unsteady on his feet and trying valiantly to keep up with two older boys as he ran to the surf with his pail. He careened past Sloan on his return trip, tripped, and fell, his water spilling on the sand.

"Need some help?" Sloan asked, crouching down to his level. Still clutching the handle of his pail in his fist, he rolled onto his rump, looked at her, and burst into wails of dismay. Sloan swept him up—baby, pail, and sand—and hugged him to her, laughing. "Don't cry, little one," she soothed, patting his back while the nanny, whom Sloan had spoken to earlier that morning, started forward and then stopped. "Don't cry. We'll help you."

He quieted, rubbed a sandy fist in his eyes, and hic-cuped. Sloan put him down and took his free hand in hers. "We'll help you," she promised again, and looked at Noah. "We will, won't we?" she said.

Noah looked down into those beseeching pansy-blue eyes of hers and then at the baby's hopeful brown ones. Silently, he reached for the pail. Sloan smiled at him. The baby smiled at him. His brain captured the moment like a snapshot.

He wanted her.

24

"Children are so much fun to be around," Sloan said a few minutes later as they walked away from the sand castle that was still under construction, with ample water now.

"*You* are fun to be around," he corrected her with a shrug that struck Sloan as significant.

"Thank you. Don't you like children?"

"You're welcome, and no I don't."

"Really?" The informality of their breakfast conversation caused Sloan to ask him a question that made her feel ill-mannered as soon as she asked it. "Is that why you've never had any children?"

"I was already twenty-five when Courtney was born, and she's cured me of any illusions I might have had about wanting a child or about a child wanting me for a parent."

"I didn't mean to pry," Sloan said sincerely. "I shouldn't have asked that."

"You may ask me anything you'd like, and I will be as honest and direct as I can. I'd prefer it that way."

Since breakfast, Sloan had been mentally preparing to give flirting her best shot, but now he was asking for honesty and straightforwardness, and that was as alarming as it was impossible. "Okay," she said lamely.

"That was your opportunity to assure me that I can ask *you* anything, and that you will also be honest and direct."

"I'm not sure that's such a good idea," Sloan said warily, and he gave a shout of laughter.

"Let's try it out, shall we?" He put a detaining hand on her arm and stopped her behind the hedge that concealed her father's fence at the beach.

"You mean, right now?"

"Right now." With startling directness, he said, "I'd like to spend time with you while you're here. Starting with tonight."

"I can't," Sloan replied, sounding absurdly panicked to her own ears.

"Why not?"

"There are three very important reasons," she said, getting control of her voice. "They are Paris, Paul, and Carter."

"Paris told me last night that you're not romantically involved with Paul. I am not romantically involved with Paris, and since none of us are romantically involved with Carter, I don't see this as an obstacle."

"I meant that I need to spend time with them."

"We can work that out. Is there anything else in the way of our getting to know each other?"

"Like what?" Sloan asked evasively, but he saw through her ploy in an instant.

"Let's not play games with each other. I've already played them all, and you wouldn't enjoy them even if you knew how to play them."

Stalling for time, Sloan looked at the small seashell she'd picked up on the beach and pretended to examine it. He waited in silence until she had no choice except to meet his gaze; then he said, "One of the things I like about you is that you are refreshingly open and honest. However, there is something that bothers you when you're alone with me. What is it?"

Sloan wondered how honest and refreshing he'd think she was if she told him the truth. *What bothers me when I'm alone with you is that I'm not an interior designer, I'm a cop working under cover, and I'm not here to reunite with my father. I'm here to spy on him. Paul isn't my friend; he's an FBI agent who is here for the same reason. Oh, and by the way, he'd also like me to find out what I can about you.* She wasn't innocent and honest; in fact, she was probably the most deceitful person he'd ever met. She was also so attracted to him that her stomach knotted just thinking about how he'd react when he found out the truth.

"Are you attracted to me?" he asked bluntly.

Sloan had the distinct feeling he already knew the answer. "You know what," she said shakily, "let's not be too honest."

He was still laughing when he leaned down and kissed her lightly on the mouth. "There, that's out of the way. The first one is the hardest. Things will be easier now."

Sloan stared at him, her mind reeling with disbelief and longing and dread.

• • •

Sloan half expected Noah to leave her at the back door, but he followed her inside. She could hear Paul's voice followed by a burst of laughter that seemed strangely discordant in this house of stultifying dignity and dark wood. "It sounds like they're all in the dining room," she remarked to Noah as she followed the sounds down the hall.

The family had finished breakfast, and Paris was looking at an open photo album with Paul leaning over her shoulder. "That tennis racquet was almost as big as you were," he remarked with a chuckle.

"She was three years old there," Edith put in. "That's the same age I was when I started my lessons."

They looked up as Noah and Sloan walked in, and Carter's smile froze. "Have you two been together all morning?"

"My father and Courtney waylaid Sloan on the beach and forced her to have breakfast with us," Noah said smoothly.

Carter relaxed, his good humor restored. "Better watch out for Douglas, Sloan. He's quite a ladies' man."

Edith was never completely good-humored, Sloan noted as the old woman gave Noah a dark look. "You ought to put a muzzle on that child, Noah. Her manners are atrocious."

"She's lonely and bored," Sloan contradicted gently. "She's extremely bright, she doesn't know anyone here, and she's surrounded by adults. Her only diversion is to shock and annoy. Children do that." In apology for having openly disagreed with her, Sloan patted Edith's shoulder and said, "Good morning, Great-grandmother."

The old lady's scowl relaxed into its habitual but less daunting frown. "Good morning," she replied stiffly.

"Sloan is very fond of children," Noah put in, helping himself to a cup of coffee from the silver pot on the sideboard. "Even Courtney."

"I don't like children," Edith bluntly reminded him. "You and I have that in common, as I recall."

"We do indeed," Noah agreed.

"That has been my only objection to you marrying Paris."

That very personal remark caused the servant at the sideboard to back out of the room through a side door, and Sloan decided to follow his lead. "I need to wash up," she said, making the first excuse that came to mind as she backed through the archway into the main hall. "I got maple syrup on my fingers when I picked up the pitcher. Excuse me."

Paul stood up. "I need to get something out of my car," he said, but when he walked out of the dining room, he went only as far as the living room across the hall. Picking up a magazine from the coffee table, he thumbed through it.

"I'm quite serious, Noah," Edith said severely in the dining room. "I haven't survived for ninety-five years only to see my family line come to an end with Paris."

"Aren't you forgetting about Sloan?" Noah asked in an attempt to simultaneously remind her that Sloan was part of the family and avoid a discussion of nonexistent marital plans between Paris and him.

"I did forget about Sloan," she admitted, looking slightly chastened. "I suppose I haven't known her long enough to automatically think of her in that way; however you're quite right."

Noah was perfectly satisfied with her answer, but Carter's next remark set off a chain reaction of surprise followed by an instantaneous blast of anger: "Whether Sloan has children or not, she can never carry on the family line," Carter said curtly. "The idea is preposterous. She doesn't know anything about being a Reynolds, and it's thirty years too late to begin teaching her. Her children will reflect her own upbringing, her own values, not ours."

"She could learn," Paris put in bravely.

"I didn't ask your opinion, Paris. Although you may already regard her as a full-fledged member of our family, no one else will. Our friends don't know her, they've never even heard of her, and they'd never accept—"

"I have a solution for your problem, Carter," Noah interrupted with an edge to his voice. "What are your plans for tonight?"

"I haven't made any specific plans for evenings while Sloan and Paul are here," he said, taken aback by Noah's tone. "I assumed Paris and you would probably want to spend some of your evenings with them going out on the town and doing whatever it is you young people like to do."

"Good. Since no one has made specific plans for tonight, you can give a party to introduce Sloan to your friends and make damned certain they accept her."

"Impossible," Carter scoffed, already shaking his head in the negative.

"Imperative," Noah contradicted coolly. "The longer you delay, the more conjecture there will be about her and about why you're afraid for people to meet her. My father has undoubtedly mentioned her to his friends, and word will spread like wildfire."

"Be reasonable! She's only going to be here for two weeks, and then she'll be gone. Besides, I think the ordeal of a party would be too stressful for her."

"She'll just have to bear up under the strain," Noah said with thinly veiled sarcasm.

"I think a party for Sloan is a terrific idea," Paris said, flinching a little under her father's icy stare but refusing to lower her gaze.

"Paris," he warned in a withering voice, "your attitude is beginning to annoy—"

"You are always annoyed when you're wrong, Carter," Edith said. "I happen to agree with Noah and Paris. We must give a party to introduce Sloan to everyone, and the sooner the better."

"Fine," he said, throwing up his hands; then he retaliated against Paris by coolly pointing out to her the negative results of her unprecedented opposition to him. "You said you wanted to spend as much time as possible with Sloan while she's here. Instead of that, you're going to have to spend it organizing a party which she isn't going to enjoy, and getting out invitations to people who will come to gape at her but who won't accept her."

"They'll accept her," Noah said icily, "if you act as if you expect them to. If you're afraid you don't have enough influence to ensure that, then I'll be happy to lend *my* influence at the party, since we know all the same people." Having thrown down the gauntlet, Noah softened his voice and looked at Paris. "You won't need to give up any of your time with Sloan, Paris. I'll have Mrs. Snowden arrange the party and handle all the details.

"Paris, I assume you have a party guest list of some sort that you can give me?" She nodded, and he said, "Fine, then all you have to do is tell your staff to get the house ready today, and I'll have Mrs. Snowden do everything else."

"I shall handle the staff," Edith announced. "Sloan and Paris can spend the day getting their hair done, and whatever else it is young women do that takes all day when there's a special party to attend."

Sloan walked in just as Edith spoke, and she looked in confusion from Paris's smile to Carter's glower. "Are we going to a party?" she asked when everyone stopped talking and looked at her.

"We're giving a party for you and it's going to be wonderful!" Paris exclaimed. "Noah, thank you so much for volunteering Mrs. Snowden. I'm afraid she'll have to handle invitations by telephone."

"Mrs. Snowden enjoys a challenge."

"I really don't need a party," Sloan ventured cautiously. "I don't want anyone to go to any trouble for me."

Carter looked at the other three. "I told you she'd feel that way," he said triumphantly.

Sloan was about to reinforce Carter's opinion when Noah arrogantly informed her, "This isn't your decision to make. It is appropriate for your family to introduce you to their friends, and a party is the ideal way to do it."

Sloan sensed the hostile undercurrents between the two men and couldn't imagine how a simple party could have caused it. She considered ignoring Noah's order to keep her opinions to herself, but Paris looked so excited that Sloan couldn't bring herself to make another protest, and Edith looked so stubborn that she knew there wasn't any point in making one.

"In that case," she told Noah with an uncertain smile, "I'd like Courtney to be invited." When he nodded, she decided to retreat from the discussion and the room, and she looked at Paris. "I think I'll go upstairs and take a shower."

Paris slid back her chair and stood up. "I keep our guest lists and Christmas card lists and all that on the computer. I'll get a guest list for you right now," she told Noah. To Sloan's surprised pleasure, Paris caught up with her in the doorway, slipped her arm through Sloan's, and said, "This is going to be so much fun! We'll do a little shopping this morning, get our hair done, have a massage. Paul said he had some errands to do . . ."

Sloan was so distressed by the prospect of being put on display like a curiosity for a bunch of strangers to observe, judge, and conjecture about that she let Paris lead her past the staircase and around it to a closed door on the right, behind the living room. When Paris dropped her arm to open the door, Sloan remembered her shower and stepped back; then she realized what she was looking at and changed her mind. The open door revealed a large, luxuriously paneled room that could only be Carter's office. It was from here that Gary Dishler emerged from time to time.

A carved mahogany desk was at the opposite side of the room, with a credenza and bookcases built into the wall behind it. Paris walked over to the desk, removed a key from a drawer, and unlocked a pair of doors on the wall behind it. She opened the doors, and Sloan's gaze riveted on the computer monitor that had been concealed behind them. The screen was illuminated, the computer ready for use, a message flashing asking for the user to type in a password.

Paris slipped into a high-backed maroon leather chair at the desk and swiveled around to the computer.

Sloan's heart began to beat with excitement as she stationed herself beside Paris. "I use FRANCE as my password," Paris said innocently.

Sloan watched Paris pull up a file named "Palm Beach Guest List" from a computer folder called "Address Lists," then send the file to a printer. She leaned down and opened another cabinet door to the right of her knee that revealed a high-speed laser printer and the computer's central processing unit.

Sloan glanced at the CPU, but her primary interest was the icons displayed on the monitor that indicated what programs and possibly what kind of information Carter was accessing on the computer. Before she could do more than glance at all that, Paris retrieved a page from the printer and sat back up, blocking Sloan's view of the computer screen. "Do you think Carter would mind if I used his computer later?" Sloan asked casually as she could. "I'd like to check my E-mail, and I'd like to send a few messages."

"It sounds funny to hear you call him by his name," Paris confided with a smile. "And no, I'm sure he won't mind if you use the computer, unless he's using it himself."

"Does he use it often?" Sloan asked, her excitement building.

"Yes, but not for very long. He can access the computer at the bank in San Francisco and see what's happening. He uses it mostly for that and for other business things."

Sloan knew the bank meant Reynolds Trust in San Francisco. "What sort of other business things is he involved in?"

"I don't know. Father doesn't like to discuss business. He says it's too complicated for Great-grandmother or me to understand." She removed the remaining pages from the printer, closed and relocked the doors, put the key back in the top right-hand drawer of the desk, and took a pencil from a leather holder on the desk.

"I'll take this in to Noah. I'm already dressed to go out . . ." she hinted. As they left Carter's office, she said happily, "We'll have a wonderful time. We'll spend the day being pampered and come home and get dressed for your 'debut.' "

Sloan left her at the staircase and headed upstairs to her room. Paris took the party list into the dining room and sat down at the table. She checked off several names on the list; then she looked at her father and her great-grandmother. "How many people do you want to invite? It's such short notice that half the people will have other plans, so we ought to figure on inviting twice as many."

"Keep it small," Carter bit out.

Noah ignored him and looked at Paris. "Check off the people you particularly want to invite, and I'll pick out the others. We know the same people."

Paris checked off several names on each of the eleven pages and handed the entire list to Noah.

"I'll have Mrs. Snowden take care of everything else," he promised, standing up. "Is seven o'clock all right with you?"

"That's fine," Edith said. "The weather has been so pleasant; I wish we could have a garden party."

"I'll see what I can do," Noah said, already turning to leave.

"Keep the damned thing small," Carter reminded him.

Edith's thoughts shifted inexorably to money. "There's no need to be extravagant," she called after him. "Feed them hors d'oeuvres, not a banquet. Two of our servants can act as waiter and bartender; we don't need to pay the caterer's staff for that."

"I'll take care of it," Noah said curtly over his shoulder.

"We'll need champagne," Paris reminded him.

"*Domestic* champagne," Edith stipulated.

He was around the corner, starting down the hall, when Paris caught up with him. "Noah," she said worriedly, lowering her voice, "maybe we should wait to give the party."

His jaw tightened. "What are you worried about? The cost? The fact that your family's skeleton is coming out of the closet? Or is it the competition from Sloan you're worried about?"

She stepped back as if he'd slapped her. "What are you talking about?"

"What are *you* trying to talk about?" he shot back.

"I—I'd rather wait and have a lovely party than toss together some shabby little affair like Father and Great-grandmother are describing. Father isn't thinking clearly. We've always given beautiful affairs, and if Sloan's party isn't like that, people will think she doesn't matter enough for us to bother. The good caterers need plenty of notice to plan menus and hire staff, and they'll all be booked solid right now. Then there's flowers and music and chairs and tables and linens—there's no way to arrange for all that in a few days, let alone a few hours."

Noah's anger with her vanished, and his expression softened. "I apologize for misjudging your motives," he said gently. "I should have known better. Leave the details to me."

Courtney and his father looked up when Noah strode into the house. "What's up?" she asked eagerly, noticing the determined set of his jaw and his long, swift strides.

"Carter is giving a party for Sloan," he replied without stopping. "Is Mrs. Snowden upstairs?"

Courtney gave an indelicate snort. "Where else would she be? She follows you from city to city, house to house, hotel to hotel, ever at your beck and call, twenty-four hours a day . . ."

It was an exaggeration, but Noah didn't bother to point that out. Mrs. Snowden's sister lived forty miles from Palm Beach, and when he went there twice a year, she accompanied him. It was an arrangement that worked well for both of them; Noah always had a limited amount of work for her to do even when he was on vacation, and in return for working a few hours each day, Mrs. Snowden got an all-expense-paid trip to see her sister.

"Good morning," she said, turning around from the file cabinet as he strode into a library that doubled as his office when he was in Palm Beach.

"How is your sister?" he asked automatically.

"Fine."

The social amenities over, Noah sat down behind his desk and nodded for her to sit down across from him. "We're going to give a party," he announced, shoving a notepad and pencil across the desk to her.

"I thought you said Carter Reynolds was giving the party," Courtney said, plopping into the chair beside Mrs. Snowden's and swinging her leg over the arm.

Noah ignored her, and so Mrs. Snowden picked up the pad and pencil. "When is the party to be?" she asked, pencil poised.

"Tonight."

She drew the obvious conclusion. "A small dinner party?"

"Something a little larger."

"How much larger?"

Instead of answering immediately, Noah scanned the pages of names and addresses of the Reynoldses' friends in Palm Beach. He picked up a pen and drew a line through names belonging to people he personally didn't like, and people he thought Sloan wouldn't like; then he slid the pages across the desk to her. "About a hundred and seventy-five people, I'd guess."

"Since it's such short notice and you want to serve dinner, I assume you want to have it at one of your clubs? Although, I really don't think there's enough time for—"

"I want to have it at Carter Reynolds's house on the lawn."

She blinked at him. "You want to give an outdoor dinner party tonight for one hundred and seventy-five people? That means hiring caterers—"

He brushed over that problem. "You can do it buffet style, the way we did the last one here, but have plenty of waiters available to pass food on trays for guests who don't want to stand in line. I want everything first class."

"Naturally," she said, but she looked shaken.

"Have plenty of champagne on hand—Dom Pérignon. Oh, and get some of those ice things, too. They look nice on the tables—"

"Ice sculptures?" she asked weakly.

"Yes. And flowers, of course."

"Of course," she echoed faintly.

"We'll need an orchestra, too. You know the routine. You've done it dozens of times for me in the past."

"Yes, but not on this short notice!" she exclaimed, looking ready to cry at having to admit there was something she couldn't do. "Mr. Maitland, I really don't think there's any way I can do all this."

"I don't expect you to do it," he said impatiently. "We just bought two hotels here. Let them do it."

Mrs. Snowden now saw a way to accomplish what was still going to be a Herculean task, logistically and diplomatically, and she rose to the challenge at once. "I will prevail on the managers of the hotels," she declared, beaming.

"I'm sure you will," he dryly replied. "You'll have to handle invitations by phone. Tell everyone that you're calling for Carter and that the party is being given by him to introduce them to his daughter Sloan."

She nodded. "I'll need some assistance. There are two women in our San Francisco office who can be relied upon to issue a telephone invitation to a last-minute party and carry it off graciously. I could fax them the list, but the phone calls will all be long distance. Is that all right?"

"That's fine."

"There's one more problem: The people we invite will very likely jump to the conclusion that they're being called at the last minute to fill in the numbers and that they weren't on the original guest list. In that case, they will be offended and they will refuse."

Noah reached for the mail she'd opened and laid in a leather box on his desk. "Then tell them we've just discovered that the original invitations were never sent out. Blame the post office, if you want. Everyone else does."

Courtney swung her leg off the arm of the chair and stood up. "It sounds like yet another boring Palm Beach party. I'm glad as hell my name isn't on that list. You couldn't drag me to one of these parties."

Noah looked up from the letter in his hand. "Sloan specifically asked that you be invited. Please don't make me drag you to it."

Instead of being belligerent and balky, which Noah expected, she looked stunned. "Sloan invited me? You're kidding."

"No, I'm not."

"Then I suppose I really don't have any choice," she said in a martyred voice. "I mean, if I don't go, she'll be surrounded by nothing but incredibly boring people."

She started to leave, then turned back. "Noah?"

"What?" he asked without looking up from the letter he was reading.

"Why are you doing all this for Sloan? Why isn't Carter or Edith or Paris taking care of the party?"

"Carter is behaving like an arrogant son of a bitch, and Edith is too cheap and too old to be trusted with the decisions. Paris was willing to take it on, but she's brand-new at defying them and they'd both end up getting their way. If they don't throw a decent party and properly introduce Sloan, she'll never be able to hold her head up around here." It was several moments before Noah realized that Courtney hadn't left. Exasperated, he looked up and found her studying him, her head tipped to the side. "Now what?" he asked impatiently.

"That explains why they aren't doing it. It doesn't explain why *you* are."

Irrationally annoyed with her probing questions, Noah glared at her. "I don't know why," he said shortly. "I suppose I felt sorry for her because Carter was acting like a snob and talking about her like she's a poor relation. It ticked me off."

"She *is* a poor relation," Courtney pointed out simply. "And you are also a snob."

"Thank you," he said sarcastically. "Are you finished, or do you have some obscure point to make?"

"As a matter of fact, I do have a point to make," Courtney

replied. "I saw this movie once, called *The Carpetbaggers*. In it, there was this rich guy who owned a big movie studio and he spent a fortune making a blond hooker into a major movie star. Do you know why he did it?"

"No, why did he do it?"

"Because he wanted to marry her, but first he had to make her *important* enough to be worthy of him."

"What the hell has that got to do with anything?"

Courtney shrugged. "It was just a thought."

"If you're implying that I intend to marry Sloan or that I give a damn what people think of her, you're wrong on *both* counts. Now, go away and let me work."

When she left, Noah reread the first paragraph of the same letter twice; then he tossed it onto his desk and leaned back in his chair, glowering at the field of bluebonnets in the impressionist oil painting on the wall across from him.

He didn't know why he'd forced the issue of Sloan's party when it was counter to his own personal objectives. Tonight, other men would meet her and find her as intoxicating to look at and as entrancing to talk to as he did. They'd recognize the same tantalizing qualities of unconscious beauty and laughing candor that intrigued him, and they'd sense that there was much more to her beneath all that. Considering that he already felt ridiculously possessive about her, the party was a hindrance.

He didn't know why he'd lost his temper with Carter or appointed himself her personal defender, except that there was something so open and unspoiled about her, a kindness and a gentle pride, that he felt absurdly protective of her even where her own father was concerned.

25

Paul was waiting in the foyer when Sloan came downstairs, ready to face what Paris happily described as a day of pampering. "I was going to drop you and Paris off and then do my errands," Paul told her, "but Paris said this beauty routine she has in mind for the two of you is going to take a lot longer than an hour or two, so I'm going to take my car, and you're supposed to ride with her. They've already brought the Jaguar around in front."

"I'll walk you to your car," Sloan said with a meaningful nod toward the front door.

Paris's car was parked in front of the porch, but Paul's car was a little further down the drive, and Sloan waited until they were standing beside it before she spoke. "There's a computer in Carter's office networked to his bank. Paris said I could use it, and she gave me her password."

"Don't get your hopes up. He's way too cautious to ever allow Paris to access his files or log onto the bank's computers," Paul said. "He'll have his own password."

"I know. I'm simply reporting what I learned to you."

"I'd like to have a copy of that list of names and addresses Paris gave Maitland for the party."

"I'll ask her for a copy," Sloan said. "I could honestly tell her that it would make a nice souvenir and help me remember everyone's names."

"Good." He glanced toward the front door as it opened. "Paris just came out of the house. By the way, in case you haven't figured it out yet, Maitland is the one who forced the issue of a party for you. I thought you might want to know."

"I could tell Carter wasn't eager to do it, but how could Noah possibly 'force' him to have a party for me if he was dead set against it?"

"You would have to have been there to fully appreciate how he accomplished it. I was impressed," he admitted.

Sloan lowered her voice as Paris approached. "Yes, but why would it matter to Noah if Carter didn't want his friends to meet me?"

"I think," he replied with a knowing smile, "you already have the answer to that. Noah Maitland is smitten."

Sloan felt a rush of pleasure because Noah cared and an even bigger one because he'd been able to outmaneuver Carter Reynolds.

"We'll be gone for hours!" Paris exclaimed happily, walking up to Paul's car. "Sloan, we're going to have 'the works'—a facial, manicure, pedicure, massage, and then hairstyling. We'll have to hurry, though, because they're fitting us in, and we have to be there on time."

"Better get going, then," Paul told them; then he got into his rented car. He waited until he was several blocks from the house before he unlocked the glove compartment and took out his cellular phone. He dialed a number and the phone was answered by another FBI agent who was sitting on the pier, wearing a cap with fishing lures stuck in the visor and holding a fishing pole in his hand. "Can you talk?" Paul asked.

"Can I talk?" the other man repeated in angry disbelief. "You're the one who'd better do some talking, Paul. You didn't tell me you're down there on your own time and your own initiative. I got a call last night from the man in the big office as soon as he found out, and he's on a rampage. He thinks you've let a personal grudge cloud your judgment and that you're obsessed with this case. I'm serious, buddy, your ass is on the line. You're going to blow your career, and even if you do turn up evidence, Reynolds's lawyers will get it tossed out of court because of the way you're gathering it—"

"But I'm not looking for evidence, and when it turns up, I won't be the one who gathered it," Paul interrupted in the weary, patient tone of someone who is being forced to explain the obvious. "I am here merely as Sloan's 'facilitator.' I had nothing to do with Carter Reynolds's decision to invite his daughter here. And if his daughter happens to come across something incriminating during her visit, it's only natural that she would turn it over to the authorities whether I was here or not. After all, she's a cop."

"I'm not the one you have to convince; you need to call the old man and convince him."

"I'm on vacation at the moment. When I make him a hero, he'll calm down. In the meantime, I'm here and conducting myself like a perfect guest who is vacationing at someone's home. I play tennis, lounge around by the pool, have dinner, go dancing. I haven't opened a drawer or even a photo album without being asked to look inside it. I'm not telling Sloan where to search or what to look for. I've never told her Reynolds is using his bank to launder money, and I've never told her whose money he's laundering. I won't have to, because fate has stepped in and put her exactly where I wanted her."

"What do you mean?"

"I mean that my gorgeous traveling companion has acquired a very persistent admirer, and no federal judge alive could rule out any evidence she gets on him, because I had absolutely nothing to do with it."

"Who is he?"

"Noah Maitland."

The agent drew a long breath and expelled it in a triumphant whisper. "Bingo!"

26

Sloan stood at her balcony railing, mesmerized by the sight below. The entire back lawn was lit with torches and dotted with tables covered in white linen and decorated with flowers and candles in glass bowls. Tuxedo-clad waiters were passing trays of champagne and hors d'oeuvres among what appeared to be at least two hundred guests. Banquet tables with huge floral arrangements had been set up on the right side of the lawn, and on the left, near the swimming pool, an orchestra was playing near a portable dance floor. On a separate table in the center of the lawn was a huge ice sculpture of graceful soaring gulls.

"Ready to make your grand entrance?" Paris asked, walking through Sloan's bedroom and joining her on the balcony.

"I didn't think this was going to be such a big, elaborate party," Sloan said.

"Noah's secretary is a magician," Paris decreed, surveying the gathering with approval. "I could never have pulled off anything like this on such short notice. Let's go."

"I'm nervous," Sloan admitted.

"So am I," Paris said with a shaky laugh. "No one has ever worn one of my designs before. Let's see the total effect."

Sloan turned from the railing and followed her into the bedroom, where she did a slow pirouette for Paris's inspection. The lemon chiffon dress had a multilayered skirt that floated around Sloan's knees with each step she took and a tightly fitted halter bodice with a square neckline and a jeweled clasp at the nape. "I will never look this good again," Sloan declared half seriously.

"The color is perfect with your tan," Paris said, standing back and studying the entire effect. "And the dress is a wonderful fit. I feel very—professional."

"You are professional," Sloan said with solemn sincerity.

"Father doesn't think so. He said I was wasting my time last month when I made these. . . ."

"Don't let him do that to you," Sloan said with quiet force. "Please don't let him do that to you. He *isn't* right. Look at me. Look at *us*," Sloan emphasized as she walked into the dressing room and stood in front of a full-length mirror. "You designed both of these dresses."

Side by side, they stood in front of the mirror, Paris in embroidered peach silk with her dark hair held back on the sides with gold clips, Sloan in pale yellow with her hair falling in a cloud around her shoulders.

"After this, my wedding gown will be an anticlimax," Sloan declared.

"No it won't," Paris said, shaking off her insecurity with a toss of her head. "Because I'll design that, too!" She turned away from the mirror. "Come along, Princess Sloan, it's time to go to the ball. Father is going to meet us on the patio, and I'll stay with you while he takes you around and introduces you to everyone."

Noah was standing near the patio, listening to a group of men who were trying to persuade him to buy into a stud farm they were planning to purchase as a joint venture.

His back was to the house, but he knew exactly when Sloan made her appearance on the lawn, because the men in his group stopped talking and started to stare. So did many of the people around them.

"Good lord, look at that!" one of the men breathed.

Noah turned slowly, prolonging the anticipation, but when he saw her, he found it hard to stay put and let her mingle with the guests. He stood there for nearly a half hour, watching as Carter moved about the guests with Sloan on one arm and Paris on his other. He saw Sloan smile as she was introduced to each person; then she listened attentively to whatever they said to her, and he watched her win everyone over with her natural poise and unaffected warmth.

Courtney, however, was running out of patience. "I think I should rescue her," she announced. "Carter has dragged her through the entire crowd."

"Stay put," Noah ordered her. "He'll bring her here in a few minutes."

"Here she comes, and without Carter, thank heavens!" Courtney happily announced a few minutes later; then she scowled as several of Noah's friends figured out Sloan's destination and began heading toward them. "And here come the wolves right after her, including our father. It's disgusting." She solved that problem by turning her back on the pack of men, including Noah; then she stepped forward and put herself between Sloan and everyone else.

"Hi, Sloan," she said with a grin. "Noah said you wanted me to come, so here I am. I even got dressed up for the occasion, did you notice?" she asked, holding her skirts out to the side to give Sloan the full effect.

Sloan took in her ensemble, which consisted of an old-fashioned prom dress trimmed in lace, long satin gloves with no fingers, and a pair of army combat boots. She looked so outrageous, and so adorable, that Sloan burst out laughing and enfolded her in an impulsive hug. "I'm so glad you're here!"

"Yes, but how do you like my outfit?"

"It's—it's *you*," Sloan replied.

"Mrs. Reynolds said I look like an overdressed refugee."

"She's very old and I don't think she sees well," Sloan said, choking back a horrified laugh.

"Aren't you going to say hello to Noah?"

Sloan had been thinking of little else since the party began, but now that the time was here, she felt self-conscious. Raising her eyes to his, she said softly, "Hello."

"Hello," he replied, his gray eyes glinting with admiration.

"You really ought to give Noah a hug, too," Courtney prodded. "You won't believe what he did to pull off this whole party just for you."

"What do you mean?" Sloan knew he'd urged Carter to have the party and she knew his secretary had worked very hard to make the arrangements, but she had no idea he'd done more than that until Courtney provided her with more of the details:

"Noah shut down the main restaurant in one of his hotels, because we needed the tables and chairs over here, and you can just bet there isn't a flower left in that hotel either. See that huge flower arrangement over there on the banquet table where all the food is?"

With an effort, Sloan tore her gaze from Noah's amused gray eyes and looked in the direction Courtney was pointing. "Yes, I see it."

"Well, this morning, that giant bouquet was on a big table in the lobby—"

"Stop it, Courtney."

She ignored him. "It's the truth. And I'll bet there's not a napkin or a waiter or a fork left in the whole pl—"

Chuckling, Noah reached behind her and gently put his hand over his sister's mouth, muffling the rest of her enthusiastic recitation. "The last time I asked you to dance," he said to Sloan, "you turned me down. What do you think my chances are tonight?"

Sloan was profoundly touched by all the trouble he'd gone to for her, and she was already sinking into the spell of his deep voice and silver eyes. "I'd say they're awfully good," she said softly.

As Sloan stepped into his arms on the dance floor, she had her first clear, full-length view of him in the torchlight, and her breath stopped. His elegant, midnight blue suit fit his tall, splendid frame to perfection, hugging his broad shoulders and narrow hips, and outlining his long legs. Against the bronzed tan of his throat, his shirt was as dazzlingly white as the smile that drifted across his face when he slid his hand around her back and moved her close against his full length. "Are you pleased with your party?" he asked as the orchestra began to play "Someone to Watch Over Me."

"Very pleased," Sloan said softly, trying not to notice how his legs felt against hers, or how solid his arm was beneath her hand, or how much his deep voice was affecting her. "I don't know how to thank you for it."

His heavy-lidded gaze fixed meaningfully on her lips. "We'll have to think of a way."

Sloan sought desperate refuge in humor. "I suppose I could give you self-defense lessons."

His silver eyes returned to hers, and his lips quirked in a half-smile. "Am I going to need them?"

"It's possible. I'm a lot tougher than I look."

"So am I."

Sloan's mouth went dry.

She was so confused by what was happening to her that she scarcely noticed how easily she danced with him or how effortlessly their bodies moved in rhythm to the sweet, familiar melody. She told herself her attraction to him was dangerous and had to stop, but when Noah's hand slid down her back and his fingers splayed on her spine, shifting her closer to him, she forgot the danger. She told herself it was only a dance, and that he probably didn't realize what he was doing.

Noah knew exactly what he was doing, and he was already thinking of doing much more. He watched the torchlight turn her hair to molten gold; she smelled like flowers, and dancing with her was like dancing with a cloud. As the music ended, she moved a little away from him and looked up, and Noah gazed at a face that was beginning to mesmerize him with its delicately carved cheeks, dainty nose, and dark-lashed, violet eyes. "After the party is over, I'll take Courtney and my father home, then I'll come back. Meet me on the beach."

"Why?" Sloan asked shakily.

"We'll invent a reason when we're there," he told her with a mocking smile.

His "reason" was as clear to Sloan as her realization that he wanted her to understand it in advance.

Paul and Paris had been dancing together, and when the couples met near the edge of the dance floor, Paul suggested they change partners.

"Noah—" Sloan said as he started away.

Startled by the sound of her soft voice saying his name, Noah stopped and turned. "Yes?"

"It would be nice if you'd ask Courtney to dance soon."

"Courtney?" he repeated, the thought of asking her to dance having never, ever occurred to him. With amused dread, Noah contemplated Courtney's combat boots, but he nodded. "I will."

When the dance was over, he located Courtney nearby. Fully expecting her to scoff at his invitation—and half hoping she would—Noah said, "Miss Maitland, would you like to dance?"

She gaped. "With you?"

"No, with the waiter," he said dryly; then he realized she was already bending down and unlacing one of her boots. Before she unlaced the second boot, she hesitated and looked up at him. "You're serious, right?"

Guilt tugged at his heart when he realized how much she'd wanted to be asked. "I'm serious."

On the dance floor, she was surprisingly adept. "Where did you learn to dance?"

She rolled her eyes. "It's a girl thing. We're born knowing how to do it. Are you going to try to get Sloan into bed?"

"Mind your own business."

"Do me a favor—let her go. You'll only end up dumping her like you always do; then she'll be hurt, and then we won't see her anymore. She's nice. I'd really like to have her for a friend."

Noah gazed at his sister's earnest upturned face, and he felt humbled by Sloan's generosity of spirit, the compassion for other people that had caused her to worry about Courtney's feelings in the middle of a party where she herself was under constant pressure and relentless scrutiny. With quiet certainty, he said, "Sloan is already your friend."

He spent most of the balance of the evening chatting with friends and wishing they would go home. Time seemed to drag, so he hit upon the idea of reintroducing Sloan to some of his friends and managed to keep her near him in that way, but only between the dances she gave to his father and every other single man at the party. He danced twice more with Courtney.

27

Sloan stood at the front door with Paris and her father saying good night to a couple who were close friends of his and who'd remained to discuss politics long after Noah and everyone else had left. Edith had retired much earlier, and Paul had evidently foreseen that Senator and Mrs. Thurmond Meade were going to linger, because he'd excused himself and gone up to bed a half hour before.

"Good night, Sloan," Mrs. Meade said. "I'm so happy to have met you. I'm going to try that recipe for key lime pie you gave me—it helped my sore arm immensely tonight."

She turned to Paris, leaned forward, and almost touched her cheek to Paris's in a now-familiar gesture that Sloan realized passed for a good-bye kiss among the fashionable Palm Beach set. "You naughty girl," she told Paris. "I can't believe you've kept your talent a secret all this time. If Sloan hadn't told all of us that you designed her dress and yours, none of us would have ever known! I heard Sally Linkley ask you to show her your sketches, but I want to see them first. It's only fair that I get first choice—I've known you longer than Sally has."

Senator Meade stepped forward and said more formal good-byes to Paris and Sloan, but when he shook hands with Carter, his compliments were enthusiastic and genuine. "You're a lucky man, Carter. You have *two* beautiful daughters. Paris has always been a credit to you, but you can be very proud of Sloan as well. She won everyone over tonight."

Carter smiled and shook hands with him. "I know she did."

When he closed the door and turned to Sloan, Carter was every bit as sincere as Senator Meade. "Sloan, I cannot tell you how proud of you I was tonight."

He truly liked her very much at that moment—not because she was likable, Sloan suspected, but because he was a narcissist and she'd added to his prestige by favorably impressing his friends. To her surprise, she had liked many of his friends tonight. She could not like him, however, and she tried hard to hide it as she smiled and said, "Thank you."

When he started up the stairs, she glanced at the antique grandfather clock in the foyer and her heart plummeted when she realized how late it was. By now, Noah would no longer be waiting on the beach for her. Fate—and Senator Meade—had interceded and saved her from doing a very foolish thing. She should have felt relieved. She felt terribly disappointed.

Paris didn't share her disappointment over the lateness of the hour. Wrapping Sloan in a fierce hug, she said,

"You were a smash! Everyone was talking about how love-ly you are, how charming, how witty—and the party was a huge success, too. That's why people stayed so late."

Sloan made it all the way to her bedroom door before she began to lose the battle against going down to the beach to see if Noah might still be there.

"Good night," Paris whispered.

"Good night," Sloan said, but she hesitated, her hand on the doorknob.

Paris noticed. "You've been up since early this morn-ing. Aren't you tired?"

Sloan shook her head, and then she confessed the rest of the truth: "Noah asked me to meet him on the beach after the party," Sloan confessed.

"He did?"

"Yes."

"Then why are you up here?" Paris asked with a smile.

That was all the encouragement Sloan needed.

The back lawn was brightly lit and swarming with activity as men and women from the hotel worked to pack up and reload everything they had brought for the party. Some of the staff who worked for Carter were helping as well, Sloan noted as she said hello to two of the maids she recognized.

No one acted as if there was anything peculiar about her apparent desire to go for a moonlight stroll on a deserted beach at one A.M., wearing a fabulous chiffon dress and dainty high-heeled sandals, but Sloan felt incredibly conspicuous, nonetheless.

She was relieved when she finally reached the beach

and turned out of their view, but her relief immediately gave way to an overwhelming sense of disappointment when Noah was nowhere in sight.

She looked in the direction of his house, but unless he was blocked by someone's shrubbery, he had obviously gone home. She took off her sandals and wandered slowly down the shore, the sandals dangling from her fingertips, half expecting him to materialize from somewhere in the shadows.

The closer she got to his house the more dejected she became. Her traitorous heart reminded her of how it had felt to dance with him and the way his gaze had fixed boldly on her lips when she said she didn't know how to thank him for the party. *"We'll have to think of a way,"* he'd said. And when she asked why he wanted to meet her on the beach after the party, his answer had made it stirringly plain. *"We'll invent a reason when we're there."*

She stopped at the edge of his back lawn, her eyes searching the terraces in the moonlight, seeing only vague shapes and dim outlines.

It was just as well, she told herself bracingly. Noah Maitland was too sophisticated, too jaded, and much too sure of himself for her. He thought nothing of trying to seduce her on a dance floor, and only two days after meeting her. He would break her heart if she gave him the chance.

She was very, very lucky to have had a second narrow escape from certain disaster tonight.

She was glad he hadn't waited.

She was thrilled he'd gone to bed.

She swallowed over a lump in her throat and started to turn. On the terrace one of the shapes moved, grew taller, and she heard her name, low and imperative. "Sloan!"

She was so elated that he hadn't gone inside she nearly broke into a run when he walked down the terrace steps and stopped there, waiting for her. He'd taken off his jacket and tie, partially unbuttoned his white shirt, and folded his shirtsleeves back onto his forearms. Somehow, he managed to look even more attractive this way than he had earlier.

Sloan stopped in front of him, happy, nervous, self-conscious, and trying desperately to seem normal. "The last of the guests stayed late."

He accepted her explanation with a brief nod; then he shoved his hands deep into his pants pockets and looked at her in lengthening silence.

Sloan had half expected him to reach for her the minute she was at arm's length, and as he continued to look at her, she wished he would. When she finally realized he wasn't going to, she attributed his hesitation to the same problem she'd been worrying about since they'd danced at the party. Since the problem had been bothering her, she naturally assumed it would be bothering him, too. Suppressing her private regret, she said quietly, "We can't do this. If Carter thinks there is anything at all happening between us, he'll blame Paris for not encouraging you more than she has."

In a noncommittal voice, he said, "In that case, I suppose I could honestly tell him I'm not interested in marriage."

"Then he'll blame *you*."

"Do you always worry about other people?"

Noah noted that she took the question very seriously, sighed, and then somberly nodded. "It's one of my many faults."

Faults? he thought with grim humor. He wondered if she knew what a real fault was. In the glow of moonlight, with the wind teasing her skirts and blowing her golden hair against her cheek, she reminded him irresistibly of a barefoot angel with sandals dangling from her fingers instead of a celestial harp.

She was the sort of woman who helped children carry pails of water to their sand castles and stopped to help elderly gardeners in pain. He thought of how elated Courtney had been because Sloan had thoughtfully suggested he dance with her, and how much Paris had blossomed in the last two days. Courtney had been right tonight—Noah had no reason, and no right, to do anything that might dull Sloan's sparkle or diminish the amazing effect she had on people.

On the other hand, she was thirty years old . . . That was old enough to know what coming here tonight was leading toward, old enough to understand the rules and play the game. Old enough to know how to handle it when the game was over.

Except, as he already knew, she didn't know how the game was supposed to be played. By her own admission she didn't even know how to flirt. A sardonic smile twisted his lips as he contemplated the havoc she could wreak on the male population if she ever bothered to learn how.

At her party tonight, he'd watched sensible, sophisticated men turn into putty when she smiled and spoke to them.

What baffled him was that either she didn't realize the effect she had on men, or she didn't care. In fact, there were only two things about Sloan he was completely certain of: She didn't know anything about men like him; and she deserved much more than what he was willing to offer.

"What are you thinking?" Sloan asked finally as the last vestiges of her courage drained away, leaving her feeling foolish and conspicuous.

"I was thinking you look like a barefoot angel," he replied unemotionally.

Sloan was stunned. She thought about who she was and why she was in Palm Beach, and her voice shook with guilty certainty. "Believe me when I tell you I'm *no* angel. I'm very far from that."

He took his hands out of his pockets and pulled her to him. "Good," he said bluntly, and lowered his head to kiss her.

It was the suddenness of his reaction, as much as the reaction itself, that made Sloan realize he probably thought she was referring to sexual conduct. She'd already deceived him about so many other things that she felt compelled to be completely honest about this one. "When I said I was far from an angel just now," she explained quickly, "I was not referring to anything having to do with—with sexual relationships."

His head lifted, his narrowed eyes searching hers. "You weren't?"

Sloan shook her head and tried valiantly to project an intelligent, mature, and open attitude about something that she felt excruciatingly uncomfortable discussing with him. "With respect to . . . those sorts of relationships . . . I haven't had what you . . . what *some people* might consider much experience."

Noah gazed down at her entrancing face and glorious eyes. The same wayward emotion that suddenly made him feel like smiling also roughened his voice. "You haven't?"

"Actually, I've only had two of those relationships."

"Only two?" he teased. "I'm terribly disappointed."

She might not have known how to flirt an hour ago, but it took her less than five seconds to notice the laughter lurking in his eyes, guess the cause of it, and encourage more of it. With twinkling blue eyes and a voice as apologetic—and insincere—as his had been, she nodded and said, "I *wish* I could tell you I've had dozens, but I've only had two."

"What a pity. Dare I hope they were both very short and completely meaningless?"

The beauty in his arms solemnly and slowly nodded, biting her lip to hide her smile. "Oh, yes," she whispered tragically. "They were *extremely* short and *totally* meaningless."

"Excellent!" He bent his head, intending to kiss the smile off her lips; then he paused, his mouth an inch from hers. "Were they really?" he asked seriously, unable to check the ridiculous impulse, the unprecedented need, to know about a woman's other lovers.

Her long lashes fluttered open and she looked steadily into his eyes; then she laid her fingers against his cheek and jaw. "Yes," she whispered achingly. "They really were."

Unable to tear his gaze from hers, Noah turned his face into her hand and kissed her palm. The tremor that ran through her when he did it seemed to shake through him as well.

On the second floor of the house, Douglas reached out to turn off the lamp beside his bed just as Courtney slammed into his room looking like a thundercloud. "You will not believe what is going on out on the terrace," she stormed, marching over to his window. "Five minutes ago, I heard Noah's voice, and I looked out my window and saw Sloan walking up to the house. Now look what's happening!" She swept back a curtain, stepped out of the way, and pointed toward the window. "Just look at that!"

Worried, Douglas rolled out of bed, hurried to the window, and peered into the darkness. His frown gave way to a slow, gratified smile as he took in the scene on the terrace below. Noah was holding Sloan in a crushing embrace, his arm angled low across her hips, holding her body against his while he kissed her and twisted them both down onto one of the chaise lounges. And Sloan wasn't resisting; she was kissing him back.

Douglas removed the edge of the curtain from Courtney's fist so that it could fall back into place. "Did you say that only got started five minutes ago?"

"Yes!"

"That's amazing," he said happily.

"He has women all over the place. I don't see why he has to try to seduce Sloan!"

"I don't think I'd call that seduction."

She was so angry she stamped her foot. "What *would* you call it?"

"Spontaneous combustion," he said with a smile in his voice; then he turned on the television set and took a deck of cards from the cabinet below it. "I'm in the mood for a late movie and one of our gin rummy tournaments."

"I'm going to bed," she said, starting toward her bedroom, where he knew she could continue spying on Noah.

"You're staying right here, my dear."

"But I'm—"

"You're planning to spy on your brother," Douglas said mildly; "however, that would not only be impolite, it would also be a waste of time, because you've already seen all there is to see. Nothing else is going to happen out there tonight; you may take my word for it." He sat down in a chair and began dealing out the first hand of cards.

"What makes you so sure?" she demanded, flopping into the chair across from him with a mutinous expression on her face.

"I'm sure because I know your brother. Noah isn't stupid enough, or rude enough, to ravish any woman on a lawn chair in his backyard."

She hesitated, considering that; then she shrugged as if dismissing the entire subject. The silent gesture was the closest she would come to admitting he might be right.

She picked up the hand he'd dealt her and glanced at her cards. "You still owe me a hundred forty-five dollars from last time," she reminded him. "If you don't pay up tonight, I'm going to have to charge you interest."

"At what rate?" Douglas inquired, arranging his cards in his hand.

"Eighteen percent on anything more than thirty days past due. I have to start thinking about my own future."

"You won't have a future if you try to charge me eighteen percent."

She won fifteen dollars more from him, and they both fell asleep watching the late, late movie.

"It's very late," Sloan whispered when Noah finally lifted his mouth from hers. "I have to go back."

"I know." Noah eased his arm out from under her, glanced at his watch, and was amazed to see it was after three A.M. He got up and offered her his hand to help her off the chaise lounge.

As she stood, Sloan looked down at her bare feet and hopelessly wrinkled dress and quickly raised her hands to her hair, trying to restore it to some semblance of order. She was suddenly mortified about her appearance and self-conscious about what they'd been doing for the last two hours. If anyone saw her sneaking into the house like this, she was going to feel like the Whore of Babylon. Worse, she probably looked like that to Noah right now.

She looked delightfully mussed, Noah thought—a fully dressed woman who'd lain beside a man who couldn't keep his hands off of her, who'd shoved his hands into her hair and kissed her until her lips were swollen. He couldn't believe he'd just spent two comparatively chaste hours with her on an uncomfortable chaise lounge, and yet, what he had done with her had been as exciting as having sex with another woman and, in some ways, more satisfying.

She walked beside him down the terrace steps, her hands clasped behind her back, sandals dangling from her fingers. Her head was bent as if she was lost in thought, and Noah began to reconsider the last hours through her eyes. . . . In actuality, he'd behaved like an oversexed, overeager, inexperienced sixteen-year-old necking and petting in the backyard without sense enough or courtesy enough to take her somewhere where they'd have privacy and comfort. He was embarrassed about his behavior; he was embarrassed because he had something to be embarrassed *about* . . .

As they neared a stand of palm trees at the rear of the lawn, Noah said flatly, "I'm sorry about all that. I shouldn't have let it go on so long or get so far. I practically molested you on a damned lawn chair."

Sloan's heart soared at the discovery she wasn't the only one feeling uncertain and embarrassed. "A lawn chair?" she repeated thoughtfully; then she raised laughing eyes to his. "Molested? Is *that* what you were doing?"

Stifling a shout of laughter, Noah pulled her into his arms.

She looked at him teasingly, and rested her hands on his chest. "My memory must be hazy, but—"

"I wouldn't want your memory to be hazy," Noah whispered, already bending his head. "I did this—" He brushed a kiss against her temple. "And this—" He trailed his lips to her ear and kissed it, smiling to himself when she shivered and pressed closer to him. "And I did this . . ." Her eyes closed and he put a light kiss on each lid before he dragged his mouth across her cheek to her lips. "And this—" He parted her lips with his and kissed her with a melting hunger, slowly exploring her mouth with his tongue, drawing her tighter to his hardening body, but when she leaned into him and began kissing him back, Noah lost his head for the second time that night. He backed her against a tree, caught her hands in both of his, and pinned them near her head while he deepened the kiss and pressed himself against her.

His tongue ravaged her mouth, his body moved slowly against hers, and her breasts swelled invitingly against his chest. He loosened his grip on one of her hands and slid his palm down her soft skin at her throat to her breast, brushing it with his knuckles and then covering it possessively. Her free hand curved round his nape, her body arched to his, and he fumbled with the jeweled clip at her nape that held the bodice of her dress up. A split second before he released it, he realized what he was doing and managed to check the impulse.

Struggling for control, he tore his mouth from hers and stared down at her moonlit face. "This is insanity," he whispered hoarsely; then he slowly lowered his head and buried his lips in hers again.

28

"Late night?" Paris asked cheerfully, perching on the side of Sloan's bed, already dressed for the day.

Sloan rolled over onto her back. "Very late," she said with a sleepy smile, thinking of Noah. "What time is it?"

"Ten-thirty."

"That late!"

Paris nodded. "It's lucky I remembered to tell Dishler not to turn on the security system when he went to bed. Otherwise, you'd have tripped the alarm when you walked past the infrared beams at the edge of the yard by the beach."

Sloan's eyes widened. She hadn't given a thought to setting off the house's security system last night. In fact, she hadn't given a thought to how she was going to get inside until she was reaching for the back door and found it unlocked. She could imagine how thrilled Carter would have been if the house sirens had gone off, the lights had all gone on, and he'd got up to discover she'd been with Noah.

"I'll get you a house key and a gate opener this morn- ing. There's a keypad at the gates, and you can turn the alarm system off there by entering a security code. If you don't, you'll trip the alarm when you drive past the first set of infrared beams. They surround the property on all sides, so there's no way to sneak past them."

She told Sloan what the alarm code was, and Sloan nodded, but she didn't want Paris to think she normally behaved as she had last night, or that she intended to continue. "I don't intend to make a habit out of . . . that," she said awkwardly, levering herself into a sitting position.

"Really?" Paris teased. "Well, 'that' has already telephoned this morning to make arrangements for tonight."

"He did?" Sloan asked, unable to hide her happy smile.

"Yes, and the four of us are having dinner tonight," she said, sounding girlishly delighted about the plans. "The dress is formal, black tie, but the destination is unknown. Noah's driver will pick us up just before sunset. That's about all he would tell me."

Sloan drew her knees to her chest and wrapped her arms around them. "What about you—did you have a good time last night?"

Paris nodded. "Paul makes me laugh, and he's comfortable to be with, but he said the strangest thing to me while we were dancing."

"What did he say?" Sloan asked, enjoying the cozy sisterly discussion of men.

"He said I intrigued him because I have so many layers. I—I'm not certain he meant it as a compliment."

"How could he mean it as anything else?" said Sloan so emphatically and loyally that they both laughed, but Paris's next statement made Sloan's smile fade.

"The interesting thing is," Paris continued, "I think Paul is the one with a lot of layers, don't you?"

"I . . . don't know."

"I'm pretty certain I'm right. I notice tiny little things about people that other people overlook. Father always says I can spot a phony across the room."

"Except for Henry," Sloan pointed out swiftly, referring to Paris's dishonest fiancé.

"True," Paris admitted with a wry smile. "And I didn't mean to imply that I think Paul is a phony, because I don't—not at all."

Sloan wasn't completely convinced Paris didn't think that. Torn between trying to change the subject or open it up further, Sloan reluctantly chose the latter. "What do you notice about Paul that seems unusual?"

"For one thing, men always like to talk about themselves, but Paul doesn't. What's more, he's so good at asking questions, and so attentive when you answer, that you never quite realize he's done all the listening and you've done all the talking. Now, if he were shy, I'd understand that, but he isn't shy at all. And that's another thing I find kind of unusual . . ."

"What do you mean?" Sloan said a little weakly.

"I mean he's not the least bit intimidated by anyone he's met, not even Father, who always intimidates younger men who aren't as—well—successful as he is."

"I'm not intimidated by him," Sloan pointed out.

"No, but men judge themselves on their accomplishments and wealth, and we don't."

She was so direct and perceptive that Sloan was having

a hard time equating this Paris with the reticent sister she'd come to know.

"There's one more thing. Paul is in the insurance business, and Father has been grumbling about the cost of the group insurance policies for his employees at the bank. Yet, when I gave Paul an opening with Father to talk about selling us one of their group plans, Paul didn't take advantage of it."

"Maybe he thought it would be bad manners to try to sell insurance to his host."

"It wouldn't have been, because I brought it up, not Paul."

"Maybe Paul was embarrassed that you did."

"I don't think Paul embarrasses very easily."

Sloan was making rapid-fire mental notes to tell Paul to start talking about himself and start selling insurance. To Paris she said something completely honest. "I don't understand men very well, so you're asking the wrong person. I can say that Paul is an honest, dependable man, probably even a gallant one."

Paris nodded sagely. "That's my impression of him, too."

Smiling, she stood up, her thoughts shifting to the day ahead. "You'd better get up and get dressed. I thought we'd go sightseeing and do some shopping. Paul's going to stay here and laze around."

"What about a tuxedo for Paul tonight?" Sloan asked as she pushed the covers aside and swung her legs over the side of the bed.

"I asked him, and he said he borrowed a tuxedo from a

friend and brought it with him—just in case he needed it here."

Sloan hurried through her shower and got dressed quickly so that she'd have time to call her mother before she left. Because she'd overslept that morning, she was going to have to call her mother at the shop, which meant it was going to be difficult for Kimberly to talk. She sat down on the side of the bed and took her credit card out of her purse.

Propping the telephone on her shoulder, Sloan placed the credit card call and braced herself for a skirmish with the owner of the shop, Lydia Collins, who had the management style of a guard on a prison chain gang.

Although Sloan rarely called her mother there, Lydia invariably behaved as if a personal call were grounds for dismissing her best employee.

"Lydia," Sloan said when the shop owner answered the phone, "this is Sloan, and I'm calling from Palm Beach—"

Lydia's professional friendliness abruptly dissolved into irritation. "Your mother is busy right now with a customer, Sloan."

Kimberly was always busy with customers because they loved her and preferred to wait for her to help them. "I understand, but I need to talk to her for just a minute."

"Oh, very well!"

She smacked the phone down on the counter with enough force to make Sloan wince, but a moment later, Kimberly's warm, excited voice made Sloan smile.

"Darling, I'm so glad to hear from you. How is everything there?"

Sloan assured her that her father and great-grandmother were treating her very well and that they seemed very nice. She saved the news about Paris for last, and as soon as she brought up Paris's name, Sloan noticed that her mother grew very still, very silent. She told her everything she could about Paris, then she finished by saying, "You're going to love her, and she's going to love you. She wants to come to Bell Harbor very soon." Finished, Sloan waited for her mother to comment, but she said nothing. "Mom, are you there?"

"Yes," her mother whispered brokenly, and Sloan realized she was crying.

Sloan's heart ached as she realized how hard her mother must have worked all these years to pretend she'd adjusted to giving up Paris long ago. Now the mere possibility of a reunion with that same daughter was making Kimberly cry. Sloan couldn't even remember her mother crying before, and she felt tears spring to her own eyes. "She reminds me so much of you," Sloan said softly. "And she loves clothes, too—she designs them." In the background, Lydia's strident voice called Kimberly's name. "It sounds like you'd better go," Sloan said. "I'll call you again in a few days."

"Yes, please."

"Bye."

"Wait—" Kimberly said urgently. "Do you—do you think it would be all right if I send Paris my love?"

Sloan blinked back tears. "Yes, I know it will. I'll tell her."

29

Edith was seated in her favorite chair in her bedroom, wearing another somber black dress, but with a large ruby and diamond brooch pinned to the bodice. Sloan wondered if she had anything brighter to wear, even a scarf.

"Great-grandmother," Paris said, pressing a kiss to the elderly woman's forehead. "You said you wanted to see Sloan before we leave."

"I would like to speak with her privately, if you don't mind, Paris."

Paris looked startled, but she nodded and left.

Sloan hadn't quite settled into the chair across from Edith before the old woman said pointedly, "What were you thinking a moment ago?"

Sloan started guiltily. "I was wondering if you would wear a colored scarf if I bought you one today."

Her white brows shot up. "You do not approve of my taste in clothing?"

"No, I didn't mean that at all."

"Do not add dishonesty to impertinence. That is exactly what you meant."

Trapped, Sloan bit back a smile. "My mother always says that bright colors are uplifting."

"You think I need to be uplifted, is that it?"

"Not exactly. It's just that you have lovely eyes, and I thought a blue scarf—"

"Now you are resorting to flattery. All of your vices are coming out into the open today," the old lady interrupted, but with a gruff smile. "As it happens, our minds are working along the same direction." She glanced at the ceiling, as if that indicated the direction she was referring to.

Sloan followed her gaze, then looked at her in bewilderment. "What direction?"

"Up. I assume that when I am gone, I will be ascending, not descending, don't you agree?"

She was talking about dying, Sloan realized, and her smile faded. "I'd rather not think about it."

At that, Edith became brisk and businesslike. "Death is a fact of life. I am ninety-five years old; therefore, I am staring the fact in the face. However, that is not to the point. I am going to be perfectly blunt with you, and I do not wish for any sort of emotional outburst. . . ."

Since she was always very blunt without issuing an advance warning, Sloan braced herself to hear something spectacularly unpleasant.

Instead of speaking, Edith reached for a large dark blue velvet box on the table beside her and passed it across to Sloan; then she began to fumble with the clasp of the brooch she was wearing. Age and arthritis had twisted her fingers badly, but Sloan knew better than to offer to help her, so she sat in perplexed silence, holding the box in her lap.

"Open the box," Edith commanded as the brooch finally came free.

Sloan opened the large flat case. Nestled in velvet was a spectacular ruby and diamond necklace about two inches wide, with matching earrings and bracelet. Since Edith was removing her brooch, Sloan thought perhaps she'd decided to deck herself out in this jewelry instead.

"What do you think?"

"Well, they're certainly bright," Sloan said lamely, recalling her suggestion of a scarf to brighten up Edith's black dress.

"Those pieces, along with this brooch, belonged to your great-great-grandmother Hanover. They have been in my family longer than any other pieces, and for that reason they have the deepest meaning for me. You have been in this family for the shortest time, through no fault of your own, and although I do not normally sink to sentimentality, it occurred to me that these jewels would be just the thing to bridge the time gap, so to speak. I wore the brooch today because it will be the last time I wear it; however, I shall look forward to seeing it on you—when you are wearing something more appropriate than those mannish pants you have on."

"On me?" Sloan repeated; then she recalled the formal dinner tonight and understood. "It's very kind of you to offer to let me wear it—"

"Silly child! I'm not loaning these jewels to you. I'm giving them to you. Ruby is your birthstone. When I'm gone, they will remind you of me and of the ancestors you never had an opportunity to know."

Shock sent Sloan to her feet so suddenly that she had to grab the velvet case before it was dumped onto the floor. Now she understood why all this had been preceded by a conversation about death. "I hope you will live a very long time and have many more chances to wear these. I do not need all this to remember you after you're—you're—"

"Dead," Edith said bluntly.

"I do not want to think about that now, not when I've only just met you."

"I insist that you take the jewelry now."

"I will *not* do it," Sloan said stubbornly, and put the box back on the table by her elbow.

"But they will be yours someday, anyway."

"I don't want to discuss 'someday.' "

"I trust you won't be as obstinate about discussing my will, because I have decided to change it so that you receive your rightful share—"

"Yes, I'm going to be just that obstinate!" Sloan interrupted, and to her shock, Edith Reynolds laughed out loud, a harsh cackling sound that was as heartwarming as it was unmelodic.

"What a stubborn creature you are," Edith accused, dabbing tears of mirth from her eyes with the corner of her handkerchief. "I cannot recall the last time anyone actually believed they could sway me once my mind is made up. Even Carter knows it is futile to oppose me once I've taken a position."

Sloan didn't want to sound ungrateful or rude, and she tempered her tone. "I just don't want to discuss your death or anything related to it. It's—depressing!"

"It frequently affects me that way," Edith said gruffly, and Sloan realized she was making a joke.

She bent down and impulsively kissed Edith's parchment cheek. "I'll buy you an 'uplifting' scarf today to counteract the effects," Sloan promised, straightening.

"Nothing too expensive—" Edith called after her.

30

Since neither of them had eaten, Paris suggested they stop for lunch first, and Sloan agreed. She was eager to give Paris her mother's message, but she was acutely aware that from now on each step Paris took toward Kimberly was going to be a step away from her father.

A waitress filled their water glasses and handed them leather-bound menus. Sloan took hers automatically and opened it. Staring blindly at the list of appetizers, she thought about the discussion that lay ahead and tried to be objective: Despite her personal opinion of Carter, she couldn't deny that he'd been a devoted father to Paris, albeit a suffocatingly controlling one, and so Paris was understandably loyal to him. It had been relatively safe and easy for Paris to take a liking to Sloan, because in doing that, Paris hadn't been forced to face the fact that her father was a liar and a villain. That wasn't true when it came to Kimberly.

Carter and his mother had made Paris believe that Kimberly was so reprehensible that a judge had issued a court order to protect Paris from her. In order for Paris to accept that that was all a lie, she also had to accept that her father and his mother were blatant liars. Sloan already knew Paris was going to find that painfully difficult to face, and she was afraid Paris would try to escape the pain in the only way she could—by ignoring Kimberly's overtures and inventing reasons not to go and see her.

The waitress appeared to take their order, and Sloan ordered the "special" without actually having read what it was. As soon as the woman walked away, Sloan decided to broach the subject of Kimberly, but Paris had something else on her mind. "What did Great-grandmother want to talk to you about this morning?"

"Jewelry," Sloan said lightly. "She wanted to give me some heirlooms, which I declined."

Paris's facial muscles tensed. "Did she also mention her will to you, too?"

When Sloan nodded, Paris put her fingertips to her temples and began to rub them as if she'd gotten a sudden headache. "I'm sorry," she said ruefully. "I know she has to die."

Sloan waited in sympathetic silence for her to say more, and Paris sighed, dropping her hands. "I saw the velvet box on her table, and I had a feeling she was going to do something like that. It's just that I hate it when she talks about dying. Maybe I feel as if talking about it will make it happen. I don't know." She shook her head as if to shake off her morbid thoughts, then she leaned forward and crossed her arms in front of her on the table. "Let's talk about something cheerful."

It was the opening Sloan needed. "Would you like to talk about your mother?"

"Okay."

"I talked to her this morning and told her all about you. I told her you wanted to come meet her."

"What did she say?"

Sloan looked directly into Paris's eyes and softly said, "She cried. I've never known Mom to cry before."

Paris swallowed as if she understood the emotional impact. "Did she say anything else?"

"Yes. She asked me to give you her love."

Paris's gaze slid to her water glass. "That was nice of her."

The emotional chain reaction Sloan had anticipated was setting in, and she racked her brain for a way around it. "I know this is hard for you. I know you were told terrible things about her, and now I'm telling you that she's one of the sweetest, kindest people on earth. There's no way to escape the fact that if I'm telling you the truth, then someone lied to you. No, not 'someone.' Your father and his mother."

"He's *your* father too," Paris said in a pleading voice, as if asking Sloan to acknowledge that relationship before Paris could form one with Kimberly.

"Of course he is," Sloan said, and she decided to use the same nonjudgmental rationale that Paul had used on the way to Palm Beach when he hypothesized about the breakup of their parents' marriage. She asked a question first. "Were you very close to your father's mother?"

"Grandmother Frances?" Paris hesitated and then

guiltily shook her head. "I was terrified of her. Everyone was. It wasn't that she was mean—although she *was* mean—but she was also *cold*."

That was exactly the sort of answer Sloan had hoped to hear. "Then let's blame her for what happened and what you were told," she said half seriously. "She probably was mostly to blame for everything, anyway."

Sloan told Paris her version of the day Carter's mother arrived in Florida in a limousine alone and departed for San Francisco with Carter and Paris. As Paris listened to the story, Sloan could see her withdrawing into herself, as if she couldn't bear to believe her father and his mother could be capable of such cruelty.

"The thing we have to remember is this," Sloan finished on a deliberately optimistic note. "At the time our father agreed to go back to San Francisco with his mother and you, he was only twenty-seven. He wasn't the man we know now. He was young, and he'd grown up in luxury, and suddenly he was burdened with a wife and two babies to support. He was probably scared to death. His mother probably convinced him she knew best. Maybe she convinced him he was desperately needed in San Francisco, since his father was so ill. Maybe he wanted to believe it. Who really knows?"

"No one," Paris said after a moment.

"There's one more factor that needs to be added into this equation: Our mother and father had absolutely nothing in common. He didn't love her. She was just a beautiful, naïve small-town girl who fell in love with a wealthy, sophisticated 'older' man and got pregnant."

"And he tried to do 'the right thing' and married her," Paris put in.

"Not exactly. When she went to San Francisco to tell him she was pregnant, his parents were there. They were so disgusted and furious that when he got home late that night, they told him to get out and take Mom with him."

Sloan wisely refrained from telling Paris that Carter had been drunk when he got home, and that his parents regarded a pregnant, small-town teenager as the final intolerable item on the long list of his irresponsible actions.

With great caution, Sloan broached the real problem that remained to be overcome. "After the marriage broke up, they told you terrible things about our mother that aren't true, and that was wrong of them, but when you think about it, it's not all that surprising."

"Actually, it was Grandmother Frances who said most of the really bad things."

"That's not a bit surprising, based on what you just told me about her," Sloan tried to joke.

"Yes, but Father heard her and he never contradicted her."

Sloan wasn't prepared for that comment, but inspiration struck and she seized on a perfect explanation. "By then, he was older and wiser, and he was probably secretly ashamed of what he did—or what he let her convince him to do. He obviously dotes on you, so he wouldn't have wanted to look like a villain in your eyes."

After allowing Paris a minute to let that sink in, Sloan picked up her water glass and thought of another good point to make. "I don't think it's unusual for divorced parents to make nasty remarks about each other to their children."

"You're right! What sort of bad things did our mother say about him?"

Sloan stared at her, a helpless smile forming on her lips, the water glass forgotten in her hand. "Our mother," she explained, "had her purse snatched by a teenager a few years ago. On the day of the trial, she testified for the *defendant* and pleaded with the judge for leniency." With a giggle, Sloan added, "She was so determined to get him off that she was absolutely eloquent!"

Paris broke into a smile. "Did she get him off?"

Sloan nodded. "The judge said he would feel like he was punishing *her* if he sent the boy to jail."

"What a nice story!"

"Not really. He stole her car a week later. He thought she was a very soft touch, and she is."

Sloan knew for certain she'd succeeded in resolving Paris's dilemma, because from that point on, Paris plied her with questions about Kimberly and kept on doing so during their bout of sightseeing and shopping.

31

The discussion about their mother had enabled Sloan to think about something besides Noah that afternoon, but her wristwatch seemed to be moving in reverse until it was finally time to get dressed for the evening. She was so anxious to see him that she hurried when there was no need for haste, and long before it was time to leave, she had nothing left to do except decide which dress to put on.

Paris strolled into her room then to help her make the choice. After inspecting Sloan's clothes and admiring what she'd brought, Paris shook her head and announced that this particular evening called for a long dress. "Not too fancy," she stipulated, "but something that floats a little when you move." Having ascertained that Sloan had nothing like that with her, Paris put her hand against Sloan's back and gently propelled her down the hall to her own room.

Paris's closet, Sloan noted with some amusement, was larger and had more clothes rods in it than Lydia's shop in Bell Harbor, and it connected to another large room filled with unfinished clothing that Paris was in the process of designing.

Sloan watched while her sister paused to pull out gown after gorgeous gown and reject each for reasons that were mostly obscure to Sloan.

"This is it!" Paris declared triumphantly, extracting a strapless white sheath from an entire rod of long gowns. "What do you think?"

Sloan thought it looked pretty much like Sara's red linen sheath, except for the color and length—until Paris zipped her into it and turned her toward the mirror.

The top of the bodice was straight and fitted like a glove to Sloan's waist; then it flared slightly over her hips and fell in a straight line to the floor. Clusters of embroidered white flowers with shining gold leaves and stems adorned the bodice and were scattered at the hem.

"Oh," Sloan whispered, "this is so beautiful."

"You haven't seen the rest of it," Paris announced as she whisked a gossamer stole patterned in white and gold leaves off a hanger and draped it over Sloan's arms. "Now we need the right jewelry," she declared, pulling open drawers that were built into the wall.

"What about my hair?" Sloan asked over her shoulder. "Should I change it and wear it down?" Instead of parting her hair on the side and letting it swing freely as she usually wore it, she'd pulled it off her face and twisted it into a loose chignon at the back of her head.

Paris was holding up two gold filigree chokers and studying them, but she looked round to give an opinion. "Your hair is perfect and so is your makeup, but you need earrings. And I"—she held up a pair that looked like long, gleaming gold raindrops—"have just the right ones!"

Sloan put on the earrings and fastened the wide gold filigree choker at her throat; then she studied herself in the mirror, marveling at the difference Paris could make in her appearance. She turned to tell Paris that, but Paris wasn't finished. She'd vanished, returning a minute later with three fresh white rosebuds in her hand. "I stole these from one of last night's centerpieces," she explained while she reached up and pinned them into Sloan's chignon.

"Does anyone have any idea where we're going?" Paul asked as a uniformed chauffeur held open the back door of Noah's Rolls-Royce for him.

"I don't," Sloan told him, as she followed him into the car, "but wherever it is, you're going to knock the ladies dead!"

Sloan's excitement and enthusiasm were so contagious that even Paul was in a lighthearted mood. "They're out of luck," he joked. "I'm already with the two most beautiful women in Florida. Paris, do you have any idea where we're going?"

She settled into the car beside Sloan, looking like a bird of paradise in a long, brightly colored silk sarong. "I do," she teased smugly, "but I am not at liberty to divulge all the information." She looked at Sloan and relented a little. "I suppose I could give you a hint: You're going to dine at the most exclusive restaurant in Palm Beach."

"Which is?" Paul prodded, grinning at her playful mood.

"It's called Apparition."

An odd expression crossed his face, and Sloan had the feeling he recognized the name. "Have you eaten there before?"

He looked truly confused by her assumption. "No. Never heard of it."

"It must be an incredibly fancy place if we need to dress like this," Sloan remarked.

A short while later, the car turned into a private marina with large yachts tucked into spacious slips along the piers. "I should have guessed—" Sloan said delightedly, turning to Paris. "Apparition is a boat."

Paris didn't answer. She was leaning forward, frowning as the Rolls glided past the last pier and stopped just inside a remote parking area where a small white helicopter was already waiting, its rotor whipping the air. "Oh, no . . ." she said as the chauffeur got out and opened her door.

Paul and Sloan followed her out of the car, but Paris took two steps and stopped dead, her gaze swinging from the little helicopter to the chauffeur. "I assumed Mr. Maitland would send the launch for us, Martin," she said to him in a slightly accusing voice.

Martin, the chauffeur, was a big man in his late forties who looked strong enough to carry the Rolls, not merely drive it, and he spoke with more authority in his voice than deference. "The launch has an engine problem today," he informed her. "Mr. Maitland expects everyone to fly out to the Apparition, where you will enjoy a very pleasant evening, I'm sure."

Sloan was taken aback by his unspoken command to get into the plane and stop hesitating, but Paris was more intimidated by the helicopter than the chauffeur.

"What's wrong?" Paul asked her gently.

She bumped into him as she backed up, trying to put as much distance between herself and the craft as possible. "I'm sorry, but I really don't think I can get into that thing. I *know* I can't. I don't even like big commuter helicopters, let alone miniature ones!"

Sloan's heart sank. She didn't mind missing out on the helicopter or the boat, but she didn't want to miss out on an evening with Noah. "Are we the only guests Noah is expecting?" she asked, hiding her distress behind a sympathetic smile. "If we are, maybe he could join us somewhere else on land?"

"That wouldn't be fair," Paris said emphatically. "Noah had his chef make a special dinner, and he planned a whole evening because he wanted to surprise you." Twisting around, she looked sadly at Paul. "I don't want to spoil the evening. You go with Sloan, and I'll go back home."

Sloan opened her mouth to veto that plan, but Paul gallantly intervened. "That wouldn't be fair to me," he said. "Sloan can go ahead, and you and I will have dinner someplace here."

"Are you certain you don't mind?" Paris asked hesitantly, gazing at him with a mixture of sorrow and melting gratitude.

He appeared to find the situation more humorous than distressing. Nodding toward the helicopter, he told Sloan,

"You'd better get going before that thing runs out of fuel." Then he turned to Paris and gestured toward the open car door. "Shall we go?"

In the car, Paris watched the helicopter lift off the landing pad and veer sharply over the water into the sunset; then she turned to Paul. "I hope you aren't terribly disappointed."

"Not at all," he said smoothly. Crossing his arms over his chest, he angled his back toward the car door and regarded her in amused silence.

A little unnerved by his attitude and his scrutiny, Paris blurted, "You must think I'm silly and neurotic."

Silently, he shook his head, indicating he didn't think that.

"I'm afraid of helicopters."

He looked at her. "That must take some of the fun out of it."

"Out of what?"

"Out of *flying* them."

Laughing, she slumped against the back of her seat and admitted defeat. "How did you know?"

"Your father is very proud of all your accomplishments. Just out of curiosity," he added wryly, "what would you have done if I'd decided to fly out there with Sloan?"

She met his gaze unflinchingly. "I knew you wouldn't do that."

In the front seat, the chauffeur was on the car phone, notifying the *Apparition* that the helicopter had just taken off with Miss Reynolds. He hung up and gazed speculatively at Paris in the rearview mirror, waiting for her decision. "We don't have to pretend, Marty," she said ruefully. "I've been caught. Mr. Maitland said he was going to make reservations somewhere else for us. Take us there."

The chauffeur nodded, made a sharp U-turn, drove to pier number three, and brought the car to a stop. Paris's forehead furrowed into a puzzled frown. "Now what happens?"

"By a strange coincidence," the chauffeur lied straight-faced, reciting his prepared speech, "the *Apparition*'s chef and captain will be returning in the copter shortly. When I telephoned Mr. Maitland just now to notify him that Miss Reynolds was on her way, he was very upset that he hadn't remembered your lifelong fear of helicopters. He instructed me to insist that you let him provide you with a substitute dinner and cruise aboard the *Star Gazer*." He nodded unnecessarily to a sixty-five-foot sailboat docked directly in front of them in the first slip.

Paris looked at Paul, her face shining with merriment. "What do you think? Is it fair to let Noah go to so much trouble?"

"It's the *only* fair thing to do," Paul said mildly, but he wasn't proof against her childlike delight in the evening. With a reluctant grin, he added, "It would serve him right if we took her out without his crew."

"Can you sail a boat that large?"

"With a little help from you." He said it so casually that Paris immediately concluded he was perfectly capable. "Can you cook?" he countered.

"Not without a lot of help from you."

He held out his hand for hers. "Let's go."

32

The *Apparition* lived up to its name, Sloan thought as the helicopter banked left and she gazed in astonished disbelief at the ship that lay below, five minutes offshore. Silhouetted against a sunset ablaze with red, orange, and purple, the gleaming white ship looked as graceful and solid as a seagoing Taj Mahal.

"Welcome aboard, miss," a man in a white uniform said, bending low and holding out his hand to help her alight from the helicopter. He showed her the way to the main deck, two levels below, and escorted her to the bow, where a table had been covered with a linen cloth and set with china and crystal for a formal dinner for two. "Mr. Maitland had an urgent telephone call, but he'll join you here shortly," he explained; then he hurried off.

Mesmerized, Sloan looked about her. She had never expected Noah to possess anything like this; she had never *seen* anything like this except in travelogues about places like Monte Carlo, where the fabulously rich put into port in gigantic yachts.

Trailing her hand along the polished railing, she

strolled slowly along the main deck toward the stern. Most of this level appeared to be taken up by a spacious saloon with large windows overlooking the sea and glass doors that opened onto the deck. The draperies were open, and Sloan was surprised that the interior looked more like an ultramodern penthouse apartment than part of a ship. The carpeting was white with shades of plum and platinum sculptured into a waving design that created a wide border at the edges and a surrealistic medallion in the center. A circular staircase with a chrome railing led to an upper and lower level. Groups of sofas and chairs, upholstered in the carpet's colors, were invitingly arranged around tables with thick glass tops. Modernistic sculptures in shining silver and gold reposed on tables; on pedestals, giant geodes displayed glittering rock interiors in a rainbow of colors including amethyst and powder blue.

Since Noah wasn't in the saloon, she rather expected him to emerge from one of the doorways she passed, but he didn't. She found him instead at her starting point on the bow. He was standing at the railing, talking on a cellular telephone, his face in profile, his voice low and harsh: "I'm not interested in any more of Warren's excuses, I'm interested in results," he was saying to someone. "Tell Graziella that if he fucks this up one more time, I'm not going to bail him out with the Venezuelan government, and he can rot in prison down there."

He paused, listening. "You're damned right I'm serious." He paused again but very briefly. "Good, then take care of Graziella and get the hell out of there." Without saying good-bye, he disconnected the call and tossed the phone onto a table. His tone was entirely different from any Sloan had ever heard him use, and she found it a little hard to equate this cold, forbidding man with the affable one she'd come to know.

He saw Sloan as he tossed the telephone on the table, and his entire expression softened.

"Hi," he said with a lazy, devastating smile that was almost as unnerving as the picture of dazzling elegance he presented in an immaculately tailored raven black tuxedo, snowy shirt, and formal black bow tie.

Sloan stopped just out of his reach, so off-balance from his ship, his helicopter, his telephone conversation, and the way he looked in a tuxedo that she couldn't think of what to say. He seemed like an unapproachable stranger. "Hello," she said in a polite, but formal voice.

If he noticed her reserve, he gave no indication of it. Leaning down, he lifted a bottle of champagne that was chilling in a silver bucket on the deck table beside him and poured some into two glasses. He held one out to her, forcing her to come close enough to take it from him.

They both looked up as the helicopter rotor began to whine, and Sloan saw three men climbing into the craft along with the pilot. "This is all a little overwhelming," she said aloud, watching the helicopter begin to lift off.

Noah restrained an urge to reach out and trace the perfection of her profile with his fingers and instead leaned an elbow on the railing, taking pleasure in the way she looked in that strapless gown, secure in the knowledge that he was going to take it off her tonight.

Sloan used the departing aircraft as a diversion for as

long as she could; then she turned to face him with an overbright smile and blurted out the first thing that came to mind: "Paris didn't come with me—she's afraid to fly in helicopters."

"What a shame," he said solemnly.

Sloan nodded agreement. "Paul stayed ashore with her."

"I'm devastated."

She saw it then—the gleam of amusement in his beautiful gray eyes that made him seem infinitely more familiar to her. At the same time, something else occurred to her, and she looked swiftly at the table, noting the flowers, the candles flickering in crystal bowls, and the place settings of china and silver. Two place settings. Two chairs. Torn between guilt over Paris and mirth at his highhandedness, Sloan settled for trying to look indignant. "You knew all along that Paris is afraid of helicopters!"

"The possibility never occurred to me," he said piously.

"It didn't?" Sloan was startled but not convinced.

Slowly, he shook his head, his eyes laughing at her expression because she clearly knew he was hiding something and she was not going to give up until she figured it out.

"You've known her for years, but you didn't know until today that she's afraid of helicopters—?" Sloan summarized dubiously. A new possibility suddenly occurred to her, and she put it into words: "By any chance, is that because Paris isn't really afraid of them?"

Noah couldn't stand it anymore. Leaning down, he nipped her ear and whispered, "Paris is licensed to fly them."

Laughing, Sloan tried to ignore the effect of his warm breath in her ear and gestured toward the table and the ship. "But why did you go to all this trouble for just the two of us?"

"I wanted to atone for last night's lawn chair."

"With all this?" Sloan teased. "Don't you ever do anything halfway?"

"I did that last night," he said meaningfully.

The subtle change in his tone and the underlying significance of his remark momentarily slipped past Sloan. "But I *liked* the lawn chair."

"You'll like the accommodations here better."

It was fair warning of his intentions, and Sloan's stomach lurched.

"Would you like a tour?"

"Yes," she said quickly, imagining a tour of engines and boilers and bilge pumps. He took her hand, linking his fingers through hers, but even the warmth of his firm handclasp couldn't banish the raging misgivings she felt at the realization he intended to make love tonight.

She'd known this moment would come, but he'd chosen the wrong time, the wrong place, because everywhere she looked, she saw unmistakable, dramatic proof that the world he inhabited wasn't merely different from hers, it was in another solar system. This was a fleeting holiday fling for him, a two-week diversion, if it lasted the full two weeks. For her, it was . . . She couldn't bear the thought, but she could no longer escape it: This was history repeating itself.

She was her mother, only thirty years later. She was

insane about Noah Maitland, and he was as unattainable as he was irresistible. She'd waited her whole life to fall in love, and now she'd spend the rest of it comparing everyone to him.

He led her one flight up the nearest exterior stairway and stopped at the first door on that deck. "This is the master stateroom," he said, swinging the door open.

Sloan tore free from her growing panic, glanced into the large, opulent room, and her gaze riveted on the king-size bed. The thick coverlet was already turned back invitingly, the recessed lighting low and seductive. In a deliberate attempt at flippancy, she said brightly, "It's not Motel Six, but I guess at sea people like you have to settle for what's available." She hated the way she sounded so much that she apologized in the next breath. "I'm sorry. That was a rude, stupid thing for me to say."

He studied her in silence, his expression unreadable. "Why did you say it?"

Sloan sighed and opted for honesty. Lifting her eyes to his, she admitted with quiet candor, "I did it because I'm nervous and uneasy. I'm used to thinking of you as you are with Courtney and Douglas." She made a halfhearted gesture that included him and the ship. "I didn't expect to find you here, with all this. I didn't even recognize the tone of your voice when I heard you talking on the phone. I don't really know you at all," she finished in a desperate, despairing voice.

Noah understood her problem perfectly, because he didn't recognize himself when she was near. Gazing at her alluring upturned face, he contemplated the sweetness of what she was saying and admired her courage for saying it—while he tried to decide whether he most wanted to bury his face in her fragrant hair and laugh at her misgivings, or bury his lips in hers and smother her doubts there. She actually regarded his wealth as a drawback, rather than his most desirable attribute, and that made her all the more unique to him—and twenty times more desirable.

In response to her fear of not knowing him, Noah took her chin between his thumb and forefinger. "You know me, Sloan," he whispered as he purposefully lowered his head. Slowly, tantalizingly, he smoothed his lips back and forth over hers, coaxing them to open for him. "Remember?" he whispered huskily, his hands sliding over her shoulders and back. Abruptly his mouth opened over hers and he deepened the kiss.

It took him less than fifteen seconds to bring Sloan's memory into sharp focus, and all her defenses began to crumble. As if her hands had a will of their own, they slipped inside his jacket and slid over his hard chest, curving over his shoulders and around his neck. He lifted his mouth a fraction from hers, his eyes smoldering, his voice thick with desire. "Now do you remember me?"

Sloan realized it was already too late to turn back, because she was never going to be able to forget him. It was pointless to deny herself the rest of the memories he'd make for her in this room. There'd be time enough for loneliness and regret in Bell Harbor. In the meantime, she wanted to be with him tomorrow and the next day, and maybe the next—as long as her appeal lasted.

He was waiting for her answer, and Sloan nodded, her voice reduced to a soft moan of surrender. "Yes." Leaning up on her toes, she crushed her mouth to his. She kissed him back with all the love and desperation in her heart, and his response was shattering. His mouth became insistent and hungry, his arms wrapped tightly around her, holding her against his rigid body, and his hands wandered possessively over her back and the sides of her breasts.

He shoved the door closed with his foot, and Sloan felt a thrill of nervous excitement, but instead of heightening the passionate exchange, he slowed it down. He kissed her until she was twisted into knots of desire—long, languorous kisses, followed by hard, demanding ones, while his hands explored and caressed her, matching the intensity of each kiss.

Sloan felt his fingers at the zipper of her gown just before he lifted his mouth from hers. He stepped back abruptly to pull off his tuxedo jacket, and the strapless gown slid to the floor at her feet. Automatically, she reached down to pick it up.

"Don't," he said, his gaze lingering on her rosy breasts, his hands swiftly unfastening his shirt.

He obviously had no inhibitions about undressing in front of her, but Sloan felt self-conscious enough for both of them.

When she turned away to finish undressing, Noah realized simultaneously that she was embarrassed and that her nude body was a miracle of ripe curves, slender limbs, and glowing skin. He unfastened the studs from his shirt cuffs while he watched her reach up to pull the pins out of her hair. With her hands raised and her head slightly bent like that, she reminded him forcibly of a painting of a nude that was hanging in the Louvre. When the last pin was out, she gave her head a hard shake, and her hair tumbled onto her shoulders in a waterfall of shining gold.

She was stunning, Noah thought with a surge of undiluted lust.

She was shy, he reminded himself.

He came up behind her and slid his arms around her, drawing her back against him. "You take my breath away," he whispered against her neck. In response, she shivered. He turned her around and brought her down onto the bed; then he stretched out beside her and leaned up on his left arm, his hand resting beneath her nape.

Sloan waited with mounting anxiety while his gaze traveled over every curve and hollow of her body. When his gaze lifted to hers again, there was no mistaking the reckless glitter in those heavy-lidded gray eyes. His hand tightened, lifting her face, and she braced instinctively for a quick assault. Instead, it was a soft stroking kiss, as featherlight and relaxing as the slow stroking of his fingertips against her nape. A very reassuring kiss.

Reassured, Sloan turned into him and kissed him back, and as soon as she did, his right hand slid over her shoulder to her breast, cupping it, his thumb slowly circling her nipple. It was a teasing touch, a tantalizing touch.

Tantalized, Sloan spread her hand over the solid wall of his chest, sliding her fingers through the short, dark matting of hair. His skin felt like hot satin over steel, his nipple hard and small as she lightly grazed it with her palm. His arm was bunched muscle, his throat a corded column. Beneath her exploring fingertips, his jaw was chiseled from granite, his cheek carved from marble. He was magnificent, she realized achingly. And he was hers. For now. The hair at his temple was smooth . . .

To Sloan these touches were a poignant discovery; to Noah they were caresses so delicate and unexpected that they were profoundly stirring. He lifted his mouth from hers, watching her in tender disbelief while she sent desire pounding through his entire body.

Oblivious to the effect she was having on him, Sloan brushed her fingertips over his mouth. His lips were sculpted from a wondrous material that was firm and warm and mobile. His brows were thick and straight; his beautiful eyes were—open.

Startled, she looked up at him. His face was hard and dark with passion, a muscle moving spasmodically in his throat. She understood what she saw; she didn't care how she'd caused it. Curving her hand around his nape, she closed her eyes, arching against him, and felt the gasp of his breath against her mouth when she kissed him.

His mouth opened over hers, demanding and urgent, his tongue stroking intimately against hers while his hand slid down her body. His fingers tangled in the tiny, springy curls between her thighs and gently gained entry. Sloan writhed beneath the sensual onslaught of fingers stroking deep inside her and the intimate stroking of his tongue against hers.

He tore his lips from hers and slid his mouth down her neck to her breasts, and by the time he returned to her lips, Sloan was clutching his shoulders, her fingers biting into his back.

His hands cupped her bottom and pulled her up against him, fitting her to his length; then he drove into her with enough force to make her body arch. Each slow, demanding thrust pushed her closer to the edge; then without warning, he wrapped his arms around her and rolled onto his back, carrying her with him.

She stared at him in disbelief, seated on top of him, and Noah chuckled at the startled expression on her flushed face. If she had been anyone else, he would have finished without doing this, but he wanted her to experience as much as his body would allow before he lost control. At least he told himself that was why he was doing it, but in some part of his passion-drugged brain, Noah knew his reason was somehow connected with her other two lovers. They had been clumsy and inept. He was neither. And he wanted to be absolutely certain Sloan knew that when they left this room.

Reaching up, he threaded his hands through the sides of her hair. "You are exquisite," he whispered. His hands slid down to her breasts, then reluctantly released them and settled on her hips, helping her to start.

She hadn't been lying about her lack of experience, Noah realized a few minutes later as he suppressed a laughing groan. She had no idea how to gauge the tempo for him; she slowed it when he wished she would go faster, changed it when he wanted her to sustain it. He couldn't predict the next moment or depend on her next movement, and because he couldn't, she now had him in a sustained state of excited suspense that was more arousing than it would have been if she had known what she was doing.

Just when he decided that, she began to watch his face and adjust to the pressure of his hips, and Noah's amusement died. The passion he thought he had under control was surging through his loins with enough force to make him grasp her hips to stop her. Pulling her onto his chest, he struggled to stop the rampage, and when he couldn't, he rolled her gently onto her back. He shifted on top of her, his hips pinning her to the bed as he began to thrust deeply inside of her. He dragged his mouth roughly across her cheek, longing to imprint himself on her mind as he was embedding himself in her body. "Open your eyes," he said, his voice reduced to a raw whisper.

Her long russet lashes flickered open. Silently, her eyes begged for release, and silently, he promised it to her. His shoulders and arms rigid with the strain of holding back, he began to increase the force of each stroke.

Sloan felt the pulsing beginning deep inside her. It quaked through until it finally exploded in a burst of extravagant pleasure that tore a low whimper from her throat. Noah drove into her one more time, his body shuddering with the same pleasure he'd given her. His head fell forward, his breathing labored. Wrapping his arm around her hips, he moved onto his side with her.

Sloan lay there, too shaken by what she'd felt to think, glorying in the simple thrill of being held in his arms. As sanity slowly returned, however, it became obvious to her that the man who had just made love to her had perfected the technique, undoubtedly through a great deal of practice with a great many women. On the other hand, she didn't think he'd found her so completely inexperienced that she bored him and he wouldn't want her again. If that were so, surely he wouldn't be holding her so close now, his hand lazily rubbing the curve of her waist. As a precaution, she decided to say something to him. "Noah?"

"Hmm?"

"I'm a very quick learner," she said earnestly.

Noah tipped his head down to see her beautiful face, and his lips quirked in a tender smile. "I noticed that," he whispered.

"What I mean is, I'll get better with practice."

The bed shook with his laughter as he snatched her into his arms, burying his face in her neck. "God help me."

Noah's laughter faded, but his lighthearted mood lingered as he held her against him. Normally an orgasm left him feeling relaxed and then energized; it did not leave him feeling absurdly happy. He could not understand why the woman in his arms had such a profound effect on him in bed and out of it. She could make him hot with a glance, cheer him with a smile, melt him with a touch. She was without greed, vanity, or guile.

She was also without dinner, he realized. He turned his wrist and looked at his watch. He'd wanted her aboard early to see the sunset, and the evening was still delightfully young.

He smoothed her heavy hair off her smooth cheek, and she looked up at him. "The evening's entertainment includes dinner and a tour," he teased.

She gave him a slumberous smile, her long fingers idly spreading on his chest. "Was that included in the price of the ticket, or is it extra?"

"Don't look at me like that or you'll get something besides dinner and the tour."

"Really?" she asked. "What?"

"Dessert."

To avoid further temptation, he reached for the telephone and instructed that dinner be served in a half hour; then he reluctantly got out of bed.

They dined by candlelight in formal attire with music playing softly in the background, but the atmosphere between them was different. Without the distraction of unfulfilled sexual desire, they were able to talk like new friends getting to know one another.

By the time dinner was over, she was so relaxed that she thought nothing of answering his question about Carter and her mother. "My mother won a beauty contest when she was eighteen, and the prize was a trip to Fort Lauderdale and a week in the best hotel," Sloan explained. "A photographer from the Fort Lauderdale newspaper was taking her picture on the beach. A cocktail party was taking place nearby—part of a rehearsal dinner for a wedding that Carter was attending—and he wandered over to see what was happening. He was wearing a white dinner jacket. My mother was dazzled. And that's what happened."

"That can't be all that happened," Noah pointed out as a joke.

"That's *nearly* all that happened. My mother had been raised by her grandmother, and she was as naïve as she was beautiful. She spent the remaining three days of her trip with him in her hotel suite. She gave him her virginity, and Carter gave her Paris. She went back home, completely convinced they were in love and that he wanted to marry her—as soon as he could win his socially prominent family in San Francisco over to the idea. Naturally, Mom was a little surprised when she never heard from her 'fiancé' again. She was even more surprised when the doctor told her that she wasn't sick with the flu, she was pregnant."

Noah lifted his wineglass, watching the emotions play across her lovely face. She was trying very hard to sound offhand, but her voice softened when she mentioned her mother and it hardened almost imperceptibly when she mentioned Carter. "Then what happened?"

"The usual," she said with a jaunty, sideways smile. "My mother went to the library and located the father of her baby by looking up his family's name in *Who's Who*." When Noah didn't smile at her attempt at humor, Sloan sobered and said lightly, "She was still so certain that he loved her and that his family must be being unfair to him that she took the rest of her prize money and bought a plane ticket. She arrived on Carter's family's doorstep at night, with her suitcase—also part of her contest prizes— but they told her Carter was out. She explained that she was his fiancée and asked if she could wait for him there. You can imagine the rest."

"Probably," Noah said, "but I'd like to hear it from you."

"You're awfully persistent," Sloan joked. Instead of being dissuaded he cocked a dark brow in inquiry and waited for her to go on. Helpless to ignore his silent command to continue, she sighed and said, "In a very few minutes, they got the whole story out of her, and they were furious." She paused, trying to think of a way to phrase the rest of the story. Carter was his friend and Paris's father, and she didn't want to needlessly tarnish his image. "They naturally felt he had done a wrong thing, and when Carter came home, he accepted responsibility and left with my mother—"

He mocked her attempt to gloss over the truth. "That's not going to fly, Sloan. I knew Carter's mother and father when they were older, and they couldn't have changed that much. What really happened?"

A little unnerved by his bluntness, Sloan straightened the napkin in her lap and finally met his unwavering gaze. "Actually," she said with a sigh, "when Carter came home that night, he was drunk, and his parents were already furious with him for a long list of transgressions. They threw him out and my mother with him. It must have been a sobering experience for him; he stopped in Las Vegas and married my mother before they went on to Florida. He had enough money left somewhere to buy a sailboat, and for the next two years he chartered it out. Paris was born; then I was born."

"Then what?"

"Then Carter's mother arrived one day in a limousine

to tell him that his father had had a stroke. She told him he was welcome back in the family fold and she told him to bring one daughter with him. They left that same day with Paris."

"Courtney is under the impression that you and your mother weren't well provided for in that deal."

"My mother was given a modest settlement," Sloan said vaguely.

"How modest?"

"Modest," Sloan said stubbornly; then she smiled and shook her head. "It wouldn't have mattered if it had been much larger. My mother is so naïve and so sweet that she would have given it away to anyone who asked her for a loan or been swindled out of it by some phony 'financial adviser.' "

"Is that what happened to the settlement she got?"

"Most of it," Sloan confirmed.

"You never refer to Carter as your father, do you?" he asked.

She gave him a laughing look and rolled her eyes. "He *isn't* my father."

Noah slowly lowered his wineglass. "He's not?"

"Not in any significant sense."

"What, specifically, do you class as 'significant' here?"

"He is my biological parent, period. A 'father' is so much more than that. A father is someone who dries your tears when you're little and looks under your bed because you're afraid a monster is down there. He makes the school bully leave you and your best friend alone. He goes to PTA meetings and your softball games, even though you're too little to play and they keep you on the bench. He worries about you when you're sick, and he worries about boys getting intimate with you when you're a teenager."

Noah grinned at the insight she'd unwittingly provided. An image of a little blond girl in a softball uniform, sitting on a bench, drifted through his mind. Her big violet eyes would be sad because they wouldn't let her play. "You played softball?" he asked, trying to remember if he knew a single woman who'd played softball as a child, rather than tennis or field hockey.

"I would be exaggerating to say that," she said, her laugh touching his ears like the soft tinkling of bells. "I was so little for my age that if I played in my own age group, my teammates mistook me for grass and ran over me. I was in my teens before I finally hit a growth spurt."

"It wasn't much of a spurt," Noah said tenderly.

"Oh, yes it was," she assured him, laughing.

On second thought, Noah decided, it must have been one hell of a maturation process, because she had a gorgeous figure, perfectly proportioned for her height. Perfectly proportioned in every way for his body . . . The mere thought made him harden, and with a mixture of exasperation and amusement, he said, "I promised you a tour."

He stood up and walked around to pull out her chair; then he draped the stole she'd brought over her shoulders.

Sloan was fascinated by the tour; she'd been on boats many times, but *Apparition* was more like a cruise ship than a boat. She explored the spotless engine room and then the galley, and when he realized she was truly interested, Noah got out the keys and showed her places he would normally have skipped, stopping to open corridor doors that concealed everything from cleaning supplies to spare nautical equipment. "I love boats," she confessed to him with glowing eyes.

"All boats?" he teased.

She nodded solemnly. "All of them—tugboats and fishing boats, slow boats and fast boats. I love the ocean and everything associated with it."

They were in the center of the ship, a level down from the main deck, and she stopped automatically at the next door.

"We can skip that one," he said firmly, putting his hand on her waist to urge her along.

Sloan was instantly curious. "Why? What are you hiding in there?"

"There's nothing in there you'd be interested in."

She burst out laughing. "Don't do that; it's not fair. Now I'm curious. I can't stand unsolved mysteries. I'm a sleuth by—" She broke off in horror. "I'm an amateur sleuth," she amended quickly, and to further distract him, she said with sham indignation, "These are the women's quarters, aren't they?—you bring women along to keep the crew from mutinying on long voyages."

"Hardly," he said, but he wasn't unlocking the door, and Sloan's fascination doubled.

"Pirate treasure?" she ventured, trying to prod him into answering. "Smuggled goods? Drugs—" Her smile faded.

He noticed, and with a resigned sigh, he unlocked the doors and turned on a light. Sloan stared in shock. The small room contained an arsenal of firearms, including a machine gun.

"Courtney saw this and refused to go out to sea with me anymore."

Sloan shook her head a little, trying to recover.

"Don't dramatize it," he warned more forcefully than Sloan thought was necessary.

Sloan registered assault weapons and others that were illegal in the U.S. "Yes, but this—this—why do you need all this?"

He tried to shrug it off as routine. "People who own boats frequently keep a gun aboard."

Sloan's uneasiness was so intense that she shivered, and Noah leapt to an erroneous conclusion. "Don't be afraid. These aren't loaded."

Sloan stepped forward. He was lying, but she tried to sound like an amateur when she pointed it out. "If that's true, then why is that belt-thing with the bullets in it hanging out of that machine gun?"

Noah muffled a laugh and pulled her out of the room, turning out the lights. "It shouldn't be there. That's an old machine gun that we confiscated from a surprise guest on the last cruise."

Sloan's mind reeled with the same refrain she'd heard earlier: She did not know him. Not really. She had gone to bed with him and done intimate things with him, but she did not know him.

Standing beside her at the railing on the main deck,

Noah sensed her withdrawal and assumed the weapons cache was the cause of it, but he attributed her reaction to the same vague panic that Courtney had felt. "Learning to use a gun is the best way to overcome a fear of them."

Sloan swallowed and nodded.

"I could teach you to shoot some of them."

"That would be nice," she said absently, trying to get a grip on her reactions. She was letting her imagination run wild, she told herself sternly, a silly mistake that was probably some sort of emotional backlash. She'd been falling in love with him almost from the moment she'd seen him in Carter's living room; she'd just joined her body with his and moaned with passion in his arms. In view of all that, it made more sense to ask for an explanation than to invent one. "It would be even nicer if I understood why you have them. I mean, we're not at war, are we?"

"No, but I do business in countries where the governments aren't always stable. Businessmen in those countries are frequently armed."

She turned fully toward him, her eyes searching his face. "You do business with people who want to *shoot* you?"

"No, I do business with people whose competitors want to shoot *them*. Or me, if I were to get in the way. For that reason, I realized several years ago that it is not only wiser, it is healthier, to do business on my own turf. This ship is my own turf. Next month, I have a meeting off the coast of a major city in Central America. It will take place aboard *Apparition*, and my colleagues will be flown aboard by helicopter."

"Maybe you ought to get into a safer business," Sloan mused aloud.

He laughed. "It isn't purely for safety; it's also for effect." She looked baffled, and Noah explained, "In a foreign port, dealing with people who are impressed by success, *Apparition* still gives me a home court advantage."

Sloan relaxed. What he said made a great deal of sense. "What sort of business do you do with those people?"

"Import/export. Basically, I'm in the business of making deals."

"In Venezuela?"

"That's one of the places."

"Does Mr. Graziella carry a gun?"

He didn't like the question, Sloan noticed. "No," he said impassively, "he doesn't. If he did, someone would take it away from him and shoot him with it."

He knew she was suspicious, and instead of saying anything to allay those suspicions, he waited for her to make her own decision. Sloan sensed that she was being tested somehow—for her potential for loyalty? Or as his lover? She liked the thought of the latter, but even if he hadn't meant that, her instincts told her he was telling the truth. In her work, these instincts were almost unfailingly reliable, and she relied on them now. "I'm sorry. I shouldn't have pried," she said, turning to the railing and looking out to sea.

"Do you have any more questions?"

She nodded slowly and somberly. "Yes, one."

"And that is?"

"Why did we skip the tour of the saloon?"

Noah was completely enthralled by her wit, her intelligence, and at the moment, by the way she looked in the moonlight in a strapless gown with her hair blowing in the breeze. He wrapped his arms around her from behind, drawing her close against his body, and his voice was already husky with awakening desire. "There's a door to my stateroom off the stairs inside the saloon, and if you go into one room, you have to go into the other, too— there are no deviations allowed on this tour," he teased.

He waited for her to react and felt a fresh surge of lust when she nodded slightly.

"There's one more problem," he whispered. "I made a mistake earlier. The package price didn't include this part of the tour. There's an extra charge—I have to collect it in advance."

His mouth touched the corner of her lips, waiting to collect, and with a shudder of surrender, Sloan turned her head to fully receive his kiss.

33

For Sloan, the next week passed in a sweet procession of sunny days and sensual nights. She spent at least part of every day with Paris and at least part of every night with Noah. His sailboat, the *Star Gazer*, became a private bower, close-by and yet private and mobile. His house on the beach became nearly as comfortable to her as her own home in Bell Harbor, and Douglas and Courtney seemed to regard her as part of their family. None of it was permanent, she knew that. She knew that only one thing from her Palm Beach trip was permanent and lasting: She was in love with Noah.

Paul and Paris appeared to have paired off, and frequently the four of them spent the day together, though they usually went separate ways for the evening. Sloan couldn't tell what sort of relationship the FBI agent was having with her sister. Paul was not the sort of man who invited questions about his personal feelings, and although Paris was perfectly willing to share hers, the truth was that she didn't know how Paul felt about her either.

That was a frequent topic of conversation between

Sloan and Noah when they were alone, but on the eighth day after her fateful night aboard the *Apparition*, Sloan didn't have him to talk to; in fact, for the first time, she had a solitary evening ahead of her, and although that would have pleased her a few weeks ago, she felt restless and alone now.

Noah had some sort of business meeting in Miami and wasn't due back until the following day. Sloan had intended to spend the time with Paris and Edith, but Paris developed a migraine headache that afternoon and had taken some medication that put her to sleep. Paul had also gone away for the day on some sort of "personal business" and hadn't known whether he'd return that night or the next morning. After an early dinner, Edith wanted to spend the evening watching game shows on satellite TV and by nine-thirty Sloan couldn't sit through another minute of them. Carter had a poker game with friends and wasn't due home until after eleven.

Sloan had an awful premonition that when she left here, when Noah was no longer near, restlessness and loneliness were going to be her constant companions. She did not deceive herself about his intentions; she'd heard enough remarks from Douglas and Courtney, and from Noah himself, to know that he was antimarriage and antichildren. What's more, she'd gotten to know some of his friends when he took her to the country club, and from things she'd heard, it was apparent that Noah discarded women as carelessly as he changed shirts—and almost as frequently.

And yet, even knowing all that and knowing how much

this was going to hurt when it was over, Sloan wouldn't have missed a moment of it if she'd been offered the choice.

Until the past week, she'd felt like an oddity around Sara and most of their old friends. Except for Sloan, they'd all been "boy crazy" as teenagers; in college, they'd slept around and fallen in and out of love constantly. Unlike all of them, Sloan had had only two sexual relationships in her entire life, and one of those relationships would never have happened if she hadn't been feeling like a complete outsider at the time.

Her mother was the only one who hadn't found that strange, although as Sloan neared thirty with no man in her life, even Kimberly began to hint that she ought to date more often. Kimberly had little ground to stand on in that regard; men asked her out all the time, and she almost never went. "I'm just not attracted to him," she would tell Sloan. "I'd rather stay home or go out with friends."

As Sloan was discovering, she was more like her mother than she'd imagined. The two of them simply weren't attracted to just any attractive, eligible man; they were attracted rarely, but when it happened, it was evidently a life-altering experience. The phrase "one-man woman" ran through Sloan's mind as she wandered out onto her bedroom balcony and looked out at the moonlight on the water.

Sloan glanced at her watch and decided to go for a walk on the beach. It was nearly ten and a walk on the beach would soothe her so that she'd be able to sleep. She put on a pair of jeans and sneakers and pulled a bulky pale pink cotton sweater over her head; then she pulled her hair up into a ponytail and headed downstairs.

When she got to the beach, she decided to turn left, away from Noah's house, so that she wouldn't see it and use it as a landmark. She needed to stop dwelling on him this way. She needed to think about her future, when he wasn't going to be around. She needed to, but she couldn't make herself do it. It was so much sweeter to think instead about the things he did and said when they were together. He was brilliant and witty and willing to talk about anything that interested her—anything, that is, except his feelings for her. Never, not even in the heat of passion, did he ever use the word "love" or talk about the future after she left Palm Beach. He never even used an endearment or called her by an affectionate nickname. In Bell Harbor, Jess called her "Short Stuff," and when he was in his Humphrey Bogart mood, he called her "Hey, sweetheart." Half the guys on the police force had nicknames for her, but the man she made love with for hours at a time called her "Sloan."

Rather than worry about all that, Sloan decided to think about all the glorious fun she'd had with him.

She was still doing that an hour later when she neared Carter's house again on her return trip. With her hands shoved into her back pockets, she gazed out across the water, smiling at the thought of how he looked sailing a boat with the wind ruffling his hair. He was as relaxed and competent at the helm of that demanding sailboat as he was driving a car, and he'd volunteered to teach her to sail it, too. As a teacher, he'd had a tendency to expect too much at first, calling out orders she didn't understand more quickly than she could follow them. She'd broken him of that during the second lesson by addressing him as "Captain Bligh" in a semiserious voice.

Sloan was so absorbed in her memory of that day that when she heard his voice, she thought for a moment she was imagining it. "Sloan!"

She looked away from the water and scanned the beach ahead; then she looked to the right. She stopped walking and stared, unable to believe her eyes. Noah was in Miami on business . . . Noah was walking toward her from the back lawn of her father's house wearing jeans and a knit polo shirt. She started walking again, and he stepped up his pace. "Going anywhere in particular?" he asked with a boyish grin, stopping in front of her.

Sloan shook her head.

"By any chance, have you been feeling sort of lost and lonely and unable to concentrate today?"

"Yes, as a matter of fact I have," she said, overjoyed because he evidently felt that way, too. "I think it must be some sort of flu!"

"A flu? Does that make you irritable and impossible to please?"

In the last week, Sloan had noticed that he had a temper and that when displeased, he could be curt and even harsh, but he never showed that side of himself to his family or to her. She gave him a look of jaunty superiority. "I wouldn't know about that. My disposition is always sweet."

He laughed and opened his arms. "Then come and share it with me."

Sloan rushed forward, and his arms closed around her

with stunning force. "I missed you," he whispered. "You're addictive." His mouth seized hers in a ravenous kiss, forcing her lips to part for his probing tongue. When he was satisfied, he turned and put his arm around her waist and started walking with her toward his house.

"Where are you taking me?"

"To the place I love to see you in the most."

It was late, and Sloan made a wild guess. "The kitchen?"

"How did you know?" he teased. "I came back tonight instead of waiting until morning because I wanted to see you. I haven't eaten since breakfast, and Claudine has already gone to bed. Courtney incinerates anything she touches, and Douglas won't touch anything in the kitchen that he doesn't plan to put directly in his mouth. Do you think you could whip up one of those omelettes like the one you made me last week?"

Sloan smothered a laugh. "It breaks my heart to think you'd have to go to bed hungry if you couldn't find a woman on the beach who can figure out how to turn on a stove. It's so sad."

Noah glanced at her face. "You don't look sad," he noted.

"You are not only handsome, brilliant, and incredibly sexy," Sloan said, trying to make a joke of what she really felt, "but you are also perceptive. I don't look sad because I have a solution."

"Am I going to like it?"

Courtney rushed into her father's study and grabbed Douglas's hand, pulling him out of his chair. "What are you doing?" he protested as the book he was reading slid to the floor.

"You have to come downstairs. Sloan is here, and you aren't going to believe this unless you see it."

"See what?"

"Noah is cooking!"

"You mean 'cooking'—as in 'angry'?" Douglas speculated, walking swiftly beside her.

"No, I mean 'cooking'—as in 'kitchen.' "

As they neared the kitchen, they stopped talking and walked softly, anxious to witness this unprecedented event without being seen.

Noah was standing in the center of the kitchen watching Sloan, who was gathering the ingredients for an omelette. "I have a philosophy about cooking," he announced in the professional tone of one who is about to expound on a theoretical analysis of a topic on which he is an expert.

Sloan grinned at him as she took an onion, a couple of tomatoes, and a red and a green pepper from the produce drawer and put them on the counter to be chopped. "Does your philosophy go something like—'I paid for the food; let someone else figure out what to do with it'?"

"Oh, have you already read my best-selling book on this subject?"

Ignoring that, Sloan said, "Would I be correct in assuming that the 'someone else' in your philosophy is probably female?"

"How did you guess?"

"Isn't that a little sexist?"

"I don't think of it that way," he declared with outrageous gall. "I think of it as delegating responsibility." The bacon was cooking in the microwave, and Noah sniffed appreciatively. "That smells delicious."

She sent him a smile over her shoulder. "Does it?"

"I'm partial to omelettes, and I'm starved."

"Want to hear *my* philosophy on cooking?" Sloan warned.

"I don't think so."

She told him anyway: "He who does not help with the cooking does not get to help with the eating."

"Okay, I'm ready. Give me an assignment. Make it a tough one."

Without turning, she passed him a knife and green pepper over her right shoulder. "Here you are. A green pepper."

He grinned at her back. "I had something more macho in mind."

She passed him the onion.

Noah laughed, enjoying himself hugely. He began to peel off the outer layer of the onion. "I hope the guys at the bowling alley don't hear about this. I'll be ruined."

"No you won't. Knives are good. They're macho."

In answer he picked up a dish towel and snapped it, landing a soft whack on her buttocks.

"Better not try that on me, Noah," Courtney said, sauntering forward. Leaning her elbows on the counter, she perched her chin on her fists and regarded him with prim superiority. "Sloan has been showing me some excellent self-defense moves. I can toss you on your—ouch," she said as the dish towel landed with more force on her rump.

She glared at him in mock affront; then she looked at Sloan. "Do you want me to take him down for that, or are you going to do it?"

Before Sloan could reply, Noah plopped a tomato from Sloan's pile onto the cutting board in front of Courtney and handed her a knife. "Sloan was just telling me her philosophy about cooking. Let me share it with you."

Courtney picked up the knife and made a halfhearted attempt to saw on the tomato. "*Eeeeuw*, this is disgusting," she said. "I am never going to get on the *Sally* show. This house is beginning to feel like real people live here."

Douglas walked in soon after, when the chopped onion was sautéing and all the preparation work was done. "By any chance," he asked Sloan, "is there enough for an extra person?"

"More than enough," she said.

Courtney was irate. "You can't eat because you didn't do any work."

"But—there's nothing left to do," Douglas replied, innocently looking around.

Noah gave him a knowing look. "Nice timing."

"I thought so," Douglas shamelessly replied, and settled into a chair at the kitchen table.

34

"It's after midnight," Sloan said as she strolled along the beach toward Carter's house, her hand held in Noah's warm clasp, his long fingers entwined with hers. Her senses were alive to his touch, his nearness, even the sound of his deep, rich voice.

"I had fun," he said.

"I'm glad."

"You make everything seem like fun."

"Thank you."

Quietly, and without emphasis, he added, "I'm crazy about you."

Sloan's heart slammed into her ribs. *I love you*, she thought. "Thank you," she whispered, because she couldn't tell him the truth.

He slanted her a sidewise smile. "Is that all?" he asked, sounding a little disappointed.

Sloan stopped. "No, it isn't," she said softly, and leaning up on her toes, she told him with her kiss what she dared not tell him with words. His arms closed around her, kissing her back, his body hardening quickly against hers.

He loved her, too, she thought.

They were partway across the back lawn, near Carter's putting green when Sloan belatedly remembered the infrared beams and her hand flew to her throat. "I forgot about those things!"

"What things?"

She laughed at her nervous fright. "The infrared beams—If the security system had been on, we'd have tripped the beams when we started across the lawn. Dishler must have seen me go out and bypassed the beams so they wouldn't be activated when the security system was armed."

"Either that," Noah joked, "or the cops are pulling up to the front door right now."

"No," Sloan reassured him. "Paris told me that when the alarm is tripped, all the house lights go on and the sirens go off."

"What?" he joked. "Haven't you ever heard of a silent alarm that goes straight to the police station?"

Not only had Sloan heard of that, she could have told him how to wire and install one. Rather than add one more thing to the list of items he was going to feel deceived about later, she said brightly, "I know all about that stuff."

He tightened his hand in a playful squeeze. "I'll just bet you do," he said, and Sloan was immediately wary.

"Why do you say that?"

"Simple logic and brilliant insight. Combined, they lead me to conclude that a woman who learns self-defense to protect herself when she's walking on the street would undoubtedly have a very good security system to protect herself when she sleeps. Am I right?" he said with smug superiority.

"I can't deny—" Sloan began, just as a shadowy figure on an upstairs balcony called softly, "Hi, you two!"

It was Paris, wearing a robe, standing at the railing.

"How are you feeling?" Sloan asked.

"Much better. I slept all day, though, and now I'm wide awake. Paul and Father both came in around eleven, but they went straight to bed. I was thinking of going down to the kitchen and making some hot chocolate. Do you want some?"

Sloan said yes; she would have said yes if she was falling asleep on her feet, but Noah shook his head and stopped at the back door. "I'm a little tired, and I couldn't ingest another molecule of anything." He wasn't too tired to give her a long and very thorough kiss good-night, or to continue to hold her in his arms afterward, which gave Sloan the thrilling feeling that he didn't like to leave her. Leaning forward, he unlocked the back door with the key she gave him and swung it open. "I'll call you in the—"

Paris's scream cut him off. "*Great-grandmother!*— No—*Help me!*"

Sloan whirled and raced through the doorway and down the back hall in the general direction of Paris's scream, with Noah right behind her. Beyond the kitchen was a cozy study where Edith had been watching television earlier, and the scene that greeted Sloan struck terror in her heart. Edith was lying slumped over on the sofa with Paris bending over her, trying to turn her over. "Oh, my God, oh, my God," Paris was moaning. "A heart attack. No one here with her . . ."

"Call nine-one-one," Sloan ordered her sister, taking over. Sloan gently rolled the elderly woman onto her back. "We'll start CPR and—" Sloan broke off when she saw the gunshot wound in her great-grandmother's chest. She sprang to her feet. "Get Paul!" Sloan shouted over her shoulder, already running. "Don't touch anything! Turn on the house lights—"

For a split second Noah thought she was running for a telephone, but there was one on the desk, and then he heard the back door crash open against the house.

"Call nine-one-one!" he shouted at Paris, charging out of the room in pursuit of Sloan. He couldn't believe the impulsive little fool was actually outside looking for a murderer.

He ran out the back door, his gaze flying over the deserted lawn; then he turned right, running along the back of the house because that seemed like the most logical route. He rounded the corner just as she dodged into the shadows up ahead. When he saw her again, she was flattened against the side of the house at the very front, looking around the corner. "Sloan!" he shouted, but she was already on the run, streaking across the front lawn, dodging shrubbery and jumping over obstacles as if they were hurdles in a footrace. He ran after her, gaining on her, too furious and frightened for her to appreciate the efficiency and agility of her movements—or to register why what she was doing looked uncannily familiar.

She stopped near the front gates. Her head drooped

forward in defeat, and her shoulders began to heave with silent weeping. Noah caught up to her, grabbed her arms, and spun her around. "What the hell—"

"She's dead," she sobbed. "She's *dead*—" The tears streaming down her cheeks doused his wrath over her recklessness, and Noah pulled her against him, wrapping his arms tightly around her. "I'm sorry," he whispered. "I'm so sorry."

In the distance, sirens were wailing, moving closer, and Noah noticed the electric gates beginning to open. He moved Sloan out of the driveway as two police cruisers arrived from opposite directions, sirens wailing, light bars flashing.

35

The Palm Beach Police Department was not only effi-
cient, it also knew how to deal with its wealthy, prominent
citizens without ruffling their feathers, Sloan noticed dully.

Within minutes after the first patrol officers arrived at
the scene, they'd sized up the situation, rounded up the
occupants of the house so that evidence wouldn't be disturbed, and notified the Palm Beach County medical
examiner. The Palm Beach PD crime scene team had
arrived soon after, secured the area, and began dusting for
fingerprints. In the meantime, two detectives began the
process of interviewing everyone in the house.

The cook, housekeeper, butler, and caretaker were kept
waiting in the dining room. Family members and friends
were placed in the living room so that they would have privacy and comfort. Since Gary Dishler ranked between the
two groups, Carter was asked to determine where he
should be kept waiting, and he chose the living room.

Captain Walter Hocklin had been summoned from his
bed to personally make certain that Carter Reynolds and
his family were not subjected to any sort of unnecessary
inconvenience by Detectives Dennis Flynn and Andy

Cagle, or the other police officers who were stationed inside and outside.

In the study where Edith's body lay, camera flashes went off again and again as the medical examiner photographed the body before it was moved. Sloan flinched inwardly each time she saw the camera flash reflected in the hallway mirror outside the living room, and she prayed Paris didn't notice or realize what they were doing.

As she sat in the living room with Noah, Carter, and the others, Sloan was a mass of bewildered futility and angry disbelief. Detectives Flynn and Cagle had finished interviewing everyone individually, but after conferring with the team in the study, they said they needed to clarify and confirm some of their information.

The detectives referred to their notes while Captain Hocklin settled into a chair and courteously explained to his audience why this was necessary: "I know you're all tired and upset," he said, but he addressed his remarks mostly to Carter and Paris. "Before we start bothering you with more questions, I'll tell you what little we know at this point. Most important to you will be the knowledge that Mrs. Reynolds did not suffer. The bullet pierced her heart and she died instantly.

"There's evidence of forced entry—a window in the room where she was found was broken and unlocked. Without your help, we can't tell what was taken, but drawers were ransacked. We have no idea how long the killer was in the house or whether he was in other parts of it. In the morning, we'll need you to look around and tell us what, if anything, is missing."

He paused, and Carter nodded curtly.

"We're going to do everything possible to get this ordeal over with as quickly and smoothly as possible. We're dusting for fingerprints in the bedrooms your family and guests are using right now, so you can sleep there tonight. Do not touch anything anywhere else. We're going to work straight through the night, and we hope to be out of here sometime tomorrow. The local press has already picked up the story, and so it will probably be national news by tomorrow. Your gates at the front of the house will keep them at a distance. Unfortunately your property is also accessible from the beach. We've put up crime-scene tape back there, and I'll place a man there tonight and tomorrow to keep people out. You really ought to hire a couple of security guards and post them back there for a few days after we're gone. Otherwise you'll be plagued to death with curiosity seekers and press."

"Gary will make the arrangements first thing in the morning," Carter said, and Gary nodded to confirm it.

"You'll be glad you did it. Now then, we've nearly finished interviewing your live-in staff, and I'd like to get them out of here until we're through tomorrow. Could you send them to a local motel, but keep them accessible for more questions?"

Carter glanced at Gary, who nodded and said, "I'll handle it."

"I understand you also employ two maids who live elsewhere. We'll be interviewing them tomorrow as soon as they arrive for work. After that, I'd like you to send them home." Satisfied that all that was out of the way, Hocklin got down to the business at hand: "I'm sorry to have to put you through more questions at this time, but it's imperative we get as much information as possible from you now, because your memories will be clearest. Detectives Flynn and Cagle have already talked to you individually, but it's helpful to gather you together as a group. Sometimes one member may say something that triggers another person's memory. Detective Flynn—" he said, nodding to the detective seated on his right.

Dennis Flynn was in his late forties, pudgy in build, average in height, with a round, jolly face that belonged on either an Irish priest or an Irish con artist. And yet, there was something about him that inspired confidence—and confidences, which Sloan assumed was probably why he'd been called out on this job.

Andy Cagle was his opposite. In his late twenties, Cagle was tall and thin, with a narrow face dominated by a pair of thick, studious-looking glasses that he was constantly pushing back up onto the bridge of his nose. There was a self-conscious awkwardness in everything he did. He actually apologized to Sloan three times for having to bother her with questions about her name and address and where she'd been that night. He looked like the sort of reticent, naïve boy-man who would rather apologize than disagree and who wouldn't know a lie if he was introduced to it by name. Sloan suspected he was actually the keener and more formidable of the two detectives.

Since Paul had instructed her to stick with their cover story, half of what Sloan told Detective Cagle had been a lie, but under the circumstances it made little difference whether she was an interior designer on vacation or a police detective working with the FBI: Edith Reynolds was dead either way. If Sloan had stayed home, Edith might still be alive. Sloan's only feeble consolation, and one she clung to, was that her great-grandmother had not suffered.

"Mr. Reynolds," Flynn began, "you said you got home around eleven P.M.?"

Sloan watched Carter's hand shake as he raked his hair back off his forehead. He was white-faced with shock, and her heart softened just a little toward him. Edith couldn't have been easy to live with, but he was clearly overwrought by the way she'd died. He nodded in answer to Flynn's question and cleared his throat. "That's right. I played poker with a group of friends until ten-forty-five. I drove straight home; that takes about fifteen minutes. I parked my car in the garage; then I went up to bed."

"Now, think carefully. When you drove up to the house, did you notice any vehicles parked on the street or notice anything suspicious at all?"

"You asked me that earlier, and I've been trying to think. It seems to me I saw a white van parked down the street."

"What did you notice about it?"

"Only that I'd seen a van like that there before one day this week."

Flynn nodded and made another note in his pad.

"You said you drove into the garage. There are four rear entrances into the house—one enters the kitchen from the garage and one enters the kitchen from the back lawn. The other two also open into the backyard but from different rooms. After you parked in the garage, which entrance did you use?"

Carter looked at him as if he were an imbecile. "I used

the door in the garage that opens into the kitchen, of course."

Unruffled by Carter's attitude, Detective Flynn made a note on his pad.

"Did you pass by the room where the victim was found on your way to your bedroom or hear any sounds in there?"

"No. I walked out of the kitchen and toward the staircase, then upstairs."

"Was it customary for Mrs. Reynolds to be alone in that room, with the door closed, in the evening?"

"Not with the door closed, but she liked that room in the evening because it looks out on the lawn, and it has a television set with a very large screen. She didn't like the solarium at night because she had to turn on so many lights in order to make it pleasant." Carter was sitting with his forearms propped on his knees, his hands folded, but now he put his head in his hands as if he couldn't bear the memory of what she had been like only a few hours before.

"Would you say it was customary for her to sit in there then, with the drapes open?"

He nodded.

"So if someone were watching the house from the beach, they would be able to ascertain that?"

His head jerked up. "Are you suggesting some psychopath has been lurking around here, night after night, waiting for a chance to murder her?"

"It's possible. Was Mrs. Reynolds handicapped in any way?"

"She was ninety-five years old. That's a handicap in itself."

"But she was able to walk?"

Carter nodded. "She got around extremely well for her age."

"How was her eyesight?"

"She needed thick glasses to read, but she's needed those for as long as I can remember."

"Was she hard-of-hearing?"

He swallowed audibly. "Only when she wanted to be. Why are you asking all this?"

"It's standard."

Flynn was lying, and Sloan knew it. Alarm bells had started ringing in her head as soon as Hocklin mentioned a broken window in the study. Edith should have been able to hear or see something that would have alerted her that someone was breaking in, and she'd have tried to flee. But she hadn't. When Sloan found her, she'd been lying face-down on the sofa. On the other hand, Sloan knew her joints were stiff and sometimes it took her a long time to stand up. Maybe she'd tried but couldn't do it in time. Either way Flynn and Cagle should know about her limitation. "Mrs. Reynolds had arthritis," Sloan said carefully, drawing Flynn and Cagle's instant attention. "I know that's not exactly a handicap, but it bothered her badly at times and made it especially hard for her to stand up if she felt stiff."

"I'm glad you thought to mention that, Miss Reynolds," Hocklin said quickly. "It could be helpful. Thank you."

She glanced at Paul, who was seated across from her on a sofa with Noah, to see how Paul was reacting to her having provided information the detectives hadn't thought to ask for. Paul was watching Paris, his expression as unreadable as it was intent.

Noah caught her eye and gave her a smile of quiet encouragement and support, and she wished devoutly that she could put her head on his broad shoulder and weep. She was a cop, and yet she hadn't been able to prevent a member of her own family from being murdered. She was a cop, schooled to notice anything suspicious off duty or on, and yet she'd quite possibly strolled within a few yards of Edith's murderer when she left the house for the beach, and she hadn't noticed *anything*.

"Miss Reynolds," Flynn said, looking at Paris after reviewing his notes. "You said you took some migraine medication in the afternoon and woke up around ten. Do you know what woke you up?"

"No. I'd been sleeping for hours, and the pills were probably wearing off."

"After you woke up, what did you do?"

"I told you—I felt like getting some air, and I went out onto the balcony."

"Did you see anything suspicious?"

"No, nothing that was suspicious."

"This is very close to time of death, and it appears the assailant entered through a study window. Your bedroom balcony isn't far from there."

"I know! But I didn't see *anything* suspicious."

"Nothing at all? Nothing the least bit unusual?"

"All I saw was Noah leaving the—" She stopped, looking so horrified that she almost made Noah look guilty. "Noah, I didn't mean—"

Detective Cagle spoke up for the first time. With that hesitant, uncertain expression, he said, "Mr. Maitland, you didn't mention that you'd come to the house. You said you'd met Miss Reynolds on the beach."

Noah seemed unconcerned with the direction the questioning had suddenly taken. "I'd started across the lawn and gotten partway to the house when I saw a woman walking on the beach who could have been Sloan, so I stopped and waited until I was sure it was her; then I walked back to the beach. Which is, technically, where I met her."

"Are you in the habit of coming here late in the evening, without calling first?"

"I called first, but no one answered."

"What time did you call?"

"Fifteen minutes before I decided to walk over here. The answering machine picked up the call."

"That's right, it did," Gary Dishler interjected firmly. "Nordstrom goes to bed early, because he gets up very early, so I handle any phone calls that come in after nine-thirty. I had heard the phone ringing when I was taking a shower, but by the time I got to the phone in my room to answer it, Mr. Maitland had hung up. I played back the message on the answering machine to make certain the call wasn't something I needed to deal with. Mr. Maitland had left a short message for Miss Reynolds. He made something of a joke about knowing she was here and coming over to throw rocks at her balcony window. I used the intercom to call Miss Reynolds's room, but she wasn't there. I paged her on the house intercom and she didn't answer. I assumed that she'd gone outdoors."

"Did you do anything else?"

"Yes, before I went to bed a short while later, I disarmed the infrared beams so they wouldn't go on with the rest of the security system, which goes on automatically at midnight."

"Why did you disarm the beams?"

"So that Miss Reynolds or Mr. Maitland could walk across the yard after midnight if they chose, without tripping the beams and setting off the alarm. It's quite simple to disarm the beams, although I had to look it up in the instruction manual when Miss Reynolds first arrived."

"Why is that?"

"Because Miss Reynolds enjoys running on the beach at early hours and walking on it at late hours. Mr. Reynolds and Miss Paris do not indulge in those activities."

Sloan had always had ambivalent feelings about Dishler, so she was surprised when he went out of his way to loyally shield her, as well as Noah, from further suspicion. He sounded like he had picked up on the detectives' doubts about Noah's phone call and Sloan's late-night jaunt on the beach and was determined to set them straight. "No one has bothered to ask me, however, I can also verify that Mr. Maitland never reached the house because I had gone to my window to open it to let in the night air. I saw Mr. Maitland start across the back lawn, stop, and then start back toward the beach."

"Did you see Miss Reynolds?"

"No, I did not. I did notice that Mr. Maitland was angling to the north of the property, not to the south, where his house lies. Knowing what I now know, I assume Miss Reynolds must have been returning from the north when he saw her, and he crossed the property in that direction to intercept her."

Cagle looked gratified and impressed and deeply, deeply apologetic. "I did not mean to imply any suspicion of Miss Reynolds or Mr. Maitland. I just wanted to know where everyone was, and when they were there, so we can rule those locations out when we're searching the grounds and house for evidence tomorrow. I haven't been with the department very long. Think of me as sort of an apprentice—"

He shot an apologetic look at everyone in the room, including Captain Hocklin, pushed his glasses up onto his nose, and tried to look invisible while Detective Flynn took over.

"We're just about finished for tonight," Flynn said. "Mr. Richardson, you said you were away for the day on business and returned about eleven P.M.?"

"That's right."

"And you rang the call button at the gate, spoke to Mr. Dishler on the intercom, and he let you in?"

"That's right."

"Thank you, sir."

"That's correct," Dishler added.

"And thank you, sir," Flynn said cheerfully.

"Miss Reynolds?" he said, looking at Sloan. "Would you mind going over the last part of the evening for me again? You said you had dinner with the victim. What happened after that, please?"

Sloan reached up and rubbed her temples without realizing her head was beginning to pound. "After dinner, I watched television with her in the room where you found her, until about nine-thirty; then I decided to go upstairs and write a letter. Mrs. Reynolds is very fond of game shows, particularly *Jeopardy!*, and I'd already sat through three of them with her. I didn't think I could handle another one. She's very intense about them and doesn't like to talk unless a commercial is on. I'd been sitting for hours, and when I got upstairs, I decided I felt more like going for a walk than sitting down again to write."

Detective Flynn was very understanding and sympathetic. "I hope you aren't blaming yourself for leaving her when you did. If you hadn't, it's likely you would have been killed by the same intruder."

"Maybe," Sloan said, feeling a surge of fury at the monster who had done this and at herself for not being there to stop it. If she hadn't been so wrapped up with Noah, this might never have happened.

A chill ran through her entire body, and she shivered. Noah saw it, and annoyance put a sharp edge on his voice as he scowled at the police captain. "You've had enough questions answered to keep you busy tonight," he said shortly. "Let these people get some rest."

To Sloan's relief, the captain stood up at once, looking apologetic. The detectives followed his lead. "You're right, Mr. Maitland."

Carter went up to bed immediately, and Paris got up to follow him. She looked like a walking ghost, her face ashen and expressionless, a handkerchief clutched in her fist, but she hadn't let herself break down in front of strangers. Sloan walked as far as the doorway with her, then stopped, and she saw Paris's control start to slip. "Aren't you coming up to bed, too?" Paris asked, her voice beginning to shake. She sounded frightened about being alone, a reaction to everything that had happened that Sloan understood from experience.

"In a few minutes," Sloan promised. "I want to talk to

Paul first. I was wondering," Sloan added gently, "if you'd mind staying in my room tonight? It's a huge bed, and—"

Paris was already nodding with relief, and Sloan wrapped her in a tight hug, trying to infuse her with some of her own strength. When Sloan turned away, she caught a glimpse of herself in the mirror, but she did not acknowledge that she looked almost as drawn as Paris or that she was shaking inside with sorrow and exhaustion.

Noah noticed the signs, however, and with Carter out of the room, he dropped the pretense of being a family friend. Ignoring Paul, he pulled Sloan into his arms and cupped her face to his chest. "Come home with me," he said in an aching whisper. "We'll look after you. Don't stay here tonight, sweetheart."

It was the first time he'd used an endearment, and the poignant tenderness of it was almost Sloan's undoing. She was so accustomed to looking after other people, of being their strength, that she almost wept at the realization that Noah was there to offer her *his* strength. "I can't," she said, but a tear slipped down her cheek. His thumb softly brushed it away, and another tear followed it. Tenderness was accomplishing what adversity couldn't—Sloan was on the brink of losing control.

"I'll be all right," she said, pulling out of his arms and impatiently brushing at her eyes. She caught a glimpse of Paul watching them, and for a moment he looked so infuriated that she froze; then she concentrated on Noah. "I'll be fine, really," she said with a fixed smile, and when he still looked dubious, she tucked her arm through his and walked him to the back door.

36

As Sloan expected, Paul had already gone up to his room, where they could talk in privacy. He'd left the door slightly open for her, and she walked inside, closing it behind her.

He was standing at the window, a drink in his hand, watching Noah walk across the lawn on his way home. "It's been quite a fucking night," he said wrathfully as he closed the window and turned around. Except for the anger she'd glimpsed when Noah was leaving, Paul had played the part of a shocked, well-bred insurance salesman all night, but now he looked as furious as he sounded.

He motioned to a pair of comfortable chairs with footstools near the bed. "What the hell is going on between you and Maitland?" he demanded.

It was none of his business, but Sloan was too startled to be offended. On the other hand, she didn't think she owed him any details, either. "What do you think is going on?" she asked mildly as she sat down across from him.

"Based on what I've observed during the last week," he said sarcastically, "I assumed the two of you were probably having a little fling. But it's more than that, isn't it? I saw that little scene before he left, and I saw the way you were looking at him tonight."

"So what?" Sloan said defensively.

His jaw tightened. "How can you be so smart about everything else, and so damned stupid about him? By your own words, he's got an arsenal on one boat and a sizable stash of firearms on the sailboat."

"People with boats keep firearms aboard! He's not selling them or trafficking in them. There are ports all over the globe that aren't completely safe. Noah is protecting his life, his crew, and his property!"

"With a machine gun?" Paul mocked angrily. "With a room full of automatic weapons? It sounds to me like he might have some sort of cargo he needs to protect."

"That cargo remark is ridiculous, and I told you, he confiscated the machine gun. Furthermore, I never said those weapons were automatic."

"You couldn't tell because you weren't close enough to examine them!"

"I had no idea you were worried about all that," Sloan said, trying to keep her temper under tight control. "If it will put your mind at rest, I'll ask Noah to show them to me again."

"No. Don't do that. Just let it alone! Look, I just don't want you to get too emotionally involved with the man. I don't give a damn if you've been to bed with him; you're both adults. However, I made the stupid assumption that that wouldn't happen, based on your past history. You sure as hell didn't sleep around in Bell Harbor!"

"How would you know?" Sloan demanded irately.

"How would I know?" he repeated with biting sarcasm. "I know when you got your first permanent tooth! How the hell do you think I know?" Leaning forward, he braced his forearms on his knees and glared at his drink as he rolled the glass between his hands. When he spoke again, he sounded more weary and worried than angry. "How involved are you with Maitland, emotionally, I mean?"

He asked the question with an almost paternal concern, and Sloan responded firmly but without any rancor. "That's none of your business."

He reached the correct conclusion on his own, and his lips quirked in a sardonic half smile as he stared at his glass and stated his conclusion: "That sounds pretty damned involved . . ."

"Paul?"

He looked up at her.

"Why are we talking about Noah when someone in this house has been murdered? Didn't anything about that session in the living room just now strike you as a little odd?"

To her relief, he didn't persist in discussing Noah. "I don't know. I suppose I was distracted. What specifically are you referring to?"

"They said a window was broken in the study and the murderer supposedly came in that way. That makes no sense. The drapes were open and she was in plain view, watching television. Even if she didn't see him at first, she would have heard the glass break."

"Maybe not, if he was quiet enough and the television set was loud enough to distract her."

"But why would a thief take a chance like that when he could have broken in through one of the other rooms? And why didn't she notice him as he was breaking in, and then try to escape?"

"Her vision wasn't good and the windows were on her left. If she was concentrating on television, she might not have seen him until it was too late."

"Her vision wasn't good, but she was a long way from being blind! She was found on the sofa, which means the murderer had to break the window, open it, crawl in, then stroll over to her and shoot her before she noticed him. Either that," Sloan finished meaningfully, "or she didn't think she needed to be afraid of whoever shot her."

"The medical examiner will be able to tell who was where when it happened."

Sloan had the feeling he was still preoccupied with Noah for some reason, and it frustrated her to the point of anger or tears. "Can't you see where I'm going with all this?"

"Yes, of course I can," he said with a grim sigh. "With the exception of the broken window, it points to an inside job."

"Sooner or later, Flynn and Cagle are going to run me through the system. I'm sure your cover will hold up, but they won't even have to glance twice to find out I'm not an interior designer in Bell Harbor."

"I'm hoping they'll do it later, rather than sooner. After

all, you're an unlikely suspect. Why break into a house you already have a key to?"

"To make it look like an outside job," Sloan said wearily. She leaned her head back and closed her eyes.

"Andy Cagle is sharp. He'll run me through the system even if it's to rule me out. You should let me tell them the truth, so they can eliminate me as a suspect and concentrate on real possibilities. I think I should talk to them first thing in the morning."

"No," he said sharply. "There's too much chance Carter would find out. I need thirty-six hours before that happens. In thirty-six hours it won't matter."

Sloan opened her eyes and stared at him. "What's happening in thirty-six hours?"

He frowned at his drink again, rolling the glass between his hands. "I can't tell you."

"I'm getting really tired of that—"

"Believe me," he said tightly, "I want to tell you, I would have told you at this point—but I can't. Not after tonight."

Sloan thought he was referring to Edith's murder tonight. She couldn't imagine any sort of connection, but it was obvious he wasn't going to give her a word to go on. "Do you have any hunches about who might have done this tonight, or is that another 'secret' you feel you need to keep?" she asked bitterly.

To her surprise, he actually gave her a complete answer. "That depends. If Flynn and Cagle have something substantial that points to an assisted burglary, I'd start with the local maids, not the regular staff who lives in. Reynolds told me more than once that they've been with the family for years. In any case, whoever the actual perp was used a nine-millimeter weapon, because I saw the casing on the floor, and he was also an amateur."

"You mean because he took so many chances by entering through the study—if he did enter that way?"

"No, because he overlooked some items a pro wouldn't have left behind. While you were outside trying to track him down, I was in the study with Paris. The diamond ring Edith always wore had been taken off her hand, but the perp overlooked a very expensive diamond brooch as well as the ring on her other hand. That's another reason for Cagle and Flynn to discount you as a suspect: Why would you go through the trouble to fake a break-in, kill her, and then leave her valuables behind?"

When Sloan didn't come up with an answer, he said, "By the way, what made you search at the front of the house rather than the rear?"

"I'd just walked through the backyard with Noah and hadn't seen anyone there or on the beach. I knew the front was a long shot, but I had to try."

Weariness was crashing over Sloan in tidal waves, and the tears she'd been fighting threatened to slip from her eyes. She thought of Edith's body on the sofa, her hair still perfectly arranged, her dress primly covering her knees. Someone had stolen her life and her jewelry, but even in death, she'd kept her dignity. Sloan drew a shaky breath and brushed away a tear. "I can't believe she's dead."

"It will hit you tomorrow," Paul said with the philosophical certainty of one who has been here and seen this all many times before. "Let's get some sleep. You're going to need it, and so will I."

Sloan hadn't realized until then how drawn he actually looked. He'd said he was "distracted," but she had a peculiar feeling he was worried. Very worried. He always seemed so utterly self-assured and resolute that it was difficult to imagine him any other way.

"I'll see you in the morning," she said.

In her bedroom, Sloan pulled off her clothes and pulled on an old T-shirt that Sara hadn't removed from the suitcases. Careful not to disturb Paris, she slipped into bed and fell into an instant, troubled sleep.

37

The call Dennis Flynn was waiting for came in at ten-thirty A.M., while he was slumped in his chair in front of his computer terminal, watching the computer banks at the Regional Organized Crime Information Center in Nashville answer his final query with another blank report. He'd already typed in all the other names on his list of family, friends, and employees at the Reynolds residence.

At the desk in front of his, Andy Cagle swiveled his chair around and pushed his glasses up on his nose. He'd already interviewed the remaining housemaids earlier and had finished writing his report. "Anything interesting coming in from ROC?"

"Nothing," Flynn said. "Zero. Zilch. According to ROC, the Reynolds household is one great big bunch of law-abiding citizens."

The phone on his desk rang, and he picked it up; then he straightened expectantly when he recognized the caller's voice. "Tell me something good," he said to the lieutenant in charge of the investigation team at the Reynolds house. "What have you got?"

"We've got a burglary that wasn't a burglary."

"What do you mean?"

"I mean that nothing seems to be missing, other than one of the old lady's wedding rings, which we already knew about last night."

Flynn's brow furrowed. "You sure?"

"We've been going room to room with the butler, the assistant, the housekeeper, and Paris Reynolds. None of them can spot anything that's been disturbed or taken except in the study."

"That's it?"

"We're still looking, but that's it so far."

"That's bad," Flynn said, watching Captain Hocklin pacing in his office. "The press is all over the place like a swarm of wasps and more of them are arriving by the minute. CNN is camped on our doorstep, the *Enquirer* is trying to sneak in through the men's room window, and MSNBC is looking for a place to park. Hocklin has already had calls from the mayor and three senators, demanding a quick arrest; he hasn't had any sleep, and he is a little cranky. Be a hero, give me something to tell him to get him off my ass."

"Okay," Lieutenant Fineman said. "Try this: The window in the study was broken from the inside."

"We figured that last night."

"Yeah, but now we're sure. Also, we've ruled out the front fence as an escape route. The flower beds are clean, no footprints. What have you got from the ME?"

"Not much so far. Time of death approximately ten o'clock. Based on the angle of entry, she was shot from a distance of three feet. She was sitting on the sofa, and the assailant was standing. That's all we've got. Keep in touch."

Flynn hung up and looked at Cagle. "Nothing's missing over there," he said, and his cheerful mask fell away. He put his hand behind his nape, wearily massaging the tense muscles. "Now what?"

"Now we stop looking for a burglar with a bad temper and start looking for someone who was in that house last night who had a motive for murder. I checked with the neighbors on both sides of the Reynolds house, and they have infrared beams that were operational last night at ten P.M., so the murderer didn't scale the fence on the sides of the property. He didn't go out the back, or Maitland and Sloan Reynolds would have seen him."

Flynn sighed. "He didn't go over the fence at the front, because Fineman just told me there are no footprints in the flower beds out there."

"Which means our man—or our woman—was very likely right there, chatting with us last night."

Flynn rocked absently in his chair, then leaned forward abruptly and picked up a pencil. "Okay, let's go down the list of names, one by one, for motive and means. Everyone there had opportunity. Wait—" he said. "Now that we know we aren't looking for a career criminal, let's give a copy of this list to Hank Little and let him start checking them out with DBT."

"I took the liberty of doing that earlier," Cagle replied with a modest smile. Access to the ROC data banks was limited to law enforcement agencies. It was free of charge and available to all the personnel at Palm Beach PD on their own computer terminals.

By contrast, it cost one dollar per minute to query the giant data banks at Data Base Technologies in Pompano Beach, and access was available to a variety of legitimate users, from insurance companies to credit bureaus. Police departments all over the country used their services, but when they went on-line, their access was cloaked to prevent anyone else from seeing who was checking out whom. "In a few minutes Hank should be wheeling over a forklift full of files," Cagle joked, referring to the enormous output of information that DBT generated on even the most uninteresting citizen.

"Okay," Flynn replied. "Let's get some coffee and start down the list."

As the junior member of the duo, Cagle accepted the getting of coffee as part of his role. He returned with two cups of strong, black coffee and put them on Flynn's desk; then he swiveled his chair around so they could work together.

"If murder was the intent, I think we can tentatively rule out the butler, cook, housekeeper, and caretaker," Flynn said.

"Why? I got the feeling during the interviews that the old lady was cantankerous as hell."

He smirked. "If she was that bad, the cook or one of the others would have helped her get dead before now. They've put up with her for years." He drew a line through those four names. "The housemaids you interviewed this morning give you any reason to believe they would risk prison to have her murdered?"

Cagle shook his head; then he took a sip of scalding coffee while Flynn crossed off two more names.

"What about Dishler?" Flynn asked.

"I don't think so. He's worked for Reynolds for several years, and he's obviously loyal. He was pretty quick to confirm Maitland's story. Seems like a long shot."

"I agree, but let's check him out," Flynn said. "What about Maitland?"

"What's his motive?"

Flynn rolled the pencil between his fingers. "I don't like him."

"Then why are we wasting time? Let's get a warrant," Cagle said dryly. When Flynn continued to scowl thoughtfully at his pencil, Cagle became curious. "Why don't you like him?"

"I had a run-in with him a year ago when I tried to question his little sister about some pals of hers who we knew were getting drugs from somewhere."

"And?"

"And he's got a temper. He's arrogant as hell, and his attorneys are a pack of Dobermans. I know, because he turned them loose on us after that minor episode."

"Then let's skip the warrant and toss his ass in jail," Cagle said straight-faced.

Flynn ignored that. "His kid sister's a brat. She kept calling me 'Sherlock.' "

"Hell, let's throw her in jail with him." When Flynn glowered at him, Cagle urged mildly, "Can we move on to someone more likely?"

"There's hardly anyone left." He looked at the list. "Paris Reynolds?"

Cagle nodded thoughtfully. "Possible."

"Why?" Flynn said. "Give me a motive."

"When I asked Carter Reynolds about his grandmother's will, he told me that he and Paris are the sole beneficiaries."

Flynn let out a mirthless guffaw. "Are you suggesting that either one of them are in urgent need of money?"

"Maybe Paris got tired of waiting for her share. Maybe she wanted to be independent of Daddy."

"But Edith Reynolds was already ninety-five. She couldn't live much longer."

"I know, but don't cross Paris off the list yet."

"Okay, I won't. What about the insurance guy—Richardson?"

"Sure, right," Cagle said with a snort. "He drops in for a visit with his girlfriend—who is not an heir to anything, according to Reynolds, and who therefore has nothing to gain by Edith Reynolds's death. Not only that, but he accomplishes the deed by remote control, because, according to Dishler, Richardson didn't return until about eleven."

"You're right," Flynn said. "I'm more tired than I realized. I forgot about the alibi." He crossed off Paul Richardson. "What about Carter Reynolds? He said he didn't get home until eleven, and Dishler confirmed it, but Dishler might lie for his employer."

Cagle nodded. "Dishler might, but I don't think Senator Meade would. He was one of the people who called this morning to demand an immediate arrest of someone."

"So?"

"So, according to Captain Hocklin, during the senator's rampage, he mentioned that he'd been playing cards with poor Carter last night while the murder was taking place."

"How did he know when it took place?"

"It's all over the newscasts."

"True," Flynn said with a sigh. "Besides, Reynolds doesn't have a motive. He's put up with his grandma for almost sixty years, and he doesn't need money."

"Not only that, but I don't think he could have faked his reaction last night. Not only did he act distraught, his face was gray with shock."

"I noticed." Flynn crossed out Carter Reynolds's name. "That leaves us with Sloan Reynolds."

Cagle brightened. "Now *that* is an interesting situation. She's never met any of them before this, never been around them, and suddenly one of them turns up dead."

"I know, but that's hardly a way for her to ingratiate herself with her new, rich family."

Cagle balked seriously at ruling her out on such a flimsy excuse. "She was there; she had opportunity."

"What's her motive?"

"Revenge for being left out all these years?"

"Nah. It would have made more sense for her to keep Grandma alive and try to ingratiate herself with the old lady. Sloan wasn't an heir, but if Grandma had lived a little longer, she might have been able to persuade her to cut her in for a little piece of the financial pie. As it is, she comes out with nothing."

"Nothing but revenge," Cagle reminded him.

"What's your problem with Sloan Reynolds?" Flynn

asked, but despite the light sarcasm that flavored his tone, he wasn't discounting Cagle's hunches. The kid was a marvel with hunches, observant as hell, and he chased down every potential lead, no matter how much effort it took. "You started harping on her as a suspect as soon as we left the house, when we were still thinking theft was the motive. Now it's murder and you're still after her."

"Among other things, the timing of her departure and return is mighty convenient. Also, I couldn't help noticing how smoothly she managed to tell us that even though Edith Reynolds wasn't handicapped, she couldn't move quickly. I had the feeling she knew we were angling toward the perp being someone known to the victim because Edith Reynolds evidently hadn't tried to escape."

Flynn thought that over and nodded slightly. "I'll buy that, but she sure doesn't strike me as fitting the profile for premeditated murder. You have to want a whole lot of revenge real bad to get up the courage to find yourself a gun, plan the thing, and then point the gun at a helpless old lady and shoot her. Besides, if she wanted revenge for being left out all these years, why not shoot Daddy for it?"

Cagle drummed his fingers on the desk, paused to push up his glasses, and looked around at Hank, who was in a glass-partitioned room, linked up with DBT. "Hey, Hank," he called. "How much longer?"

"Not long."

"You know what I think?" Cagle said.

"You've got to be kidding. I never know what you think or why you think it."

Cagle ignored the good-natured gibe. "There's only

one significant detail we haven't verified. Do you have the name of Edith Reynolds's attorney—the one Reynolds said had prepared her will?"

Flynn picked up his notebook and begin flipping through page after page of notes. "Wilson," he said finally.

"Let's go have a personal chat with Mr. Wilson," Cagle said, standing up and stretching. "The exercise will do us good—help build up our strength so we can go through the DBT records."

38

Paul was sitting out by the pool, watching the crime team meticulously searching through the bushes at the rear of the house. "They're looking for a weapon," he told Sloan as she sat down on the edge of a chair beside his.

Sloan nodded absently and raked her hair off her forehead.

"Gary Dishler was looking for you," he added. "Maitland's telephoned twice, and he wants you to call him back—immediately. The crime scene team won't let him past the line."

"Gary told me. I'm going to go over there in a few minutes, but I need to talk to you first."

Paul heard the tension in her voice, he saw how pale she was, and he felt guiltier at this moment than he'd felt in years. She was going through hell, and he was about to make it a hundred times worse for her. He had an insane urge to pull her off to the side, tip her chin up, and beg her forgiveness in advance. *"Forgive me. You didn't deserve this. I've been so proud of you so many times. I think you're wonderful."* "What's up?" he asked.

"I've been tagging along with Paris and Lieutenant Fineman, and also eavesdropping when I can get away with it. Nothing is missing, Paul. No one broke in here, and nothing was stolen except for the diamond ring. I saw the crime team picking up glass from the broken window. Most of it was outside in the shrubbery, not inside. Someone intended to murder her. I believe it was meant to look like a burglary that went bad. And I believe the murderer was someone living in this house. Someone she knew."

He was listening attentively, but his attention shifted to Paris the moment she appeared outside with a tray of soft drinks. "I agree."

"I'm going to become a chief suspect."

His gaze flicked to her. "You? Why you?"

"I'm the long-lost daughter. I come here for the first time, Edith is murdered, and her ring disappears."

"A grudge murder? If you were going to take someone out for that, you'd take good old Carter, who's neglected you until now, or maybe Paris, since she's had all the goodies all these years instead of you."

On one level, Sloan knew he was right, and she felt a little better.

Paul continued watching Paris for a moment as she stopped to talk politely to each crime-scene-team member and to offer him something cool to drink; then he gave Sloan his attention and tried to add on smiling reassurance. "Now, if you were a beneficiary of Edith's, that would be different."

Sloan smiled with the memory. "She wanted to make me one. She called me into the solarium and tried to give me some heirloom jewelry, then started talking about changing her will. I refused to discuss any of it."

Paul's smile faded abruptly. "Did you happen to mention any of that to Paris?"

"I don't think so—yes, I did. It came up at lunch later that day."

His jaw tightened, he turned his head toward Paris, watching her with blazing intensity. His curse was low and infuriated. *"Son of a bitch!"*

"You can't be thinking what I think you are!" Sloan scoffed.

He seemed not to hear; it was as if every fiber of his being was concentrated on the scene he was watching. "Son of a bitch!"

"You're being ridiculous!" She grabbed his arm to get his attention, and he tore his gaze from Paris.

"Am I?" he mocked bitingly. "Stop being a blind fool about your sister, Sloan. Open your eyes. This is reality: Your sister didn't want you to come here in the first place. I never had the heart to tell you that, but I knew it from our informant."

Sloan brushed that aside. "I know that. Edith told me. For her entire life, Paris was led to believe my mother and I were some sort of trash—worse than that. Of course she felt that way, but not after we met."

"Right," he sneered. "It took Paris less than a day to reverse the feelings of an entire lifetime. In one day, she turned herself into your loving big sister. Doesn't it strike you as a little too 'nice'?"

"No! It doesn't!"

"Then consider this. For thirty years, she's been an emotional slave to her father and great-grandmother, but you walk in here and in less than a week, Great-grandma starts lavishing you with her brand of affection; then she wants to cut you in for part of Paris's share of her money. Not only have you stolen Great-grandma's love and money from Paris, you've also stolen the man she was supposed to marry. And after all that, you think Paris doesn't hate your guts? And while we're on the subject, don't you find it just a little odd that 'sweet, gentle, timid' Paris would fly helicopters for a hobby?"

"You don't understand her—"

"Neither do you," he snapped. "It would take a team of shrinks to figure her out, and I'd be afraid to read their report."

Staggered, Sloan gazed up at him. "You hate her, don't you?"

"Hate her?" He laughed tightly. "Half the time she scares the hell out of me."

"My God, I think she's half in love with you, and you think she's some kind of monster."

"She's either a monster or a saint, and I don't believe in saints. That leaves the monster."

Sloan shook her head, completely bemused and immensely saddened. "I thought you cared about her. I really did." Sloan couldn't stop staring at him, searching his face for some sort of clue as to the man he really was. "I know this assignment is 'business' for you, but sometimes, I'd catch you watching Paris with a funny smile . . . almost a tender smile."

"She's easy to watch," he said bitterly. "Look at her—" He tipped his head toward Paris, who was chatting with one of the men. "She's beautiful, she's graceful, she's well-bred. She's a little shy until you get to know her, and then she blooms in front of your eyes, and you think you're the reason."

Sloan was becoming more stunned by the moment. She hadn't misjudged Paul's attraction to Paris. He was very attracted—and completely against his will. Sloan found that situation encouraging and amusing.

"Tell me something," she said. "If Paris was all the good things you think she is and none of the bad, sick things you think she is, then how would you describe her?"

Paul's eyes lifted briefly and unwillingly to the subject of their discussion as she reentered the house. "I'd describe her as a miracle."

Sloan stood up, suppressing a smile. "That works for me."

He shrugged. "Unfortunately, I don't believe in miracles."

Shoving her hands into the back pockets of her slacks, Sloan gazed down at the man sitting in the chair. "Paris is just like my mother—they're like little willow trees. They seem fragile and they bend in the breeze, but you can't break them. They won't let you. Somehow they always find a reason, a way, to go on thriving. You start out thinking they're weak and they need sheltering, and they do. But while you're shielding them, they're sheltering you. My mother baffled me forever, and until now I'd never met anyone like her. But my sister Paris is just like her."

Paul looked at her steadily, debating whether he ought to point out the truth, and then he decided to do it. "You're wrong, Sloan," he said quietly. "That's not Paris. That's you."

He got up and walked away, leaving her staring after him in amazement.

"Mr. Richardson?" Paul turned at the sound of the butler's voice. "You have an urgent telephone call from your office."

Paul hurried up to his room and picked up the phone. It was the call he'd been waiting for, and the news was not only good, it had come a day sooner than he'd expected.

"Paul," the other agent said, using terms that would be meaningful only to Paul while he relayed the news that a federal judge had just signed a search warrant authorizing the FBI to search Maitland's boats. "Sorry to bother you on vacation, but we have great news. The client signed the contract. I have it in my hand. Do you want to wait until tomorrow to countersign it? Or shall I bring it down there today?"

"Today. Definitely today. The Reynolds family won't miss me or mind if I'm gone because there's been a death in the family."

"I heard. So sad." The man paused an appropriate moment to sound as if he cared; then he asked Paul whether he wanted only the FBI involved when they boarded the boats today, or whether Paul wanted participation from the Coast Guard and/or the Bureau of Alcohol, Tobacco, and Firearms as well. "There are a couple details about the group policy I wasn't clear on. Do you want an exclusion clause for smokers?"

"No, don't exclude them."

"What about accidental death coverage?"

"Include that, too. That makes it a solid package. No loose ends, no matter what happens. How soon can you get the package put together?"

"We went ahead with plans in the hopes the client would sign the contract. I can have everything ready in an hour or two if I move fast."

"Get moving. I'll meet you out at the job site and show you around personally. The more daylight we have the better."

Paul hung up and breathed a sigh of relief.

39

Rather than returning Noah's telephone call, Sloan went to see him. She had something to tell him, and she didn't want to do it on the phone.

Courtney had been enrolled in a Palm Beach private school, and it was Douglas who let her in, gave her a reassuring hug, and told her how sorry he was about Edith. "Noah is upstairs in his office, and he'll be very glad to see you." Confidingly, he added, "You may interpret that to mean he's like a caged bear because he hasn't been able to talk to you and find out how you are."

Upstairs Sloan waved at Mrs. Snowden, who occupied a small office next to Noah's.

Noah was on the telephone, carrying on what sounded like an important phone call, when he looked up and saw Sloan in his doorway. "I'll talk to you later," he said, and unceremoniously hung up on whomever he was talking to. He came around his desk and wrapped Sloan in a fierce embrace. "I've been worried sick about you. How are you holding up, darling?"

"Okay," Sloan whispered, her cheek pressed to the

reassuring strength of his chest. He'd called her darling, and the sweetness of the word combined with the tenderness in his voice was so touching that Sloan had to fight a sudden impulse to cry.

"Have the cops found anything significant over there?"

"It's what they *haven't* found that's significant," Sloan said, reluctantly lifting her face off his chest and tipping her head back.

Noah took in her pale complexion and the haunted expression in her violet eyes. "Tell me about it on the way downstairs. I'll have Claudine fix us something to eat. You look like a ghost. I wish you had stayed here last night and let us look after you."

The concept of being looked after by someone who was actually more capable than she was a new one to Sloan, and in her emotional state, it was as poignant as being called darling.

He put his arm around her waist as they walked downstairs. "I have something to tell you, and I'd like to do it privately, without Douglas," Sloan said. He nodded and took her to the living room, a dramatic area with a soaring ceiling, white marble floor, and full-length windows that looked out over the front lawn, where a fountain was splashing water over a life-size bronze sailfish. Noah's house was airy and light and so much more beautiful to Sloan than Carter's.

"Very little was stolen last night," she began as he sat down next to her on the sofa, but Noah's first priority was evidently looking after her. Before she could tell him anything more, he reached for the telephone and pressed the intercom button. He asked Claudine to serve them lunch in the living room; then he gave Sloan his full attention.

"No one broke into the house," she began again. "Someone wanted it to look like a break-in, but most of the broken glass was outside, which means the window was broken from the inside. The only thing missing so far is a ring Edith was wearing, but her other ring and her brooch hadn't been taken from her. The motive wasn't robbery, Noah; it was murder."

His brow furrowed slightly as he tried to imagine why anyone would want to murder Edith. "Are you certain?"

"As certain as anyone can be without an admission from the person who did it."

"That's almost unbelievable. She rarely went out; she couldn't have made an enemy of anyone. Who could possibly want to murder her?"

Sloan drew a long breath and looked straight into his eyes. "I think the police will put me on top of the suspect list."

"You?" he said with a laugh. "You?" he repeated. "Why in God's name would anyone think you would want to murder her or that you're capable of violence?"

Sloan was entirely capable of dealing in violence, but she couldn't go into that. Instead, she told him why the police would suspect her. Noah listened in silence, his amusement slowly vanishing as she spoke. He was not, Sloan realized with relief, naïve about the workings of the law, nor did he try to convince her that she had nothing to worry about because she was innocent. In fact, he did something that amazed her.

As soon as she finished speaking, he reached for the intercom and spoke to Mrs. Snowden. "Find Robbins wherever he is, and then get Kirsh on the phone. He's staying here in town at the Windsor."

He hung up, and in answer to Sloan's questioning look, he said, "Robbins is my security chief, and Kirsh is one of the best criminal lawyers in Florida. He's at my hotel."

Sloan's eyes widened. "Kenneth Kirsh?"

"The very same," he said with a reassuring smile.

Mrs. Snowden had Kirsh on the line in less than a minute, and Noah picked up the phone. "Ken, I need you over here right now." He'd scarcely hung up when Mrs. Snowden buzzed him on the intercom again to say that Robbins was on the line.

Noah picked up the phone. "Where are you?"

"Good. You can be here in two hours." He listened for a minute. "This is more important."

Kenneth Kirsh was a little shorter than he'd seemed when Sloan had seen him on national news programs talking about the last guilty criminal he helped escape punishment. To law enforcement officials everywhere, he was a scourge. To Sloan at that moment, he looked awfully good.

He listened attentively while she told him what she knew and what she feared would happen. He did not dismiss the possibility that Sloan would be treated like a major suspect, but like Paul he found some reassurance in the fact that Sloan had nothing financial to gain by Edith Reynolds's death. "I take it you haven't been con-

victed of any violent crime in the past?" he said half jokingly, and when Sloan told him she hadn't, he smiled and
handed her his card. "Call me if they bring you in for
questioning." He reached out and shook Noah's hand.
"Thank you for thinking of me. I'm flattered," he said.

Sloan was still digesting the fact that the arrogant
Kenneth Kirsh was flattered by an opportunity to stop his
vacation and report to Noah's house when she looked at
her watch. "I need to go back to the house," she told
Noah. "I don't want to leave Paris alone too long. Carter
is handling funeral arrangements, but Paris has her hands
full and she looks ready to drop."

"I want to make a couple more phone calls to make
sure we're prepared for any eventuality, so I'll let you walk
back alone this time," Noah said, pulling her into his
arms for a kiss.

"I think I can manage that," Sloan said, trying to tease.

"Yes, but I don't like it," he said with a somber smile at
her upturned face. "I like walking you home. I'd like carrying your books, too, and passing you notes after class."

Sloan looked at him in confusion, and he kissed her
again before he tenderly explained, "You make me feel
like a high school boy in love for the very first time."

In love? Sloan searched his tanned face, noticing the
tenderness in his eyes, the smile touching his firm lips,
and she knew he meant it. His smile deepened as she
gazed at him, and she realized that he was *telling* her he
meant it.

40

"This must be one hell of an emergency for you to pull me off the Atlanta job," Jack Robbins said as he closed the door to Noah's office two hours later. "What's up?"

Noah looked up at the stocky, energetic man who was in charge of security for all of Noah's ventures around the world. Like many of the men who headed security for high-profile clients, Robbins was a former FBI agent. At fifty, he was the image of a pleasant, physically fit, easygoing businessman. Beneath that image, he was tough, tenacious, and tireless. Noah regarded him as one of his greatest business assets. He was also the only employee whom Noah allowed to be a friend as well.

"I'm not sure what's up," Noah replied, leaning back in his chair. "It's probably nothing, but I want to make sure it keeps being 'nothing.' Did you know Edith Reynolds was murdered last night?"

"It's been all over the newscasts, but the way I heard it, it was a burglary that went bad."

"I don't think it was." Noah told him who Sloan was and then relayed the information that she had given him.

When he was finished, he said, "They're going to be looking for someone to pin this on who had access to the house or was around at the time of the murder."

Robbins frowned in confusion. "You can't think they'll seriously consider you a suspect?"

"I wouldn't give a damn if they did."

"Then why am I here?"

"I don't want them to consider Sloan as one."

Robbins studied his employer in silence for a long moment and began to grin. "So that's the way it is?"

He expected Noah to either deny it or ignore the comment. Instead, Noah nodded. "That's the way it is."

Robbins's smile widened, and he said softly, "I'll be damned."

"Probably. But before you are, I want to make sure they find the real killer, rather than contenting themselves with Sloan because she's the newcomer on the scene. Palm Beach doesn't exactly have a high homicide rate, and the cops aren't used to investigating them."

"If Sloan Reynolds is an heir, she's going to be their logical choice, no matter how inexperienced they are."

"Then let's help them find a better choice." Noah slid a list made up by Sloan across the desk and Robbins picked it up. "Those are the names of the people who were at the house that day and evening. One of them either murdered Edith or they let the murderer inside the house. Use your connections, run them through the system. One of them will turn up dirty if you dig deep enough. I'm afraid the local cops will decide Sloan is their murderer and stop digging. I want you to dig and keep digging until you find dirt, and I want it done fast."

Finished, Noah waited for Jack to stand up and get at the task. "Any questions?" he asked.

"Yeah, one—" his friend said with a grin. "Do you happen to have a picture of this woman?"

Noah misunderstood his reason for asking that. "I don't need you to check Sloan out," he said impatiently. "I want you to check out the others. Sloan couldn't hurt a fly. Hell, she's afraid of guns when they're locked in a room."

"I don't want to check her out; I just want to have a look at the woman who finally got under your skin."

"Get out of here and get busy. I don't even want Sloan's name bandied around in the press as a *possible* suspect." Despite his last statement, Noah had a sudden impulse to show off the woman he loved, and he reached into his desk drawer. "On the other hand," he said as Robbins stood up, "I don't want your curiosity over Sloan's appearance to distract you from your work." He slid the newspaper story about Sloan's party across the desk. At the top was a wide-angle picture that took in much of the general scene that night. Sloan was in the foreground with her father.

"Blond, huh?" Jack joked. "I thought you liked brunettes."

"I like that blond."

"Where's she from?"

"Bell Harbor. She's an interior designer."

"Whoever designed her exterior did a spectacular job," Jack said admiringly. "I see Senator Meade graced the affair with his crooked political presence."

"Naturally. He and Carter find each other eternally useful," Noah added, but Jack wasn't listening. He slid the clipping toward Noah and pointed to a couple who were dancing in the background.

"Paris, Sloan's sister."

"I know Paris. Who is the guy she's dancing with?"

"A friend of Sloan's who came along with her to lend moral support while she met her family for the first time. He's in the insurance business."

"What's his name?"

"Paul Richardson. Why?"

"I don't know. He—looks familiar."

"Maybe he sold you insurance. Check him out along with all the others on your list."

"Will do."

"Mrs. Snowden will show you up to your room. Do you need a computer to use?"

"No." Jack lifted his briefcase, which contained his laptop computer. "I never leave home without it."

41

Andy Cagle slouched contentedly in the passenger seat as Dennis Flynn put the car into gear and pulled away from the curb in front of Grant Wilson's building. The attorney had been delayed in probate court, and they'd had to cool their heels for over two hours in his office before he returned, and then they had to convince him he was in possession of material evidence that would help solve this murder.

The effort had been worth it. What they'd discovered had them both in a state of excited disbelief, because making an arrest in this case was going to be much easier than they'd imagined.

"I'm almost afraid to believe it," Flynn said. "Why do you think Edith Reynolds didn't tell Carter that she'd changed her will and made Sloan an heir?"

"I don't know. Maybe she thought he'd argue. Maybe she didn't think it was any of his business. Maybe she never got around to telling him."

"It doesn't matter," Flynn said with a grin. "All that matters is that Wilson said Edith assured him she'd discussed the new will with Sloan."

Cagle shoved his glasses up on his nose and nodded with satisfaction. "Yep. And the only way Sloan could make sure that Great-grandma didn't change her mind later, when Sloan was gone, was to bump her off right now."

Flynn nodded. "We've got motive and opportunity. We need the weapon. Should we bring her in for questioning and see if we can drag the location out of her, or should we notify the team at the house and tell them what we know? They can start combing her room and keep going from there."

"Let's try to find it without alerting her that we're onto her."

Flynn picked up his cellular phone, called Lieutenant Fineman at the Reynolds house, and filled him in on the latest development.

As Flynn was about to hang up, Cagle had an inspiration. "Tell the boys to be sure and search the shrubbery line along the north side of the property all the way down to the beach. Maitland said she was coming from the north when he saw her that night. She probably wasn't stupid enough to hide the weapon in her suitcase or somewhere we'd be able to find it easily. And tell them to make sure she doesn't catch on to what they're doing. I don't want her moving the weapon."

Flynn spoke into the telephone and relayed that message along with a suggestion: "Keep her busy writing out her recollection of the night or something." He hung up. "Let's go make the captain's day," he said dryly. "If they find the weapon in time, Hocklin will have time to primp before he faces the nation on network news."

• • •

News of the early breakthrough in the Reynolds murder spread through the police department and brought on a mood of pure elation.

"Pure luck, you guys," the sergeant joked as he walked by.

"Congratulations," Hank said as he dumped an armload of DBT reports on the former suspects onto Andy Cagle's desk. "I guess you won't be needing these anymore."

Cagle sorted through the reports and pulled out the only file he was interested in; behind him, Flynn answered his telephone. "We'll be right there!" Flynn shot out of his chair and grabbed his jacket. "They found the murder weapon," he told Cagle. "Nine-millimeter Glock, and one round is missing from the magazine. Let's go get a warrant signed."

Cagle was already on his feet, pulling on his jacket. "Where was it?"

"You aren't going to believe how dumb this broad is," Flynn said, shaking his head. "She had it stashed under her mattress. Like, we'd never think to look there."

42

Sloan was in the dining room with Paris, trying to write out a longhand report on the events of the night before, which struck her as an absurd waste of time, while Paris answered constant telephone calls from horrified family friends. Lieutenant Fineman was hovering in the hallway talking quietly to someone from the crime investigation team. The front doorbell rang, and Sloan glanced up as Nordstrom walked down the hall to answer it. When she looked up a moment later, Detectives Cagle and Flynn were walking swiftly into the dining room.

Sloan saw the cold, determined expressions on their faces, and the ballpoint pen slid from her fingers.

"Sloan Reynolds," Flynn said, pulling her out of the chair and shoving her to the wall. "You're under arrest for the murder of Edith Reynolds." He yanked her arms behind her and cuffed her. "You have the right to remain silent—"

"No!" Paris screamed, bracing her hands on the table and swaying as if she were about to faint. "No—"

"It's a mistake," Sloan promised over her shoulder as

she was rushed outside. "It's a mistake. It will be all right."
Two police cruisers were waiting in the driveway, engines
running, and Sloan was shoved into the backseat of one of
them.

The press were staked out at the street, and a commotion went up when they realized the police were taking
someone from the house. As the car passed through the
gates, cameras were aimed at her in the backseat and
Minicams were shoved at the car windows.

In the front seat, Andy Cagle turned around and eyed
her as if she were some sort of deadly bacteria. "Interested
in talking, or would you prefer to wait until after we book
you?"

The phrase *You're making a mistake* leapt to Sloan's
lips, but she bit it back because it was just too trite to be
uttered. She'd heard it hundreds of times from every guilty
creep who'd ever been brought in for questioning or to be
booked, and she couldn't bear to hear herself say it.

They drove past Noah's house, and she saw the fountain splashing over the sailfish behind his gates. She wondered how long it would be before he heard the news.

Paul had left the house on some sort of urgent errand
and had said only that he'd be back "later." Cagle and
Flynn obviously didn't plan to question her before they
booked her, so Paul wouldn't get to her before she was
processed through the system, and that made her furious.
She did not relish being fingerprinted and photographed
with a number in front of her chest one damned bit! That
hadn't been part of the deal when she agreed to come to
Palm Beach.

What she couldn't understand was why they didn't seem to think they needed to question her. She forgot Cagle had asked her a question until he reminded her: "Does your silence mean you'd prefer to talk after you're booked?"

"No," Sloan said as calmly as she could. "My silence means I'm waiting for some explanation about why you don't seem to think you need proof."

Flynn looked over his shoulder while he waited for two trucks to respond to his siren and clear out of his path. "Now, what makes you think we'd do a nasty thing like arresting you without any proof?"

The gleeful arrogance in his tone caused Sloan to enjoy a brief fantasy about doubling up her fist. "You can't have any proof because I didn't commit the crime."

"Let's save this little chat for a few minutes until we can do it face-to-face," he responded, stepping on the accelerator and swerving around the trucks.

The front entrance of the police station was surrounded by a mob of television crews, newspaper reporters, and photographers, and Sloan was certain that was precisely why she was taken in through the front of the building instead of another entrance: Flynn and Cagle were parading their prize in handcuffs for the mob to photograph and film.

Sloan had a fleeting thought of her mother seeing this on the evening news, and that made her feel worse than anything else . . . until Flynn and Cagle put her into a room with a two-way glass window and shoved a plastic bag with her gun in it across the table at her. "Recognize this?"

After she got over the shock of seeing it, Sloan was

almost relieved that her gun was all they were hanging their arrest on. She opened her mouth to say that it was hers and she had a permit to carry it, but before she could, Flynn robbed her of the ability to speak: "Guess where we found it—under *your* mattress! Now, how do you suppose it got there?"

She'd hidden the weapon in a much less obvious place than under a mattress, and she'd checked that morning to make certain it was still where she'd left it. "I don't"—she leaned forward, gazing at her own nine millimeter Glock—"know how it got there," she said honestly. "That isn't where I had it hidden."

Flynn turned all warm and friendly. "Now you're doing this the right way." Sliding his chair forward, he glanced at Cagle. "Why don't you get Miss Reynolds a glass of water."

"I don't want a glass of water," Sloan informed Flynn, but Cagle ignored her and left the room. "I want answers! You found that under my mattress?"

Flynn gave a shout of laughter. "You're something else, lady. This is a first. Let me explain how this works, Miss Reynolds. We ask the questions. You give the answers."

Sloan's mind was whirling with shock and alarm as she reached an unthinkable conclusion. Ignoring his lecture on protocol, she said, "How many rounds were in the magazine?"

"Nine. One round is missing. Isn't that a coincidence? And you want to hear another coincidence? I think ballistics is going to tell us that the slug that killed Mrs. Reynolds came from this gun."

Sloan stared at him, chills beginning to slither up her spine. This morning she'd checked to make certain the weapon was still where she'd hidden it, but she hadn't seen any reason to check the magazine to see if it was still full. "Oh, my God!" she whispered.

Andy Cagle slid into the chair at his desk and reached for the DBT data on Sloan Reynolds. Something was bothering him about the way she'd reacted to seeing the gun—no, something about the way she was reacting to the whole ordeal of being brought into a police station for booking. He began scanning the file.

"Nice work, Andy," Captain Hocklin said as he strolled back into the building after having made a brief statement to the press announcing the arrest of Sloan Reynolds for the murder of Edith Reynolds. He patted Andy's shoulder to show his appreciation; then he stopped when Cagle looked up at him, his expression dazed and alarmed. "What the hell's the matter?" Hocklin said, instantly anticipating the worst because Cagle never looked alarmed about anything.

"She's a cop," Cagle said.

"What?"

Cagle held up the thirty-five pages of information on Sloan Reynolds. "She's a cop," he repeated.

Hocklin's first thought was that if he had to tell the media he'd made a mistake today, he was going to look like a world-class ass; then he relaxed a little. "So what—cops don't make much dough, and she wanted her fair share from the old lady."

"Maybe."

"Did she deny the Glock was hers?"

"No. She denied having hidden it under the mattress. Anyway, it's registered to her. Look, right here—" He pointed to the DBT report.

Hocklin ignored it. "She had motive, means, and opportunity. Book her."

"I don't think—"

"I gave you an order."

"But we could be making a mistake."

"Book her, and if we're wrong, we'll apologize."

Cagle glowered at Hocklin's back as the captain walked away; then he heaved himself out of his chair. He walked into the room where Flynn was trying to question Sloan Reynolds. "Excuse me," he said automatically to her; then he looked at Flynn. "I need to talk to you out there." He jerked his head toward the door.

Flynn looked puzzled, but Sloan wasn't. She knew the moment Cagle looked at her and said "Excuse me" that he'd found out her secret. Based on the sheaf of papers in his hand with data printed from top to bottom, she assumed he'd finally bothered to run her through DBT, because she wouldn't have turned up in the ROC files when he checked with them. Now that they knew, she was still in something of a predicament because she couldn't tell them why she'd lied about being an interior designer, and she couldn't tell them she was working for the FBI.

She expected Flynn and Cagle to walk back in and start treating her more like a puzzling enigma than a murderer. In that she was wrong.

"Miss Reynolds," Flynn said flatly, "will you come with me, please?"

Sloan stood up. She couldn't believe they were going to release her this easily. "Why?"

"You already know the procedure. You've been through it before, only on the other side."

"You're actually going to book me?" she burst out angrily. "Without asking for any explanations?"

The two detectives looked at each other. Cagle shoved his glasses up on his nose and managed to look both sheepish and angry. "We'll ask you for explanations later. But if I were in your place when we start asking, I'd tell us to shove the questions up Captain Hocklin's ass, and then I'd demand that we contact your attorney."

Sloan had her answer: Hocklin wanted her booked, regardless. Hocklin, she realized bitterly, had probably already announced it to the flock of reporters outside.

She went with them, refusing to give them the satisfaction of uttering a word. She knew what hotel the attorney was staying in, and if he wasn't there, she knew she could call Noah and Noah would find him. There wasn't much point in contacting Paul, since he'd probably expect her to sit around in jail until he got the thirty-six hours he said he needed.

43

Jack Robbins leaned back in his chair, watching his computer download files from Data Base Technologies, but his thoughts kept returning to the newspaper clipping and the male face that seemed distantly familiar.

He shook his head as if that would dislodge the unsettling thought. Leaning forward, he typed in a query for "Reynolds, Sloan." On the bottom of his computer screen the words "Now Online" were flashing, followed by the names of the entities who were currently searching DBT's database.

When he typed in her name, he didn't expect to turn up anything extraordinary, and he wasn't curious about the details of the woman's personal life. He was simply doing the job he was paid a great deal of money to perform—which was to insulate Noah from potential problems of any nature. In Jack's mind, the possibility that the woman who made Noah's face and voice soften might also become a suspect in a murder case constituted A Very Big Potential Problem.

DBT came up with seven matches for the name "Sloan Reynolds" and provided the social security number and city of residence for each name. Only one of the matches lived in Florida—Bell Harbor, Florida. He chose that one. She was going to be easy to single out, he realized with relief. When the download was complete, he went off-line and pulled up her file on his computer disk.

The first section of information provided all her addresses for the last ten years, the taxable value of every home she'd lived in, and the names of whomever she'd paid a mortgage payment to or made a rent payment to. She owned a very modest house, Jack noted.

The next section listed the names of anyone who had ever lived with her at any address, or even received mail at her address. Evidently, she'd never had a live-in boyfriend, not for even a month.

He held down the "page down" key a split second too long, and his computer jumped to a later section that listed the names and phone numbers of all her neighbors at all her addresses. Instead of returning to where he'd left off, he scrolled backward from that point. She didn't have a car, which struck him as odd, but she owned an inexpensive boat. She'd never had a lien, judgment, or bankruptcy, either. She'd never been involved in a criminal, a civil, or even a motor vehicle problem.

She was incredibly clean, Jack thought as his scrolling took him back into the first section. She was a saint. She was . . . He stood clear up out of his chair, staring at the screen on his laptop. . . .

. . . She was a cop!

She was a detective on the force of the Bell Harbor Police Department! She was no interior designer; she was a cop. And for some reason, she didn't want Noah to know it.

Jack slapped a floppy disk into the laptop and transferred her file to it. While that was happening, he picked up the telephone and called local telephone information for Bell Harbor. He asked the operator for the number of the Bell Harbor Police Department; then he dialed that number.

"Detective Sloan Reynolds, please," he said to the man who answered.

"She's on vacation until next week. Can anyone else help you?"

Jack hung up and headed for Noah's office, the floppy disk in his hand. He reached Noah's office doorway at the same time Mrs. Snowden did, and the unflappable Mrs. Snowden, who appeared to be shaken up for the first time since Jack had known her, rushed forward and cut him off.

"Mr. Maitland," she burst out.

Noah was on the telephone with the head of an aeronautics company in France, and he frowned at her and then at the two flashing lights on two other phone lines. "I'm sorry to interrupt you, but Paris Reynolds is on line two. It's her second call. You were on the phone when she called the last time, but now she says it's urgent."

Noah said an abrupt good-bye to the French industrialist and lunged for line two, but Jack stopped him. "Don't take that call yet, Noah! I have something to tell you."

Noah paused, his arm outstretched toward the phone. "What the hell is it? Didn't you—"

"She's a cop, Noah."

In all the years he'd worked for Noah Maitland, Jack had never seen him immobilized by any emotion or any event. The worse the pressure, the greater the disaster, the more energized he became until it was dealt with. Now, however, Noah stared at him as if unable to absorb what Jack had just told him. "You're out of your mind," he said finally, reaching for the flashing button on the telephone again. "Sloan is afraid of guns."

"Listen to me, Noah," Jack said sharply. "She's a detective with the Bell Harbor police force. I don't know what she's doing here, but she's obviously under cover."

A sudden collage of images flashed through Noah's mind—Sloan in the backyard with Carter, tossing him on the ground. Sloan showing Courtney some self-defense moves. Sloan, chasing down a killer, dodging obstacles and leaping hedges like a graceful gazelle. No . . . Like a *cop!*

He reached for the phone, slowly this time, and picked up Paris's call. He listened for a moment. "How long ago did they take her in? All right, calm down. Your father is upset, and he's not thinking clearly. I'll handle it and call you back." He hung up the phone and looked at Jack, his expression completely blank. "Why would she lie to me?"

Before Jack could begin to speculate, Mrs. Snowden reappeared in the doorway. "Ross Halperin is on the phone, and he says it's an emergency."

Courtney collided with her as she raced into Noah's office. "Sloan's been arrested!" Courtney cried, lunging for the television set and turning it on.

"I'll take Halperin's call," Jack said, reaching for the phone to talk to Noah's chief counsel. When he hung up, he looked at Noah and hid his wrath behind a flat, terse voice. "The FBI got a search warrant. At this moment, they, along with the Coast Guard and the ATF, are swarming all over your boats looking for a stash of illegal automatic weapons."

Noah slowly stood up. "What? Why in hell would she lie to me?"

Courtney was standing in front of the television set, swearing at the commercial that was interrupting the cable newscast. "Noah, look, dammit—" she said, pointing, but the news story that came on wasn't about Sloan.

"It's been a tough day for the rich and famous in Palm Beach, Florida," the newscaster announced. "Within the hour, two yachts belonging to tycoon-socialite Noah Maitland have been impounded and boarded by the FBI, Coast Guard, and ATF. We have footage."

Jack recognized the profile of the FBI agent standing at the *Apparition*'s stern at the same time Noah did.

"*Richardson!*" The name exploded from Noah like a curse.

"Your girlfriend's a cop, Noah," Jack said flatly, "and her 'boyfriend' is FBI."

"Courtney!" Noah snapped. "Get out of here."

She took one look at Noah's face and started backing out of his office. Despite her flippant, disrespectful digs about her brother's business dealings, Courtney had never really believed Noah did anything wrong. "Sloan's a cop?" she said, looking dazed. "And Paul's an FBI agent? And they both wanted to take the yachts away from you? But why?"

He turned and looked at her, a muscle ticking in his clenched jaw. Mrs. Snowden drew her the rest of the way out of Noah's office and hesitantly said as she closed the door, "Mr. Maitland—Sloan Reynolds is on the phone."

Standing behind his desk, his gaze riveted on CNN's coverage of the takeover of his property, Noah reached out and pressed the speaker button on the telephone. Sloan sounded calm but a little shaken. "Noah, Mr. Kirsh isn't in his room at the hotel. I've been arrested."

"Have you now?" Noah said silkily. "Do you only get one phone call?"

"Yes—"

"That's too damned bad, Detective Reynolds, because you just wasted it." Reaching out, he disconnected the call.

Shoving his hands into his pockets, Noah watched the invasion of his personal property. He remembered Sloan's reaction to the weapons she'd seen on board, the questions she'd asked him about them. And then she'd gone to his stateroom with him to make love. They'd made love for hours that night—after she'd pried enough information out of him so that her coconspirator could bluff a federal judge into issuing a search warrant.

He thought of the way he'd held her hand and confessed that he was crazy about her, and the way he'd told her he felt like a teenager in love for the first time. "Bitch!" he said aloud.

The newsclip ended, and he turned back to his desk and went into action; he told Mrs. Snowden to get four people on the phone for him. Two of them were attorneys, one was a retired federal judge, and the other was a Supreme Court justice. When he finished rapping out those instructions, he told Jack what he wanted done. "Got it?" he snapped.

"Consider it done," Jack replied.

"When I'm finished with that son of a bitch," Noah said in a murderous voice, "he won't be able to get a job as a crossing guard!"

44

Paul made certain Maitland's ships were secured for the night and under guard; then he wearily walked over to his rented car. The ten P.M. news came on as he pulled out of the marina. *"It's been a bleak day for two of Palm Beach's most respected families,"* the newscaster said. *"This afternoon, Sloan Reynolds, daughter of financier Carter Reynolds, was arrested for the murder of her great-grandmother, Edith Reynolds."*

Swearing under his breath, Paul made a U-turn in the street, slammed down on the accelerator, and headed for the police station.

In her cell at the police department, Sloan was listening to the same broadcast, but it was the second half of it that brought her to her feet in an agony of disbelief:

"A short while later, the FBI, in collaboration with the Coast Guard and a team from the Bureau of Alcohol, Tobacco, and Firearms, seized and boarded two yachts belonging to billionaire Noah Maitland. Sources close to the investigation report that the FBI has reason to believe Maitland has been using the yachts to transport illegal weapons."

The exterior of the police station looked modern and manicured; the interior was well-lit, but the officers standing around and working on reports looked as if they were having a quiet night. "Who's in charge?" Paul snapped at a cop who'd been getting a drink from a water fountain.

"Sergeant Babcock; he's over there talking to the dispatcher."

"Are you Babcock?" Paul said, interrupting a chat the two were having about the seizure of Maitland's yachts.

Babcock straightened. "Yeah, who are—" Before he could ask the question, an open case with FBI credentials was in front of his face.

"What can we do for you, Mr. Richardson?"

"You're holding one of my people. I want her released to me. Now."

The lockup was empty except for one drunken teenager, who was waiting to be picked up by his father, and Sloan Reynolds, whose arrest had made Captain Hocklin famous and euphoric that day. "Who are you talking about?"

"Sloan Reynolds."

The sergeant paled, the dispatcher gaped, and officers stopped writing reports and turned around, openly eavesdropping. "Are you telling me Sloan Reynolds is working for the FBI?"

"That's what I said. Are you holding her here or not?"

"Well, yeah, but I can't—I don't have the authority—"

"Who does?"

"That would have to come from Captain Hocklin himself. But he goes to bed early, and he was up late last—"

Paul picked up the telephone on the dispatcher's desk and thrust it at him. "Wake him up," he snapped.

Babcock hesitated, studied the look on the FBI agent's face, and did as he was told.

Sloan signed for her belongings, which constituted her purse and watch, and walked in stiff silence to Paul's car in the parking lot. "We'll check in to a motel for the night," he said. "I'm sorry, Sloan. I had no idea they'd busted you until I heard it on the ten o'clock news."

In an odd, soft voice, she said, "I'm sure you were very busy or you'd have come sooner."

Paul glanced uncertainly at her and decided to wait until she'd settled into a room before he told her exactly what had kept him.

He stopped at a decent-looking motel, got two rooms next door to each other, and left her outside hers. "I need to make a phone call; then we'll talk."

She said nothing, but put the key in the lock of her room and walked inside, leaving the door a few inches ajar.

Inside the room, Sloan walked over to the television set and turned on CNN. They were having a field day showing films of federal agents swarming over Noah's boats. They were making him sound like a criminal who made his money transporting and selling illegal weapons. She saw Paul at the edge of one quick shot.

When Paul walked into her room, Sloan was standing at the foot of the bed, still watching the news footage of his raid on Maitland's boats. "I know how you must feel," he began soothingly.

Her arms dropped to her sides, and she turned fully

toward him, her face a study of emotions that he didn't quite recognize. "Did you find anything?" she asked in an odd voice.

"No, not yet," Paul admitted. With a resigned sigh, he said, "Look, I know you must want to tear into me for all this. If it will make you feel better, do it."

"That won't make me feel better, but this will—" Her right fist slammed into his jaw, snapped his head back, and sent him reeling backward.

Grabbing for the wall to steady himself with one hand, Paul lifted his other hand to his jaw. For someone as small and slender as she was, she packed a hell of a wallop. She took another step forward. Caught somewhere between pain, admiration, and annoyance, he held up his hand and said ominously, "Enough! That's enough. I'll let that one pass, but there isn't going to be another."

Deprived of an outlet for her anger, she seemed to wither before his eyes. She slumped down on the foot of the bed, wrapped her arms around her stomach, and rocked slowly, as if she were trying to physically hold herself together. Her hair fell forward, hiding the sides of her face, and her shoulders began to shake.

Her silent, anguished weeping was even harder on Paul than her right hook. "I'll try to make things right somehow."

She stopped rocking and lifted her tear-streaked face to him. "With whom?" she said, her voice choked with tears. "With Noah? Before he knew what you were doing today, he was moving heaven and earth to try to protect me from being arrested. An hour later, he hated me so much, he hung up on me and left me in jail."

"I can't help that."

Fiercely, she cried, "What can you help? Can you help Paris forget that I've smeared her family's name all over the world news? Can you help her forget that I was hauled out of her home in handcuffs? She was screaming when they took me away. Do you hear me?" Sloan finished hysterically. "She was *screaming!*"

Paris was an Academy Award caliber actress, in Paul's opinion, but he knew there was no point in saying that, or in trying to make Sloan believe that the only thing Paris could possibly have felt was relief because her sister was being arrested for her own crime. He didn't know whether Paris would now play the role of sweet, naïve, supportive sister while Sloan was under suspicion of murder, or if she'd decide she didn't have to bother. He hoped, for Sloan's sake, Paris might decide to do the former. It would make things a little easier on Sloan if she was allowed to come back there. He nodded to the telephone beside the bed. "Call her," he said. "If she was that upset over what was happening to you, she may want you to come straight home."

The hope that flared in Sloan's eyes, the hesitant way she reached for the phone and then picked it up, made Paul feel as sick as he'd felt when he realized Paris had to be the murderer.

The phone call was extremely short, and when Sloan hung up, there was no more hope in her eyes. She looked up at Paul, her voice dead. "Gary Dishler said that Paris told him to tell me she and Carter never wanted to see or talk to me again. He's putting our luggage on the porch right now.

If we don't pick it up within a half hour, it will be sent off with the trash in the morning."

"I'll go get it," Paul said, feeling a sudden urge to put his hands around Paris's slender, "fragile" throat and choke the life out of her.

Sloan nodded and tiredly reached for the phone. "I'll call my mother and Sara. They must be out of their minds with worry if they've heard about this."

The police department was apparently providing security while the crime scene team still had work to do, because two police cruisers were parked in the driveway, but the team had obviously knocked off for the night. So had the media, Paul noticed with relief as Gary Dishler answered his call at the gates.

Paul took the luggage from the porch and put it in his car; then he walked up to the front door and rang the doorbell.

Dishler answered, his face like stone. "As I told Sloan Reynolds a few minutes ago, she is not welcome here. Neither are you."

He started to close the door, but Paul stopped it with his right hand and removed his credentials case with his left. He knew damned well Dishler knew he was FBI by now, but the showing of credentials was a necessary formality before Paul pressed his authority. He held the open case at eye level in front of the assistant. "Now that the formalities are over," Paul snapped wearily, "get Paris Reynolds down here."

"The FBI has no authority here."

"A crime was committed here that involves someone working for the FBI. Now, do you want to get Paris down here, or do you want me to walk out to that car, pick up my telephone, and have this place crawling with agents in an hour?"

"Wait here," Dishler snapped, and closed the door with a bang. When it opened again, Paris was standing on the threshold in a pale brocade dressing robe, her face a cold, beautiful mask. "Haven't you done enough damage to everyone?" she demanded.

Unperturbed, Paul handed her a card with his cell phone number written on the back. "Call me at that number if you decide you want to talk."

She looked down her patrician nose at him. "About what?"

"About why you killed your great-grandmother."

For the second time that night, Paul was caught off guard by a woman. Her open hand crashed against the side of his face; then the door slammed in it.

45

"Are you going to try to see Maitland before you go back to Bell Harbor?" Paul asked Sloan the next morning. She looked as pale and haunted as she had last night, and he felt even guiltier because she didn't seem to have the strength left to be angry with him.

She put a case containing her toiletries into her suitcase and zipped it closed. "Yes, but it won't do any good," she said without looking at him. She hadn't looked at him at all, except when she opened the door to let him in.

"Would it make you feel better to know that I feel lousy about this?"

"I don't care how you feel about anything."

Paul couldn't believe how bad that made him feel. She had trusted him and done her job, and he liked her tremendously. "Okay, would it make you feel better to know why I'm after Carter and what brought me here?"

"Why tell me now when it was 'classified' before?"

"I want you to know now."

She glanced at him for the first time; then she looked away and shrugged.

Paul took her arm and forced her to sit on the bed; then he sat down in a chair across from her. "I know Carter is laundering money for a South American drug cartel that deposits cash at Reynolds Bank and Trust. The cash is accepted, credited to bogus accounts, and the IRS forms are bypassed. The money is wire-transferred by Reynolds Bank into the cartel's offshore bank accounts, where it becomes nice, clean money. Ready for spending."

She looked him right in the eye, and what she said was painfully astute. "You don't *know* Carter is involved in any of that; you *think* he is; that's all. If you had any proof, you'd have wiretaps and search warrants."

"Our informant met with a strange accident the day he was going to hand us some proof. The cartel we're dealing with is a pack of animals, but they're more cunning than most of their competition. They've hired prestigious law firms to represent their legitimate business interests here, and they're slowly acquiring political clout. Senator Meade is a particular friend of theirs. I want to take Carter down, but even more, I want to find his contact with the cartel."

"What does any of that have to do with Noah?"

"Maitland is Reynolds Bank's biggest depositor; he has an astonishing number of bank accounts there. He also has nice big boats that periodically go to Central and South America—"

"So does the Holland America cruise line," Sloan mocked bitterly.

Paul ignored the sarcasm. "Maitland has some questionable 'business associates' in those ports."

"Known criminals?" Sloan countered.

"No, but let's not argue about that. Let's stick to the

issue: Someone has to smuggle the cartel's cash into the States and into Reynolds Bank and Trust. I think Maitland is the one. I also think he brings in drugs with the cash from time to time."

She nodded slightly and got up; then she picked up her suitcase and purse.

"You don't believe any of that, do you?" Paul said.

"About Noah, no. About Carter—I don't know."

She turned at the door. "I've been released under your authority, but I haven't been cleared of the murder charge yet. I'd appreciate it if you'd handle that."

Paul stood up and looked helplessly at her. She had so much quiet dignity and she was so disgusted with him that he felt like one of the creeps he'd been talking about.

"Good-bye," she said.

He nodded silently because he couldn't think of anything to say.

46

The problem with Palm Beach estates was that many of them, including Noah's, had electric gates at the street that prevented unwelcome visitors from getting to the front door.

As Sloan feared, she had become one of those visitors. Mrs. Snowden informed her of it as Sloan waited in her rented car outside the gates. In a tone as frigid as her last name implied, Noah's secretary said, "I am to tell you that if you ever come near this house or anything else belonging to the Maitland family, Mr. Maitland won't bother with the police. He will deal with you himself." She paused, as if uncertain that a personal warning was necessary, and then obviously decided it was: "I wouldn't put him to the test if I were you. Good-bye."

Unwilling to cry where Mrs. Snowden could see her on a closed-circuit monitor, Sloan started to put her car in reverse; then she saw Courtney bounding down the front steps toward her.

Sloan got out of the car and walked over to the gates. Courtney stopped on the other side and raked Sloan with a contemptuous glance. "How could you!" she demanded with bitter fury. "How could you do this to us when we were never anything but nice to you!"

"I know how it looks," Sloan said achingly. "I don't expect you to believe this, but I had no idea any of that was going to happen." She swallowed before she could go on. "I—I loved your family, every one of you."

Courtney's gray eyes were so like Noah's that Sloan was unconsciously memorizing the color of them in the sunlight, even though they were glaring at her with cold animosity. "I'm not stupid enough to believe any of that."

Sloan accepted her condemnation with a nod. "I don't blame you." She started to turn; then she realized something so poignant that she had to blink back tears before she could turn back. "Thank you for not accusing **me** of being a murderer as well as a spy."

Courtney dismissed her gratitude with an indifferent shrug. "I'm not stupid enough to believe you killed Edith."

Sloan turned away because there was nothing more to say, but Courtney wasn't quite finished. "I stayed home from school because I figured you'd come here, but you'd better never come back. Noah's gone and you're lucky. He isn't just mad. He hates you."

Sloan nodded. "I understand. Do you think, if I waited awhile and wrote him a letter, that he'd at least read it?"

"Not a chance," Courtney said as she turned her back on Sloan and walked away.

Courtney waited until Sloan was pulling out of the drive; then she turned and walked backward slowly, watching her leave. She lifted her palms to her eyes and pressed hard to keep the tears back.

47

Sloan had been too miserable during the drive back to Bell Harbor to worry about what impact the news of her arrest would have on her life and job in Bell Harbor, but within hours of her return, she had no doubt.

When Sloan called her mother at Lydia's shop to tell her she was home, Kimberly ignored Lydia's complaints and actually took the rest of the day off "for personal reasons." Sara terminated a meeting with an important client and arrived immediately after Sloan's mother; then they both doted on her as if she were ill, bringing her small treats and favorite foods in attempts to restore both her mood and her appetite.

Sloan didn't realize they were doing this because she looked ill. With her arms wrapped around a throw pillow, she sat curled tightly into a corner of the sofa and told them what she knew about the murder.

They'd both recognized Paul aboard Noah's boat when they saw him on the news, and Sloan saw no reason not to tell them the truth about her relationship with Paul. Rather than upset her mother, however, Sloan let them believe it was Noah Maitland that Paul had gone to Palm Beach to investigate, and she left Carter out of the picture. She told them about Paris and Carter and people she'd met and things she'd done, but she left out her brief love affair with Noah. She didn't know how to discuss him or if she could do it without breaking down.

When she ran out of things to talk about, Kimberly went into the kitchen to make Sloan a cup of tea while Sara made an attempt to lighten Sloan's mood that backfired badly. "Did you see any Mr. Perfects anywhere?" she teased.

Sloan had to fight to control her expression. "I . . . well . . . yes."

"How many?"

"Not many. One."

"Only one? Palm Beach is the gathering place for an awful lot of Mr. Perfects. You must not have been looking around."

Sloan closed her eyes and saw a tanned male face with a square jaw, beautiful gray eyes, and an insistent mouth leaning toward her. She swallowed. "He was as perfect as it gets."

"Did you meet him?"

"Oh, yes," Sloan said weakly. "I met him."

"And did you go out with him?"

"Yes."

"And?" Sara prodded.

Sloan's voice dropped to a whisper, and she had to clear her throat. "We liked each other."

"How much did you like each other?" Sara's smile

wavered as she watched Sloan's face and listened to her voice.

Sloan laid her cheek against the pillow she was holding and swallowed. "A lot."

"Do we have a name?" Sara asked.

"Noah Maitland."

"Noah Maitland?" Sara uttered. "*Noah Maitland?*" Like many residents of Bell Harbor, Sara subscribed to the *Palm Beach Daily News* and kept up on the social whirl there. "Listen to me. Even if he weren't an arms smuggler, you wouldn't want him. He has a different rich, glamorous woman with him in every picture I've seen of him, but he never sticks with any of them."

Before Sloan could reply, her mother returned from the kitchen with the tea and spoke up, her voice gentle but firm. "I don't think Sloan should give up hope that all this will work out. Edith's murderer will be found, and then Paris and Carter will realize she was innocent, and they'll forgive her. And so far, no one has said that anything illegal has been found on Noah Maitland's boats. I'm sure he's innocent or Sloan would never have—" She glanced tenderly at her unhappy daughter and said with certainty, "Or else Sloan would never have fallen in love with him. The truth will come out about his innocence, and Sloan can apologize to him. I'm sure he's a kind, gentle man who will understand and forgive her." She looked at Sloan. "Isn't that true, darling?"

Sloan thought of her last phone call with Noah and lifted teary eyes to her mother. "No."

A few minutes later, Sloan realized she had to take

immediate steps to help her get over all this. She reached for the phone and called the police department. "Matt, this is Sloan," she told Lieutenant Caruso. "I'd like to come back to work tomorrow instead of Monday, if you can use me."

"Are you back in town?" he asked, and when she said she was, he told her to report for duty in the morning. Caruso hung up the phone and strolled over to Jess Jessup's desk. "Sloan is home. I told her she could come to work tomorrow. I hope that's okay with Captain Ingersoll. I mean, she's been charged with murder . . ."

Jess stood up. "Caruso, you're an ass."

"Where are you going?" Caruso called after him.

"You can reach me on the radio if you need me," he replied, but before he left, Jess stopped at the dispatcher's desk. "Sloan is back," he told the dispatcher. "She's at home."

Before Jess reached his car, the dispatcher had put the word out to the officers on duty around Bell Harbor.

Within ten minutes, a parade of police cruisers began to arrive in front of her house.

Jess arrived first, and Sara answered the door. They had not seen each other since he'd appeared at her house after the barbecue on the beach, and Sara faltered when she saw him standing there. "Come out here a minute," Jess ordered, drawing Sara forward onto Sloan's porch. "How's she doing?"

"She's fine," Sara said firmly. "She's terrific."

Jess wasn't deceived. "How is she really doing?"

"Fair."

He nodded as if he expected that; then he did the last thing Sara expected him to do or wanted him to do. He reached out and tipped her chin up, and his smile was without mockery or flirtation. "Do you think we could bury the hatchet for her sake for a while?"

Sara nodded warily, taken aback by the gentleness in his face as he looked at her. "I'd like that, Jess."

For the rest of the afternoon and evening, a steady procession of police cruisers arrived at Sloan's house and disappeared after a little while. Boxes of pizzas and sandwiches from fast-food restaurants accumulated on the living room table as Sloan's friends on the force invented excuses to come by and say hello.

Sloan knew better.

They had come to show their support and to cheer her up. It worked until Sloan went to bed that night. Alone in her bed, there was nothing to distract her from remembering Noah. She fell asleep thinking about the times she'd lain against his side after they'd made love, her head on his shoulder, his hand idly caressing her, until they both slept. Or made love again.

48

Paris wasn't fooled one bit by Detectives Cagle and Flynn's courteous tone. They were sitting in her living room the day after her great-grandmother's funeral, and they were trying to make her incriminate herself in her great-grandmother's murder.

"I'm sure you can understand why we're baffled," Flynn was saying. "I mean, if Sloan killed Mrs. Reynolds, why would she wipe her prints off her own gun and then 'hide' the gun where we couldn't miss it? Her prints on her own gun wouldn't have incriminated her. The *gun* incriminated her because it fired the shot that killed Mrs. Reynolds."

"I told you before," Paris stated, "I don't know the answer to that."

"Sloan said the gun was still in its original hiding place, not under the mattress, on the morning after Mrs. Reynolds's death. She checked. Do you think someone else could have put the gun under the mattress?"

"Who?" Paris countered angrily. "The servants had all been sent home by you. The only people in the house that morning who didn't work for you were Paul Richardson and Sloan, my father and me, and Gary Dishler."

"That's the confusing part," Cagle put in.

"Yes, isn't it?" she countered. "You obviously don't think Paul Richardson or Sloan could be guilty."

"Richardson is FBI and he has no motive. Your sister has an unblemished record as a police officer and she was working for him. Believe me, if all that weren't true, your sister would be staring at a lifetime in prison. Now, let's see, who does that leave us with—who had a motive for wanting to see your great-grandmother dead and Sloan in prison, and who was here to move the gun under the mattress?"

Paris stood up, ending the interview, and motioned to Nordstrom, who was hovering in the hallway. She was through with being nice to people who treated her badly. "Nordstrom," she said coldly, "please show these men to the door, and lock it behind them. They are never again to be allowed past the gates."

Flynn dropped his friendly pretext. "We can get a warrant."

Paris nodded toward the door. "Do it, then," she said. "But until you have one, kindly get out and stay out!"

When the front door closed behind them, Cagle looked at Flynn with a wry smile. "That was a genteel way of saying 'fuck off,' wasn't it?"

"Yeah. I'll bet she was just as genteel when she pointed that Glock at her great-grandmother's chest and pulled the trigger."

Paris wasn't feeling genteel. She was panicked. She

paced slowly back and forth across the living room floor, trying to think of who the murderer could be. She wasn't as willing as the police were to discount Paul Richardson or Sloan. Paul was obviously a liar and a phony, and he was fully capable of using people ruthlessly. He knew how to use a gun, and he would know how to fix things so it looked like someone else was guilty. He had no heart. He had broken hers. The problem was . . . he actually seemed to believe that *Paris* had killed her great-grandmother.

Sloan was as dishonest and heartless as he was. She'd pretended she wanted Paris to think of her as a real sister; then she tricked her into loving her like one. She'd filled Paris's head with touching stories about their mother and made Paris yearn to be part of their family in Bell Harbor. In retrospect, it was easy to see that Sloan had only accepted their invitation to come to Palm Beach so that she could smuggle an FBI agent into their midst, and then they could both try to destroy Noah.

Absently rubbing her throbbing temples, Paris went over what the detectives had said and what they'd implied. They seemed to be absolutely convinced that Sloan was telling the truth, and that whoever put her gun under her mattress was the killer. The police were convinced it wasn't Sloan or Paul, and Paris knew it wasn't her father or herself.

That only left Gary Dishler.

At first the idea seemed absurd, but the more she thought about it, the more she realized how little she actually liked the man. When he'd come to work for her father a few years ago, his position as assistant had been well-defined, but now he seemed to be in charge of every-thing. Generally, he treated her father with deferential respect, but there had been a few times when she'd heard him use a clipped, impatient tone that was completely inappropriate. She'd seen him lose his temper with a housemaid and fire her on the spot because she'd touched some papers on his desk.

The more Paris considered it, the more unpleasant and unsavory Dishler seemed to her. She couldn't imagine why he would want to hurt her great-grandmother, but she wasn't entirely sure he was incapable of it.

Her father was going through condolence cards in a spacious second-floor study with connecting doors to his bedroom on one side and to Gary Dishler's office on the other. The hallway door into Dishler's office was open, but the connecting door was closed. Paris carefully closed the hallway door into her father's study so they'd have complete privacy. "We have a problem," she said as calm-ly as she could.

"What is it?" he asked, slitting open another envelope.

Paris sat down on a chair in front of his desk. "Do you know how Gary really felt about Great-grandmother? I know she was rude to him from time to time."

"She was rude to everyone from time to time," Carter pointed out philosophically. "What has that to do with Gary?"

Paris drew a fortifying breath. "The police were here a while ago. They believe that whoever put Sloan's gun under the mattress also killed Great-grandmother, and they are convinced it wasn't Sloan or Paul."

"Don't get involved with all that, Paris. It will drive you crazy if you try to sort it out. Let them handle it."

"I don't think we can afford to do that."

He looked up, frowning. "Why not?"

"Because the police are already convinced I did it. I had the biggest motive and the best opportunity."

."That's ridiculous! It's insane."

"It's insane to go to jail for something I didn't do, but that happens to people all the time. There's only one person who could have moved that gun the morning after Great-grandmother was killed, and it's Gary Dishler. Outside of Paul and Sloan and you and me, he was the only other person the police allowed to stay on the premises after her body was found. You didn't do it and I didn't do it. That leaves Gary."

An odd expression crossed his face as she finished, an expression almost like fear, but it vanished so quickly Paris couldn't be certain. "The police won't even bother asking him about it, and I think I'm going to be arrested. I think we ought to hire our own private detectives or something. And I think I ought to have a lawyer ready."

Anger, not fear, was tightening his face as she stood up and said, "Will you think about doing both those things?"

He nodded curtly, and Paris left him. She'd started down the stairs when she heard a door crash into its frame, and she turned and darted up the stairs. Her father's study door was still open, but Dishler's hallway door was closed now, and Paris almost moaned aloud at the thought Dishler would be the one he asked to get her a lawyer and hire the detectives. Then she realized her father had looked angry enough to confront Dishler himself and try to wring the truth out of him.

Fear for her father made Paris violate the precepts of a lifetime. She rushed into her father's office, closed the door, and leaned over his desk to the telephone. She pressed Gary Dishler's extension number, and the phone was immediately answered. "What is it?" he snapped.

"Gary? Oh, I'm sorry," Paris said as she carefully held down the number three on her father's telephone, which enabled the room-monitoring feature. "I meant to dial the kitchen."

"That's extension thirty-two," he said, and hung up. Gary had chosen the new phone system, and he'd shown her how to use the room-monitoring feature when her father was recovering from his heart attack. Now Paris was putting it to a new use. The conversation in Gary's office came over the speaker phone, and Paris listened to it with a mounting sense of disbelief and horror that turned to terror.

"I told you to calm down, Carter!" Dishler warned in a voice Paris had *never* heard him use before. "What are you saying?"

"You heard what I said. My daughter has just informed me that she is likely to be arrested for Edith's murder."

"Which daughter is that?" Dishler asked needlessly.

"I only have one daughter who counts," Carter snapped. "And she has just presented me with a rather convincing argument that *you* must have moved that gun. Which makes you a murderer."

Instead of hearing Dishler react with a violent denial,

as Paris expected, she heard his chair make a noise as if he had leaned back in it, and when he spoke, his voice was grotesque in its calm lack of concern.

"You had a serious problem, Carter, and your business partners recognized it as soon as I reported it. They asked me to handle the problem before it blew up and the fallout destroyed all of us."

"What problem?" Carter demanded, but he sounded alarmed and defensive.

"Come now, you know what problem," Dishler said snidely. "The problem is that Edith changed her will before either of us realized it. She cut Sloan in for a piece of her estate, a large portion of which is the Hanover Trust. Sloan's part of the trust should have given her fifteen million dollars. But the Hanover Trust only has five million dollars total, because the trustee—that's you and your bank—has been milking it for a decade to keep the bank operating and to cover your losses everywhere else. Am I correct?"

After a silence, Paris heard her father say, "I could have persuaded Sloan to leave the money in the trust and to be satisfied with interest payments. I'd already persuaded Paris to do that—"

There was a crash, as if Dishler had slapped his hand on the desk. "Sloan Reynolds isn't Paris: She's a cop. If she decided she wanted to withdraw the principal and you couldn't hand it over, she'd have raised a stink. That stink would have covered you and spread to Reynolds Bank. Your partners in that bank couldn't allow that to happen."

"Stop calling them my partners, damn you! We had a

business arrangement, not a partnership. They bailed me out when the bank was in trouble in the eighties, and in return I agreed to launder some money for them over the years. I've let them put their own people in a few key positions, and I've tolerated having you around, but nobody ever talked about murder."

"There was no choice. If I'd known ahead of time that Edith was going to change her will to include Sloan, the old woman would have died a natural-looking death before she could sign it, and there would have been no problem.

"Unfortunately, I didn't know anything about it until Wilson left here with the new will signed and witnessed by your servants. I consulted with your partners, who consulted with their attorneys. It turned out that the only sure way to prevent someone like Sloan from being able to claim her inheritance was if it appeared that she had murdered in order to get it. Your partners advised me to handle the matter."

Paris heard her father make a sound like a groaning curse, and Dishler said with a vocal shrug, "It's just business, Carter. Nothing personal. It was handy that she had her own gun."

Carter's voice dropped to a defeated whisper. "How did you know? When did you find out she was a cop?"

"The day before poor Edith's demise, I asked your daughter what her opinion was of the rare Persian carpets downstairs. She described the colors in the Aubusson—she didn't know the difference. That, combined with the fact that she showed no real interest in any of the decor, made me suspicious.

"It took me five minutes on the computer to discover she was a cop and one phone call to verify it. It took your business partners fifteen minutes to come up with a plan and give me instructions." Irritably, he added, "It took me thirty minutes to find where she'd hidden the damn gun. Now, can we end this unpleasant discussion?"

In the office next door, Paris heard the strain in her father's voice as he asked, "What about Paris? They'll arrest her for it."

"Now, you know I would never let that happen. Sloan will be taken care of tonight, and the matter will come to an end."

"How?"

"Are you sure you want to know?"

In the office next door, Paris held her breath, her hand hovering over the button that would turn the speaker phone off. But, she had to know what they were saying about Sloan.

Her father must have nodded, because he didn't speak, and Dishler's answer chilled her blood. "Tonight, with a little persuasion, Sloan is going to have an attack of guilt and shame that causes her to write a note, confessing to killing her great-grandmother. And then she is going to blow her brains out. Women don't like to mess up their looks when they die, but she's a cop. She would be more likely to take a quick, certain route, don't you—"

Paris slapped the intercom button off and fled from her father's office, stumbling as she raced down the hall. Her father's bedroom suite was at the end of the north wing of the house, hers was at the end of the south wing. As she passed the central staircase that led down to the foyer and divided the two wings, she saw one of the maids walking down the hall with an armful of fresh linen, and she made herself slow to a walk.

She had no idea yet exactly what she was going to do; her crazed emotions blocked logic except for two trains of thought. She had to warn Sloan, and she had to leave the house without making anyone suspicious about why she'd left or where she was going.

"Hello, Mary," she said to the maid. "I just remembered I'm going to miss my—manicure appointment. I'm in a terrible hurry."

In her room, she grabbed her purse and car keys and started for the door; then she remembered throwing Paul Richardson's card in a drawer with some vague thought of writing a stern letter of complaint to his superiors about the accusation he'd made.

She saw the card, but her hands were trembling as if she had palsy and she dropped it twice.

Nordstrom was in the downstairs hall. She needed to give him a message for her father so that he wouldn't suspect why she wasn't going to be home for dinner. She tried to think of where she could say she was going on the day after her great-grandmother's funeral that wouldn't strike him as odd. "My father is meeting with Mr. Dishler, and I don't want to disturb him. Will you tell him that . . . that Mrs. Meade called, and I'm going over to discuss some of my designs. I think it will help cheer me up."

Nordstrom nodded. "Certainly, miss."

49

Paris glanced at the clock on the dashboard as she lifted the Jaguar's car phone from its cradle in the center console and saw that it was a little after four o'clock. If she completely ignored the speed limit, the drive to Bell Harbor would take an hour or even less. It would take her longer than that to arrange for a plane, fly to Bell Harbor, and find transportation once she landed. She decided to drive. Either way she couldn't get there before dark.

Cradling the car phone on her shoulder, she kept one eye on traffic while she dialed the number Paul had scrawled on the back of his card. Her hands were still shaking, but she had urgent details to handle, and that kept her from thinking about the unthinkable.

The phone at the number Paul had written gave out a tone as if it were a pager, and Paris put in her car phone number, hung up, and waited for a quick return call.

Sitting in his Palm Beach motel room, Paul listened with resignation to the verbal blasting coming across the phone line from the special agent in charge of the FBI's Miami division. The cellular phone he carried was lying on the nightstand, and a small light on it began to flash, indicating a call was coming in. Paul reached over and switched it to its pager mode to keep it from ringing . . . and further antagonizing the angry man on the other end of the phone.

"Do you understand what's happening here, Paul? Am I making this clear? It's going to cost the bureau a fortune in man-hours just to answer the first deluge of complaints that Maitland's attorneys filed in court today."

"What, specifically, is he accusing us of doing?"

"I'm so glad you asked," Brian McCade replied with biting sarcasm. There was a shuffling of papers as he picked up Maitland's attorneys' papers. "Let's see, this one accuses us of illegal search and seizure, then there's entrapment . . ." Paul listened silently to the long litany of legal accusations. "Wait, I missed this one," McCade said bitterly. "This one charges us with 'malicious incompetence.' "

"I never heard of that one. Since when is incompetence a violation of the law?"

"Since Maitland's attorneys decided to try to make it one!" McCade said furiously. "His attorneys are probably writing new law with some of these. I can see this going all the way to the Supreme Court for rulings."

"There's nothing I can say, Brian."

"Yes, there is. In one of these complaints, Maitland is demanding a formal, public statement of apology because you didn't find anything illegal on either of his boats. He wants you to say you're sorry."

"Tell him to go to hell."

"Our attorneys are drafting the legal equivalent of that reply; however, I don't think it's appropriate unless you honestly feel that he got the stuff you were looking for off his yachts without you knowing it."

Paul expelled his breath in a long sigh. "There's no way he could have. He flew back after he had the last meeting in South America aboard the *Apparition*. We kept that ship under surveillance on its way back here, and we've had it under surveillance every hour of every day that it's been in Palm Beach."

"So, what you're telling me is that no contraband was brought aboard in South America or you'd have found it."

Paul nodded; then he said it aloud. "Right."

"And there was nothing aboard the *Star Gazer*, either?"

"Nope."

"So, basically, Maitland is innocent."

Paul thought of the personal lives he'd destroyed over his wrong hunch, and he felt far worse than he could let McCade know. "That about sums it up. Although, legally you can hang your hat on the machine gun we found. That constitutes an automatic weapon, which constitutes 'illegal.'"

"Thank you for that enlightening observation. Now, what do we say about the fact that the damned thing is practically an antique, and one that he confiscated to boot?"

Paul sighed again and thought of Sloan and the way she'd steadfastly defended Maitland because her own judgment was more reliable than his. "Do you think it would be worthwhile for me to try to pay Maitland a visit and try to soothe his sensibilities?"

"He doesn't want soothing, he wants blood—yours."

"I have to talk to him to straighten out another matter," Paul said, thinking he had to at least try to convince

Maitland that Sloan had no idea Maitland was a target of the FBI's investigation.

"Don't go near Maitland," McCade warned, growing angry again. "By doing that, you could jeopardize our defense. Did you hear me, Paul? That's an order not a suggestion."

"I heard you."

As soon as they hung up, Paul got two more calls from his men in Palm Beach. He gave them each detailed instructions; then he got a glass of water and brought it over to the bed. He got out his suitcase and began to repack.

Paris waited fifty minutes for Paul to call back; then she accepted that she needed to formulate a plan and rely on herself. Her hands were perspiring on the steering wheel, the speedometer was at 110 miles an hour, and she half expected to be pulled over at any moment for speeding.

She needed to stay calm and think. With her right hand, she opened her purse and felt around for a pen and something to write on; then she picked up her car phone and called directory information for Bell Harbor.

The information operator informed her that Sloan's number was unpublished.

"Do you have a listing for Kimberly Reynolds?" Paris asked.

The operator gave her the phone number and address, and Paris wrote it down. "I'd also like the phone number for the Bell Harbor Police Department."

Paris wrote that down and called it first. She asked for Detective Sloan Reynolds, and the operator at the police station put the call through. Paris's tension mounted as she waited expectantly for Sloan's voice.

A man answered her phone and said he was Lieutenant Caruso.

"I need to speak with Sloan Reynolds," Paris said.

"I'm sorry, ma'am, but she went off duty at three o'clock."

"I have to reach her right away. I'm her sister and it's urgent. Could you give me her home phone number?"

"You're her sister, and you don't have it?"

"I don't have it *with* me."

"I'm sorry but it's against policy to give that out."

"Listen to me," Paris said in a strained, impatient voice. "This is urgent. Her life is in danger. Someone is going to try to murder her tonight."

The man on the other end of the phone evidently decided she was a crank caller. "Would you be referring to yourself, ma'am?"

"Of course not!" Paris exploded. Realizing that neither hysteria nor a temper tantrum was going to get her anywhere with this fool, Paris tried again. "I am her sister. Do you know Sloan Reynolds personally?"

"Sure do."

"Then you must know that she was in Palm Beach until a few days ago visiting her family."

"Yep, and her great-grandmother was murdered, and Detective Reynolds was arrested and then released. We've had two calls here from people who wanted to confess."

Paris decided he was an idiot. "Who is in charge there?"

"That would be Captain Ingersoll, but he's off today."

"Then who is second in charge?"

"That would be me."

Paris hung up on him.

Finished packing, Paul reached automatically for his car keys and cellular phone. The flashing light indicated an unanswered call, and he remembered one had come in while he was on the phone with McCade. He'd had two more lengthy phone calls after that. The number he was supposed to call wasn't one he recognized.

Paris's hand was shaking uncontrollably as she picked up the paper on the car seat and read Kimberly Reynolds's phone number. She reached for the car phone just as it began to ring, and she jerked it out of the cradle.

"This is Paul Richardson," a familiar voice said. "Your telephone number came up on my pager—" Those were the most wonderful words Paris had ever heard in her life. She was so relieved she had to choke back tears. "Paul, this is Paris. I'm in my car on the way to Bell Harbor. You have to believe me because the Bell Harbor police think I'm a crank and they won't do anything. And if you won't help—"

"I'll believe you, Paris," he interrupted in an amazingly gentle and reassuring voice. "And I'll help you. Now, tell me what's happened."

"They're going to murder Sloan tonight! They're going to make her write a suicide note and confess to killing my great-grandmother, and then they're going to shoot her!"

She half expected him to blow the whole thing off or to make her explain again in detail while the remaining minutes of Sloan's life ticked away.

"All right. Tell me who 'they' are, so I know the best way to stop it."

"I don't *know* who they are. I just overheard a conversation about how it's going to be done tonight."

"Okay, then tell me who you heard discussing it."

The moment of betrayal had come. Her father had loved her and raised her . . . Her father was perfectly willing for Sloan to die tonight to protect his "business" . . . Her father hadn't exactly been hysterical when he realized his own grandmother had been murdered for the same reason. Paris had loved her so much. She loved him. She loved Sloan.

"Paris? I have to know who is involved or I can't be as effective!"

She swallowed and wiped her left arm over her wet cheek. "My father. My father and Gary Dishler. I heard them talking about it. Dishler works for some people he refers to as my father's 'partners,' and the 'partners' told him to kill my great-grandmother, so he did it." Tears were pouring down her cheeks in torrents, blurring the cars and the road ahead. "They told him what to do to Sloan, but he isn't going to do it himself. They've hired people, I think."

"That's what I needed to know. I'll call you back."

Paris hung up. Paul would help her save Sloan. He would also arrest her father.

She thought of her proud, handsome father being taken out of his house in handcuffs. She thought of murder trials and accusations and ugly newspaper stories with his picture in them. Her tears came faster and faster. "I'm sorry," she told him aloud. "I'm sorry, I'm sorry, I'm sorry."

50

An FBI helicopter was at the marina, and Paul was on his way to it when he made a call to the Bell Harbor Police Department. He also got Lieutenant Caruso.

Paul identified himself, and before he could draw a breath, Caruso said, "I recognize your name from the TV reports. You were with Sloan in—"

"Stop talking and start listening," Paul snapped. "She's in danger. Someone is going to try to get to her, probably at her house—"

"I'll bet you mean that broad who just called here. I figured she was a crank, but just to be on the safe side, I paged Sloan and left a message on her answering machine at home."

"Did she answer your page?"

"Nah, not yet, but—"

Mentally Paul riffled through the officers he'd met with Sloan the night of the barbecue. One of them stood out; he'd been sharp enough to be suspicious of Paul that night and to question Sloan's story about firecrackers that sounded like gunshots. "Where's Jessup?"

"He's off duty too. Who else do you want—"

"Listen to me, you ignorant bastard, and I'll *tell* you what I want. Get off your ass and find him; then have him call me at this number!"

Days were short in March, and the sun was already going down when the Bell Harbor exit off the interstate came into view. Paris needed directions to Sloan's house, but each time she called Kimberly's number at home, she got an answering machine.

Kimberly was probably still at work, Paris thought frantically. She told herself to stay calm, to think of other ways. She suddenly remembered that Kimberly worked in a boutique, and Sloan had talked about the owner. The owner had an old-fashioned woman's name, and the boutique was named after her. Paris had been especially interested in the kinds of designer merchandise that . . . that . . . LYDIA carried.

She grabbed the car phone and asked for the number of Lydia's Boutique. She was so relieved that she almost laughed when Lydia grumbled about a personal phone call for Kimberly.

"This is Kimberly Reynolds," the soft voice said, sounding understandably curious about the identity of her caller.

"This is Paris, Mrs. Reyn . . . Mother."

"Oh, my God. Oh, thank God." She was squeezing the telephone receiver so hard that Paris could hear the sound in her own phone.

Paris flipped on her lights and slowed to an exit speed that wouldn't hurtle her into the traffic backed up at the stoplight near the end of the exit ramp. "I'm in Bell Harbor. I have a problem. I need to find Sloan right away."

"She should be at home. It's after five, and she was working an early shift, but if she's working on a case, she often works later."

"I'm just exiting off the interstate. Could you give me directions to her house from . . ." Paris paused to read the street sign. ". . . From Harbor Point Boulevard and the interstate."

Kimberly complied with a gentle eagerness that touched Paris's heart even though it was pounding with anxiety. "Sloan keeps a spare key in a place you'd never think to look," she added, and told Paris where to find it. "If she isn't home yet, you could go inside and wait for her," she added.

"Thank you very much." Paris was already making a left turn in accordance with Kimberly's directions. She suddenly realized she didn't want to end this first conversation with her mother yet. Holding her breath with uncertainty she said, "Do you think I could come over and see you later?"

A teary laugh escaped her mother. "I've been waiting for thirty years to hear you say that. You . . . you won't forget?"

"I promise I won't."

Minutes later, Paris found Sloan's house. A light was on inside, and a plain white, late-model car with an unusual license plate that read BHPD031 was parked in the driveway.

Certain that BHPD stood for Bell Harbor Police Department, Paris found a parking spot on the street in front of the house, grabbed up her purse, and got out of her car. The wind had picked up, and a few raindrops spattered the driveway. Although night had fallen, the street seemed safe and well-lit. Her plan was to knock on the door, tell Sloan what was going to happen, and then drag her out of that house immediately. Paul could take care of the rest.

The plan seemed perfectly sensible and easy to accomplish, yet the closer she got to the front door the more uneasy she felt. She stepped onto the porch and lifted her hand to knock; then she hesitated for another look around. Across the street on her right, the beach was partially lit by large mercury-vapor lights on tall posts, and the light was bright enough to illuminate a female figure walking quickly along the sand in the distance and then breaking into a run. Paris recognized her and was so relieved and happy that she called out to her without thinking about the noise of the wind and surf.

"Sloan—" Her greeting turned into a muffled scream as the door suddenly opened, a hand clamped over her mouth, and she was dragged inside.

51

The threat of rain that had made Sloan break into a run turned out to be little more than a few raindrops, and she changed her pace to a slow walk. Normally the ocean soothed her; it sang to her, but since she'd returned from Palm Beach, she'd found no consolation there. Before she went to Palm Beach, she'd loved her quiet hours alone at home. Now she couldn't stand to be there, either.

Bending down, she picked up a smooth round stone; then she wandered back toward the waves, and with a flick of her wrist, she tried to make it skip across the water. It should have skipped; instead it hit the water and sank. Because of the day she'd had, this seemed absolutely fitting.

She'd gotten home at a little after three o'clock and spent most of the intervening time sitting on an outcropping of rock to the north of the picnicking area.

She'd watched clouds roll in and obliterate the setting sun while she tried to hear the music. On still evenings, the sea played Brahms lullabies to her; on stormy nights it was Mozart. Since she'd come back from Palm Beach, the music was gone; now the sea harangued her; it gave her keening sounds and bleak whispers that plagued her even in her sleep.

It complained to her that her great-grandmother was dead but her killer was free. It whispered to her that she had loved and lost because she'd let everyone down. It counted off her losses with each pitch and toss of the waves. Edith . . . Noah . . . Paris . . . Courtney . . . Douglas.

Sloan stood there, her hands in her pockets, listening to the bleak refrain, and it sent her back to her house even though she knew she wouldn't be able to escape it there either.

She cut across the street at an angle, head bent, tortured with memories, followed by the sad, urgent whispers. She was so preoccupied that she'd nearly reached the back door before she looked up and realized her house was dark at the back. Since she'd returned from Palm Beach, she'd started leaving a light on in the kitchen and one in the living room so she wouldn't walk into a dark emptiness. She'd turned the kitchen light on earlier; she was sure of it.

Wondering how she could specifically remember doing something that she obviously hadn't done at all, Sloan reached for the back door; then she saw the small broken pane of glass and jerked her hand back. She whirled, flattening herself against the house; then she ducked into a crouch.

Keeping below window level, she made her way toward the front of the house, noticing the living room lamp was still on. She did a swift calculation of probabilities and appropriate responses: she had absolutely no way of knowing if there was someone still in there or why they'd broken in. Thieves broke in quickly and got out quickly, but they wouldn't normally turn out some of the lights.

She had a house key with her but no car key and no weapon. Her Glock was still in the custody of the Palm Beach police, her loaner-replacement was in her purse in the bedroom. Her thirty-eight was in the desk in the living room. If there was anyone in her house, the sensible thing to do was leave, go to a neighbor's, and call for assistance.

That was her plan until she rounded the front corner of the house and saw a familiar Jaguar convertible parked on the street. Paris's car. Had Paris broken into the house and left her car right there in plain view? The idea was so bizarre it felt eerie.

Sloan quietly retraced her steps to the rear of the house and moved to the back door, silently turning the knob while she automatically stood to one side out of the line of fire. She heard something inside then. A movement? A whimper? A word?

She stole a quick glance into the darkened kitchen through the broken window and was pretty sure that the room was empty, the swinging door that connected it to the living room closed.

Her senses were alive now, tuned to any nuance of sound as she stole into the kitchen and carefully pried the swinging door open with a finger.

Paris was sitting at the desk in the living room facing the kitchen, white-faced with terror, while a man with his back to Sloan held a gun pointed at her. Praying there was only one man, Sloan pulled the door open a little further.

Paris saw her, and on a desperate impulse she started talking, trying to distract everyone, trying to give Sloan a clue. "Sloan won't write a confession that she killed my great-grandmother just to get my father off the hook. She'll know you intend to kill her as soon as she does."

"Shut up!" the man hissed at her. "Or you won't live long enough to find out if you're right!"

"I don't see why it takes three of you with guns to try to kill one woman!" She knew at that moment that Sloan and she were going to die; she sensed it with a terrifying fatalism.

"Now that you've showed up," the man to the left of the kitchen door told Paris softly, "it's going to be two women."

Paris assumed Sloan would retreat, but what she actually did was so ghastly to watch it was unthinkable. Sloan opened the door further into the kitchen, held up her hands palms up to show she wasn't holding anything, and stepped into the living room. "Let her go," she said calmly. "It's me you want."

Paris screamed, the man at the desk whirled around, and the other two grabbed Sloan's arms and slammed her into the wall, each holding a weapon at her head. "Well, well, welcome home!" one of them said.

"Let her go, and I'll do whatever you want," Sloan said so calmly that Paris couldn't believe it.

"You'll do what we want or we'll kill her while you watch," the one by Paris said as he moved around to her side of the desk. He grabbed her by the collar and dragged her up off the chair, shoving her toward one of the men with Sloan. "You," he said, pointing his gun at Sloan, "get over here. You're going to write a letter."

"I'll write," Sloan said as she was shoved forward with enough force to make her stumble. "But you're making a mistake."

"You made the mistake when you walked in the door," the gunman by the desk said as he grabbed her and yanked her into the chair.

"If you want to go on living when you leave here," Sloan warned, "you'll pick up that phone and call who-ever sent you."

He pressed the barrel of his gun to her head. "Shut the fuck up and start writing."

"Okay. Let me get some paper out of the desk, but lis-ten to me—my sister has nothing to do with this. No—don't shove that gun into my head any harder. I know you're going to kill me. But you're not supposed to kill her. Call your boss and ask."

To her left, Sloan noticed a shadow move in the hall-way that led from her bedroom, and she felt sweat break out on her forehead as her adrenaline escalated. She bab-bled harder, faster, trying to distract her captor so he wouldn't see the shadow. "She's the one they're trying to protect by killing me. Tell your boss—"

The thug grabbed a fistful of her hair and yanked her head back. He shoved the gun against her mouth. "Say another word and I'll pull this trigger."

She nodded slowly, and he moved the gun away and released her hair.

"What do you want me to write on this paper?" she

asked, opening the drawer slowly. With her right hand Sloan pulled out a tablet, while her left hand closed around the butt of the thirty-eight. Using the tablet for cover, she got the gun into her lap and slid closer to the desk to hide it.

"What do I write?" she repeated.

He pulled a piece of paper out of his pocket and slapped it in front of her on the desk.

In Paris's mind—just before everything went black— the slap of the paper coincided with simultaneous explosions from every direction and a sudden sharp pain in her head. The last thing she saw before she slipped into a pit of darkness was Paul Richardson's face, and it was contorted with fury.

52

The atmosphere at Bell Harbor General Hospital was distinctly festive, despite the fact that the little hospital was under siege by the same frenzied media that had descended on Palm Beach to cover the murder of Edith Reynolds. The attempted murder of Sloan and Paris Reynolds the night before had caused an uproar of grim conjecture and wild theory.

The local TV stations preferred to credit Detective Sloan Reynolds and Officer Jess Jessup with all the acts of courage and daring that night, and to overlook the heroics of two FBI agents who'd participated in the raid that night.

The national media found it very curious, and very exciting, that one of those FBI agents had made headlines only days before during the search and seizure of Noah Maitland's yachts.

The announcement a few minutes ago, shortly after dawn, that Paris Reynolds had regained consciousness signaled the beginning of a celebratory mood. And—it was hoped by the hospital staff—the departure of the throngs of reporters at their doors.

"Mr. Richardson?" A smiling nurse stepped into a private waiting room on the third floor. Lowering her voice so she wouldn't wake up Kimberly and Sloan she said, "Miss Reynolds is awake. If you'd like to see her alone for a few minutes, this is your chance."

Paul stood up. After waiting at the hospital, hour after hour, for Paris to regain consciousness, he suddenly had no idea what to say to her.

He panicked a little when he saw that her eyes were closed, but as he sat down beside her bed, he realized her breathing was strong and even and her color was vastly improved.

He took her hand in his. Her eyes opened, and he watched her register who he was. Now he waited for her to remember *what* he was—the bastard who had doubted every honest, decent thing she'd done and then committed the final, vicious injustice of accusing her of murdering the great-grandmother she had loved. He felt he deserved the same treatment he received the night she slapped him and slammed the door in his face.

She looked at him, her confusion disappearing completely. She swallowed and made her first effort to speak in two days, and Paul braced himself. Her voice was barely a whisper. "What took you so long?" she asked with the barest trace of one of her smiles.

He gave a hoarse laugh and tightened his hand on hers.

"Was I shot?" she asked.

He nodded, remembering the gruesome way it had looked to him when a stray shot ricocheted off something and grazed her head.

"Who shot me?"

Paul leaned his forehead on their clasped hands, closed his eyes, and told her the truth. "I think I did."

She was very still, and then she began to shake with laughter. "I should have guessed that."

Paul looked into her eyes and tried to smile. "I love you," he said.

53

Paris left the hospital at the end of the week and went to her mother's house to recuperate. Paul took vacation days to be with her, Kimberly hovered over her, and Sloan came over every day to visit.

Kimberly and Paris seemed to be thriving, but Sloan was growing thinner and paler by the day, and Paul knew it was because of Maitland.

Since Paul felt the breach was entirely his own fault, he was more than willing to try to heal it for her, despite the fact that he'd been told to stay away from Maitland. What prevented him from doing it was that Maitland refused to see him. Paul had called him twice to ask for a meeting, and the man wouldn't take his calls or reply to the request.

Paul was thinking about all that while Paris, Sloan, and Kimberly were chatting in Kimberly's living room on a sunny afternoon, two weeks after Edith's death.

The doorbell rang, and since no one else seemed to hear it, Paul got up and opened the front door. Staring back at him with narrowed eyes was Courtney Maitland.

"We came to see Paris," she informed him. "What are you doing here? Trying to confiscate the china?"

Paul looked over her shoulder and saw Douglas getting out of the car, and the framework of a fragile idea took shape.

"I'd like to talk to you both privately before you go in to see Paris," he said, stepping outside and forcing Courtney to back up. He closed the door behind him so they couldn't brush past him. While Courtney glared and Douglas glowered, Paul said simply, "I did your family a grave injustice, and I did the same thing to Sloan. I would like to try to make it right with everyone if you'll help me."

Courtney sniffed. "Why don't you just wave your FBI badge and mumble incantations. Isn't that how *you* make things happen?"

Again, Paul ignored her and addressed Douglas. "Sloan had absolutely no knowledge of what I intended to do with those yachts, Douglas. She had absolutely no idea I was interested in Noah for any reason whatsoever. When she agreed to go to Palm Beach with me, Sloan knew only that we suspected Carter Reynolds of illegal activities. You've read the newspapers. You know he's confessed to everything and that we have Dishler in custody. Dishler is talking his head off."

He paused, trying to gauge their reactions, but he couldn't tell what they felt, so he pressed on: "I was right about Carter. I was wrong about Noah. What matters is that you weren't wrong about Sloan when you thought she cared about all of you. You've heard about what she did—she risked her life to save Paris's. She trusted me, and I betrayed that trust, but I did it out of duty and in the belief she was wrong about Noah and I was right."

He paused again, and Douglas looked at Courtney, as if to see what she thought.

"Courtney," Paul said, "she talks about you to her mother and Paris all the time. She misses you."

"Why should we believe anything you say?" Courtney asked stubbornly.

Paul shoved his hands in his pockets. "Why on earth should I lie about it?"

"Because you're a jerk?" Courtney suggested, but without force.

"I'm obviously wasting my time with all this," Paul said curtly, reaching for the door to open it. "None of *you* care about Sloan. Just forget it. I'm tired of trying to make amends to people who aren't interested."

He opened the door to go inside, but Courtney put her hand on his sleeve. "How much does Sloan miss us?"

He turned back. "Unbelievably. How much does your brother miss her?" he fired back.

She looked down, her loyalties at war inside her head; then she looked up. "He misses her badly enough to be leaving for Saint Martin today, which he doesn't like, and when he's there, he's going to join a bunch of people he doesn't like. Then he's going back to San Francisco to stay."

"Get me in to see him, and I'll try to make him listen."

"He'll throw you out," Courtney predicted delightedly. "He's not in love with you. We need to make him see Sloan, and it has to be somewhere he can't throw her right out."

They looked at each other, arrived at the same conclusion, and walked into the house.

"Hi, everyone," Courtney called.

Her voice made Sloan whirl around in disbelief. "We can't stay long," Courtney continued, hurrying forward to kiss Paris on the cheek. "Cool bandage, Paris."

Sloan looked past her to Douglas, who opened his arms. He hugged her and whispered, "Courtney's going to take you and Paul to Noah. Go with her. If you wait, Noah will be gone. He's leaving in a few hours." He trailed off distractedly, looking over her shoulder, and dropped his arms. "Who on earth is that?"

Sloan was so anxious to leave and so afraid of the outcome that she had to study her mother before she could answer. "My mother. Would you like to meet her?"

"My dear," he said with a slow smile, "I would like nothing more."

54

Noah slid the last sheaf of papers into a briefcase and carried it downstairs to the foyer where his suitcases were waiting to be loaded into the car by his chauffeur.

He stood in the foyer, his hands thrust into his pockets, taking a last look around. He had designed this house himself. He loved the shapes and forms of its rooms, its soaring ceilings and panoramic views. Now, he was glad to be leaving for a while. Wherever he went in the house, memories appeared of Sloan and his gullible obsession with her; they greeted him in its rooms and followed him down its hallways.

He glanced into the living room and saw Sloan there on the sofa, worried about being arrested.

Noah's footsteps echoed on the polished wood floors as he wandered from room to room.

He went through the kitchen doorway and she was there, making late-night omelettes: *He who does not help with the cooking does not get to help with the eating*, she'd warned.

"Give me an assignment. Make it a tough one."

She'd handed him a knife and a green pepper.

"*I had something more macho in mind,*" he'd explained. She'd given him the onion.

Noah opened the back door and walked out on the terrace, standing there. On his left was the umbrella table where she ate breakfast with Courtney and Douglas and himself for the first time. Courtney had been demanding the details of the evening before when Noah "crashed and burned," and Sloan had burst into infectious laughter. *I don't know the first thing about flirting. . . . If I'd had a telephone, I'd have called my friend Sara from the dance floor and asked her what to say.*

Noah tore his gaze from the table and looked straight ahead. She'd met him there on the lawn near the terrace, late at night, after her party, looking like a barefoot angel with her sandals in her hand. "*With respect to . . . those sorts of relationships . . . I haven't had what you . . . what some people might consider much experience. Actually, I've only had two of those relationships.*"

"*Only two? What a pity. Dare I hope they were both very short and completely meaningless?*"

"*Yes,*" she'd whispered, laying her hand on his cheek. "*They really were.*"

They'd ended up on the chaise lounge on his right that night, where he had behaved like a teenager, necking and petting. The beach stretched out in front of him. He'd met her on the beach the night Edith died; he'd come back from Miami early because he missed her. He'd walked her home after she made him help with the cooking. "*I'm crazy about you.*" He had meant "I love you." Thank God he hadn't said that. It would be one more idiotic thing he'd have to berate himself for now.

Noah turned back and walked into the house. Of all the women he'd known, he wondered what streak of mental instability, what fluke of human chemistry, could have made her the one woman he'd wanted above all others.

He could not understand how he could have been so damned naïve. He would have bet everything he had that she was as in love with him as he had been with her. Actually, he *had* bet on her and in the end, she'd cost him a damned fortune. The unsavory publicity resulting from the FBI's search of his boats had damaged his reputation and, even though the FBI hadn't found anything, the mere fact that they'd suspected him would linger in people's minds for years to come.

Sloan Reynolds was as delicate and beautiful as an orchid; she was Mata Hari in a ponytail.

He stopped in the doorway of the family room and looked at the videotape sticking out of the VCR. For days after Paris and she were nearly killed, the television news programs had had a field day running film footage they'd gotten of Sloan doing her job as a cop. Even though Courtney regarded Sloan as a complete traitor, she'd been fascinated with what she saw on television and, with typical innocent insensitivity, she'd taped everything she saw and then badgered Noah to watch it.

According to Courtney, the Bell Harbor Police Department had been featured on an episode of a series about "Real Police in Action" or something like that.

Sloan had been part of a drug bust that was filmed while it was actually happening.

The videotape beckoned to Noah. This was his last chance to see it before he left. Courtney and Douglas were visiting Paris, and he was alone in the house. He walked over to the television set, turned it on and inserted the tape.

The television screen lit up, the tape began to run, and Noah felt a new surge of fury when he remembered he'd actually volunteered to teach Sloan to shoot so the "delicate little angel" wouldn't be afraid of guns!

On the television screen, the "angel" was wearing a jacket with POLICE stenciled across the back, and she was crouched at the side of a police cruiser, a gun clasped between her hands, covering her buddies as they charged across the front lawn.

In the next film clip, Sloan wasn't merely covering her pals, she was in the lead, running toward a building and flattening herself next to the front door, gun clasped in her hands, held high.

Noah hit the OFF button. He despised her in that videotape.

But if she hadn't betrayed him, he would have thought she was utterly magnificent.

He remembered he'd left one report upstairs that he needed to take with him, and he went up to his office to get it so that he could leave. He was leafing through the files in his desk drawer when he heard voices coming down the hall. When he looked up Paul Richardson was standing in the doorway with Courtney on one side and Douglas on the other.

Douglas saw the ominous look in Noah's eyes. "Noah, would you just listen to what Paul has to say?"

In reply, Noah reached for the telephone and pressed the intercom button. "Martin," he said to his chauffeur/bodyguard, "I have an intruder in my office. Get rid of him." He shifted his gaze to his desk, found the report he was looking for, and stood up, moving around his desk. "When I walk past you, Richardson," he said as his father and sister wisely backed out of his way and a little down the hall, "if you so much as twitch, I will consider it an aggressive move, and I will delight in throwing your ass over that balcony. Do we understand each other?"

In response, the FBI agent stepped further into Noah's office, shoved the door closed, and turned the lock, effectively blocking out Douglas, Courtney, and Martin, who was bounding up the stairs. Leaning his shoulders against the door to further prevent anyone from getting it open, Richardson folded his arms over his chest, and regarded Noah impassively for a moment.

On the other side of the door, Courtney and Douglas could be heard reassuring Martin that he wasn't needed. Paul had no doubt that Noah was enraged enough and fit enough to take him on himself right now, but he was banking on the fact that Noah wouldn't want to expose a fifteen-year-old girl to a violent scene involving himself, even if she could only hear and not see it. He was also banking on his ability to diffuse Noah's wrath before he decided that Courtney had precipitated the scene and could pay the price by having to listen to a fistfight.

"Noah," Paul said finally in a relaxed, conversational

tone, "I've had a lousy two weeks. In fact, I haven't been through anything like this in over five years."

Noah leaned his hip on the front of the desk, a muscle drumming in his clenched jaw, his attention on the door behind Paul as he listened for an indication that Courtney was still out there or that she'd gone.

Paul knew it, and so he talked a little faster, and a little friendlier. "Do you remember the Zachary Benedict case from five years ago?"

Maitland's gaze flicked contemptuously to him. No one was likely to forget the worldwide furor over the Academy Award–winning actor/director who'd been wrongfully convicted of killing his wife. Benedict had escaped from prison and taken a hostage named Julie Mathison, who'd fallen in love with him. Paul had recaptured him in Mexico when Benedict risked his freedom to rejoin Julie, and the violent scene in the Mexico City airport had been televised around the globe.

"I can see from your expression that you remember that debacle. I was the agent in charge of apprehending Benedict. I'm the one who took Julie Mathison to Mexico and used her as bait in the airport."

"Tell me something," Noah snapped, "do you ever go after anyone who is guilty?"

"Not in your case, obviously. And not in Benedict's case either. I went to see Benedict when he was finally acquitted and released from prison after Mexico City, and I pleaded successfully on Julie's behalf. He forgave her."

"What the hell does this have to do with me?"

"I'm getting to that right now. You see, there were two

major differences between Julie's situation with Benedict and Sloan's with you right now: Julie went to Mexico City to help me apprehend Benedict because I persuaded her that he was guilty. I would never have been able to persuade Sloan that you were guilty."

Paul glimpsed a flicker of reluctant interest in Noah's eyes and charged ahead. "In fact, I didn't bother to try. Sloan came to Palm Beach with me to help me check out Carter Reynolds. She had no idea that I thought you were bringing in the cash that Reynolds was laundering for the cartel. I kept her in the dark for several reasons. One of those reasons was that Sloan is an idealist; she's loyal and she is very smart. If she'd ever suspected I was using her to glean information that could be used against you, I think she would have blown her cover and mine to shield you."

"Am I supposed to believe that?"

"Why would I lie?"

"Because you're a conniving son-of-a-bitch."

"Courtney shares your opinion," Paul said wryly. "She phrased it a little more politely, but her tone and her meaning were identical. However," he continued briskly, "that's off the subject. I said there were two major differences between Julie Mathison's and Sloan Reynolds's situations. The second one is this: Julie felt guilty for betraying Benedict after she did it. She was willing to put up with Benedict's fury and his refusal to see her or let her explain. Sloan, on the other hand, has nothing whatsoever to feel guilty about. She has as much pride as you do, so think carefully before you walk on it any longer."

Paul shoved away from the door. "I know I've given you a lot to consider." He glanced at his watch. "You have a half hour to decide whether or not to screw up your life and Sloan's."

"What the hell is that supposed to mean?"

"It means she's waiting for you on the *Apparition*. So give it some thought. She isn't there to plead with you. She'd never plead. She wanted to tell you she was sorry about what happened and to say goodbye to you properly."

Turning he reached for the door, then he stopped and turned halfway back. "There's one more thing," he said with a smile. "I'm going to marry Paris, and as I learned to my immense discomfort one night she has a surprisingly strong right arm."

Maitland caught the gist of that. "She slapped you?" he concluded dispassionately.

"Exactly."

"Why?"

"I accused her of murdering Edith."

"That sounds like a good reason to me," he said with biting amusement.

"An hour before that, I also discovered that Sloan packs even more power and she's quicker than Paris."

Interest flickered in Maitland's eyes. "Sloan slapped you too?"

"No. She nailed me with a right hook that almost sent me to the floor."

"Why?"

Paul sobered. "Because she'd just found out I'd used her to get to you." He'd said everything he could think of to say to vindicate Sloan, but when he searched Noah's impassive face for a clue as to how he felt, his expression was completely unreadable.

Noah sat there after Paul was gone, thinking over what he'd said. There was no way of knowing for certain that the FBI agent was telling the truth about Sloan. There would never be proof. And yet, he did have proof. He'd always had it. The proof had been in Sloan's eyes when she looked at him, in her arms when she clung to him, in her heart when she made love to him.

That was proof enough, Noah decided. He stood up, eager to see Sloan, and then a thought occurred to him and he started to laugh. Richardson was not going to get off free. After publicly damaging Noah's integrity and shedding doubt on his character, Richardson was going to be stuck with Noah for a brother-in-law!

He was still smiling about that when he walked into the foyer and Courtney intercepted him at the front door. "I guess this is goodbye," she said, looking somewhat subdued for Courtney. "Paul said he didn't think anything he said made much difference to you. Don't be angry with me for bringing him here, okay? I don't want you to go away angry with me." She leaned up on her toes and to Noah's shock she put her arms around his neck and gave him a kiss goodbye.

"If I didn't know better, I'd think you were actually going to miss me," he teased.

She shrugged. "I will."

"Really? I didn't know you even liked me."

His suitcases were in the car already, and he reached down and picked up his briefcase. She was watching him, trying to detect his mood, Noah knew, and she was clever enough to pick up on something that was giving her hope. "I would like you a whole lot *more* if you'd forgive Sloan."

Over her shoulder, Noah saw Douglas standing in the living room, watching him with the same hopeful expression on his face that Noah heard in Courtney's voice. Eager to leave and see Sloan, Noah winked at his father and turned toward the door. "Well, okay if it would really make you like me a whole lot more."

That was all she needed to hear. She started pushing her new-found advantage to the limits. "You know," she added irrepressibly as he opened the door, "what I'd really like more than anything is if you'd *marry* Sloan and stay in Palm Beach."

Noah laughed, wrapped his arm around her, and kissed the top of her springy curls. She took that as a "yes" and followed him out onto the porch. "Noah," she called eagerly as he slid into the back seat of the car, "I'd make a really terrific *aunt!*"

His shoulders shaking with laughter, Noah closed the car door.

55

The helicopter's rotor was still whipping when Noah reached the main deck, looking for Sloan. He passed one of the crew who was securing the deck furniture in preparation for getting under way, and rather than waste time looking for her, Noah said abruptly, "Is Miss Reynolds aboard?"

The crewman knew only three significant things about Miss Reynolds—the rumor among the crew was that she'd been a close friend of the FBI agent who'd caused his employer's ship to be impounded; she'd been accused of murder; and she'd been brought aboard by his employer's young sister who told the crew to keep her presence a secret. The man decided his safest course was complete ignorance. "No sir, not as far as I know."

Noah nodded and frowning, he walked up the exterior steps to his stateroom. It would have been impossible for the launch or the helicopter to have arrived without the crewman on deck noticing that. Apparently, Sloan had changed her mind about coming to talk to him, which seemed very odd.

Shoving his hands in his pockets he stared at the king-size bed where he'd shared so many hours of stormy passion and quiet conversation with Sloan and he began to wonder how much truth there'd actually been in Richardson's defense of her. The woman Noah had watched on that videotape wouldn't have been afraid to confront him if she were innocent.

Sloan stood in the doorway behind him, working up her courage. She'd had a few hours to think about the reality of what had happened between them, and despite Courtney's belief that Noah would be willing to forgive and forget, and everything would be rosy once he saw her, Sloan didn't think that was true. This wasn't a fairy tale. The reality was that she loved him with all her heart, but she had brought him nothing but public humiliation. The reality was that Noah had never said he loved her, he didn't believe in marriage, and he didn't want children. Besides that, they were from two entirely different worlds. The most she could hope for now was honesty during this last visit and perhaps, someday, his forgiveness.

She stepped forward, shaking with nerves, fortified with determination. Noah had his back to her, his hands shoved in his pockets, head slightly bent, as if he was lost in thought. "I came to say goodbye," Sloan said softly.

His shoulders tensed, he turned around slowly, his expression unreadable.

"I came to ask you to forgive me, and I know that will take you a long time." Sloan paused to steady her voice, her eyes pleading with him to believe her and understand. "I don't blame you for how you feel about me. I wanted to tell you the truth so many times, but Paul was afraid you'd say something to Carter." Trying to keep her voice from shattering with the love and sorrow she felt, she drew a long breath and then went on. "I should have told you anyway, because I knew in my heart you wouldn't. But in a way, it's best that things came to such a quick end for us. It would never have worked out for us."

He spoke for the first time. "It wouldn't?"

"No." She gestured toward the elegant stateroom. "You're you . . . and I'm . . . me."

"That's always been a tremendous drawback for us," he said, straightfaced.

Sloan was so shaken that she didn't catch the thread of amusement in his voice. "Yes, I know, but that wouldn't have stopped me from falling more hopelessly in love with you every day. You don't want marriage, and I would have wanted to be your wife."

"I see."

"I love children," she said achingly. Tears were blurring her vision so badly that she could hardly see him.

His gaze on her, Noah reached down slightly and pulled the cover back on the bed.

"And you don't want children."

He unbuttoned the collar of his shirt.

"I would have wanted to have your baby."

He unbuttoned the next button. . . .

Every table in the exclusive Palm Beach restaurant was occupied and people waiting for tables were crowded into the bar and in the foyer at the front.

The telephone at the maitre d's desk rang and he picked it up. He listened to the caller, frowning because he couldn't hear. "I'm sorry, who is it you wish to speak to?" he asked, cupping his hand over his free ear in an effort to block out the noise. "Yes, the Maitland party is here now. I'll call her to the phone."

The maitre d', whose name was Roland, was new at the Remington Grill. He located the table reserved for the Maitland party on his chart, then he threaded his way through the restaurant to a table at the back.

Three women were seated there: One of them was a stunning blond in her early thirties; one of them was an elegantly dressed blond in her late forties who looked enough like the other woman to be her mother; and one of them was a dark-haired teenager in an appalling outfit who didn't look like she belonged with the other two women or amidst the exclusive clientele of the Remington Grill, either.

Since Roland wasn't certain whether the caller had

asked for Mrs. or Miss Maitland, the maitre d' took the safe path. "Pardon me, Ms. Maitland," he said to the three laughing females. "I have a telephone call at the desk for you."

All three women looked inquiringly at him.

"For which one of us?" the teenager inquired.

"For *Ms. Maitland*," Roland emphasized, a little annoyed at the trouble he was being put through.

"You're new here, so let me explain," the teenager said pertly, clearly relishing his predicament. "You see, I am Miss Maitland, and this"—she nodded to the younger blonde—"is my sister-in-law, Mrs. Noah Maitland. And this"—she indicated the older blonde—"is my sister-in-law's mother, who is Mrs. Douglas Maitland. However," she added, laying down her trump card with a mixture of glee and pride, "she is also, *my* mother."

Roland's brows levitated with suppressed ire. "How delightful."

Sloan slid her chair back and took pity on the man. "That call is probably for me. Noah telephoned from Rome and said he might be able to come home tonight instead of tomorrow."

Noah walked quietly upstairs and deliberately surprised his three-year-old daughter in her bedroom. "Daddy!" she exclaimed, rushing toward him in her robe and pajamas while the housekeeper disappeared into an adjoining room. "You're back early!"

Normally, Noah would have swept her into his arms, but he was hiding a present for her behind his back, so he grinned at her instead.

"Aunt Courtney was here today!"

"I can tell," he said tenderly.

She tipped her head to one side and it made her long blond corkscrew curls dance. "How can you tell?"

"Your dreadlocks."

Sloan found Noah on the terrace with their daughter on his lap. They were sitting in the moonlight, whispering about something. "Daddy's home!" Ashley exclaimed.

Noah looked up and saw Sloan, and his eyes were warm with love and a silent greeting.

"We've been telling secrets," Ashley confided. Beaming, she leaned close for Noah to whisper another secret to her. Then she looked at him and said, "Can I tell Mommy that one?"

"Yes," Noah said solemnly.

Ashley matched his tone. "Daddy says he loves you very, very, *very* much."

Visit
❖ **Pocket Books** ❖
online at

www.SimonSays.com

Keep up on the latest new
releases from your favorite
authors, as well as author
appearances, news, chats,
special offers and more.

SIMON & SCHUSTER
A VIACOM COMPANY
www.SimonSays.com

Pocket
Books

2381-01

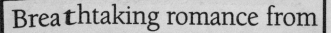

Breathtaking romance from

JUDITH McNAUGHT

A Gift of Love
(A collection of romances from Judith McNaught,
Jude Deveraux, Andrea Kane,
Kimberly Cates, and Judith O'Brien)

A Holiday of Love
(A collection of romances from Judith McNaught,
Jude Deveraux, Arnette Lamb, and Jill Barnett)

Almost Heaven

Double Standards

A Kingdom of Dreams

Night Whispers

Once and Always

Paradise

Perfect

Remember When

Something Wonderful

Tender Triumph

Until You

Whitney, My Love

POCKET BOOKS

3010-01